Books by Alina

The Holbrook Cousins
- The Successor
- The Screw-up
- The Scion

The Frost Brothers
- Eating Her Christmas Cookies
- Tasting Her Christmas Cookies

The Svensson Brothers
- After His Peonies
- In Her Candy Jar
- On His Paintbrush
- In Her Pumpkin Patch

Check my website for the latest news:

http://alinajacobs.com/books.html

IN HER Pumpkin Patch

A HOLIDAY ROMANTIC COMEDY

ALINA JACOBS

Summary: Pumpkin spice, fall festivals, and nostalgic movies, Harrogate is the perfect place to celebrate Halloween. My grouchy billionaire boss hates Halloween. But I have the perfect trick planned. I'm going weasel enough information out of my boss to write a killer article for a big payday. His washboard abs are sexy in that costume though. Maybe instead of playing a trick, I'll give him a treat!

To discounted Halloween candy—
you are my ride or die

In this town we call home
Everyone hail to the pumpkin song!

CHAPTER 1

Penny

Fall—a time of hayrides, pumpkins, apple picking, cozy sweaters…and failure.

I was travelling by train to my small hometown with a torn duffel bag filled with my meager possessions and broken dreams. At least I had a temp job as an account manager at Svensson PharmaTech waiting for me. It wasn't my dream job as a journalist, but hey, I'd taken what I could get. Going home, tail between my legs, would be unbearable if I was going to be unemployed.

The worst? I didn't even have overbearing parents or a childhood bedroom to crash at. Instead, I was going to be staying at my now-deceased foster mother's house. Her granddaughters, the twins Morticia and Lilith, lived there now. Yeah, they were identical and creepy and finished each other's sentences, but it was a free place to stay—though the twins claimed the house was haunted. But beggars can't be choosers.

A haunted house would be fitting, though, since it was fall, which was, in my opinion, the best time of the year. I loved sweaters, apple cider, and pumpkin-spice anything. Too bad I couldn't afford nice new fall outfits and accessories. I had barely been able to scrounge up some business-casual clothes for my new job.

Be positive, I ordered myself. It was my favorite time of year, and I was going to enjoy it, dammit, even if I did have a crappy temp job and a failing baking YouTube channel. I was going to make soups, pies, and cheesy pasta. Mimi's house had a large kitchen, though it was old. I was going all out for Halloween. The fall holiday season in Harrogate was fun! There was the Halloween festival and handing out candy to trick-or-treaters...

I sighed and stared out the window. It was overcast and drizzly. The weather didn't even have that wow factor of the crisp blue sky and orange, yellow, and bright-red leaves. My small hometown was improving, mainly thanks to the investment from the Svenssons, but the train still sucked. It was packed with people going back to Harrogate from various weekend trips away.

The child in the seat next to me sneezed, getting snot all over my plaid skirt. Where were his parents? I tried not to swear as I blotted the fabric. To cheer myself up from the reality that I had officially failed as a journalist, I had dressed for fall, complete with boots, a scarf, and a cute sweater with smiling pumpkins, which also looked like it had snot on it.

The kid sniffled. His nose was running. I sighed and pulled a tissue out of my purse and handed it to him. He looked at me.

"Seriously, you need me to wipe your nose for you?" The kid blinked. He was a little greasy but otherwise cute: chubby cheeks, blond hair, and big gray doe eyes. I gingerly blotted his nose.

"Where are your parents?" This kid was tiny—probably a toddler. He had his ticket pinned to his shirt.

"Who does that?" I muttered. "I thought that was something that happened in the olden days on orphan trains." I was suddenly nostalgic for rainy days in Mimi's attic, reading *American Diaries* books and eating caramel popcorn.

"You're not going to bite me if I look at your ticket, are you?" I asked the kid, curious about how far he'd come. Maybe he was a child of a broken home, sent to visit his father for the weekend.

He pulled at the ticket, and I unfastened it for him then peered at it.

Davy Svensson – unaccompanied minor.
Yellow Ridge Wyoming to Harrogate

"That's—" I took out my phone, "fifty-seven hours? You've been on the train for *fifty-seven hours*? Who sends their toddler on a train for fifty-seven freaking hours by themselves?" Where before I had found the kid weird and annoying, now I was feeling protective. My mother had been terrible and would leave me alone randomly, hence my stint in and subsequent aging out of foster care.

I felt terrible for the kid. And incensed. How dare his parents treat him like this?

"Who's your dad? Is that who you're going to meet?" I demanded. "A Mr. D-bag Svensson, I assume?"

The kid whimpered and looked sad.

I took a turkey sandwich with brie, apple slices, and arugula on ciabatta out of my bag. I had stopped by the Grey Dove Bakery before I left Manhattan. Yes, I splurged. Now that I'm not paying rent, I can do that, right? Don't judge me! I'm terrible at money and math. That's why I majored in journalism.

I fed the kid bites of sandwich as I stewed about his neglectful father. "Eat that, and you can have a cookie. It's a special Halloween cookie!" Yeah, I really went all out. How could I not? Chloe, owner and baker extraordinaire, had carefully wrapped the sugar cookie in Halloween-themed tissue paper.

"I have three cookies," I told Davy when he had eaten his half of the sandwich. "You want a bat or a witch or a pumpkin?"

He pointed to the pumpkin. "Thank you," he said softly, cookie crumbs raining all over his shirt.

"We're train buddies," I told him as I dusted him off. He grabbed my hand then immediately fell asleep next to me.

I had always wanted a giant family with a bunch of kids. I wanted to host elaborate Halloween parties, and my huge house would be decorated top to bottom, and the kitchen would be filled with yummy baked goods.

Life did not work out like that. Now I had three children named student loans, credit card debt, and poor decision-making skills to keep me company. I ate the other two cookies and the rest of Davy's. He'd just sneezed on me, so I guessed I already had whatever germs he was carrying.

I stewed as I thought about someone sending their kid on a train alone like that. He must have been so frightened! That sent me into a spiral thinking about my mother. Trisha had left me with my father when I was just a kindergartener to run off to Europe with her much older boyfriend. She rarely called. When she did, it was just to make promises she had no intention of keeping. When my father died, the state of New York tried to contact my mother, but she had dropped off the radar. She didn't resurface until I aged out of the system. Like a dummy, I welcomed her back into my life again and again. She would always dangle nice things in front of me. Trisha was now an editor at the *Vanity Rag*, and she was constantly promising she would run one of my articles.

My phone rang, playing spooky Halloween sounds. Davy stirred, and I hurried to answer it before he woke up.

"Penny, darling!"

Speak of the devil—or rather, speak of my mother.

"Hi, Trisha," I said, trying to keep my voice neutral.

"Why don't you ever call me Mom?" she complained. "You are my daughter, after all."

"Are you calling about the article I sent you?" I said, gritting my teeth. I had submitted an article about the Wild West of knitting: people stealing yarn, sabotaging projects, and lying about patterns. It was nuts and would make a fascinating article. I was sure of it.

"Our readers don't want to hear about that," Trisha said with a fake laugh.

"Oh. Okay. Well, I appreciate you calling to tell me in person."

Ugh! I couldn't believe I had fallen for her lies *again*!

My mother snorted. "I didn't call about that. I heard through the grapevine that you are going to be working at Svensson PharmaTech."

"I'm not technically working *for* them, I'm just a temp."

"Of course you are."

There was that underhanded dig. Every time I had to talk to my mother, my self-confidence did a nosedive, and I had to self-medicate with copious amounts of cake.

"Great conversation, *Mom*."

"Don't get snippy with me, Penny," Trisha said, a harsh undercurrent in her voice. Then it softened. "I was calling to see if you had availability to do some freelance work."

In spite of myself, I perked up. Was this my big break?

"I have a fantastic idea for the next issue," my mother continued. "The Svenssons have been in the news recently with the popsicle scandal, and people are interested. They're the new hot topic—all those good-looking brothers, polygamist cult victims turned billionaires. We want you to do an in-depth exposé on them. Really get to know them, learn about their family, their habits, their interactions."

"That sounds a little unethical..." I said uncertainly.

"They're public figures," Trisha insisted.

I blew out a breath.

"If you can write a good story on them, you could parlay that article into a book, a TED talk, a *Good Morning America* appearance, maybe even a movie," Trisha said. "You could be one of the top investigative journalists of your generation."

Against my better judgment, I saw dollar signs and glory pass before my eyes. Then I thought better of it.

"I don't know, maybe I shouldn't," I said.

"Trust me, Penny," Trisha said, using that tone that always made me believe whatever she was saying. "The Svenssons are terrible people. Men like that don't become billionaires by being nice. They have skeletons in their closets. Ask me how I know. Evan Harrington's investment firm bought our magazine last winter, and they are determined to wring every cent out of it. We want you to expose them."

"Can I think about it?"

"We need an answer now. There are other people we can ask, too, you know. You're not that special." She sniffed. "Look, we really want this story to happen. We'll give you an advance."

An advance! Well then. Penny had bills to pay. But when I had signed up to be a journalist, I'd had visions of being like Erin Brockovich and exposing things people in power were trying to sweep under the rug. I had imagined saving lives and making a difference, not airing someone's family drama all over the newsstands.

I looked down at Davy asleep on my lap. *Good men don't send their sons across the country by train all alone.*

I had never been able to stand up to my mother on my own behalf, but maybe I could be in Davy's corner.

"You know what?" I said. "Sign me up."

"That's my girl!" my mother said.

Against my better impulses, I felt a flush of joy that my mom seemed proud of me.

I woke Davy up as we pulled into Harrogate station. There was a break in the rain. The sun was setting; the historic buildings and the tall clock tower were silhouetted against the orange rain clouds.

I loved *Gilmore Girls*, and the New England town of Harrogate feels like the closest you can get to Stars Hollow. It even has a town square with a bandstand. The Halloween festival is held there every year. I snapped pictures of it from the window as the train chugged into the ornate station.

"I'm so excited for Halloween in Harrogate," I said to Davy as he yawned. "You're going to love it!" I picked him up and carried him off the train. He had a small grocery sack holding a few clothes and a stuffed animal.

I bounced him in my arms and looked around the train station.

"Look at the decorations!" There were workers in the station stringing up fake spiderwebs and arranging displays with hay bales, pumpkins, and colorful leaves. I breathed in. It smelled like fall. "It's going to be so awesome! You can go trick-or-treating."

He nodded and wiped his eyes.

"Davy!" a deep voice barked.

A tall man with gray eyes, broad shoulders, and military-short hair stalked over to me. He was wearing a suit with a black overcoat that brushed around his knees. Must be Mr. D-bag Svensson in the flesh.

"What are you doing with him?" he demanded, glaring at me with steely eyes.

"And a Happy Halloween to you, too," I said tartly as the tall man snatched the kid out of my arms.

He glared down at me. He was hot in a sort of growly, dangerous way. Unfortunately, he did not seem to like me. And honestly, I didn't like him very much.

Davy's lower lip started trembling.

"You shouldn't have let Davy travel across the entire country by himself!" I scolded the man. "He didn't even know what stop to get off at! You're his father. You should have gone and picked him up." I jabbed my finger in his face as I chastised him. Actually, he was so tall, my finger came up at chest height. I poked him. "He could have been hurt."

Jab.

"Kidnapped."

Jab.

"You are a terrible parent!"

The man grabbed my hand with his larger one then seemed to realize he had touched me. He released me and stepped back.

"I'm not his father. Davy is my little brother."

Davy's trembling lip turned into full-blown crying. I winced as he screamed like a murder victim in a haunted house and reached for me. I held out an arm to him.

His older brother snatched him away.

"I don't need judgment from a girl who wears a sweater covered in pumpkin pom-poms," he sneered. "Of course someone like you is infatuated with such a childish holiday. I bet you drink pumpkin-spice lattes and decorate cookies and post pictures of orange candles on your Instagram," he barked over Davy's screams.

"And I bet you sit at home alone on Halloween with the lights off, refusing to hand out candy to children!" I screeched.

We glared at each other.

"I don't know why I'm even wasting my time on you," he huffed.

"Poor Davy. He should come live with me. We'd bake cookies and make candied apples. He shouldn't be subjected to some Halloween-hating Grinch."

"That's—those aren't even the same holiday. You know what? Never mind. Stay away from my family," he snarled.

I watched him stalk off. Now I was doubly glad I had taken that freelance job for my mom. That Svensson was going down.

CHAPTER 2

"I can't believe the nerve of that woman," I snarled as I buckled Davy into his booster seat.

My little brother was still screaming. I've been trying to rescue my brothers from the cult at younger and younger ages. I had a plan. The noose was tightening around my father. I refused to leave any more of my siblings in that environment. I'd hated every minute of my childhood that I'd spent stuck in that polygamist cult with an inattentive mother.

I loved my family and would do anything for them. Which was why I had lost my temper when that curvy redhead had looked at me with such scorn, as if I was going to hurt Davy.

He was still letting out that ear-piercing scream, and I patted him on the head as I finished securing the booster seat.

I could not deal with that girl right now. I had several irons in the fire. My brothers were useless, I was trying to make sure my company, Svensson PharmaTech, stayed well ahead of the competition, and then there was the small problem of Halloween approaching.

The holidays always made my brothers various shades of morose. I had no patience for it. Yes, our childhoods had been toxic and would make a salacious Netflix miniseries, but we couldn't dwell on the past. But my brothers' mood swings were coming, and it was just one of those things I had to plan for.

The phone rang through my car speakers. Legally, in Harrogate, we are not supposed to talk on the phone while driving. Deputy Mayor Meghan Loring had had the law passed to mess with Hunter. Their unrequited-love situation had to be resolved soon. I needed to check my calendar and see when I could work on that. With Mace and then Archer each having their own crises, dealing with Meg and Hunter had fallen by the wayside.

"Garrett," Hunter said over the speaker. "Bad news... What is that? Do you have a banshee in the back seat?"

"I don't need Halloween references from you right now," I said shortly. "It's still September. Halloween season should not start until October first. Thanksgiving season begins on November first, and Christmas shouldn't start until Black Friday. I don't understand why commercial entities seem to think otherwise. I will not be pushed to celebrate holidays any earlier than I deem appropriate," I said over Davy's screeching. "I do not want to see Halloween decorations in August."

"Whatever. Listen, we—"

Police lights flashed in the side mirrors as sirens blared. Fuck. I pulled over to the side of the road.

Of course Davy had gone silent and was staring wide-eyed at the blue lights. Maybe I could use Davy as an excuse. He was cute, though a little smelly. I rolled down the window.

"Be charming," I ordered my little brother.

Susie, one of the Harrogate city police officers, walked up to the window and sighed. "Garrett, you can't talk on the phone, even if it's on speaker, while operating a vehicle. You know that."

"Yes, Officer, I understand," I said, handing over my license. "See, one of my younger brothers just came in to town. Surely you understand how that is." While I have many admirable traits, being charming and flirty is not one of them. Archer might have been able to talk himself out of a ticket. It would seem I was unable to do so.

"This is your last warning," Susie said, taking out her notebook and my license.

"I know. I won't do it again, Officer."

"No, this is your last strike," she said, shaking her head. "You just lost your license."

I opened my mouth. No sound came out. I shut it. "I need to call my lawyer."

"Step out of the car," Susie said.

"Officer, it's cold. Look, I have the kid. He's sick and shivering."

Susie poked her head into the car as I stepped out. Davy smiled and waved.

"Could I have one more warning? Please?" I tried to smile. It might have been more of a grimace.

"Nope. You can wait in the cruiser for your ride."

I called Hunter from the police cruiser, Davy wriggling on my lap. "*This is your fault*," I spat into the phone. "You need to come pick me up. I lost my license."

Hunter was struggling not to laugh. "You know the law."

Wrong fucking thing to say. "*Don't you dare*. This is your fault," I hissed. "If you hadn't mistreated Meghan, none of this would have happened."

Davy, the novelty of the police cruiser wearing off, had started screeching again. He continued screaming for the next sixteen minutes. I know because I counted.

This town isn't that big—how does it take Hunter sixteen minutes to drive over here?

The big idiot finally showed up, completely unremorseful.

"Sorry I'm late. We had the town hall meeting," he said over Davy's screams.

I ignored him as our brother Parker loped over to my car.

"Be careful," I warned him. "Don't scratch it."

"I don't see why you care," he scoffed. "How long do you lose your license for?"

"Twelve weeks," Susie said. "Shorter if he does some community service."

"What am I going to do without a license?" I snapped at Hunter.

"Maybe Remy can drive you in the bus." Hunter was not acting as contrite as I thought he should.

"At least now that he's in a bad mood, we can tell him we lost," Parker said.

"*You lost*? Jesus, you all had one job. I knew I should have been at that town hall."

"Wait?" Susie said, pausing at the police cruiser. "The plastic straw ban actually passed?" She looked miffed. "I'm not sure if I want to drink my iced tea through a paper straw."

"You can also use the metal ones," Parker said unhelpfully.

"This is not going to work for me," I said. "I cannot drink my coffee out of a metal straw. Or paper. Neither of those will work for me."

"It's better for the environment," Parker said with a smirk as I buckled Davy back into the booster seat. "Put him with Hunter. I don't want to ride with him. Davy smells like stale popcorn and salami."

Davy cried the whole way home. I rolled down the window to let the cold fall air in.

Usually after bribing my father to send one of my little brothers to me, I dumped the kid off on Mace. But Davy was the first new kid since Josie had come into the picture. Now Mace spent all his time with his new girlfriend. Not that I minded—it made him less of a Neanderthal.

Archer was the next-best bet. Though obnoxious, he was good with the kids, probably because he was basically one. Lord knows how he managed to talk Hazel into agreeing to be his fiancée. I needed to make sure Archer didn't do something dumb to drive her away. Again. He split his time between Manhattan and Harrogate. When he was in town, he was at Hazel's café. It was doubtful Hazel would want a small child running around her business.

His conference center should be a success as soon as I could disabuse him of the notion that he would be treating it like his personal fiefdom. I patted myself on the back for making sure Archer had chosen a good site. His other option had been the now-defunct zoo. I still couldn't believe he had wanted to bring in penguins.

Maybe Parker could be in charge of Davy?

My younger brother fiddled with the radio.

"I know what you're thinking," Parker said, "and I'm busy. I'm working. I'm the only person developing cutting-edge technology. Svensson PharmaTech would be nothing without me. I have to concentrate."

He was defiant. I was determined to stamp that out. I stared at the side of his head. Most of my brothers were wary of me. Some of them were out-and-out afraid.

"Are you really?"

Parker snorted and drove through the gate and down the drive to the roundabout in front of the estate house. My older brother Remy was waiting on the wide stone steps that led up to the huge front door. The building was a nineteenth-century mansion. It was too ornate for my taste, but it was the only place large enough to hold my entire family. And there was an excessive amount of Svenssons.

Hunter pulled up behind us as I took Davy out of the car.

"Davy!" Remy said, sweeping our little brother into a huge hug. Davy tugged at Remy's bushy beard.

"I have a present for you!" My older brother took out a stuffed goat. Hunter scowled as we walked into the house. I had half a mind to buy Remington a goat one of these days. He constantly talked about it, and Hunter always shot it down. Davy sniffled as he petted the stuffed animal as my two dozen youngest brothers crowded around him.

"Don't let him get it dirty. He needs a bath," I ordered.

"My friend will like this," Davy said his a high-pitched voice.

"What friend?"

"From the train."

I ground my teeth but forced myself to stop. Who did that girl think she was?

I was adding her to my shit list along with Hunter and Mace and Archer. In fact, I was putting the whole town on the list. First I lost my license, then the straw ban passed. How would I even get to the office tomorrow? I ran through the list of people I didn't care for right now as I sprayed Davy off in one of the upstairs bathrooms. He hollered as if I was burning him alive.

"He is cute now that he's clean!" Archer said when I brought him down to the kitchen. Several of my younger brothers were there, eating a snack Josie, Mace's girlfriend had made for them.

Josie, picked up Davy and snuggled him. "He's so warm!" Davy immediately started crying. "Wow, tell me how you really feel!" Josie said, handing him to Hazel.

"I know you have more important things to do," I told her point-blank. "There's no need to coddle Archer."

"I don't mind being over here," Hazel said as she, too, tried to make Davy laugh.

"Find a YouTube video," Archer suggested. "Kids love YouTube videos."

"I'm not setting him in front of the TV so he can grow up like you," I scoffed.

"We made him some pizza toast," Josie said, shoving a plate at the screaming Davy.

"I brought stuffed animals," Archer said, pulling a raggedy stuffed jack-o'-lantern out of his bag.

"Where did you even find that?"

"The dollar store. It makes a noise."

The toy made the sound of a dying pigeon. Davy kept crying. He reached for me.

Mace snickered. "He only wants Garrett, poor kid."

I looked at Mace. He froze, and the smile fled from his face. I picked Davy up. He immediately stopped crying and looked around.

"This is not going to work for me," I said. "I have to work."

"But it's almost Halloween!" Josie gushed. "Aren't you excited?"

"Can we have a Halloween party?" Nate, one of my middle-school-aged brothers, asked.

"We have the fall festival," I said irritably.

"You shouldn't have asked in front of him," Mace said to Nate. "Garrett hates fall and Halloween."

Hazel gaped at me. "How? Fall is the *best* time of the year."

"I don't hate it. I wouldn't waste that much energy. It's merely an annoyance. I dislike fall. It's damp. There are dead leaves and all the Halloween junk and the pumpkin-spice everything. There are the excessive amounts of smelly candles and the creepy straw decorations. Plus all the inane parties and costumes."

Hazel looked at me in bemusement. I snapped my mouth shut.

The girl from the train station had been like fall personified.

But she's not wet.

I beat that thought down as if I was taking a shovel to a zombie.

CHAPTER 3

Penny

I grumbled as I dragged my duffel bag through the train station. I tried to put the asshole Svensson out of my mind. Poor Davy. I hoped he would be okay. I also hoped his brother stepped on a rake.

Where were the twins? They were supposed to pick me up. A horn blared, and an antique black hearse pulled up in front of the train station, seeming to appear out of the dark. Morticia, or maybe it was Lilith, rolled down the driver's window. The twins had the same alabaster skin and long black hair.

"Get in," Morticia said, tapping her black-painted fingernail on the steering wheel. "Lilith, scoot over."

"New ride?" I asked as I tossed my bag into the back and squeezed in next to Lilith. Morticia sighed and pulled away from the curb. We passed the blond Svensson, highlighted under a streetlamp, stuffing a still-screaming Davy into the car.

"We have to drive an antique," Morticia explained. "It's the ghost. He doesn't like anything but classic cars."

"Right." I leaned back in the itchy horsehair seat. I was squished next to Lilith. "Why don't you modify it to have more seats?"

Morticia turned to me, teeth sharp. "Then we wouldn't have room for our art pieces… or a coffin."

Salem, the twins' black cat, wound around my legs after I staggered out of the hearse. I looked up at the creaky old Victorian house. It was the closest place in the world I had to a home. Four stories tall, with a glass-enclosed turret, the huge house was a true Victorian mansion. It had tall ceilings, a wraparound porch, and a third-story ballroom that Mimi had always used to host big holiday parties.

I picked Salem up while Morticia dragged my duffel bag up the steep wooden steps to the front door.

"Watch that third step," Lilith warned. "The board is rotten. You'll crash right down to the cellar."

Morticia fitted an ornate skeleton key into the lock. It turned with a loud clank, and the front door creaked inward.

The first time I'd ever come to this house, I'd been barely a teenager. Mimi, Morticia and Lilith's grandmother, had welcomed me with open arms. She had been my foster mother until I'd aged out of the system. Even after, I would always come back to the house for holidays. Halloween was Mimi's favorite. She would dress up as a witch and turn the whole foyer into a mini haunted house and decorate the yard. She had died a year ago. I missed her every day.

"Did you have issues with the house when you moved in?" I asked the twins.

"A bit. It was vacant for months," Morticia explained as I followed her into the kitchen.

"I told her we should have sold it," Lilith added.

"No!" I protested. "You can't sell this house! I love it!"

"It's so large," Morticia said, setting the kettle to boil water for tea. "We really only need the carriage house out back. It wouldn't be right for the house. It needs a rich couple to fix it up."

"If I had money, I would buy it, and you could live in the carriage house," I said wistfully.

Morticia snorted as she measured tea leaves. "Honestly, we'd give it to you, but Mimi took out multiple loans on it. Plus the upkeep costs are insane. It really needs a full remodel. And art doesn't pay that much."

"You have some work for the Harrogate art trail," I countered.

"It's not going to last," Lilith said, passing out cups. "We'll be done with our contract by Christmas."

"After that," Morticia said, sipping her tea, "who knows."

"Thanks for letting me crash here anyway," I said.

"How long is your temp position?"

"Until I get fired probably."

Lilith smirked. "Maybe you'll find a rich man. There are loads of them bopping around Harrogate now. We have quite the startup scene."

"I can't rely on a man. I need to make my own fortune. If I could make my baking YouTube channel profitable..."

"Your sex ASMR baking channel?" Autonomous Sensory Meridian Response videos, short hand for videos that feature sensual sounds like whispering, soft petting, or nails running across silk, all usually done by pretty girls. But of course if you asked the men that watched them, it was totally about how relaxing the sounds were. Girl? What girl? You mean a girl was doing it? Nope, never noticed.

"It's not sex baking!" I exclaimed, face red. "I just talk in a soft, calming voice while I make cakes."

"Yeah, but I've read the comments on your videos. You have a lot of guys who get off on watching you bake and do your sexy voice."

"I don't read comments," I sniffed.

"Start a Patreon and do baking in your underwear for your paying subscribers," Lilith suggested. "I bet you'd make enough money to buy this house in no time."

"That's unsanitary! No, I need something else."

I looked up at the ceiling. It was cobwebby and needed to be cleaned. And I needed to come clean to the twins about my mother.

"I cannot believe you're going to trust her," Morticia said once I'd relayed the conversation and Trisha's job offer to write a tell-all on the Svensson brothers.

"Could be bad," Lilith said. "This could be your epic and bloody downfall."

Morticia swirled her tea around in her cup. "We should do a reading. We'll see how your fortunes will fare in Harrogate. With something this serious, it's the only way."

After tea and snacks, I slowly walked through the house, the happy memories flooding back and bringing tears to my eyes. The furniture was exactly as Mimi had left it, though it was all covered with white sheets. The place felt a little spooky, like a real haunted house.

There was the bedroom with the hundreds of dolls and the study with the creepy animatronic animals from the Mast Brothers' chocolate factory, where Mimi had worked until it closed. Now it was going to be a swanky conference center. I hope they kept some of the creepy elements. It would be so cool to have a Halloween party there.

As I walked through the house, I hated to admit it, but the twins were right; the Old Victorian house had fallen on hard times. Several light bulbs were out or at least flickering. The stained woodwork was dusty, the tall windows were dark and dirty, and the chandeliers were covered in cobwebs. Mimi hadn't had the energy to keep the house up in her old age. Then it had sat vacant. It did need someone who could afford to take care of it.

At least Mimi hadn't gone full-on *Grey Gardens*, mainly because the twins kept her in check, though they weren't all that much better. I had been out back to their art studio. It was a pack rat's nest.

I pushed aside one of the heavy drapes that hid a secret passageway for the servants. Playing here as a kid had been magical. I still loved the house. I took my bag up the narrow back staircase to the turret. It was my favorite room, and it was very cozy with the rain pattering on the large panes of slightly wavy glass.

As I set down my bag and pulled the sheets off the furniture, a whistle shrieked. It was from the speaking tube. Back in the day, the servants would blow a puff of air into one end of the tube, and the other person knew to open their end to talk.

"Hello?"

"Tarot reading in the music room," Morticia said, voice tinny through the metal funnel.

In the library, the twins had removed the white sheets from the furniture. An old pipe organ that took up most of one wall lurked over us.

"We need to see what the future has in store for you," Morticia said. It was still raining outside, giving the room an eerie vibe. The Victorian-era gaslights flickered on the walls. Lilith and Morticia sat side by side, their angular faces, high cheekbones, and pointed chins spooky in the flickering light.

"Sit," Lilith said. Sage burned in a ceramic dish on the table. I sneezed.

"New man in your life?" Morticia asked, setting the tarot cards on the table.

"God, no. Geez, is this that kind of reading? I'm here for my work life. I have loans and credit card debt to pay back. I haven't even been within the spray zone of a man since…" *Since an hour ago.*

That does not count! I told my brain furiously.

I tried to ignore Morticia's gaze as I shuffled the oversized tarot cards then cut the deck. If I was going to deal with Douche-face Svensson and my mother, I needed all the help from the spiritual realm I could get.

Morticia studied the three cards in view. Lilith clicked her tongue. Mimi had used to do my tarot card readings. I suddenly missed her horribly. She was more of a mother than my own had ever been.

"What does it mean? Am I going to have riches and success in my future? Was I clear on the fact that I am up to my tits in debt?" I asked.

"The tower, the wheel of fortune, and the magician," Morticia said in a rapt voice.

"That's good, right? Wheel of fortune means my financial condition is about to change, and it can only get better."

Salem meowed, rubbing against my leg.

"Yes, but the tower means you are flirting with danger."

Thunder boomed, and I jumped. "That's literally my life."

"The magician means that new opportunities are coming, and possibly where you least expect them."

"So unexpected enormous riches are coming my way if I can be risky and ballsy." I pumped my fist. "Good to know."

"Or it could mean you're going to gamble and lose everything."

CHAPTER 4

Garrett

Mornings at the Svensson estate were chaotic. My two dozen youngest brothers acted like a pack of wild dogs, fighting for food and squabbling. Josie used to cook, then Archer's girlfriend, Hazel, had taken over. I'd had to put the kibosh on that, because the two women had more important things to do than make meals for thirty-odd people three times a day.

Now we rotated. It was Remy's turn for breakfast today.

"Breakfast burrito?" he offered. "It's steak, hash browns, eggs, and cheddar."

I took it from him wordlessly.

Remy bent down. Davy was plastered to my leg.

"I have a mini burrito just for you."

I sat Davy down by Billy and Oscar and the rest of my youngest brothers so I could read the paper in peace. Davy's lower lip started trembling. I swiftly picked him back up. I had had to listen to him shriek for hours the previous night, and I did not want to repeat the experience. Davy sat on my lap and munched on his mini burrito while I tried to read the local paper. It was all about the Halloween fair and the *Macbeth* play the community center was putting on.

"They're still looking for volunteers," Archer said. "Can't you do community service to get your license back sooner?"

"I would rather pay the fine," I growled.

"But then you'd have to wait," Mace said. He and Archer were identical twins, which meant I held them both in identical contempt.

Before I could say anything, Davy tried to climb down from my lap, almost squeezing his burrito out over my suit.

"Davy, you and I are going to have to come to some sort of agreement," I told him in a low voice. "You're ruining my image."

"Come here, Davy," Archer said, reaching over to try and grab him. Davy shrank back.

"He only wants Garrett," Mace said with a laugh.

"I don't know why," Archer grumbled. "He's the least good-looking."

Davy was too young to go to school with the rest of my younger brothers. Fortunately, I had had the foresight to insist that one of the amenities offered at Svensson PharmaTech be a day care. Davy did not appreciate it. He screamed as soon as I handed him to Donna, one of the day care workers.

"He'll stop eventually," Donna said, patting Davy on the back softly.

His screaming was giving me a headache. Had I still possessed my driver's license, I would have picked up cold-brew iced coffee on my way to the office. That sure would have eased the tension in my forehead right now.

"You need another assistant, Mace," I snapped at my brother. Ever since the situation with his last assistant had gone south, my older brother had become gun-shy. He was the CEO, and his office suite included a room for an assistant. Archer had recently moved his things into it.

"I need coffee," I told him.

"I can't drive you," he replied.

It was irksome to have to rely on my brothers. Curse Hunter and the cell phone law.

"Also, I don't know how you're going to drink it with the straw ban," Mace added.

I fumed. "What are you doing that is so important?"

"We have the temp coming in."

"Excuse me?"

Mace gave me a mild look. "She's going to help with the accounts."

"I don't need help."

"We are chasing that acquisition for Thalian Biotech. It would be huge for PharmaTech if Sebastian sold us his company."

"I have it under control."

"Fine," Mace said. "Then you can use the temp to take you to the coffee shop. Actually," Mace said, clapping his hands together, "that's a great idea! The temp can be your chauffeur-slash-assistant."

"Is *this* what you've been up to lately?"

Mace nodded. He seemed terribly pleased with himself. Moron.

"I refuse. Send the temp back."

"Too late!" he said. "The receptionist just sent me a chat saying Penny is here."

CHAPTER 5

Penny

I had fallen asleep to the hypnotic sound of rain on the ancient tin roof. Fortunately, the storm had blown over by the time I woke up. I threw open the windows and breathed in. The air was crisp after the rain and smelled faintly of apples and smoke.

"Smells like fall!" I sang.

My last job had really been several jobs cobbled together to afford rent and baking ingredients. I wrote content for blogs with titles like "Which Avenger Are You? If you walk around like you have a pregnant guinea pig in your pants, you might be Captain America!" I also did random side hustles like being paid to wait in lines so people could score *Hamilton* tickets.

At night I made cakes. I had a small YouTube channel called Queen of Tarts with a small but dedicated fan base. Some of them even donated. My fans said the ASMR videos helped them sleep. Unfortunately, the reality was that I didn't actually break even on my baking channel. I should quit, but baking was my emotional outlet.

I told myself I was investing in a brand. I was hoping to build up enough of a following that I could be accepted as a contestant in the *Great Christmas Bake-Off*. That was how Chloe, the winner of the show last Christmas and girlfriend to billionaire Jack Frost, had kick-started her successful franchise. I hadn't made the cut this year, but maybe next year. I should have asked the cards about it the night before.

"You are going to be positive," I ordered myself as I picked out my outfit. "You have a job. Actually you have two jobs."

I still wasn't sure that I should even try to write that tell-all about the Svensson brothers. Last night, I had deluded myself that it was all a dream, except that there was money in my PayPal account the next morning from Trisha.

"You can do this," I told myself as I dressed. "This is your big break. So what if it's a little unethical, it's not like you're writing for the *New Yorker*. It's the *Vanity Rag*; it's a high-society tabloid with nicer pictures and paper. Besides, that Svensson yesterday was a dick." *A big, thick dick...* "No brain."

I tried to focus on something wholesome, like dressing in my fall best.

Svensson PharmaTech was fairly conservative, so I left my blinking jack-o'-lantern sweater at home, at least for the first day. Mimi had collected sparkly brooches, so I pinned a fall-themed piece on my lacy blouse and tucked the blouse into a plaid pencil skirt then pulled a more subtle sweater on, buttoning only the top button. Black tights, patent leather penny loafers, and a black headband completed the look. I spun around in front of the tall antique mirror in the room. I was really feeling the *Chilling Adventures of Sabrina* vibe!

Mimi had a Vespa in the carriage house. It was a cream model with red accents. I felt pretty cool riding down the street between trees sporting yellow, red, and orange leaves. As I turned onto Main Street, a freight train rumbled past right down the middle of the lane. The gleaming white letters on the side read "Svensson PharmaTech." It was another cool, unique thing about Harrogate. I waved to the conductor.

On the way to my first day on the job, I stopped at Ida's General Store.

"There's my favorite cake baker!" Ida said, waving to me when I walked in. "Back in Harrogate?"

"Just for a temp position." *And dirt on the Svenssons, but she doesn't need to know that.*

"I'm actually here to purchase some ingredients for my next cake," I said, giving the older woman a hug. She and Mimi had been friends, and I admired the no-holds-barred way Ida led her life.

"Ooh! I love your Instagram!"

"Thanks, Ida. I saw your comments."

"You have a lot of admirers, if you know what I mean!" she said, waggling her eyebrows. "Might want to take them up on some of those offers."

"No, thanks," I said.

"Don't knock cake sex until you've tried it," she said, sighing happily. "Speaking of which, I loved the Nutella crepe cake. Maybe you could do a fall version?"

"I'm thinking fall themed, like a pumpkin-spice princess cake."

"Yum. You know, if you're up there working at the Svenssons' company, you might catch a billionaire," Ida continued, refusing to give up on my love life.

Yeah, trap him in this article... But think of the student loans you can pay off!

"Maybe..."

"The way to a man's heart is food. And a sexy Halloween costume!" Ida winked.

"I'm not sure about that," I said. "I've been emotionally eating and my cake YouTube videos haven't been helping. Someone has to eat that cake after I bake it! Shameful secret: I have eaten a whole cake in about a day and a half. I don't know if I'd look so hot in a sexy Halloween costume."

"Men like something to grab onto," Ida assured me.

"Well, I have a lot." My blouse was a little tight over my boobs. Summer had ended late this year, and I had only just taken out all my fall clothes. They were slightly snug. Okay, maybe a little more than slightly.

"If you really want to be in the Halloween spirit, we're putting on the annual *Macbeth* play," Ida said. "We need a young person for Lady MacB. If you have a boyfriend locked up in that old haunted house, bring him along too. Rehearsals are starting soon."

"I guess it depends on who I would be acting against. So a tentative yes?"

My Vespa chugged up the hill to the glass-and-steel Svensson PharmaTech offices. I'd never been there. The company had just been building the facility when I'd left for college almost a decade ago. When I walked into the lobby, it contained warm woods, white terrazzo floors, and actual live trees.

"They totally need to dress these up for Halloween," I said to myself as I took out my phone. "With some hay bales, café lights, and pumpkins, this would be awesome for a Halloween party."

I was so busy taking selfies that I didn't even notice the other woman standing next to the reception desk.

"Bronwyn?" My enemy from high school, Bronwyn had gone out of her way to make me feel terrible. She had spread nasty rumors about me, insulted me in the hallways, and lied to the teachers and told them I was cheating off her paper.

"Penny McCarthy," she said looking me up and down.

"Do you work here?" I asked. "I'm here for a new temp position."

She stared down her nose at me and flipped her glossy hair. The rain had made my own hair even frizzier than normal. Suddenly I was back to being the abandoned, friendless teenager.

Bronwyn sneered at me. "It figures you're just a temp. Some of us didn't waste money on a journalism and basket-weaving degree. I went for accounting, and now I have a cushy job. And I'm going to land one of the Svenssons as a husband. Just you watch."

I glared at her.

"I'll take you up to Mr. Svensson," she said, waving to the receptionist.

How has Bronwyn been hired for a real job and not me? I fretted as I followed her. *Wait, I don't care. You're an adult, Penny. So what if you're a temp. Your real job is journalist. You're going to write an awesome article. You'll get a book deal. Bronwyn will be so jealous.*

I followed her into a conference room. There, glowering at me, was Mr. D-bag Svensson from the train station. He was flanked by several of his brothers.

"Garrett," Bronwyn said, "this is the new temp, Penny."

His eyes narrowed when he saw me. "I didn't ask for her. Send her back."

"With pleasure," Bronwyn simpered.

"I guess you still haven't found any Halloween cheer," I snapped.

CHAPTER 6

Garrett

Mace hissed at me, "Garrett, we need the extra hands. We're trying to buy Thalian Biotech. We need full marketing packages. We need a welcome committee."

"What can you do?" I asked the curvy redhead. *Don't think about her curves. That's inappropriate.*

"I can write. I'm a journalism major."

"See, unqualified," I said to Mace. "Unlike Bronwyn."

Bronwyn beamed. Penny snorted then covered her mouth, pretending it was a sneeze.

"You got me an assistant unannounced," Mace countered.

I glared at him. "Yes, because you are useless and incapable of multitasking. I am operating on a higher plane than you."

I turned to the redhead. "Do you have any experience at all being an assistant?"

"I was a camp counselor once," she offered.

"Typical Mace, you can't even find someone reputable."

"I know several girls who are very qualified assistants," Bronwyn said. "They'll be better than some temp."

"Would you please give us a list of names?" I asked.

"They need to be vetted," Mace said. "But Penny is here now. She can fetch your coffee and print things for you."

"I can get my own coffee."

"No, you can't," Hunter said. "You lost your license."

Fuck, that's right. "A terrible inconvenience."

"Penny can be your chauffeur," Mace offered.

"No."

"I'm not driving you around," Hunter warned. "So either you're going to walk, or Penny can drive you."

"Do you know how to drive?" I asked her.

"Of course!" Penny said, glaring at me.

"Great. You can be Garrett's new chauffeur and assistant," Mace said.

"Why don't you show her around, Bronwyn?" Hunter said.

"No," I said. "Bronwyn, you have important work to do. Penny's not going to be here that long, just until I get my license back. She doesn't need a grand tour. I do not want or need an assistant."

"I have a conference call," Mace said, cutting and running.

Hunter followed him after setting a stapled stack of papers on the table. "She needs to sign the NDA."

Bronwyn left. Then it was me and Penny. She pulled out an orange pen with a sparkly bat topper and silently signed the NDA.

"So," she said. She wasn't wearing what the workers at Svensson PharmaTech usually wore. She was dressed more like a preschool teacher, in what I could only describe as a fall costume. The brooch of a purple witch on a broomstick drew the eye right to her chest. The blouse was tight over her tits.

I killed that thought. How was the girl from the train station in front of me? It was troublesome.

Penny tucked a red curl behind her ear. "All signed."

I stared at the sparkly orange ink.

"Do you need me to get you coffee?" Penny asked uncertainly. "Sorry, I thought I was just coming here to do account management, not be a personal assistant."

"Follow me," I said, turning and marching out the door.

Penny trotted behind me as I walked to my office. "Do you need help on the big super-duper secret project?"

"No."

I needed her to stop talking. Even when she was silent, her presence was overwhelming. Or maybe it was the smell of pumpkin spice. Was she wearing a perfume? Did they even make pumpkin-scented perfume?

Focus.

I had to think. I had a to-do list. Get my license back. Get Hunter and Meg back together so I could talk on the phone in peace. Convince Sebastian to sell me his biotech company.

"Mr. Svensson," Penny said, interrupting my thoughts. "I'm actually pretty good at—"

"Penny," I told her firmly, "we don't need your help. The only reason you're still here is because Hunter is a fucking idiot!" I raised my voice. Hunter walked over to the glass wall of Mace's office and slammed his palm on it.

"Read a book," I told Penny. "I will call you when I need you to drive."

Mace's suite had an attached office for an assistant. Mine did not because I did not need an assistant. Except now I had an assistant. She sat on the couch against the wall while I went through emails.

As I made notes, I watched her out of the corner of my eye. Penny started off sitting back straight, legs pressed together. As the hours wore on, Penny shifted on the couch. She rested her head against her hand, curling her feet under her. Geez, she was distracting. I looked at the clock. I'd had the same spreadsheet up for the last twenty minutes, and I couldn't really remember what I had been looking at. Also my whole office smelled weird. Not bad but sweet and a little spicy, like cinnamon and pumpkin.

We had an upcoming meeting with Sebastian, the Thalian Biotech CEO. I needed to concentrate on the acquisition. It was important that Sebastian sell to us and not to the Holbrooks. At least Bronwyn was working on it. Unlike Penny, Bronwyn was qualified.

Bronwyn came into my office and looked down at Penny. "Do you want me to find another office for her?"

"We are at capacity here," I reminded her. "That's another issue we have not yet addressed: Where will we put all the employees if we purchase Thalian Biotech? Sebastian will have questions about it. The Holbrooks have plenty of space, of course."

"I'll look into some land options," Bronwyn said.

"I can do it!" Penny offered eagerly.

"We need someone qualified," Bronwyn said. The rest of whatever she was going to say was cut off by a horrible screaming. Mace and Hunter stuck their heads out of his office. Donna was walking down the hall with Davy, who was writhing and flailing in her arms.

Mace winced at Davy's screams. "Is he hurt?"

"He's just upset," Donna said. "He hasn't calmed down in the last several hours. He's screamed nonstop since Garrett dropped him off this morning. He's upsetting the other children. He's not that well socialized."

"You're expelling him?"

"No," Donna said diplomatically. "But he's very upset, and since you all are here, it might help him to calm down." Davy's face was almost purple.

I smelled that same sweet pumpkin-spice scent behind me, and Davy immediately stopped crying and smiled.

"Hi, Davy!" Penny cooed. He reached out to her, and she picked him up.

"I like your pin," Davy said. He hiccupped then patted the sparkly brooch.

"I'm busy," I told Mace. "Davy can't stay here."

"He really should be socialized," Mace said.

"He can stay with Remington," Hunter said. "We have an important acquisition to try to win. I can't have him running around."

"I'll drive you back home, and you can pick up your car," Mace said, grabbing his jacket. "Or I guess it's Penny's car now."

CHAPTER 7

Penny

The Svensson estate was insane. So were the Svenssons. Garrett and Mace sat in the front of the car, arguing. I was sitting in the back of Mace's car with Davy. The little kid smelled a lot better than he had the last time I'd seen him.

I still wasn't sure what my job was supposed to be. I had been bored out of my mind all morning. I'd alternated between looking up information about the Svenssons online and texting with Morticia and Lilith about how awful Bronwyn was. I also snuck glances at Garrett in between text messages. If Davy was the cute, cuddly model, Garrett was the hard-ass. He hadn't smiled once—not even when Donna had brought Davy upstairs.

"Your brother's mean," I whispered to Davy, making him giggle. I thought I saw Garrett stiffen for a second.

"Are you going to decorate for Halloween?" I asked when we pulled up in front of the estate, which had been built out of huge chunks of gray stone with ornate detailing, floor-to-ceiling windows, and several turrets that put Mimi's haunted Victorian mansion to shame. I was in awe. "You could have an *awesome* party here!"

I tried to take in as much information as possible for my article. During the mind numbing-hours I had spent on Garrett's couch researching the Svensson brothers, I hadn't found much information—only gossip and speculation. Hot billionaires, big house, tight-knit family. So far there hadn't been anything super salacious that people probably didn't already know. The Svensson brothers went to work then went home. Sounded pretty normal. But everyone had skeletons in their closets—especially in a house this size.

"Are we going inside?" I asked as innocently as possible.

"No," Garrett said. "My car is out here."

A large man with a big bushy beard came out from a side entrance. "Welcome, friend of Garrett," he said, hugging me.

"Remington, you can't just hug people you've never met," Garrett snapped, pulling him off me.

Remy hugged Garrett instead, and I laughed at the face he made.

"This is our oldest brother," Garrett explained when Remy released him.

"I have a meeting," Mace said, waving as he handed me Davy's booster seat.

"Hungry!" Davy said as Mace drove off.

"Me too!" I told him.

"Remy's going to feed you," Garrett said.

"Bye, Davy!" I called. Davy looked like he was about to start crying.

"If you're good, Penny will come visit you," Remy said to Davy, bouncing him up and down.

"That's right!" I exclaimed, ignoring Garrett's scowl. "I'll come by and make Halloween crafts, and we'll make cupcakes."

Davy blew me a kiss, and I blew one back.

"We're friends!" he called happily.

"We *are* friends, Davy! Now I have to drive your brother to work, because apparently he broke the law. Don't be like Garrett."

I turned to the sleek black sedan that glimmered in the sun. A Tesla. *Very snazzy.*

"This is a nice car."

"Don't scratch it," Garrett warned. He was standing possessively by the driver's-side door.

"I need to drive." I held out my hand. "Keys?"

Garrett glowered at me and didn't move.

"I'm a great driver," I told him. "Very careful."

He slowly moved around to the other side of the car while I readjusted the seat and the mirrors. I smiled at him as he sat in the passenger's seat and buckled his seat belt.

"You will be very happy with my chauffeuring service," I told him. "Oh, you know what? I'm going to buy a cute little chauffeur's outfit with a matching hat and gloves."

I wanted to see how far I could push him. With the way Bronwyn was acting, it was doubtful I would even last the week, so why bother acting professional at all? I didn't know how I was going to get enough info for the article if I wasn't even allowed inside the house.

"It will be a really sexy chauffeur outfit, you know, with fishnet tights. I saw one for sale as a Halloween costume," I continued as I started the car. It made an almost imperceptible purr. "Mmm," I moaned. "This is a *nice* car."

In New York City, I was reliant on trains, buses, and my own two feet for transportation. I had always envied the girls in their exquisite designer shoes who were helped in and out of town cars. Now it was my turn. Well, sort of. I was the driver. But still—no more stinky buses.

"Where to, O Great CFO?" I asked Garrett. "We're getting lunch, right? I'm starving."

"I suppose," he said. "I really need coffee."

"Any preferences? Any coffee shops with cute girls that you want to hit on?"

"No," he snarled.

"I'm teasing!"

"Just drive," he said.

I pressed on the gas. The car jerked forward and ran into a bush. I screamed.

"I thought you said you were a good driver!" Garrett yelled, throwing open the car door. We inspected the damage.

"You can just buff that out," I told him with more confidence than I felt. "I saw this product on an infomercial. It's made by the same people that sell that super-duper sticky tape that can hold a boat together."

"That tape is a scam," Garrett said, getting back into the car.

"Don't tell me that! It's like finding out Santa isn't real!"

"I thought you were a Halloween nut," Garrett said.

"I love all holidays equally, but some more equally than others."

I drove Garrett over to the coffee shop. He didn't make any more conversation. He was typing emails on his tablet the entire time. Now that I was in a confined space with him, I couldn't help but notice the sort of clean masculine scent that permeated the car. It was better than freshly baked bread. I just wanted to bury my face in Garrett's chest and inhale. I wiped my mouth. I was starting to get a little drooly.

He's a terrible person, Penny. Honestly, you would think by now you would have better decision-making skills.

"Just circle the block," Garrett said as I pulled up in front of the Grey Dove Bistro. It was the Harrogate franchise location of Chloe's Manhattan restaurant. He didn't wait for my answer as he climbed out of the car and slammed the door shut.

Fuck that. The way Chloe organized the Grey Dove Bistros was that there were some similar menu items but also some that were unique to each location. This one had the donut Danish. They were all over Instagram. There was no way I was passing that up. Besides, I was starving. A whole morning of doing nothing except search the internet for dirt on the Svenssons had made me work up an appetite.

I parallel parked the Tesla and only banged into the car behind me a little bit. Then I ran across the street to the café. It was in an old, historic building. There was art on the walls depicting corgis and dachshunds in Halloween costumes, smiling silly doggy smiles while sitting next to various fall baked goods.

Garrett was standing off to the side, waiting for his order. He scowled when he saw me.

"I'm starving," I told him when he stalked over to me.

"I have a lot of important things to do. I can't wait for you to order lunch."

"More important than lunch? Did you even eat today? Maybe your blood sugar's a little low, and that's why you're so grouchy." I almost felt his forehead, but one, he was so tall that his head was way up there, and two, I didn't want to press my luck.

"You don't want a sandwich, Garrett?" Hazel, the franchise owner, asked. I recognized her from Instagram. She had her poofy hair in a ponytail and was wearing an apron that had pumpkins and latte cups embroidered on it.

"I'm fine," Garrett said firmly.

"What would you like to order?" Hazel asked me. I was slightly, okay, *insanely* jealous of her, though I absolutely loved her. Owner of a successful franchise. Artist extraordinaire. Hot rich boyfriend. Archer Svensson seemed like the fun Svensson brother, especially compared to Garrett the Grouch, looming in the corner.

"I'll take a country ham on sourdough, a pumpkin-spice latte, and three donut Danishes. I'm super excited about eating a donut Danish. I'll have a chocolate, a classic vanilla, and a pumpkin spice."

Out of the corner of my eye, I saw Garrett grimace.

"Coming right up!" Hazel chirped as I tried not to wince at the total on the cash register. That credit card debt was just piling up.

I waited next to Garrett for my coffee. He studiously ignored me.

Hazel put a plastic container of iced coffee on the counter. "Sorry this took so long, Garrett. No one orders iced coffee in the middle of fall."

"You know I have to have iced," he said.

"Here's your straw," Hazel said.

"What. Is. this."

I looked at him. "It's a straw. It's made out of paper."

He picked it up with a scowl as if it was roadkill.

"We use those in New York City," I told him. "They're better for the environment."

"I need a plastic straw," he said to Hazel.

"Sorry, they're illegal in Harrogate now," she said.

I tried to bite back a snicker. Garrett looked as if his whole world was crashing down.

"Surely you have some in the back. The bill was only passed last night at the town hall meeting," he complained.

"All restaurants had to dump their straws out to be recycled," Hazel said and left to go take another order.

"This is terrible. This is the worst day of my life," Garrett muttered to himself. "I'm going to kill Hunter."

He was back on his phone while I waited for my latte and lunch.

"Do you mind if I eat here?" I asked Garrett, half expecting him to jump down my throat about daring to tell him how to use his time. He grunted, still on his phone, and followed me to one of the metal café tables by the window.

I noticed his coffee was still on the counter, so I grabbed it and set it and the straw in front of him.

"I'm not drinking that," he said as I took a bite of the donut Danish. It was basically a normal donut with crème brûlée in the hole. The pastry crackled nicely under my teeth, and the vanilla-flavored cream was smooth and rich but not too heavy, so it was a nice counterpoint to the donut.

"Paper straws won't kill you," I said, sticking the white-and-blue–striped straw into his coffee cup.

"I can't even order any straws," he spat. "They're all sold out on Amazon. And some places refuse to ship single-use plastic to New York State."

"Most of the state has a plastic straw ban," I told him. "Plus the tariffs with China are making it hard to import goods."

He cocked his head slightly and studied me.

"Don't act so surprised," I said, inspecting my sandwich. "I told you I majored in journalism. I follow the news, local and international."

Ida came over to me right as I took a big bite of the sandwich.

"I have you down for Lady Macbeth," she said loudly.

I swallowed. "I said it was tentative, Ida."

"You'll need to convince one of these good-looking guys to play opposite you. You've never had a romance like a theater romance. You could have him do it." She jerked her thumb at Garrett.

"No," Garrett said. He was glaring at his coffee.

"Ignore him," I told her. "He hates Halloween. I would have thought you would be Lady Macbeth, Ida?"

"My sister, Edna, refuses to allow me to be the lead in the play. She wants you to do it, Penny."

"If Judge Edna wants me to play Lady Macbeth, I'm not going to cross her. Some people might be afraid of witches and zombies, but hell hath no fury like Judge Edna. She rules her courtroom with an iron fist."

"Ain't that the truth? Rehearsals start next week," Ida called over her shoulder as she went to go talk to Hazel.

"Don't you want a sandwich?" I asked Garrett.

"I have protein bars at my office. Aren't you done yet?"

"No. You can't rush this," I said, picking up the pumpkin-spice donut Danish. The caramelized sugar crunched under my teeth as I bit into it. I closed my eyes and chewed slowly. When I opened them, Garrett was watching me, expression unreadable.

I held out the donut Danish to him. "Want a taste?"

"No, thank you."

"They have metal straws, you know," I told him as he sipped his coffee with obvious distaste.

"That's even worse. You'd never be able to keep them clean."

CHAPTER 8

I ate three CLIF bars for lunch. I should have ordered a sandwich, but my whole day had been ruined. I seethed as I fished chunks of the paper straw out of my coffee. Then I forced myself to calm down. The only way to fix the situation was to have a composed, level head. I forced myself to relax my shoulders. This would have been easier to do if Penny hadn't been sitting there right in the corner of my vision.

Clear head. Dispassion.

Start with the most pressing matter. That would be acquiring Thalian Biotech. I had that under control. I'd had a meeting with Bronwyn yesterday about the numbers. Sebastian would see how much his company could expand with the resources of Svensson PharmaTech at his disposal.

Next: my license.

I could wait out the whole sentence or do community service. Neither was desirable. Table it.

Next: the straw ban. *I need plastic straws. This is America. I should be able to purchase a plastic straw, surely.* But I didn't have time to waste searching the internet for them. I looked over at Penny. She was scrolling slowly through her phone. I needed to find something for her to do. I emailed IT to bring a laptop for her then walked slowly around my desk.

Penny hurriedly closed her phone when she noticed me standing over her, but not before I saw that she was looking at office Halloween decorations on Pinterest. She smiled up at me sheepishly.

"Since you're here, you can help me," I informed her.

Dennis from IT knocked on the doorframe. "Here's your computer. It's all set up and ready to go."

"Thank you," Penny said, smiling sweetly at him. His face went red, and he started stammering. Budding work-place romance? Not on my watch.

"That's all for now, Dennis. Penny, I will take you on a brief office tour." I turned the opposite direction from where Dennis had gone. Penny trotted after me.

"This is the breakroom. There are healthy food items. Svensson PharmaTech is about physical well-being. We don't allow donut Danishes or the like in the office."

Penny nodded enthusiastically and took notes. "No joy, no candy, no donuts. Got it!"

"That wing over there"—I pointed through the window to an adjacent building—"houses Research and Development. My brother Parker runs that division."

I led Penny back to the C-suite offices. "Across the hall is Mace's office. Sitting on the couch is Mace's intern, my younger brother Adrian. It is unclear what value he brings to the company."

"I do stuff!" Adrian protested.

"I would find a desk for you," I told Penny, "but we are very tight on space. We are opening a new facility in downtown Harrogate next year, which will free up floor area here. For now, you will work in my office."

Mace's assistant's office was free, but for some reason, I didn't want Penny over there. Besides, all of Archer's things were in there. It wouldn't do.

I opened the laptop for Penny. "What I need you to do is very important." She perked up. "You need to find me plastic straws."

Her shoulders slumped slightly. "Sure thing, boss."

"Price is no object," I continued. "My coffee was ruined today. I cannot have a repeat of this tomorrow."

Mace knocked on my doorframe. Parker and Hunter stood slightly behind him. Hunter looked annoyed, while Parker looked wary.

"Go away," I said.

"We need to talk about the Thalian Biotech acquisition."

"It's not on the calendar."

"Hunter's leaving tonight for Manhattan, and he wants an update."

I sighed and stood up.

Mace looked expectantly at Penny. "Aren't you going to bring your assistant?"

My brothers really needed to remember who ran things around here. "She's the chauffeur."

"Maybe she could offer another opinion."

"She's not qualified."

"Sometimes people who are far removed from the situation can come up with interesting solutions."

I herded them across the hall to Mace's office and closed the door. I looked at my brothers suspiciously. "What is this meeting really about?"

Hunter cleared his throat. Parker looked between our older brothers.

Honestly. They were like penguins, choosing which one to sacrifice over the edge of the ice shelf to draw out the sea lion. Parker seemed to have been selected for this purpose. My younger brother swallowed and stood up straighter.

"The Holbrooks are trying to move in on our territory. We need to win Thalian Biotech, not just to add to our research portfolio but to make sure the Holbrooks can't compete in our market sphere."

I stared at him unblinking through his insipid speech. He began to wither under my gaze.

Hunter blew out a breath. "Are you in the game or not?"

"You can't obsess over straws..." Mace began.

I blinked.

Mace flinched.

My smile was downright feral. "I have everything under control, I assure you."

CHAPTER 9

Penny

After the meeting, I took Garrett back to the Svensson estate. When I drove into the roundabout, I parked the car and turned it off.

"What are you doing?" Garrett asked as he opened the door.

"I'm giving you your car back."

"No. Just bring it tomorrow morning when you pick me up. Seven a.m. Don't be late."

"All righty then."

Garrett was already out of the car and heading back into the house. I could barely make him out in the dark. The temperature had dropped. It was cold, and I wanted a hot bath and pasta—and another donut Danish, but I couldn't really afford the ones I had already eaten today, so that was a no go. I cranked up the heat and turned on the radio. It was fall, so I had my vintage Halloween songs from the 1930s and

1940s on Spotify. The croons of the Boswell sisters singing "Heebie Jeebies" came from the speakers.

I tried not to feel depressed. It was only my first day, and Bronwyn was trying to have me fired and Garrett outright despised me. Also, I hadn't learned much about the Svenssons that wasn't available online.

The NDA I had signed was only about business dealings, not their personal lives. When I eventually wrote the article, I would have to be careful to write only true things. I could not write anything speculative. I needed proof; otherwise I had no doubt Garrett would come after me with everything in his arsenal. There were at least three lawyers in the Svensson clan. I did not need to be sued for libel.

The moon was bright and low in the sky when I parked in front of the rambling old Victorian house. Salem wound around my feet, meowing as I pushed open the large front door. The house needed a good cleaning. Even for a Halloween party, it was grungy.

I put the bag of groceries from Ida on the counter. I was going to make a cake for my Queen of Tarts YouTube channel. For the next six weeks up until Halloween, I was creating fall-themed desserts. First up: pumpkin soufflé cheesecake. I set up the camera and lights, shooed Salem off the counter, and washed my hands.

I pressed a graham cracker-and-melted butter mixture into the springform pan and put it in the oven. I was going to layer my cheesecake to make a beautiful gradient. As I narrated in my soft ASMR whisper, I made the cream-cheese mixture with pumpkin and meringue. I poured it over the graham-cracker crust and put it in the oven to bake while I made a pumpkin mousse. I smoothed the mousse over the cheesecake once it was cool. Then I made a rich orange-caramel glaze to pour on top. Finally, I sprinkled a graham-cracker-spice mixture on top of the caramel and put it in the fridge to set.

It was late by the time I finished, but the video was looking good. I had a fair number of active subscribers, but I didn't earn enough to even cover the ingredients. Plus I had splurged and bought a high-end camera, microphone, and film lights, so really I was in the red with this failing side hustle. My Hail Mary was the *Great Christmas Bake-Off*. There was prize money if you won, and the exposure would boost your social media following. Maybe I could finally make money off ads. I sighed and uploaded some pictures of the finished product to Instagram.

Salem meowed as Morticia and Lilith slunk into the kitchen.

"You should make a black cake next," Morticia said.

"How's your art?"

"We had a meeting today with Archer Svensson. He wants to commission several big sculptures in the conference center courtyards."

"The old Mast Brothers chocolate factory?" I said. "I love that place. You should do a meercat!"

"We told Archer we had some of the animatronic puppets in the house. Mimi had several." Mimi had been a known pack rat.

"Archer doesn't want anything that on the nose," Lilith said. "Also, for someone who is supposed to be an art collector, he doesn't have good taste. I showed him several sketches of abstract sculptures of important Harrogate figures."

"You didn't show him the Romani queen statue, did you?" I said, aghast.

"It's a work of high art," Morticia sniffed.

"I'm sure Archer doesn't want a statue about the Romani queen at his brand-new conference center," I told the twins. "It is supposed to be for nice events. You can't have people in business suits show up and see a bunch of creepy statues!"

Morticia sniffed. "Penny has no taste. Please ignore her, Romani queen."

"She's buried near here," Lilith said.

Morticia nodded. "You should go leave her an offering at her grave site. It's in the abandoned cemetery to the east outside of town."

"She likes Coca-Cola," Lilith added.

"We made her an offering two days ago," Morticia said, inspecting her black nail polish. "And the next day, Archer asked us to stay on and create more artwork for the conference center."

I shushed them as I videotaped the cake being cut. I narrated, trying to ignore Morticia and Lilith's smirks.

"Are you still going through with the article?" Lilith asked.

"Learn anything juicy?" Morticia added.

"Nope."

"Everyone has a dark secret," Morticia said and picked up the knife. "Everyone."

She sliced herself a piece of cake.

"Delicious."

There was a crack and a bang outside. I ran out. Morticia and Lilith sauntered behind me. Morticia raised a dark eyebrow as we inspected Garrett's car. A tree branch had split off and gone straight through the passenger-side window.

"It's the ghost, Bobby," Lilith said. "He doesn't like modern cars."

"He died right in the front room watching *Jay Leno's Garage*," Morticia said.

"I don't care where he died, Garrett's going to kill *me*. I can't believe I'm going to have to buy Garrett a new car," I groaned.

"It's a bad omen," Morticia said. "I'll burn some sage."

Penny showed up the next morning with a black garbage sack billowing in the passenger-side window of my car. I sent Remy an email to have another car brought in and to send this one to a shop.

"My house is haunted," she said breathlessly. Music blared from the speaker as I buckled myself into the car.

"What is that?" I asked as we drove away.

"Oh, sorry!" she said, turning off the radio. "I was listening to Halloween carols."

I thought for a moment then turned her music back on, listening closely. "This is from *The Nightmare Before Christmas*," I said slowly.

"Yes," Penny said. "That's a Halloween movie."

"No, it's not," I said. "It is clearly a Christmas film."

"I guess you're entitled to your opinion even if it's wrong," she sniffed as she turned the car onto the main road. "Do you need coffee?"

Did I need coffee? Yes. Did I want to drink it out of a paper straw? No. Maybe I could drink it quickly.

"You know, you can call ahead for your order," Penny told me when we arrived at the Grey Dove Bistro.

"It's better to order it fresh," I countered.

"I have a surprise for you!" Hazel said as she took Penny's drink order. She was purchasing another huge container of pumpkin-spice latte.

"We have pumpkin-spice cheesecake lattes now," Hazel said. "I just invented it. Do you want to try it?"

"Um, yes, of course." Penny was excited.

I tried not to gag.

"We also have pumpkin hummus," Hazel said. "It's actually better than it sounds."

"I'll try it!" Penny said. "I need something for lunch."

"I thought you were eating another donut Danish," I said.

Penny nodded. "That too!"

Penny bounced up and down while we waited for our orders. "Stop it," I told her.

"You need to get with the Halloween program," Penny said, ignoring my tone. "It's not even October yet. Buckle up, pumpkin-cup. Oh!" She squealed when Hazel slipped the giant frothy orange monstrosity piled with whipped cream across the counter toward us. Penny took a long sip.

"It's *so* good," Penny said and made a moaning sound that was seriously destroying my concentration. "Garrett." She held the cup out to me. "You should try some. It will put you in the fall spirit."

"Never."

"Hazel even made little Halloween marshmallows," Penny added.

She took a bite of a donut Danish. There was that moan again. I gritted my teeth.

"I love pumpkin everything!" Penny exclaimed.

Hazel put my cup of iced coffee on the counter. Then I heard a *clang*, and there was a metal straw. Penny choke-laughed on her donut.

"I know you don't like the paper, so I found a metal straw!" Hazel said brightly.

The only reason I didn't completely lose it was that she was Archer's girlfriend. "Thank you," I forced out, taking the straw. I had no intention of using it.

Penny took big gulps of her coffee as we walked out of the café. I opened the door for her since her arms were full of pumpkin goods. My whole car smelled like pumpkin-spice latte. I couldn't even roll down the window because it was broken.

"Do you want some hummus?" Penny asked me, opening the container when we were back in my office.

"I thought you were saving it for lunch."

"I've had a rough day," she said. "And it looks like you did, too, what with the metal straw."

"It's disgusting."

"Maybe it could just be your personal straw. You know, then it would only be your germs in it," she said, sitting on the edge of my desk. She was wearing a wool sweater tucked into a red plaid skirt. She leaned over to rummage in the paper sack for the bread.

I saw a slight stripe of creamy-white skin before she tucked her sweater back into her skirt. I shook my head. I did not want to be my father, infatuated with every woman who walked past me. If for some godforsaken reason I ever settled down, as they said, it would be with one woman for life.

"You're hangry," Penny said, holding out a wedge of pita with pumpkin hummus on it. "You need protein in the morning."

"I already had Bulletproof coffee."

"Then why do you need more iced coffee?"

"It's part of my routine."

"Maybe you should mix it up a little," she coaxed, holding out the slice of pita.

I took it from her hand. I was not letting her feed me.

"It is tasty," I said grudgingly. "Though Hazel is an excellent cook, so it's not surprising that whatever she made would taste good."

"You need a mini fridge and a microwave in here," Penny said, settling down on the couch. I needed to find her a desk, if only because watching her lounge on the couch was starting to be a bit much. It was almost intimate the way she put her stocking-clad foot on the edge of the sofa. Her legs in the black ribbed tights swung back and forth, almost giving me a view under her skirt. Did she know? Was she doing this on purpose?

Focus. I forced myself to look back at my screen.

While Penny sat on the couch and typed on the laptop, I went through my most complex and most important plan.

My father was a scourge on the earth. He'd fathered more than a hundred children with nine wives. I had almost rescued all of my brothers out of the cult. The older ones were scattered around. The youngest ones were all in Harrogate. There were two more baby boys in the compound. They would be easy enough to grab. My father willingly took bribes from me for the boys. But there was still the matter of the Svensson sisters.

In a polygamist cult, for obvious reasons, girls were in high demand. This was a delicate situation. It required a scalpel, not a machine gun. If he thought I was trying to rescue my sisters, my father would have them all dispersed to the ends of the earth. It would take years to track them all down.

"I found it!" Penny yelled triumphantly.

I growled low in my throat. I had almost forgotten she was in my office. "What?"

"Plastic straws. I ordered them, had them sent to South Carolina, and I have a guy who's going to drive them up here in a week." She pumped her fist. "I am on a roll. What else do you need me to do?"

I looked at my to-do list. "Win the biotech company."

She grinned.

"Sebastian is coming here in a few days," I told her. "We need to make sure we all know everything there is to know about him. Favorite foods, how he takes his coffee, everything. We've started a dossier on him, but perhaps you can add to it."

Penny nodded.

"Talk to Bronwyn. She's started on the dossier already."

CHAPTER 11

Penny

The last thing I wanted to do was go talk to Bronwyn. But Garrett had asked for a dossier, and there was only so much surfing on the internet I could do.

Bronwyn was on her phone headset when I knocked on her office door. She swiveled around in her chair to stare at me.

"Yes, I know," she said into the headset. "Poor girl showed up in a Halloween outfit. Garrett was horrified, as he should be."

Great. Love it when people talk about me when I'm right there.

"Really? I think we would be good together too. He's going to see how invaluable I was in winning the Thalian Biotech company, and then he'll realize we were made for each other."

Gag. Who would want to date, let alone marry Garrett Svensson? He was crazy. Hot, yes—I wasn't blind or delusional—but seriously, who would want to listen to him complain about straws for the next fifty years?

"Well, his brothers are dating their employees. Josie was Mace's assistant, you know."

I tapped my foot.

"Of course we'll do drinks tomorrow!"

"Not that it's any of my business," I said dryly when she ended the call, "but I couldn't help overhearing. Something tells me that Garrett doesn't want a crazy bitch for a girlfriend."

"You're just jealous," Bronwyn scoffed. "All you do is drive Garrett around."

"You don't know. Maybe that's part of my Machiavellian plan. Spend a lot of alone time with Garrett in a car. Maybe I'll casually get lost and end up in a romantic overlook."

Bronwyn's mouth was a thin, angry line. "Garrett doesn't want someone like *you*. You're not good enough for him."

"Get over yourself," I said, rolling my eyes. "There is nothing about Garrett that would make me want to touch him with a ten-foot pole."

I mean, maybe I *could* touch him, sexually speaking, but only to make Bronwyn angry. Not because Garrett was superhot.

"Garrett's going to fall in love with me as soon as I win him this biotech company. We're going to be engaged after a tasteful one point eight years of dating, then we're going to get married at his family estate." Bronwyn smiled. "You won't be invited."

"I'd rather eat a slug than come to your wedding," I said. "Speaking of the super-awesome project, Garrett wants me to finish up the dossier on Sebastian."

"I'm doing that!" Bronwyn screeched.

I winced. "Now I am. Send me everything you have, please. Don't want to make Garrett angry, do you?" I batted my eyelashes at her.

"Fine," Bronwyn spat. "You're still going to fail."

I spent the rest of the afternoon researching Sebastian. Bronwyn did send me files, but I doubted they contained all that she had collected.

Garrett had his scowl back on. A desk that had magically appeared in his office along with one of those uncomfortable but expensive plastic chairs. I much preferred the couch.

Shifting in the squeaky seat, I emailed an old coworker of mine. She wrote back that she was working on a big article about Sebastian. She would send me her notes if I promised to bake her sister's baby shower cake.

"Make any progress?" Garrett asked me.

I looked up. It was dark outside. The sun had almost set over the skyline. I admired the silhouette of the historic city from our vantage point six stories up.

"Sebastian sounds like a very nice man. I doubt the two of you will get along at all."

The tendons in Garrett's jaw formed tense lines. I could practically hear him grinding his teeth.

"Are you ready to be driven?" I asked sweetly. I was ready for a bath and a big slice of cake. My butt hurt. I was going to burn that chair.

"No," he said and sat back down.

I sighed.

Morticia: *We're right outside your office.*

Lilith: *The Harrogate Trust wants us to add some Halloween cheer to the art walk.*

Penny: *I think it should be fun cheer, not like chicken bones or anything.*

Morticia: *Come see what we have.*

"I'm going to use the little girls' room," I announced.

Garrett grunted. I really needed a break from this room and this man.

The art walk was right outside the Svensson PharmaTech offices. It was going to be connected through town to Archer's new convention center and hotel complex. I didn't take my jacket so that Garrett wouldn't know I was sneaking out. I regretted that decision as soon as I stepped outside. It was freezing.

The air was sharply cold and smelled smoky. The moon was just starting to peek over the tree line.

Trees draped with glowing chandeliers marked the entrance to the art walk. Teeth chattering, I hurried down the path. It was well lit, and massive sculptures marched down the path, casting spooky shadows. Morticia and Lilith were a short ways in.

Long black hair swinging, the twins were inspecting various metal jack-o'-lanterns, burnt-wood sculptures, and hay bale structures they had set up.

"Do you think we should have pumpkins?" Lilith asked.

"Or these lanterns, or both?" Morticia added.

"This is supposed to be an Instagramable moment," Lilith said, "according to Josie."

"We need to make the art walk look festive," I said, inspecting the options. "I like the jack-o'-lanterns, but I think they're a little too small."

Lilith nodded.

"Could you hang a fall-themed wreath or something off the lampposts? I do like the hay bales." I shifted one of the bales around and squeezed two of the metal jack-o'-lanterns around it. I propped a wooden cat next to it. "Can you fabricate some sheet metal to look like ribbons, and maybe some brooms? Then you can have nice little displays. Oh! You should laser cut verses from creepy poems on sheet metal and wood. Then each spot is a little different!"

"I knew you were basic enough to help," Morticia said, patting me on the head.

"I feel like you're being mean," I said, pouting.

Morticia looked down her nose at me. "I would say I don't like to judge people, except that we do. We love to judge people."

"I'm not giving you any more cake."

Lilith snorted. "We'll see you later after you finish driving around that oaf."

As I left, the twins turned as one back to the Halloween display. They were so weird.

I hurried back to the office. It was windy; dead leaves swirled around my feet. Head down, I hugged myself against the wind, cursing because I had foregone my jacket.

In the dark, strong, muscular arms grabbed me. I shrieked and started flailing ineffectively.

"Stop it!"

"Garrett?" I looked up to see his irritated face.

"I saw you go into the art trail through the window," he said, releasing me. "It's closed after dark. Harrogate has improved but not that much. It's dangerous at night. You could have been killed." His face had an intensity that was a little unnerving.

"I didn't know you cared that much—"

"We would have been sued."

"There it is." I said, shrugging him off and hurrying back toward the warmth of the building.

With his long legs, Garrett quickly outpaced me. He slowed down to match his pace to mine and looked at me critically. Then he took off his jacket and wrapped it around me. "I don't want you getting sick," he said to my incredulous look. "Do you have any idea how difficult it is to have a house full of people? The kids are constantly bringing germs back. One person gets sick, then it spreads like a refugee camp."

"Sounds gross. I guess I won't be hosting a Halloween party at your house after all."

He was taken aback. "Why would you want to do that?"

"Sebastian is very excited about Halloween," I told him with a smirk. "I found out all about it in my dossier research. He's very much looking forward to the holiday. You all should tell him you're hosting a Halloween party. That will help convince him to sell you his company. I bet the Holbrooks aren't going to do that. I am pretty good with Halloween games, like pin the tail on the pumpkin—"

"Pumpkins don't have tails."

"I can make graveyard dip! It's marshmallow fluff, gummi worms, and crushed Oreos."

"That sounds disgusting."

"You need some Halloween spirit. Shoot, we should decorate the office."

"We will never have an office Halloween party or decoration," he said in a clipped tone.

"You'll see that I'm right," I told him. "Sebastian and I are kindred spirits. Maybe I'll even dress up in a sexy Halloween costume for him when he comes."

Garrett's eyes widened slightly, and he practically sprinted away from me while I doubled over laughing.

CHAPTER 12

Garrett

It was silent in the car as Penny drove me back to the Svensson estate. Her comment about wearing a sexy Halloween costume had thrown me. What would she even wear?

"We're here!" she chirped as the car pulled up in front of the house. I turned to look at Penny in the dark. "Unless you want to go for a late-night romp in the graveyard."

"Why would I want to do that?"

"The Romani queen is buried near here," she said, turning to face me. "We could go make an offering. Maybe it would help you win that company."

"No, thank you," I said, climbing out of the car.

My little brothers were lined up nicely in the dining room when I walked in. Josie was serving portions of grilled fish.

"There's the future Macbeth!" Remy called out.

"Excuse me?"

"Ida said you're playing Macbeth in the fall festival production," Archer said. "I'm proud of you, Garrett, venturing out of your comfort zone like a baby bird leaving the nest."

"I'm not playing Macbeth."

"But you could earn your license back more quickly," Hunter said. "I went down to the city to try to negotiate your fine. Judge Edna said she would give you your license back if you played Macbeth in the play. She'd count it as community service."

"Isn't that illegal?" I asked. "It's basically bribery."

"Small town," Josie said. "Also, Edna really doesn't want Ida to play Macbeth in drag, and Art has that bum foot."

"And a drinking problem," Mace muttered.

"So you know she's a little desperate."

Archer snickered and scooped a large spoonful of grilled eggplant onto Nate's plate. "Garrett doesn't want his license back. He clearly likes being driven around by the cute redhead."

"Why don't you and Meg play the Macbeths?" I shot at Hunter. I did not want the conversation to derail to the state of Penny's physical attributes, as impressive as they were.

"Please," Mace snorted. "Meg still hates Hunter. Aren't a whole bunch of people murdered in that play? Meg would probably stab Hunter for real."

I needed to bring those two back together. It was the only way to keep my quality of life from deteriorating any further. Mace handed me a plate of food, and Davy crawled into my lap as I ate.

"Remington, would you please come fetch him?"

"He's too short to sit by himself," Remy said, beaming at me. "Why don't you take him to work with you tomorrow?"

"You should take us!" Oscar said. "We need to learn from the best about how to run a company."

"Flattery will get you nowhere," I told him. "Besides, you have school."

"But we have a real business plan. We almost have a prototype for our product," Billy said.

"You can show me when you're done," I promised him. "But not for a few weeks. Sebastian from Thalian Biotech is arriving in a few days. We need to make a good impression. My sources tell me his meeting with the Holbrooks went very well. We have the added disadvantage that we're not in Manhattan, so he would be moving his employees."

After dinner, I walked outside. It did really feel like autumn. The season always made me feel slightly anxious. When my father had kicked us out of the cult, Hunter, Greg, and Remy had made it seem like we were just camping. It had been the middle of summer, it was warm, and we hung out in the brush and fished and hunted. Then fall hit, along with the bitter cold, and it suddenly wasn't so much fun anymore. The change in the weather brought back the anxiety of being a child and listening to my older brothers' panicked whispers at night when they thought we were asleep.

Remy came out onto the terrace, Davy draped over his shoulders.

"He should be in bed," I said.

"It's not that late, it just turns dark early. Davy wanted to see the stars. I told him you knew all of the names of the constellations."

I looked up at the night sky.

"Hazel made cookies. Here, I brought you one."

"I don't care for sweets."

"But it's a happy bat, for Halloween!"

Remy was probably my favorite brother. He stayed in his lane and didn't get in my way. He was a military veteran, and his money had been what Hunter and Greg used to hopscotch our family net worth into the tens of billions. Now he puttered around the estate, ran his foundation, entertained the kids, took care of the grounds, and generally annoyed Hunter, which I wholeheartedly approved of.

"You can eat it, Remy," I told him.

He took a big bite of the cookie, crumbs tumbling down his beard. "Having a bunch of bakers in the family sure is convenient," he said around the treat.

"Sure is."

He rocked on his heels. That was what he did when he was going to ask for something he knew I did not want to say yes to.

"Davy and I were talking earlier today—"

"Oh, you and Davy were having a conversation, were you?" I said. "That's interesting, especially since Davy can barely string together sentences."

"Davy intimated that he might like a Halloween party."

"No."

"How about a fall festival?"

I sighed.

"We could do hayrides," my older brother said.

"We don't have horses."

"Could get some goats," Remy said, bouncing Davy. "Could be fun—bobbing for apples, jack-o'-lantern carving contest..."

"We're not having a Halloween party."

The next morning, Penny screeched to a halt in front of the house. There was a headlight missing on the car.

"Get out," I told her.

"And happy fall morning to you too!" she said. "Did you sleep well? Have good dreams?"

"I had a nightmare that my car was further damaged, and oh look, it is."

"It's the ghost," she said, hopping out of the car. "He hates modern cars. Maybe you have an old Ford pickup or something?"

"We do not. Those old cars are dangerous. They don't have airbags," I said, frowning. "You get in a wreck, and the steering wheel goes straight through your rib cage."

"Then they bury you and you come back as a zombie!" She giggled.

"Car accidents aren't funny," I said.

"I know!" She stared at me, eyes wide, lips pressed between her teeth. "But the thought of you as a zombie is kind of funny!"

A new Tesla pulled up alongside the ruined one. Remy jumped out. "Penny!"

"Remy! He's the best hugger," Penny said, clearly delighted.

I did not want my brother hugging Penny. I pulled him off. "We're late."

"You run the company," Penny said with a laugh. "Can you really be late?"

"You're late," Hunter said when we walked into my office, Penny trailing me. "We have a meeting about the Thalian Biotech acquisition."

"Sorry," Penny said. "It was my fault. We had to find a new car."

Hunter scowled at Penny. I was seriously about to punch my brother in the face, which was weird because violence was not my style. I preferred to lull my victims into a sense of complacency then crush them and everything they loved.

"Maybe you do need to find a new chauffeur," Hunter said. "Time is money, and I don't want her costing us this company."

"Penny is doing a fine job. She has a very detailed dossier on Sebastian," I told my older brother. "And you need to remember that I'm the one who not only keeps this company afloat but makes sure our entire family doesn't end up in the poorhouse. If I let you all run riot with the finances, Archer would have blown all the money on a zoo."

Hunter blinked. "Fine. Penny, show us what you've been working on."

CHAPTER 13

I had just stuffed the last bite of my donut Danish (I really needed to cut back!) into my mouth when Garrett's brother said that. He and his brothers looked at me expectantly. I chugged my coffee then promptly choked on it. Garrett patted me twice on the back. His touch shot straight through me down to my pumpkin patch.

Geez, Penny, get it together.

The truth was, I wasn't really prepared to present anything. I had a few notes on my phone, but thankfully my friend had sent me the files on Sebastian the night before. There were tons of good personality information. In gratitude, I had promised my friend a three-tiered raspberry-chocolate cake. I would sure have liked a slice of that cake right about then.

"I can give you a rundown," I rasped, "if you'd like."

"Five minutes," Hunter said.

I skimmed through the files again while chugging the rest of my pumpkin-spice cheesecake latte. Next time, I was ordering two of them. I needed it if presenting to Garrett and his brothers was going to be a regular occurrence.

Bronwyn was waiting when we walked into the glass-enclosed conference room. Mace and Parker were already there. She had her various charts and graphs up on the screen. From what I could tell, they were all about how much money Thalian Biotech and Sebastian as the owner and majority shareholder would make.

Bronwyn turned up her nose when she saw me. "I thought this was supposed to be a confidential project."

Then why was she blabbing to her friend on the phone about it?

"Penny has apparently been putting together a dossier on Sebastian," Hunter said. He still sounded skeptical.

"I doubt it's as thorough as the one I made," Bronwyn said triumphantly.

I knew she was hiding information from me.

"Let's hear it," Garrett said, sitting at one of the chrome-and-leather chairs. "We need to know everything there is to know about Sebastian."

Bronwyn pulled up a profile on the screen. "Sebastian is very impressive, but not as impressive as you, of course, Garrett," she said with a laugh.

I was satisfied to see that Garrett's expression remained neutral.

"Sebastian went to Stanford and started his company five years ago," Bronwyn continued. "Based on his TechCrunch interview, he's very into exercise and technology. He likes to read biographies and wakes up early to work out. He also takes care of his younger half brother, so I know he'll be glad to see how much money he can make for his family. I have several graphs showing how much money he's going to earn with this acquisition." She looked smug.

"That's it?" I scoffed.

"No," Bronwyn said in annoyance. "He also likes dogs."

"That's not a character profile. You just read his Wikipedia page!" I yelled at her.

Garrett looked between us. "What information do you have, Penny?"

Annoyance at Bronwyn gave me a boost of confidence as I walked up to the front of the room and not-so-subtly pushed her aside. "Sebastian is a billionaire and a CEO, yes. He also has a half brother. These facts tell us literally nothing about him."

Bronwyn glared at me.

"Let me tell you about who Sebastian really is," I said, staring at Garrett and his brothers. "He's a man that cares about his family, about his quality of life. He also cares about his employees. This goes beyond money, though that is important for him. He wants to leave a legacy; he wants to make a difference. Did you know that when he started the company back in college, Sebastian had an opportunity to start a generic social media company that would have probably been able to sell to Facebook for a billion after a couple of years? Instead, he took the more difficult path, because he believed the world needed people to do something crazy, to really push the boundaries."

Hunter and Mace were nodding along with what I was saying.

"Did you know Sebastian is very much a person tied to the idea of *place*? He's from upstate New York. On holidays, he always goes home. He believes in work-life balance and achieves it by hiring talented people and then trusting them to do their jobs. He wants to be involved with his little brother and not just be a shadowy ATM. When we sell Svensson PharmaTech to him, we're also selling Harrogate. We're selling the small-town culture."

Garrett looked at me blankly.

"So in conclusion," I said, "you all should host a Halloween party, preferably at the Svensson estate."

Garrett's mouth clamped down in a thin line. "Never."

I pulled out my phone and showed them a picture of Sebastian and his little brother on his Instagram account. "You guys have a lot in common. Sebastian really likes kids and would appreciate our town. It's very family friendly."

"How does that lead you to think we need to host a Halloween party?" Hunter asked.

"You need to show him what a warm place this is and how similar you guys are," I said. "Show him you come from the same backgrounds and value the same things. It's not a stretch. I know you are good men. You care about the community and each other."

Bronwyn was glaring daggers at me, but her expression changed to sweet as she looked at Garrett. "I can help you plan a party," she said.

I still needed to write that article. I needed to be in that house. "I'm sure you're too busy!" I chirped, giving her a fake smile. "I can help plan the party. After all, I'm just the temp. I can do the office decorations too."

"That seems overkill," Garrett said. "I don't want the office to look like a Halloween store."

"Why do all of you hate Halloween?" I exclaimed. "It's the best holiday ever! There's no weird sentimental flare-ups like with Christmas and Thanksgiving, which are all about repressing your emotions in order to deal with your family. Halloween is pure. It's about spooky fun, cool decorations, and excessive amounts of candy. What's not to love?"

"She makes a convincing argument, Garrett," Mace said.

"A Halloween party isn't going to help us win this company."

"No," I retorted, "but neither is showing Sebastian a bunch of boring graphics."

"We need to show Sebastian that we also have enough space for his employees," Bronwyn interjected. "Parties won't help make him overlook the issue. He's not an idiot."

"Just develop more land in town," I said. Garrett and Mace looked at each other.

Garrett's tone was flat when he spoke. "The city tends to fight us every step of the way."

I had done some coverage of similar development projects during my ill-fated career as a journalist. There was one thing successful developments had in common... "So offer some type of amenity to the community," I said.

"We've already built several parks," Garrett retorted.

"Archer keeps saying he wants a zoo," Mace said.

Garrett's lip curled.

"I meant something they can't say no to, like a job creator," I said hastily before Garrett could start an argument.

"We need a better answer," Hunter said, making notes on his notepad. "The Holbrooks have acres of land out in Connecticut. Especially because of Wes Holbrook's facilities."

"That family has the worst luck," Parker said.

"I don't believe in luck," Garrett sneered. "Luck is for the weak. It's what little minds rely on when they cannot comprehend the intricate web of dealings that must be laid to achieve your goals."

"All right, there, Machiavelli," Mace said. "Before Garrett starts plotting his path to world domination, let's assign action items."

"Penny will start putting together a tentative party plan and schedule," Hunter said, "and Bronwyn and Adrian can start looking at land options."

I nodded, hoping I didn't look gleeful. Finally, I would be able to start collecting real dirt on the Svenssons.

CHAPTER 14

Over the next few days, Penny threw herself into planning an itinerary for Sebastian. She also went way overboard on Halloween. Her whole desk was decorated. She had lanterns with little LED lights and pumpkins and other squashes. There was an excessive number of candles, along with garlands constructed of colorful leaves and strands of lights.

"He's making a decision at the end of October, right?" Penny said, perching on the edge of my desk. "So we'll have a Halloween party in early October, at your house. That will be more family friendly. We'll have games and whatnot. I'll need to go over to the house and plan it out."

I felt a rush of happiness at the thought of Penny at the estate. Which was… odd.

"Then I'll have another party that's more adult." She winked at me. "I'll try to convince the twins to have it at Mimi's house."

"Mimi?"

"My foster grandmother."

"We also have the big Halloween festival the weekend before Halloween. Still looking for someone to play Macbeth," she said, pushing my leg slightly with her foot. "That's enough for Sebastian to have the full Harrogate Halloween experience, I think."

She chattered on about the particulars of each party. I was only half listening. Her chest was right at my eye level. The way the sweater stretched over her tits was… distracting. They rose and fell as she talked.

"… which we'll use to decorate your office," I heard her say in the laundry list of Halloween events.

"Decorate my office?"

Penny nodded excitedly. "This whole office will be filled with fall. You can't just buy it, either. It needs to feel DIY but high-end."

"No."

"Yes!" Penny replied. "It's not like you have to make anything. I know some artists who can help. We'll make the lobby space very festive. You could even have a desk-decorating contest!"

I scowled. "Don't decorate my office. I want it pristine."

She looked up at me expectantly. I sighed then took out my credit card and handed it to her.

She jumped up and down with glee. "I can't wait! I love shopping and decorating." She texted someone while I mentally tallied how much the décor was going to cost.

"Don't go overboard," I warned.

"I won't! I'm just going to buy some hay bales, cute fabric, and some lights. It will barely be anything. Pinky pumpkin promise."

"Uh-huh," I said.

She pulled on her red wool cape. "Do you want me to buy you a coffee or a snack or anything while I'm out? I hate to think of you stuck here, starving, while I'm gone," she teased.

"I'm fine," I said as I walked her downstairs.

"I can't believe your straws aren't here yet," Penny complained when we walked through the lobby. "The shipment said they were delayed. Can you believe that? Maybe we can find some other sort of material. I'll test some other straws out for you, you know, give them a good hard suck, see if they can withstand a milkshake or something else creamy."

My head was reeling. I opened my mouth then shut it. Penny laughed.

A big black hearse pulled up in front of the office. Two identical young women were in the car, one driving. They were even wearing black lace gloves and silk scarves over their hair.

"These are our Halloween decorating experts," Penny said as she opened the door of the hearse.

"I suppose they do look the part."

"You seem to be warming up to Penny," Mace said when I went into his office to talk to him about space for Thalian Biotech. My brother Liam and his cofounder, Jack Frost from Platinum Provisions, were in Mace's office. My older brother Greg was there, too, a look of annoyance firmly affixed to his face.

"She's fine," I said, trying and failing to avoid thinking about her *sucking on something*. I looked at Mace. He looked at me. Liam and Jack looked at each other and snickered. "The space for Thalian Biotech, if you don't mind."

"I had Adrian look into it," Mace began.

"Adrian," I scoffed. "He's barely made a dent in the money he lost."

"It wasn't his fault it was stolen," Mace said. "And the authorities recovered some of it."

"Jack and I did not drive all the way out here to listen to you rehash last summer," Liam said.

"We have a meeting with the architect to walk the site in an hour," Jack added.

"You all have a lot of space over there," Mace said.

"We can't put them in the development with Platinum Provisions," Liam retorted.

"Why not?"

"We need the space," Jack said. "There's been a lot of interest in the medical device work we'll be doing with PharmaTech. I'm anticipating we'll grow much more quickly than previously thought."

"We need to have a legitimate and desirable space for Sebastian," Greg said, looking up from his phone. "Hunter was telling me about how you all have been spending your time with that temp worker, planning Halloween parties instead of finding space."

"The Halloween parties are a good idea," I snapped, unwilling to let Greg shit talk Penny.

Greg's lip curled back. "The fact that it is *parties*, multiple, plural parties, is a problem."

"Just FYI," Jack added, "the Holbrooks were showing Sebastian around Frost Tower the other day. They were giving him a tour of Mark Holbrook's space."

"Did he seem impressed?" I asked.

"Yes."

"Was your tower decorated for Halloween?" I demanded.

"Uh, yeah. Chloe did some decorations."

"Was it hay bales? Did you have those animatronic puppets? What about the fake spiderwebs?"

"No puppets," Jack said.

Greg cursed under his breath.

"Shut up, Greg."

"But a lot of pumpkins. Chloe was going for tasteful yet homey."

"He ate in Chloe's restaurant," Liam said. "I met him briefly. He seems nice. He was impressed with the restaurant."

"Was it decorated too?"

"You get weirder and weirder every time I talk to you," Liam said.

"He took a lot of pictures of the space," Jack added. "I know Greg hates holidays, but I think we can all point to the impressive turnaround of Frost Tower's financial situation as an example of how nice decorations can sell a project."

I texted Penny.

Garrett: *The credit card has no limit. Feel free to go all out. Aim for tasteful yet homey.*

Penny: *Sure thing, boss.*

Garrett: *No animatronic puppets.*

"We need to have a legitimate idea about where to put the factory," Greg said. "Not decorating tips."

"Didn't you say you two were looking at some other property nearby?" Mace asked. "Greg, what about the portfolio of foreclosed properties we bought over the summer? Can we put any of those together?"

"The only one that would be big enough would be the old belt factory on Sixth Street," he replied. "It shares a block with several properties in the portfolio."

"That could work. It's a nice building," Mace said, looking at the pictures of the property on the screen.

"It needs a lot of work," Liam said. "We were looking at that one potentially."

"If Sebastian is easily wooed by hay bales and pumpkins, surely he'll like the building. It has character," I said.

"We need to run it by Meg and bring her over to our side," Mace said. "As the deputy mayor, she has a lot of sway."

"They'll approve it," I said. "It would be great for the city."

"I'm not so sure," Mace said. "At the town hall meeting, Meg was fielding a lot of questions about the town letting the Svenssons take over everything without giving back."

"Don't let Hunter come," Liam said with a snort.

"We need a lawyer there. Maybe we should bring Josh in?"

"Their firm is busy," I replied. "Besides, I keep hoping that Meg and Hunter will, at some point after gazing into each other's eyes long enough, see that they were meant to be together."

CHAPTER 15

Penny

"I'm assuming we can't have any wax corpses in the lobby of Svensson PharmaTech?" Morticia asked.

"Please don't," I said.

"What about roadkill skeletons? Lilith found a skunk last night—"

"No! Please no," I practically shouted. "We want cute Halloween decorations."

The twins were both wearing perfectly round sunglasses, making them look like some sort of horror movie characters. Morticia's driving gloves rustled as she carefully navigated the ancient hearse through the parking lot.

Lilith sighed. "I suppose we can do very basic Halloween decorations. No one wants to take any artistic risks these days. How disappointing."

"I'm trying to help Garrett win the company," I said. "Then he'll like me and I can write my article, then I'll be back to Manhattan with a book deal and a swanky magazine job."

"For some reason, we thought you would be staying in Harrogate," Lilith said, looking at me over her sunglasses judgmentally.

"And I thought you said you were selling Mimi's house," I shot back.

"Potentially. It would have to be the right buyer," Lilith said. "Someone with money to keep the house up."

"And someone with the good taste not to paint all the stained woodwork white," Morticia added. We all collectively shuddered.

The first place we stopped at was Ernest's farm. "I'm glad you're back in Harrogate," he said, giving me a big hug.

"We will need hay bales and pumpkins," Morticia said. She and her twin sister opened lace parasols and walked through the pumpkins, pointing out the ones we wanted.

"He gave you his credit card?" Lilith said, thin black eyebrows raised as I paid Ernest.

"What?" I protested. "It's company business."

"All black," Lilith said, plucking the heavy metallic card out of my hand. "I approve."

Next, we went to a thrift store and selected accessories and furniture that gave off spooky and fall vibes. At the fabric store, Morticia found bolts of burlap and black and orange lace.

"I can't say this is my best work," Morticia said when we were back at the PharmaTech main lobby, stringing up lights and arranging pumpkins. "But it should be Halloween enough for someone named Sebastian."

"Nothing wrong with having a basic fall display!" I said as I arranged big wicker baskets full of colorful branches of leaves and sticks of dried flowers.

"You should have let us put up some squirrel skeletons," Lilith said as she hung several large metal spiders on one of the walls.

"No skeletons," I said, placing a white pumpkin and several yellow and green squashes on a metal table. "Besides, I feel like this is actually pretty Instagram-worthy."

I was on a ladder stringing up lights when I overreached to hang a strand and felt myself fall.

"*Oof!*"

Garrett caught me and set me gently on the floor.

"You have very strong shoulders."

"I lift weights," he said matter-of-factly. He stuck his phone in my face. "This is what we are aiming for."

"Is this Frost Tower?" I said, looking at the picture.

"You know of it?"

"I am a card-carrying member of the Grey Dove Bistro rewards club. I'm over there way too much, actually. Probably why I'm a little on the heavier side. Good thing I didn't squash you."

"You're perfectly proportioned," Garrett said.

"Go me!" I said and pumped my fist. If I hadn't known any better, I'd have thought I saw the hint of a smile around his mouth.

He turned to inspect the decorations. Morticia and Lilith watched him like cats checking out a toy. Garrett stared back at them. Unblinking, they huffed and went back to hanging the metal cutouts of Halloween scenes I had begged and pleaded with them to lend me for the atrium.

"Does it feel festive enough?" I asked him. Several of his employees were already gathering around, taking selfies.

"Hashtag PharmaTech Halloween on Insta, ladies!" I called to them. "We are totally going to have an awesome Halloween party," I said, starting back up the ladder.

Garrett took the lights from me and climbed up instead. "There was some contention amongst my brothers on the number of parties," Garrett said, long arms making quick work of hanging the lights on the trees growing in the atrium.

"You have to have a kids' party and a company party, and then an after-hours one where you can really let loose," I said as I held the ladder steady. "I'm making a bunch of Halloween-themed cocktails, like the Witch's Tit."

Garrett sucked in a breath.

"I put a little boozy cherry on top to symbolize—"

"Yes, I understand. I don't live under a rock," he said slightly irritably as he climbed down the ladder.

"This is going to be the best Halloween ever. Sebastian is going to—"

"That's supposed to be top secret," Garrett murmured.

I leaned up to whisper in his ear, "Sebastian is going to hand you his company. Trust me. I know how to character profile someone."

Was it my imagination, or did I just make Garrett Svensson shiver?

CHAPTER 16

Garrett

Penny insisted on leaving early that day.

"I need to see your estate," she said, turning the car onto Main Street.

The train horn blared, and Penny honked back and waved to the conductor.

"Remind me to have that train decorated," she said. "Oh, and we should have a haunted house, and a candy corn-eating contest!"

She was still listing off things for the party when we stopped by the Grey Dove Bistro.

"Grilled cheese sandwiches and potato, bacon, and cheddar soup," Hazel said as she handed us a box. "I packed extra. Archer is supposed to be cooking tonight, and you know how he is."

"That smells amazing," Penny gushed, looking into the boxes.

"I heard we're having a Halloween party," Hazel said as she set a box of cookies on top of the big boxes of soup and sandwiches. "I have so many ideas for snacks and treats!"

"Remy was thinking we should have hayrides," she said as we pulled through the tall iron gate of the Svensson estate. "I love horses. Do you all have some?"

"When were you talking to Remy?"

"Your brother is in charge of the grounds, right? Mace gave me his number."

My little brothers were all home from school, and they stampeded to us when we walked through the front door.

"Remy said we're having a Halloween party," Peyton said, jumping around me.

"We are!" Penny said, walking through the house, spinning around to take it all in. "Wow, this place is amazing! You could have two thousand people here and not even realize it."

"You should see the backyard," I told her.

"Davy!" She picked up my youngest brother and snuggled him to her chest. As the kids washed up, I took Penny out to the backyard. It was expansive, with a wide stone terrace leading down to a lawn. In the summer it was green, but now in the fall the grass was brown and dry.

"This is amazing," Penny said in awe as we walked around the grounds. The sun was already setting. The lights that lined the bridle paths and walking trails into the woods that started at the edge of the lawn glowed softly.

"The Harrogates originally built this house in the late eighteen hundreds," I told her as we walked around so she could take pictures and make notes. "Building big estates to show off your Gilded Age money was very in vogue. We bought it because one, it was cheap, and two, it was the only place big enough to fit all my brothers."

"It's nice that you all care for them so much," she said, touching my arm softly.

She looked down then back up, the setting sun making her hair glow like fire. "I wish I'd had some family to take me in when my mom up and left. You're doing a really good thing."

"I worry about them sometimes," I admitted to her. "Like maybe it's not enough."

"You're a good man. You're doing a good job with them." She rubbed my arm. "Davy seems better, at least."

She looked back at Davy. He was eating dirt out of one of the potted plants at the top of the wide stone stairs leading up to the terrace.

"Or not," she said, running up to grab my little brother.

"Gross, Davy," she said as I fought with him to pull the root of whatever dead plant he was eating out of his mouth. "We have yummy soup and grilled cheese. Don't eat that!"

"I'm hungry," he complained.

"I'll make you a dirt cake for the Halloween party, how about that?" she offered. "We'll decorate it like a graveyard with ghosts and zombies and everything."

Remy was handing out food when we walked back into the dining room.

"Are we saving any for Hunter?" Remy asked as he handed Nate a bowl of soup.

"No. No, we are not."

The kids were more or less well-behaved at dinner.

"Are you going to come help Garrett cook tomorrow?" Peyton asked Penny.

"Don't talk with your mouth full," I chastised him.

He swallowed then continued, "This is so much better than what Garrett makes."

"I didn't make this," Penny said. "But I'm sure Garrett makes you nice dinners."

"They're boring," Billy complained.

"It's not as inedible as Mace's cooking," Isaac said. He was a teenager, and they were all hungry all the time. "It's just bland."

"Food shouldn't be fun; it's about energy," I said.

"They still need to eat. They're growing boys," Penny said. "If the food isn't tasty, they won't eat enough."

"When I cook, I carefully calculate out what they're supposed to be eating," I said.

"Do you all switch off cooking?"

"Yes, but Mace and Archer have their girlfriends cook for them," Billy interjected.

"Well, that's not sending a great message," Penny said with a laugh.

"Exactly," I said. "That's why I cook."

"But Hazel is a much better cook than you," Arlo said.

"Well, it's difficult to do better than outsourcing food to Hazel," I growled at them playfully.

Nate laughed. "I bet you're a better cook than Garrett, too, Penny."

"I can come by and help cook," Penny said.

"I already had all the ingredients for grilled seafood delivered," I countered.

"Gross," Henry said.

"Gross!" Davy shrieked.

"You've never even eaten fish," I told him. "You spent the entirety of your life until now living in the desert."

"I had fish sticks," Davy said with an exaggerated frown.

"That's not real fish," Penny said to Davy.

"My fish won't be that bad," I told him.

"You should come cook!" Arlo said to Penny.

"No. She has more important things to do," I told my little brothers.

"I need to come back over in the daylight anyway," Penny said.

"You don't—"

"I'll come by," Penny said firmly. "I think between the two of us, Garrett and I can come up with something better than bland fish."

CHAPTER 17

Penny

Trisha called me on the way back to the old rambling Victorian house.

"Any progress?" she demanded before I could even say hello.

"Just came back from having dinner with Garrett's family," I told my mother.

"Garrett Svensson?" Trisha seemed intrigued. "Already on a first-name basis. Interesting. I suppose you do take after me after all."

I felt guilty. My mother wasn't a person I really wanted to emulate.

You don't actually have to write the article, I told myself. But I'd taken the advance. *Besides, Garrett is an asshole.*

But was he, though? Garrett had been… I didn't want to say nice, but there was a softness with him when he interacted with his younger brothers. He was mean to the adults, sure, but the little ones… There was something about a man going all soft and cuddly around children that made my ovaries flip-flop.

"You think you can have something together for the December issue?" Trisha asked.

"Of course," I said automatically.

"Good girl! You'll be editor at *Vanity Rag* before you know it!"

I was still feeling guilty when I walked into the Victorian house.

Salem meowed reproachfully when I almost tripped over him in the dark.

"Lay it on, why don't you?" I said, petting him. "I'm not writing anything *terrible* about the Svenssons."

"Not writing what?"

I shrieked and almost dropped my laptop.

Morticia and Lilith were sitting in the dark in two tall wingback chairs.

"Why are you just sitting in the dark?" I demanded, flipping on the lights.

"We're communing with the spirits," they said in unison.

I tried to calm my heart rate down. "Unnecessarily creepy, but whatever. I'm going to go commune with some baking," I told them, heading to the kitchen.

"Turn the lights back off," Morticia called after me.

The kitchen was my safe space. While I enjoyed cooking, I was obsessed with baking. I had a recipe in my head for a caramel apple cheesecake.

I set up the camera and lights and cut out parchment paper to line the pan. I measured out all my ingredients then slowly beat the cream cheese by hand. My videos were enjoyed by people who were trying to relax. Therefore, I couldn't use electronic appliances. I didn't want to lull the viewer into a half-sleepy state, dreaming of yummy baked goods, then suddenly startle them with obnoxious mixer shrieks. Plus it was meditative to bake by hand. I needed to calm down. The article was stressing me out.

When the cream cheese was smooth and fluffy, I added the eggs then whisked in brown sugar and melted butter, creaming them together.

I narrated my steps softly and slowly sifted the flour. Watching it dust the batter was hypnotic. Almost as hypnotic as watching Garrett...

Whoa, where did that thought come from? It's been a dry spell, I told myself. *He's attractive, and society has primed you to think rich dickwads are hot.*

Garrett really was hot though. Too bad it was fall and not summer; I would forego chocolate for a week if I could see him shirtless. *You can't think about sex while baking. Baking is supposed to be wholesome,* I chastised myself, smoothing out the batter in the pan then dropping in chunks of salted caramel.

While it all baked, I whisked the caramel sauce in a double broiler and made a cinnamon-apple compote. When the cheesecake was cool, I carefully removed it from the pan, setting it on a platter painted with smiling spiders, bats, and jack-o'-lanterns. I poured the caramel over the cheesecake then topped it with the apples.

I cut a generous slice. After taking video of the various angles of the cheesecake, I finally took a bite.

"Delicious," I whispered.

It was the type of thing I ate and then looked around and was like, Hey, where did all this cake go? I could have easily eaten the whole cheesecake.

"The spirits say you should give us a piece of that," Lilith said as she and Morticia seemed to appear in the kitchen.

"I'm taking it to the Svenssons."

"The Svenssons?" the twins said.

"I'm cooking for them tomorrow."

"Cooking?" the twins chorused.

"Are you just going to repeat everything I say like a couple of ghosts?" I demanded. In unison, the twins turned to each other, exchanged a look, then turned back to me.

"We're feeling bad energy from you," Lilith stated.

"It's the energy of being broke and having too little self-control around baked goods," I retorted, switching off my camera and unhooking my microphone.

After slicing off another morsel for myself and then wrapping up the cheesecake, I went up to the bathroom. It had an old claw-foot tub with a brass telephone-style faucet. I turned on the water as hot as it would go then lit way too many candles. I needed some self-care. A nice romance novel and a long soak would help me clear my head.

As the water ran, filling the bathroom with steam, my phone buzzed. It was Garrett. My heart yammered.

It's from the sugar, I assured myself. *It is totally not because you're a weirdo who gets all hot and bothered because her boss texts her in a professional capacity.*

I peeked at the message.

Garrett: *Were you serious about coming over tomorrow?*

Penny: *Of course! Besides I promised your little brothers they wouldn't have to eat boring fish.*

Garrett: *Ok. You don't have to if you don't want to.*

Penny: *I love cooking. You're not going to get rid of me that easily.*

Was he onto me? Suddenly I didn't know if a relaxing bath was going to help undo the knots in my stomach. My whole life, I had wanted to be a journalist. I'd wanted to work for a reputable paper, exposing the lies of shady politicians and making a difference. Instead, I had taken the worst of the worst writing jobs to pay rent and student loans. I had done a lot of crappy things in the name of a paycheck, but for some reason, this article on the Svenssons seemed like the worst.

"I'm not going to reveal anything incriminating or embarrassing. Maybe I'll write a sweet piece that makes them all look great!" I said to my reflection in the mirror.

Even as I told myself that, I knew my mother wouldn't accept such a thing. She wanted the scandal—the titillating details! That's what sold.

Garrett: *Thank you. I'm glad you're coming.*

I stared at the phone. Was that a typo? Did he mean he *wasn't* really glad? I stuffed a bite of cheesecake into my mouth, letting the caramel coat my tongue.

Penny: *Tired of eating your own cooking?*

Garrett: *Mace and Archer have their girlfriends around when they cook. It helps to have more people to corral the kids in the kitchen.*
Penny: *I'm good at kid corralling!*

Ah, so that was it. Garrett didn't want me there for him, he wanted me there as a babysitter. A part of me was a little miffed. It wouldn't be so bad for Garrett to want me, right? Then I thought about the article. It was better that we stayed strictly professional. He was going to hate me when this article came out.

CHAPTER 18

Garrett

"You almost veered off the edge," I chastised myself after texting with Penny. I wasn't even sure what had spurred me to contact her. What did I care if she showed or not tomorrow? I didn't even like her.

But if I was being honest, I was perhaps *mildly* sexually attracted to her. Okay, not mildly if the dream I'd had the previous night was anything to go by, but it was not as if I needed a girlfriend. She would just be a distraction.

One day in the distant future, I would find a nice accountant or an insurance claims adjuster and settle down. She would have a capsule wardrobe of interchangeable separates in all neutrals, with hair cut medium length an even two inches below her shoulder. She would run marathons and be vegan. She wouldn't be anything like Penny.

Penny was all curves and soft sweaters, and she smelled like pumpkin spice. I wondered if she tasted like it too. I forced myself to bury the feelings. I refused to be the asshole who lusted after his assistant. She was causing me to go against all of my rules. Normally I didn't text, preferring not to leave an electronic trail.

In the estate, we had a club room, where we kept the alcohol. I rarely drank, preferring to keep a cool head. Penny was making me hot, and I didn't need to dump an accelerant on the fire.

I did like the room, though. It was wood paneled and had thick carpets that muted sound. I could think without distractions. I sat in a leather chair and stared at the fireplace. Penny would probably insist on having a fire going. I didn't have any wood, though.

Get yourself together.

I took out my tablet and started making notes. I read over my list. Penny seemed to have the profile of Sebastian under control. But there was the issue of space.

"I can't believe you didn't leave me anything to eat!" Archer said dramatically from the doorway.

"Go away. I'm thinking."

"You're thinking?" Archer held up his hands. "I'll think too."

"Spare me. You have one brain cell bouncing around in your skull like the Windows screensaver. You'll give yourself a stroke."

"I hope you're thinking about where to put the factory for Thalian Biotech," my older half brother Greg said, pushing past Archer. "And not Halloween parties."

Eli and Tristan crowded around him. They were our college-aged half brothers and Greyson Hotel Group's interns. While Archer was a marginally effective CEO on the days he decided to show up to work, he was, in my opinion, a terrible influence on Eli and Tristan. They had been cocky when they'd started working for him, and since starting their jobs, they had become much worse. I made a mental note to knock them down. A little humbling never did a man any harm.

On the weekends, my older brothers tended to come to Harrogate. Most of them, the ones I was still in contact with anyway, lived in Manhattan and were only slightly useful.

"I hope you brought food with you," Archer complained as Walker, another half brother, went to the liquor cabinet and started pouring drinks.

Josh came into the club room with a bucket of ice. It was getting too crowded for me.

"Garrett's cooking tomorrow," he said. "The kids were complaining. Apparently it's fish."

"Maybe we can order pizza," Parker suggested.

I picked up my stuff.

"You're leaving?" Josh said incredulously.

"We came all this way," Walker said, affecting a New York Jewish grandmother's accent. "We never see you, you don't call, you don't write..."

"Because I'm too busy making sure you all don't trip, fall, and drown in the Hudson River. Yes, Walker, I'm talking about you. You're the one who went on a date with a literal Russian spy last night."

"Wait, what?" Walker yelped.

"You did what?" Hunter snarled.

"She's under investigation by the FBI," I said. "I feed the bureau... information. In exchange, they slip me information. She bugged Walker's phone; fortunately I had the device taken into FBI custody. Within the week, she should be arrested and in jail. Whatever they found is enough to incriminate her."

"You were behind the bum who stole my phone this morning?" Walker yelled, eyes bugging out of his head.

"Your phone was stolen, and you didn't report it?" Hunter said with a frown.

Walker looked chagrined. "I was hoping I would be able to get it back," he mumbled.

I pulled a phone out of my pocket. "This is your new one."

"Garrett knows all," Josh said in awe. Eli and Tristan looked at me, wide-eyed.

"That's right." My brothers just needed to be put in their place and be reminded of who pulled the strings around here.

"Maybe you could do something about those traitors in Seattle," Hunter said.

"Salinger is going to get what's coming to him," I said sagely. "I have a plan."

"Of course you do," Hunter said dryly, setting a glass on the mahogany bar top.

And I had a plan for him as well. Penny's Halloween talk had the nebulous beginnings of a plot in my brain. Soon I would be able to drive and talk on the phone and drink my coffee out of a plastic straw the way God intended.

"I feel like the bum was a bit much. You could have just had me take it off him," Greg said in disapproval.

"Garrett just did that to be mean, I bet," Tristan said, taking a long swig of his scotch.

"That is eight-thousand-dollar scotch," Hunter said, smacking him lightly on the shoulder and taking the glass away. "If you can't appreciate it, you aren't allowed to drink it."

"We'll bring you a juice box," Archer said, sitting across from me. I glared at his feet. He scooted over on the couch.

Mace came into the room. "The kids are all watching Netflix." He looked at me oddly. "Also, they said that Penny is coming to cook dinner tomorrow night?"

"Oh hell no!" Archer exclaimed. "You give me so much shit about having Hazel cook on my nights."

"You are pretty judgmental, Garrett," Mace added.

"I don't have to explain my reasoning to you," I snapped. "Penny will be here tomorrow. If you don't want to eat what she's cooking, I'm sure Remy can kill a squirrel and boil it for you. You can all eat it in the bunker."

CHAPTER 19

Penny

"Going to make dinner for the boss?" Morticia and Lilith asked from my doorway. I jumped and stifled a scream. The twins were quieter than Salem. They just seemed to *appear*.

"He's not my boss. I'm a temp, basically a contractor," I said irritably.

"She has feelings for him," Lilith said.

"No I don't." *Just run-of-the-mill sexual attraction.*

"He's a good-looking male specimen," Morticia said.

"You sound like you're about to dissect him in the mortuary in the basement like on *The Chilling Adventures of Sabrina*," I told her.

"Aunt Zelda is my kindred spirit," Morticia said with a sigh.

"She's going over to Garrett's house to 'bake his cake,'" Lilith said with a smirk.

"Do not use cake as a sexual innuendo. Don't ruin that for me; cake is all I have left. Also, I already baked the cake, so there. I'm going over to make fish pasta and snoop around for my article that I have to write so I can pay off the student loans I took out to get a useless journalism degree."

"I can do this!" I said, trying to pump myself up as I walked up the steps to the Svenssons' front door a short while later. It swung open before I could even knock. I hastily put away my phone. Trisha had texted me a barrage of messages wanting all the dirty details about the Svenssons and their escape from the cult.

Miniature versions of Garrett peered at me around the heavy wooden door.

"I don't understand why you all can't act like normal people. Every single time someone comes to the door," I heard Garrett bark, "you stampede over."

They scattered and Garrett appeared, looming large in the doorway.

"I brought cake," I said, holding up the large cake carrier. "I only ate a couple of slices."

Garrett ushered me inside. Several kids crowded around me. They were wearing various superhero costumes.

"There was some sort of Halloween event at their school. Apparently it's going to be an all-month thing," Garrett explained dryly. He led me through the massive dining room with the four crystal chandeliers and into a kitchen that was bigger than every single apartment I had ever lived in in New York City combined.

I set the cake down on the counter and looked around. On the island were metal pans of raw seafood laid out on ice, all organized by color.

"Halloween is a big deal in Harrogate," I told Garrett as three Captain Americas raced past me to the sink.

"We're going to help!"

"They are?"

"Josie and Hazel have been teaching them how to cook," Garrett explained. "They said they will not have useless males running around, though I think their general sentiment was that the older Svenssons were too far gone to save."

"I do love a man that's good with his hands," I quipped.

Garrett's eyes widened slightly.

"You know, for chopping and banging."

"Banging?"

"Meat. You know, like pounding chicken." I winked at him and turned to inspect the seafood.

Otis handed me an apron. "We made this for you in school. We had art today."

"Thank you! How adorable!" There was a somewhat wobbly bat on the front of the apron and lettering that said, "Have a batty Halloween!"

"I love it," I said, hugging him. "Now, who here has ever made pasta?"

"What are you making?" Garrett asked as he watched me swirl egg yolks and salt and a little water in the flour mound I had made. I had set up each kid with his own mound. They all seemed familiar with the process. Between the dozen or so crowded around the large island, we should be making enough pasta to feed an army... Or an ex-polygamist cult.

"A nice hearty seafood pasta dish, perfect for fall. It has a tangy creamy lemon and shallot sauce. It's tasty and surprisingly easy to make. The trick is to time the cooking of the fish, shellfish, shrimp, and scallops."

Garrett grunted in approval.

"I hope they like this dish," I said lightly. "I guess you all didn't eat a lot of fish in the desert."

Garrett peered at me. I tried to look innocent and harmless. Was he onto me? I wouldn't have been surprised; Garrett was obviously very perceptive. I half wanted him to call me out so I could end this charade. After the kids had given me the apron, I felt like a grade-A bitch coming in their house and lying to them.

"There were silverfish in the compound," Billy said, handing me a perfectly round, smooth yellow ball of pasta dough.

"Silverfish are gross," I said. "My cat, Salem, catches them in our house."

"You have a cat?" Arlo exclaimed. "You should bring him to the Halloween party."

"You can't bring the cat here," Garrett said, scooting Arlo out of the way so he could set several heavy metal pasta makers on the counter. "He wouldn't like the crowds."

The kids chattered to each other happily, the novelty of me in their kitchen having quickly worn off.

"What are you dressing up as for the Halloween party?" I asked him. "Wait, let me guess... a really sexy vampire?"

"No."

"I have a ton of glitter. I can make you a moody sparkly vampire."

"Not my style."

"Okay then, how about an Anne Rice vampire? I think you'd look very tasty dressed up in a waistcoat and those super-duper-tight pants from the Victorian era—you know, not to objectify you or anything, just to be period accurate." I winked at him.

"I figured you would insist on some sort of themed couple costume," Garrett said, turning back to cleaning the mussels. "Not that I'm volunteering."

I thought I saw a slight smile around his mouth.

"Really? Because on the theme of tight pants and waistcoats, we should be Elizabeth Bennet and Mr. Darcy. There's a Halloween costume contest at the fall festival. We should enter. I'm sure Ida could drum up some votes for you. She could be our campaign manager."

"Campaign manager?" Garrett said. There was a slight flash of teeth. Was that a grin? His eyes almost crinkled.

"The costume contest is very competitive," I said. "People go all out. There's backstabbing and saboteurs. One year, we thought Ida had murdered Art to win the contest. He collapsed dramatically on stage. Turns out he was just drunk. But you can see that people in this town take Halloween very seriously."

Garrett fastened one of the pasta makers to the countertop. His sleeves were rolled up, and I admired the way the tendons and muscles in his forearms flexed. *He could knead my pasta any day of the week.* Also, now that I had the image of him dressed up as Mr. Darcy, complete with a top hat, I couldn't scrub it out of my head. Clearly I had problems.

Garrett turned to me. "Where do you want me to stick it first?"

CHAPTER 20

Garrett

"Stick it?" Penny said.

"The dough?" I asked.

"Ahahaha!" Penny was slightly flushed.

"Isn't that how you work the pasta machine?" I asked with a frown. "You have to put it through the part that rolls it flat, then you have to put it in the part that cuts it."

"Exactly!" Penny said. She sounded a little shrill. "Just have to make sure the dough isn't too thick, or it might not fit."

Her eyes had a sort of glazed look. The last thing I needed was for her to faint in the kitchen. Our insurance premiums would rise. I grabbed Penny and guided her to a stool. "You look a little woozy."

"Yep, woozy."

I handed her a La Croix out of the fridge, and she sipped it while my little brothers ran the pasta dough through the machines. When the dough had all been sliced into long strands, Penny jumped up.

"You can just tell me what to do," I offered. "I think the kids are all pasta-ed out. Go set the table and I'll call you when it's ready," I told them. "I don't want anyone wearing costumes during dinner; you need to be dressed and washed." They scattered out of the kitchen carrying plates, cups, and utensils.

"I'll do it, I don't want overcooked fish."

In several large pans, she made the sauce then poached the fish, shrimp, scallops, mussels, and lobster while the pasta boiled.

"Normally I would plate it," she said, staring at me while I hoisted the huge pots of boiling water and drained the pasta in the sink. "But I think we'll just put the pasta in the pans. It will be easier."

I turned to look at her, and her words trailed off. Was that a little bit of drool coming out of the corner of her mouth?

"Sure is convenient to have a man around to lift heavy stuff," she said, clearing her throat.

"I'm sure you can manage on your own."

"But it's so much better when someone else is there to give you a hand," she said.

I froze. Was she implying what I thought she was? Surely someone wouldn't use food innuendos for sex. As soon as I thought the word *sex*, it was as if my brain had run into a brick wall. I picked up the colanders of pasta and moved to dump them into the large pans of steaming fish.

"You have to do it nicely," Penny said, grabbing my forearm. Her hands were soft and warm against my bare skin. Coming into contact with her was like being Tasered.

Using tongs, Penny carefully took out servings of noodles and swirled them in the sauce. The way she made those motions with her wrist was almost hypnotic.

Could be on your dick.

My brain was betraying me. Clearly I was losing my mind. Next thing I knew, I was going to be living out in the middle of nowhere in a trailer with no plumbing or electricity.

"Are you done?" I growled more harshly than I meant to.

Penny looked up at me, her green eyes glistening from the steam. Her mouth was slightly open. The only thing separating us was the pot of pasta.

"No. I have to make it look decent."

"My brothers are animals. They won't care."

"Are you an animal?" she whispered. "I see how you're looking at me as I use the tongs, watching me like a starving man, parched in the desert." Penny took out another mound of pasta. She swirled it then reached for another serving. "Like you could just ravish anything that crossed your path."

My pants are not getting tight. I am in control of my own person.

"I'm not thinking about you in that way. You work for me," I snarled at her.

The tongs dropped with a clang, and Penny jumped slightly. "I just meant that you seem like a man who's tired of eating crappy bachelor food and wanted some good home cooking, not... the other thing," she said, groping for a towel.

"I am *very* sorry." I set the pot down with a clank. "I would never think of you in that way, ever."

"I was just joking!" she said then looked down at her feet. She looked back up, defiant. "But glad to know you wouldn't even think of me that way. Sure does make a girl feel special."

She turned to pull the bread out of the oven, and I rubbed my jaw in frustration then carried the pans out to the dining room.

Archer showed up as we sat down to eat.

"Typical," I said.

"Why are you so angry? I cook on my nights!" he exclaimed.

"No, you don't—Hazel cooks," I scoffed.

"I just made sandwiches," Hazel said. Archer's fiancé was covered in flour.

Though I didn't act it, I was glad they had showed up. There was tension between Penny and me, and I was reeling from our exchange. It had forced me to confront feelings I was trying to bury that needed to *stay buried*. Penny was my employee for fuck's sake.

CHAPTER 21

Penny

"I made cake," I announced cheerfully after dinner. Internally, I was still kicking myself for half flirting with Garrett. I should have just doubled down. Instead, I had acted like some scared, hurt teenager when the hunky football player said she was too weird like in that movie, what was it called? Oh wait, yeah, it wasn't a movie. It was my life in high school.

"It's caramel-apple cheesecake." I looked at all of Garrett's brothers then back down at the cake that was missing a few slices already. "I don't know if there's enough to go around..."

"They don't need all that sugar anyway," Garrett said. The faint traces of humor were gone from his face. He didn't seem fully present.

Was he angry with me? I'd thought we had developed some sort of a rapport. I probably shouldn't have teased him in front of his brothers. Now I would lose my temp job and any hope of getting paid for the article. Maybe when the twins sold Mimi's house, I could secretly live in the attic and sneak down to bake or steal food in the middle of the night from the new owners.

I wanted nothing more than to cut a huge slice of the cheesecake and huddle under a nest of blankets on my bed.

Hazel handed me a cake cutter. "I've been trying to cajole Platinum Provisions into making a cake server that doesn't suck and crush the cake or leave half of it behind. This is what they sent me."

I tried it. "They may need to do a little more work," I said diplomatically. Hazel snickered. Between the two of us, we parceled the cheesecake into two dozen slices. I tentatively handed a dessert plate to Garrett.

"No thank you," he said, his attention not wavering from making sure his brothers weren't eating with their hands.

"I'll take his," Archer said, plucking it out of my hand and taking a huge bite. "That's amazing!"

"I don't see how you can taste it," Mace said. "You just shoved the whole piece into your mouth."

"I guess I'll be going. I still have to prep for Sebastian—he's coming on Monday," I said super casually, trying not to make puppy-dog eyes at Garrett. *Have some self-respect, Penny.* I straightened my shoulders.

"Do you need to take any food to Ticia and Lilly?" Hazel asked.

"I think they have some rats they're going to suck the blood out of," I said dryly. "Also, I think they might curse you for a thousand years if you call them by those nicknames."

Hazel laughed. "They're so funny!"

"You are braver than me!" I told her as I put my coat on.

"I'll walk you to your car," Garrett said abruptly, standing up.

"You mean your car," I replied as he followed me outside.

"Possession is nine-tenths of the law," he replied, holding the front door for me. My boots clacked on the flagstones of the roundabout as I walked through the dark. I was hyper-aware of Garrett next to me.

"I'm safely at my car," I said, touching the driver's-side door lightly. Garrett loomed in front of me. Dry leaves rustled in the cold breeze. An owl hooted. I shivered.

"Don't you need a warmer coat?" Garrett asked.

"Maybe, but this one is stylish."

Garrett looked at me, his eyes silver in the waning moonlight. I shivered again. Branches scraped against the windows on the estate. I told myself I was shivering from the chill and the spooky noises, but really it was because of Garrett. He was so intense and so close to me.

"I guess I'll be going." I opened the car door.

"Penny," he said, stopping the door from opening.

Was this it? Was he going to fire me?

"When I said I wasn't thinking about you in *that way*, I meant it."

"Fuck you," I said, shoving him out of the way, momentarily not caring that he could fire me and ruin my life.

He caught my arm then released me, running a hand through his hair. Garrett hissed out a breath between gritted teeth. "I meant that I *wouldn't*, not that I didn't want to. Have a good night."

I slowly sat down in the driver's seat, and Garrett shut the door and stalked off.

Fuck me.

CHAPTER 22

I took a freezing shower after making sure all the kids were in bed at a reasonable time. Then I tried to meditate and do tai chi. I needed to clear my mind. Sebastian was coming tomorrow morning. Convincing him to sell us Thalian Biotech needed to be my singular focus—not Penny.

There was a soft knock on my door, and then it opened. Davy padded in.

"You're supposed to be in bed," I told him.

He handed me a plate covered by a napkin.

"I saved some for you," he said. "You didn't eat any." He seemed proud of himself.

If I were my father, I would have screamed at him for disobeying me and thrown the plate against the wall. But I refused to be my father. So I bent down to look him in the eye.

"Thank you, Davy, that was a very thoughtful gesture."

"Are you going to eat it?" he asked hopefully and handed me a fork. I looked at the plate. It was a small sliver, not even two bites. I wasn't a sugar person, but Penny had made this cheesecake. I ate it in one bite.

"It's yummy, isn't it?" Davy asked, clearly delighted I was eating it.

I nodded and chewed. It was better than yummy. Yummy did not do it justice. It tasted like being with your family and like fall—but nice, happy, cozy-around-a-fire fall, not desperate winter-is-about-to-come-and-we're-all-going-to-freeze-to-death fall. It wasn't super sweet either. There was the smooth tang of the cheesecake; the graham cracker crust had bite, as if it contained oats. The caramel was slightly chewy, and the apples made it lively.

"Penny is really nice. She should be your girlfriend," Davy said to me, patting me on the head.

"She is nice," I said, picking him up and squeezing him. "Now you need to go back to bed."

The thought of Penny as my girlfriend chased around my head that night. Usually I aim for a solid seven hours of sleep a night. I barely slept thirty minutes.

Penny was bright and cheerful the next morning when she picked me up. Impressive organ music blared out of the car speakers when she pulled up.

"This is to hype you up!" she shouted over the music.

Was that what we were going to do? We were just going to pretend that what I'd said the previous night had never happened? Fine. I could do that. But I had spent the night a little too hyped.

"I'm fine," I growled.

"You need to be in a better mood than that," she retorted. "We need to make a good impression on Sebastian. Do you have another, friendlier version of yourself? Maybe we could lie and say that Archer is you. People like him."

"I'm likable," I said.

"Really? Give me your best 'Happy Halloween'!" she shouted, clapping her hands.

"No."

Sebastian was scheduled to be there at lunch. Before he arrived, Penny put some more finishing touches on the decorations in the lobby and my office. It was like a haunted house. I was smacked in the face with a ghost when I walked down to the lobby to wait for Sebastian.

"We should take some of these down," I said, trying to untangle fake spiderweb from my tie.

"Wait until you see the conference room," Mace said. "It's very festive. Puts you right in the spirit." He was struggling not to laugh.

Maybe I would have Davy hide worms in his bed, though I didn't want to do that to Josie. Maybe when she was out of town...

"He's here!" Penny said and hurried outside. I followed her as a car pulled up in front of the building and a tall brown-haired man stepped out. We shook hands with Sebastian and led him into the lobby.

"This is intense!" Sebastian said, smiling broadly as he looked around.

"Halloween is a big holiday in Harrogate. We have a fall festival and everything!" Penny gushed.

Sebastian smiled down at her. I felt that he held it several beats too long to count as a strictly professional smile.

"I can tell," Sebastian said. "I love all those quirky things about small towns."

"We're all full of quirks!" Penny said with a laugh. Was she flirting with him?

"I was walking along the art trail earlier," he said to us. "It was very impressive. I can't wait to bring my little brother out. Though, there were these two twins—"

"Creepy? Pasty-white skin? Look as if they belong in a horror film?" Penny asked.

Sebastian nodded.

Mace nudged me and whispered, "I think we should just hang back and let her charm him."

Sebastian did seem charmed, all right, I noted in annoyance. He was staring at Penny as if she was a tasty Halloween treat.

"They're not paid actors, believe it or not," Penny was saying. "They're honest-to-goodness local characters."

"Like Ida?" Sebastian asked as we walked up to the conference room.

"We should have locked her up," Mace said to me under his breath.

"I hope she didn't manhandle you!" Penny exclaimed, touching his arm lightly. I was seriously going to throw someone out the window.

Sebastian laughed. "She cornered me and gave me a whole pitch about the town."

"Sorry," I interjected, physically shoving myself between Penny and Sebastian. "This was supposed to be a confidential meeting."

Sebastian grinned. "It's not really a secret anymore. There's tons of speculation online, and *TechBiz* is running a big article in their next issue."

Bronwyn was waiting in the conference room, pulling up the presentation on the screen. She shook hands with Sebastian.

"Hungry?" Penny asked him.

"Did you make all that?" Sebastian asked her gesturing to the spread Hazel had had sent over to the office. He was being way too nice. He was obviously flirting with Penny, and I didn't like it one bit.

"We had lunch catered from a local restaurant." Penny giggled and tucked her hair behind her ear. "I just baked the cake!" she said as she shoved a plate at him.

Parker was clearly struggling not to smile next to me. I didn't trust myself to speak. I'd probably throw Sebastian out after beating him with the scarecrow Penny had strung up next to the smartboard.

"We planned a working lunch," Mace said, as Bronwyn passed out printouts.

Sebastian listened intently and asked smart questions while eating the food. Penny sat across from him, taking notes. Periodically, he would turn to her and ask her opinion about something that had been said. Bronwyn seemed annoyed. I was annoyed too.

While I discussed the financial projections, Penny dished up the cake. "Some of these boys—*men*, although sometimes they act like boys—don't like sweets. But this isn't super sweet. You'll like it," she coaxed, sliding me and Mace a slice.

"I love sweets," Sebastian replied.

"Me too. Mace is the one who doesn't like sweets," I said, shoving half the slice into my mouth. Penny looked at me in confusion.

"Wonderful! This is a spiced-pecan and caramel cake," she said, sliding Sebastian a piece. He inspected it carefully then looked up at her.

"Wait, are you the Queen of Tarts baker?"

"I—yes," Penny said, blushing. "It's a silly hobby."

"I thought your voice sounded familiar, and then I recognized the cake," Sebastian said.

I forced myself to relax the death grip on my fork.

"I love your videos," he continued. "You didn't tell me you had a celebrity in the house, Garrett!"

"Penny is an excellent baker," I said. I didn't like how delighted Sebastian was to be in Penny's presence.

"She makes these amazing ASMR baking videos," Sebastian said. "They are literally the only thing that helps me sleep."

"I'm glad you like them," Penny said. "You're probably the only one."

"Please! There are tons of us in the comments. Everyone loves you! I can't believe I'm actually eating one of the famous Queen of Tarts cakes."

"Penny has been a great asset to Svensson PharmaTech," I interjected before Sebastian could propose marriage or something else obnoxious. "She's also organizing several Halloween events in Harrogate."

"You are? I love Halloween!" He was making googly eyes at her.

This was not working for me. I couldn't figure out why I cared if Sebastian was flirting with Penny. I barely knew this woman. But she had made dinner for my brothers, and she cared about my company.

"We're hosting a big Halloween party in a couple of weeks at the Svensson house," Penny said. "You should come by and see their estate. It's wicked cool." She winked at him.

I was going to stab someone. Maybe Parker, if he didn't wipe that smirk off his face.

"Then there's the Halloween festival. You definitely should come. We're going to have a costume contest and a cake contest and a giant pumpkin-carving contest. We're also putting on a production of *Macbeth*."

"How fun! I should bring my brother. I love these kinds of events. It really puts you in the holiday spirit."

"I know!" Penny gushed. "Too bad you don't live here. You could play Macbeth."

"Maybe I'll have to move here then."

"As much as we'd love for you to make a quick decision," I said firmly, "I'm afraid the spot has been filled. I'm playing Macbeth."

"*You are*?" Mace said, almost choking on his cake. I kicked him hard under the table.

"Oh, right, Garrett mentioned that last night," Mace said. "Our company likes to be involved in the town events."

As Mace went on about the Harrogate Trust and the Art Zurich Biennial Expo the town had won a few months ago, I watched Sebastian, trying not to look too smug. He thought he was going to impress Penny with his money, his charm, and his love of Halloween? Well, he had another thing coming. I had more money, I was better looking, and I could out-Halloween the best of them.

CHAPTER 23

Penny

"Sebastian was really nice!" I gushed that evening when the Thalian Biotech CEO had left to travel back to Manhattan. "He seems to really care about his company's impact on the environment and the community and how he treats his employees. And he loves Halloween."

Sebastian and I had chatted about our favorite Halloween movies on the drive over to look at the Platinum Provisions site and the site Greg was planning on giving Thalian Biotech.

"He's as if a jar of mayonnaise became self-aware," Garrett said later after Sebastian had left and we were back in the office.

Mace snickered. "Thank you for all your work, Penny. If Sebastian does agree to sell to us, it's all because of you. You really charmed him."

Garrett glowered.

"Did I do something wrong?" I asked when Garrett and I were alone in the car.

"No, of course not. You were perfect. You are perfect," he said.

He thought I was perfect?

"Wait," Garrett said, looking around. "Where are we going?"

I glanced at him then back at the road. "You said you were going to play Macbeth."

"Shoot, that's right. I did."

"The play is going to be on a big outdoor stage. It's from the early twenties, all painted wood. Archer is letting us do rehearsals in the old Mast Brothers chocolate factory," I told him, "so we're heading there. The factory buildings there are big enough to hold the stage."

"Double, double, toil and trouble; Fire burn, and cauldron bubble!" Ida called out when we walked in. "Hark! Is that Lady Macbeth I see?"

"Ida," her sister Edna said tersely, "that's not anywhere in the play. Do you even know your lines? Does anyone here know their lines?"

"I'm ready!" I called out as Garrett helped me shrug off my coat. His fingers barely brushed the skin on my neck. I shivered. And was it my imagination, or did his hand linger on my back before setting the coat on a nearby chair?

"I've brought us a Lord Macbeth," I announced, taking Garrett's hand and leading him up to the wooden stage. "They won't bite," I whispered to him.

"I will!" Ida said. "You tell them, Bert!"

Bert was asleep on the steps leading up to a fake doorway.

"Thank you for stepping up, Garrett," Judge Edna said. "As you can see, Bert does not have the stamina and vigor required to play Macbeth."

"You're supposed to say MacB," Ida countered. "Someone could be cursed if you say the name."

"That's a silly superstition," I said, and Garrett's mouth quirked. I suddenly wanted to kiss him. Was there kissing in this play?

"Places! Here's a script," Edna said to Garrett. "You're a smart young man. I'm sure you can have everything memorized in the next few weeks."

"I already have the entire thing memorized," he said, handing the script back to Edna.

We all stopped to stare at him.

"You do?" I asked. "All of it? Everyone's lines?"

"Of course," Garrett replied matter-of-factly. "I have all of Shakespeare's plays memorized as well as his sonnets."

"Did you hear that, Ida?" Edna said. "Garrett's shown up to work, unlike some people."

"But I have to play several characters," Ida complained. "He only has to play the one."

"Places!"

Surprisingly, Garrett was actually a very convincing Macbeth. The play started off with three witches—played by Ida, Bettina, and Dottie—in the woods, telling a prophesy. Macbeth happened upon them in the woods.

As Garrett delivered the first soliloquy, I watched in rapture. Something about the set of his jaw and his shoulders gave him a noble authority. We all applauded when he was done.

"Maybe we should put some kissing or dry humping in this play," Ida whispered to me. "I could change the script."

"You can't just rewrite Shakespeare," I whispered back.

"He wouldn't mind, the randy old bard."

"How'd I do?" Garrett said, half smiling as we walked to the car. His overcoat was open, a cashmere scarf draped around his neck. I wanted to unwind it then undo him. I furiously rubbed my nose.

"You're a really good actor," I said.

"I'm pretty good at a lot of things you don't know about," he replied.

"Oh yeah? Like what?" I said, resting my hip against the Tesla. He leaned over me, and I pressed back against the car. Part of me hoped this was part of a joke, and part of me hoped it was very real.

"Did I make myself clear about how I wanted to think about you but couldn't?" Garrett asked in that deep voice.

"Yes," I croaked. "Crystal."

"It would break a lot of rules for me to be that way with you," he murmured.

"Good thing there's no kissing in *Macbeth*, just lots of witches and stabbing and blood. Perfect, gory Halloween play."

It was as if Garrett was a vampire, pinning me with his gaze.

"How do you do it?" he said.

"Do what?" He was mind-bogglingly close.

"Smell like that? You always smell like fall, like nice fall." His breath was warm on my cheek, blowing out in a puff of steam.

Kiss me! This is the part of the movie where you kiss me! I shrieked internally.

Garrett straightened up. I wanted to scream like a banshee.

"I should go home," he said abruptly.

Funny, because I was about to burst into flames.

I tried to cool down as I drove him back to the Svensson estate. My libido and the rational part of my brain were having a knock-down, drag-out, dirty fight. My libido wanted me to hike up my skirt and straddle Garrett as soon as I put the car in park. The rational part was all like, "No, Penny, do not kiss your boss, don't lose your job and your only hope of writing that article! Think of your student loans, think of your credit card debt! Why won't anyone *please* think of Penny's terrible financial situation?"

I put the car in park. I did not hike up my skirt. Before Garrett left, he put a hand on my arm.

"Thank you for your help today." He might have said something else, but I was breathing in his unique masculine scent and tracing the strong jaw in my mind and trying not to drool. I really had it bad for this guy. It was just lust, I told myself. One good roll in the hay, and I would so be over him.

"Have a wonderful fall evening!" I called out.

Garrett looked over his shoulder at me, confusion on his face and that same quirk on his mouth. I wanted to see him smile and laugh. And have his babies.

"Geez, Penny," I muttered. "Get it together."

A long stint of baking and sugar was in order. Just what the doctor ordered. I plotted what I was going to bake as I locked the car when I was back at the Victorian house.

"Or you could go see the Romani queen."

I shrieked and whirled around. There were Morticia and Lilith, standing right beside my car.

"Where did you come from?" I yelled.

Morticia held out a shovel. "Securing more decorations."

"I don't even want to know," I said as I followed them up to the dark Victorian house. Salem wound around my legs when I went inside.

"So have you smashed your boss yet, or are you two just staring into each other's eyes?" Lilith asked.

"What? Where did you hear about that?" I demanded. I looked around at the melted candles and the burned incense in the living room. "Did the spirits tell you something?"

"No dummy, we saw it on the town Facebook group," Morticia said.

"I'm all over the Facebook group?"

I pulled out my phone. There were Garrett and I, locked in an embrace on the stage.

Love blooms in Shakespeare.

"Ida. Argh! This is going to cost me my job!"

There was a horrible screech and a crash. We ran outside.

"Oh my god, I'm so sorry!" a woman yelled, running over to us. Garrett's car sagged on the ground. All the tires seemed to have ruptured, and the windshield was blown out.

"I barely scratched it!" she said in shock. "I thought I saw something, and I jerked the wheel, but I swear, I barely scratched your car!"

Lilith patted the woman's hand.

"No," Morticia shook her head. "*That* is what's going to cost you your job."

CHAPTER 24

Garrett

"What am I doing?" I muttered as I walked into the house. The kids had already eaten. Archer was sitting at the dining room table with Hunter, Mace, and Parker. They were rehashing the meeting with Sebastian.

"There's Mr. *Shakespeare in Love*!" Archer called out when he saw me.

"What are you talking about?" I growled.

"You and Penny." Archer clasped his hands to his chest. "I can't believe my baby brother has a girlfriend."

"And one of your employees, at that," Hunter said, staring at me.

I glared back at him. "I'm not dating her."

"According to the Harrogate Facebook group, you are," Archer said.

"You spend entirely too much time on social media, Archer. Give me that." I snatched the phone from him. There was a post from Ida featuring Penny and me reciting lines.

"We're plotting to kill Banquo," I said.

"Who? You don't mean Sebastian, do you? Because we need him to sell us the company first," Mace said.

"I heard he was all over Penny," Hunter said with a frown. "This is a lawsuit waiting to happen."

"She's not technically an employee," Mace said. "She works for the temp agency. She's a contractor, legally speaking."

"You're free and clear to bang her," Archer said cheerfully, "but then you have to marry her."

I, oddly, did not have a problem with that.

"You should have just peed on the side of the building to show dominance," Parker said. "You would have been more subtle."

Hunter smirked. Mace struggled not to laugh, and Archer collapsed in a fit of giggles.

"*All of you*," I hissed, "*are going to regret this*."

"We're just teasing!" Mace called out.

"He doesn't mean that, does he?" I heard Mace mutter as I stalked out.

I didn't have time for little minds. I needed to figure out what I was going to do with Penny. I knew what I wanted to do to her: push her against the couch in my office, push up her skirt, *fuck her*.

I filled up the bathroom sink with cold water and dunked my head in, did three hundred pushups, and still felt wound up.

I scrolled through my phone and searched for "things to help you fall asleep." The first result was Penny's website with photos and links to her YouTube videos. There were soothing pictures of cakes, ingredients, and baking tools. Front and center was a photo of her in fall colors, standing at a counter and stirring batter.

I clicked on the video link and lay back on my bed, hypnotized as I watched her slowly, methodically bake cakes. Periodically she would whisper instructions; her voice made my scalp tingle.

I was still… tingly the next morning. I went out to the trails in the woods on the estate property and did sprints in the cold of the fall morning. Then I forced down my Bulletproof coffee after an ice-cold shower. I barely had the patience to listen to my brothers' chatter during breakfast.

"I think we're ready to start our company!" Billy said from his spot next to me.

"Don't talk with your mouth full," I told him absently.

"Can you help us set up a corporation for our toy company?" Oscar asked.

"Talk to Hunter," I said. "He's the lawyer."

Hunter glared at me from across the table.

"We need a loan though," Oscar said.

"You need to have a product first. Show us a prototype of whatever it is you're selling."

"A paper airplane launcher."

"Heaven help us. They really are spending too much time with Archer," I said.

Archer yawned dramatically and made smacking noises with his mouth that he knew annoyed me immensely. I threw a napkin at him before he could scratch himself.

"If you had the paper airplane launcher, you could just hit him that way," Billy said.

I smirked. "You should have led with that."

"So we can have a loan?" Oscar asked me.

"Here's three hundred dollars," I said, taking out my wallet.

"Yes!" my little brothers said excitedly.

"I can't believe you don't appreciate everything I've done!" Archer said, yawning again. "I'm mentoring the next generation of Svenssons. Just look at how amazing Eli and Tristan are!"

"Either of you!" I barked. "What's the projected burn rate on the conference center Archer is building at the Mast Brothers site?"

Eli and Tristan looked at me blankly.

I shook my head and stood up. "Currently it's a hundred and fifty thousand dollars. You all need to find some tenants."

"You need to get laid!" Archer yelled at me as I left.

I paced outside, waiting for Penny. I felt as if I was going to crawl out of my skin.

There was a roar, and I peered down the driveway as a huge antique hearse, belching exhaust, trundled down the drive. Penny pulled the hearse to a screeching halt in front of me.

I waited a long minute. Where was my car?

Penny leaned over the passenger seat and cranked down the window. Her tits jiggled with the motion. Her sweater wasn't super low-cut, but at the angle, I could see the cleavage and the line where her breasts met. I wanted to rub my cock between them.

I wrenched the door open. Penny almost tumbled out of the car. I caught her awkwardly, one hand dangerously close to the underside of her breasts, the other on her waist.

"Apologies," I muttered.

"I'm so sorry! I wrecked your car! Actually the ghost did," Penny blurted as she sat up on the wide leather bench seat. "There was a bang and a *sheeesh* and all the tires popped off and the windshield is kaput," she said, flailing her hands around. "But this hearse is battle ready. Plus, there's enough room in the back to get feisty, if you happen to swing that way!"

CHAPTER 25

Penny

"Get feisty in the back?" Garrett said after a moment.

I gave him a quick glance. *You're going to get fired, Penny.* "Sorry, off-color joke. The getting feisty, that is. I meant more that it's a hearse and it transports corpses, so you know, if you're *really* in the Halloween spirit ”

"Just so you know, that's horribly illegal," Garrett said flatly.

"Right, but regular sex isn't," I said. "Like, I can have sex with a guy in the back of the hearse and not get arrested."

"You can't in a public place," Garrett said sharply.

Why was I talking about sex with Garrett?

"Well, get in. We're going to be late," I told him, patting the bench.

"No," he said, his jaw set.

"No?"

"No. I refuse to show up to work in a hearse. We'll take a new car."

I shut off the engine and raced after Garrett as he walked to the garage. "Slow down! I'm shorter than you and wearing heels. Why are your legs so long?"

But when Garrett clicked the button to open the garage door, there were no cars left.

"What the—" He looked around. "Where are all the cars? I'm going to kill Archer."

"I can drive!" I protested. "The hearse is fine!"

"I put up with a great deal, but I refuse to ride in that monstrosity," Garrett thundered. "There are lines a man just cannot be expected to cross!"

Five minutes later, we were rumbling down Main Street into downtown Harrogate. The hardwood trees that lined the roadway sported colorful red, orange, and yellow leaves.

Garrett had sunk far down in his seat.

"Don't pout," I told him. "Think of it as a Halloween adventure. Besides, Remy said he can't get you a new car for another day or so."

Garrett growled and slumped further.

"Maybe," I giggled. "Maybe I can buy a coffin and you can hide in it while I drive you around."

"That is grossly unamusing," he snarled.

"I think it's pretty funny!" I said, snort-laughing.

"Park far, far away," Garrett told me as we pulled in to the PharmaTech parking lot.

"No way!" I told him as I parked in the CFO's marked spot. "I'm wearing heels, remember?"

Several of Garrett's brothers were loitering under the awning to the entryway.

"When Remy said you were going to roll up in a hearse, I didn't believe him," Archer said. "Yet here you are."

"It's a bad omen," Parker replied as Garrett slunk past them. I tried and failed not to giggle.

"Hey, look on the bright side," I called after him. "You survived your first hearse ride! Not many people can say that!" Garrett's brothers roared in laughter, and I joined in. "Ah, I kill myself!"

The receptionist waved me over.

"Oh, look, Garrett, your straws are here!"

"You ordered plastic straws?" Mace asked.

"Of course! I need to make sure Garrett is well taken care of."

"Wow, Garrett, she buys you contraband straws, drives you around in the hearse, bakes cakes—you need to marry her," Archer said, throwing his arm around Garrett's shoulders.

"Since you have straws," I told Garrett, "do you want to go get your iced coffee?"

"Not if I have to ride around in that hearse."

"You'll get used to it."

"There's not even any legroom," Garrett complained as I pawed through the duffel bag stuffed full of plastic straws. "The bench doesn't adjust."

"Just stretch out in the back," I told him, zipping the bag back up.

"Throw a white sheet over him and you've got an impressive Halloween costume," Archer said, causing all of Garrett's brothers to start laughing again.

"All of you," Garrett hissed to his brothers. "All of you are on my list."

He turned to me. "Fine, Penny, we'll get coffee. Anything to get away from these useless idiots."

"It's Halloween," Parker said with a smirk. "I think you should call us pumpkin heads or something more festive."

CHAPTER 26

Garrett

I slumped down as far as I could go in the front seat of the hearse. It smelled weird, like paint thinner and formaldehyde. The thing was probably crawling with germs.

We stopped in front of Hazel's café, and Penny looked around furtively. She pulled a plastic straw out of the black duffel bag.

"They'll confiscate them," she explained, tucking the straw into her purse. "Since we're here, we can have a working breakfast and talk about your Halloween party."

"I thought you were planning it," I said as I held the door open for her.

"Yes, but I want to run everything by you," she said as we stood in line. "Grey Dove Bistro has the best breakfast! They've have crepes, eggs Benedict, and those fluffy Japanese soufflé pancakes."

"We have special pumpkin pancakes for fall," Hazel said when we approached the counter.

"I'll take those," Penny said. "And a pumpkin-spice latte, extra whipped cream and caramel drizzle."

"Would you like pumpkin syrup on your pancakes?" Hazel asked.

"Yes. Yes, I would."

"Isn't that somewhat of a pumpkin-spice overload?" I asked.

Penny and Hazel looked at me aghast. "There is never too much pumpkin spice!" Penny said.

"For you, Garrett?" Hazel asked.

"Just my iced coffee."

"You need some food," Penny said. "You can't party plan on an empty stomach."

"You're planning the Halloween party?" Hazel squealed. "I'm so excited! Ooh, put a caramel apple booth."

"I thought this was a party, not a fair," I said.

Hazel looked between Penny and me. "I think Archer might have invited all of the schoolkids when he went to hype his zoo idea."

"We are *not* building a zoo."

"He promised a petting zoo at the Halloween party," Hazel said. "Sooo... Better trap a raccoon or something and throw some hay down."

I sucked in a breath.

"I think Garrett's hangry," Penny said, squeezing my arm.

"That's because the only thing he drinks is that nasty Bulletproof coffee," Hazel said.

"He needs some protein. How about a crepe?" Penny asked me.

"We have the creamy, cheesy mushroom crepe," Hazel said. "I went mushroom picking yesterday, found loads of them. They're nutty and savory."

"So tasty," Penny said. "He'll take it!"

Penny grabbed a metal stick with a black bat cutout with the number thirteen on it.

"Morticia made these," Penny told me. "Or maybe Lilith. I always think that it must be weird to see someone else walking around with your face." She looked up at me. "But then, I guess you must be used to it."

"I don't have a twin," I said, pulling out her chair for her.

"All your brothers—you guys look nearly identical," she said.

"My father worked hard to find sister wives that were all slim, blonde, and blue-eyed," I said dryly.

"What was it like?" Penny asked softly.

I sipped my coffee. Maybe it was the plastic straw, maybe all of Penny's energy was rubbing off on me, but I didn't blow her off.

"It was…" I looked out the window. "Difficult. My father is not a good man, but he liked to build himself up as if he was a god. On a good day, he was neglectful, on a bad day, abusive. He didn't even drink—the cult rules banned alcohol—so you can't even blame his behavior on addiction. He was, he is, simply a terrible person."

Penny reached across the table and took my hand, softly rubbing her thumb across my knuckles. She didn't say anything, for which I was grateful.

Hazel came over with our food.

"This looks amazing!" Penny said, releasing my hand.

Hazel looked between us but didn't say anything. There was a small, knowing smile on her face as she slid the plates in front of us.

"Enjoy!"

"Look at these pancakes," Penny said, jiggling the plate. "Aren't they amazing? They're so fluffy." Penny drenched the stack of pancakes with syrup and took a huge bite.

"So good," she said with a little moan that made my teeth rattle and my pants feel tight. She cut off a piece of the tall pancake and held it out to me. I gingerly took the fork from her hand.

"You're not going to let me feed you?" she teased.

"I can't be the only person appearing on the Harrogate Facebook group day in and day out," I replied.

"You spice it up!" she said. "Otherwise it's people complaining about the train schedule and the state of their grass. Do you like it?" she asked excitedly as I chewed the fluffy piece of pancake.

"It does taste like fall," I acknowledged.

"I know. Isn't it awesome?"

"The crepe is pretty good, too," I said, taking another bite.

"Better than Bulletproof coffee?" Penny asked.

"Yes," I admitted.

She looked expectantly at my plate.

"What?"

"Can I try some?"

I cut off a piece and held it out to her. She leaned forward and ate it off the fork.

She made that moan again. "It tastes like the forest in autumn!"

Remy knocked on the café window. Davy was with him.

"Does he have Davy on a leash?" Penny asked, cocking her head.

"Apparently," I sighed as they came into the café. Remy unclipped Davy, and he raced to Penny and climbed onto her lap. She fed him a bite of pancake.

"Yummy!" Davy yelled.

"See, Garrett, someone likes pumpkin spice."

"Of course he likes it; it's carbs and sugar," I scoffed.

"Davy has very discerning taste, don't you?" Penny cooed. "Are you excited for the party?"

"Halloween. I'm going to be a spaceship."

"What should Garrett be for Halloween?" Penny asked him.

"You're dressing up?" Remy exclaimed, voice booming around the café.

"He should be Aquaman," Davy said.

Penny grinned at me. "Yeah, Garrett shirtless and covered in tattoos. I could get behind that."

CHAPTER 27

Penny

I didn't know what to think after the breakfast meeting with Garrett—or was it more of a breakfast date? But I had invited-slash-cajoled him into going—it wasn't as if he invited me. But he didn't protest, either, and last night he had almost tried to kiss me, probably. I was, like, ninety—okay, maybe seventy—percent sure of that.

It wasn't as if I could even force him to have a conversation or throw myself on him and start making out. Garrett was in yet another meeting. I was in his office, flipping through Pinterest, looking for party planning ideas.

Penny: *It's so awesome. I get paid to plan parties!*
Morticia: *I thought you were being paid to write a salacious tell-all.*
Lilith: *If you're going to get laid might as well do it now.*

Penny: *I feel like you're going to judge me if I sleep with my boss slash guy I'm writing an article about.*

Morticia: *Yes but even we can see he's attractive. When was the last time you got any?*

Penny: *Too long…*

Lilith: *There are several practicing sects of Wicca that believe sex is divine.*

Morticia: *There are also some that say it will bring about the end times but you know…*

Penny: *That doesn't make me feel good.*

Lilith: *Just don't do it on the thirteenth. It's a Friday.*

Penny: *I can't anyways, that's when we're having the Halloween party.*

Penny: *You're coming right?*

Lilith: …

Morticia: *Isn't it for kids?*

Penny: *Yes, but you'll survive. They don't bite. Besides, you have to help me decorate.*

Penny: *They have a tiny house they want to turn into a mini haunted house. They have teenagers, so I was thinking we should make it extra creepy.*

Lilith: *Fine. We'll be there.*

Morticia: *Someone has to make it suitably haunted.*

I looked up to see Bronwyn tapping her shoe on the polished concrete floor.

"Garrett's out, but I'll take a message for him," I said sweetly.

"I saw you went on a breakfast date," she sneered. "Though I suppose I shouldn't really call it that. Garrett clearly doesn't like you if he took you to that grungy café."

"One, don't insult Grey Dove Bistro. That is my ride or die. Two, it wasn't a date, it was a working breakfast. *I* asked *him*. He didn't refuse."

"You're trying to manipulate him," Bronwyn spat. "And steal him from me."

"Steal him from you! How many dates have you gone on with him?" I shot back.

Bronwyn pursed her lips. "We have had several late nights in the office."

"Clothes on or off?"

"Don't be disgusting!" she shrieked. "You were always like that in school: weird, friendless, overweight. Don't kid yourself that you're the type of girl a man like Garrett wants. He wants someone like me. Once I help him win Thalian Biotech, he's going to see that we are perfect for each other."

"I doubt he wants a conniving bitch," I hissed. "You're a backstabbing gold digger. You were the one who spread all those slut-shaming rumors about me in high school."

"I don't know what you're talking about," Bronwyn sniffed.

"If you try to sink your claws into Garrett, I'll tell him all about how you treated people in high school," I threatened.

"Me? You're the conniving one. I know you're up to something," Bronwyn said, eyes narrowing. "And I'm going to find out. If I can't have Garrett, you can't either." She turned on her heel and flounced out of the office.

I leaned back against the couch and reached for my coffee, trying to calm down. All the anger that I'd thought I left behind when I went to college was back and bitter in my throat. I took a swig of coffee then immediately choked on it.

Coughing, I muttered, "Shit, the article. What if she finds out? She'll ruin everything!"

I felt the familiar pit in my stomach about the article. I really shouldn't write it. I was lying to myself and thinking I could write a positive article, and maybe it wouldn't be that bad. Maybe my mother might go for it if I made it funny enough. Who didn't like funny articles about kids? My mother, that's who. I sagged.

My phone buzzed. Speak of the devil.

Trisha: *Any updates?*
Penny: *Working on it. Been spending time with them.*
Trisha: *Any juicy tidbits, just between us girls?*

I gritted my teeth.

Penny: *Oh lots. Not that I can share them with you yet!*

I would parade around town in a garbage sack before I told my mother a single detail of Garrett's personal family tragedy. That was something he had told me in confidence. No way was I going to betray that.

Trisha: *I've told the higher-ups about the article. They're very interested. If it pans out, we're willing to offer you a permanent position, with a career progression path.*
Penny: *Awesome! I'll get back on it!*

I was jittery the rest of the afternoon. I needed to do something about this article. I was going to have a heart attack. Then I really would need the hearse.

"Drink too much coffee?" Garrett asked early that evening when he was done with his meetings. There was a softness around his eyes that hadn't been there when I first met him.

"I'm a pumpkin spice addict!" I quipped, holding up my third cup of coffee. I had ordered two to go from Hazel that morning. They were large ones with whipped cream, powdered nutmeg, and a caramel drizzle. A pile of whipped cream remained in the bottom of my last cup.

Garrett shut the door to the office. "Penny," he said.

I slurped my whipped cream.

"I wanted to ask if you wanted to go out."

"Outside?"

"Out with me, to dinner or drinks at a bar."

You're going to betray his trust and ruin his life. Even if it's the nicest article in the world, he won't like it.

I wanted to say yes though. But I cared about him too much. *And you have to write that article. Think, Penny, you'll have an actual real job with health insurance and a 401(k) and dental. After all this sugar, you're going to need dental. Besides, maybe Bronwyn was right and Garrett doesn't like girls like you.*

"I don't think that's a good idea," I said, looking down at my cup. "I mean, we work together."

"Apologies," Garrett said in a clipped tone. "I misread the signals."

No you didn't! I mentally screamed. *Well, maybe just the biggest signal, which is that I'm a crappy person who is seriously considering selling you out.*

I licked the whipped cream off my lips then mentally face-palmed when he looked at me like a leopard eyeing a piece of meat.

"Do you need to go home now?" I asked meekly.

The drive was silent and tense. I had both hands on the wheel of the hearse as I navigated down the dark road to the Svensson estate.

"I've ordered a new car," Garrett said when I dropped him off. "Actually several. We will not be using this hearse anymore."

"Okay," I said softly. "Good night."

Without responding, he walked up to the ornate front door.

I felt like crying as I slowly drove back to the old Victorian mansion. I parked the hearse then slunk inside. Morticia and Lilith were in the living room. Before them on the table was a plastic doll on a white sheet. The twins were slowly removing the head. Morticia—or maybe it was Lilith—was wearing a set of Victorian glasses that had several layers of lenses.

She peered at me. "It's for the haunted tiny house."

I sighed. "I had a horrible day and too much caffeine and probably too much sugar. I'm going to go bake a cake."

Lilith grabbed me by the shoulders and shoved me down onto one of the large wooden chairs. She handed me the head of the decapitated doll. Its lifeless eyes stared at me accusingly.

"You don't need sugar," she said simply.

"I know I'm getting soft," I said, poking my midriff. "At first I thought all the fat was going to my boobs, but now I think it's migrating down to my tummy."

"You don't need cake," Morticia said, peering at me through the steampunkish glasses. "You need to go talk to the Romani queen."

"We will prepare an offering you can take to her," Lilith said. "Think about what you're going to ask her."

I already knew. I wanted Garrett.

CHAPTER 28

Garrett

What the hell was wrong with me? I never should have asked Penny out on a date. I was in the home office, stewing. When Penny had dropped me off, I walked straight past my brothers and upstairs, ignoring their cries to come eat dinner. I was too worked up to eat. Besides, I'd had that crêpe for breakfast with Penny.

How had I misread the signals? I needed to withdraw from the play—that much was obvious. I also needed to find Penny her own office. Maybe we could finally evict Archer from Mace's assistant's office and put her there. Or I could put her with Bronwyn. They seemed to know each other.

I couldn't believe I had broken my own rules. What had gotten into me the last week? Penny. She was unlike anyone I'd ever thought I would be attracted to.

The door swung open, and Archer barged in. He had a plate of tacos with him. "Remy made Memphis-style tacos.

They have pulled pork and coleslaw. They are extremely addictive."

"Go away."

"Hey, I brought these up here especially for you. I could have just lied to everyone and taken them to the library and eaten them."

"You aggravate me."

"Aren't you hungry?" Archer said, waving the plate in my face.

"I'm working," I growled.

"Working on how to get into Penny's pumpkin patch?"

I glared at him. "That is an incredibly inappropriate comment."

"But accurate, right?" He waggled his eyebrows. "Remy said he saw you two having a long, romantic brunch, and Hazel said looks were exchanged."

"Nothing happened."

"She held your hand!"

"Lies."

"Davy took a picture." Archer pulled out his phone, scrolled, and stuck the screen in my face. There was a picture of Penny and me. She was laughing at something I'd said. I looked… not like myself.

"You sure you don't want these tacos?"

I shook my head.

"You can tell your older brother what's wrong," Archer cajoled, patting me on the head. He jerked his hand away when I slapped at it. "I have quite a lot of experience in the woman department, and I am currently engaged to be married."

He waggled his left hand in my face, displaying the tattoo reading I BELONG TO HAZEL around his left ring finger.

"I can't believe you got that tattoo, on your hand no less. It's so unprofessional."

"It's romantic." He gazed at his hand.

"You aren't even married yet," I said, crossing my arms.

"It's my engagement tattoo. It's the twenty-first century, Garrett. Get with it. Plus chicks dig tattoos. I was watching a YouTube video on how to do prison-style tattoos. We could give you a real sexy tattoo. That will really have Penny jumping you in your office, glass windows or not," Archer said as he took a huge bite of a taco.

"We aren't having this conversation."

"I knew you weren't bringing him those tacos!" Mace yelled from the doorway.

"Garrett said he didn't want them!" Archer protested through the mouthful of food.

"Then you should have brought them back downstairs and shared them with the group," Hunter said, coming in and sitting at his desk.

"Garrett's having woman troubles," Archer said. "He's lost his appetite."

"You did eat all those pancakes at breakfast, Garrett," Hunter said.

"Don't even start with me."

Hunter stared at me. "And you had a plastic straw."

"Penny ordered some online."

"Aww. If that's not love, I don't know what is!" Archer said. "Smuggling in plasticware!"

"At least Penny is better than any of Archer's girlfriends, Hazel excluded," Hunter said, looking back at his computer.

"I think she's friends with Hazel," Mace said. "They went to high school together. She would fit right in."

"Stop trying to dictate my life."

"You should ask her out," Mace said.

I clamped my mouth shut.

"Come on, we can role-play," Archer said, standing up, half-eaten taco in his hand. "Pretend this taco is Penny, and pretend like you're going to ask her out."

"I already asked her out." I mumbled.

"You what?" Mace shouted.

"Are you deaf or just dumb?" I snapped.

"When was this?"

"Was that the breakfast date?" Archer demanded.

Hunter wrinkled his nose. "I hope that wasn't your first date, Garrett. Honestly, you'll give the Svensson brothers a bad name if people think that's the best you can come up with."

"You're one to talk, considering we're all still paying for the aftereffects of Meg," I hissed at him.

"And that's why you should all learn from my mistakes and plan better dates," Hunter said.

"That was *not* what I planned. I am excellent at planning. Way better than any of you. That was a working breakfast," I retorted.

"Hazel said there wasn't much working going on," Archer stage-whispered.

"So you asked her out after?" Mace pressed.

"This evening." I looked at the window. "She said no."

"She said no?" My brothers were flabbergasted.

"Ouch."

"Rejection."

"Ask her again!" Archer demanded.

"She said no. I'm not going to turn into a stalker. I'm her boss. I never should have asked."

"Technically—" Archer began.

"There's no technicality."

"Ugh, there's going to be a lawsuit. Should we fire her?" Mace asked Hunter.

"Absolutely not," he said in horror. "Then it really would be a lawsuit. Just shunt her off to another department."

"She's planning all the Halloween stuff," I said.

"She never should have been in Garrett's office to begin with," Hunter said, ignoring me. "I don't know what kind of operation you all are running over there."

I did not want Penny to leave the office. I—well—I enjoyed having her around, even if she did insist on all those Halloween decorations.

"She shouldn't be driving him around anymore either. Honestly, I thought you had more sense than that, Garrett," Hunter admonished. "Considering all the grief you've given me."

I suddenly couldn't take my brothers anymore.

"I'm going for a run," I announced brusquely.

The several hundred acres of the old Svensson estate contained several cottages, fake ruins, bridle paths, and walking trails. It was pitch-dark and freezing cold when I ran outside. My feet pounded the ground as the cold air burned my lungs.

I hated to admit it, but Hunter was right.

I increased my pace. Lights marked the paths closer to the main house. Farther back into the estate, there weren't any lights. Slivers of moonlight shimmered through the bare trees.

I ran for miles to the back of the estate property. It backed up onto an old historic farmstead. There was a cemetery back there if I remembered correctly. While the Svensson estate contained its own family cemetery, the one on the farmstead wasn't maintained. At the town hall meetings, periodically someone would suggest that the Svenssons should take over the upkeep. I told them we would be glad to once we owned the land. The issue was of course tabled.

I slowed as I approached the high wrought-iron fence at the edge of our property. Peering through the darkness, I saw a light bobbing. Grave robbers? Vandals? I squinted. The figure was wearing a familiar red cape. It couldn't be... The figure stumbled, and the lantern light lit up their face for a second.

It was Penny.

What is she doing in a graveyard in the middle of the night?

Thoughts of grave robbers or vagrants crossed my mind. Harrogate had improved, but out in the more rural areas, there were still the Rust Belt town problems of poverty, violence, and drugs.

She could be hurt.

She probably didn't want to see me after what had happened earlier. I would stay in the shadows, I decided. But I couldn't live with myself if anything happened to her.

CHAPTER 29

Penny

The Romani queen had been the high priestess of a group that had fled to America in the early nineteenth century. She had died and been buried in Harrogate. Legend had it that you could go to her grave with an offering, and she would grant you a wish.

The twins swore by her; I had always been skeptical. But now I was desperate. I parked the hearse on the edge of the abandoned farmstead, squeezed through the gate with the busted lock, and then spent the next thirty minutes stumbling around in the dark, looking for the grave.

"How are there so many dead people here?" I whispered softly. I had a lantern that the twins had given me. They swore that the Romani queen liked drama. I didn't think the lantern had a lot of oil left. It was sputtering, casting creepy, flickering shadows on the ground that made my skin crawl. I should have just brought a flashlight.

As much as I loved Halloween, being in a graveyard in the middle of the night was actually super disturbing. An owl hooted, and I jumped.

The graveyard wasn't well maintained. The tall, dry grass rustled. A stick cracked. I whirled around. Was someone out there? Was I being followed?

"Why do you have to go to the grave site at midnight?" I muttered to myself.

The twins had insisted that was the only time to go, that the Romani queen wanted you to prove that you were serious about your request.

I wasn't even sure what my request was. I wanted Garrett, but then I had rejected him, so the Romani queen might just ignore that request. I should probably ask for my student loans to be repaid or my article to be successful or maybe to generally put my life back on track. I was almost thirty and had never held a real job, just a series of freelance and temp gigs.

"Oh, there it is!" In front of me was a huge grave with a raised stone bed and an elaborate headstone in the shape of a weeping marble angel. There were pieces of jewelry, cigars, dead flowers, and other offerings on the grave.

"Geez, I hope I don't accidentally summon her ghost," I mumbled as I pulled out the offerings the twins had given me. I lit the incense then set down the whole cake they had insisted I bake, along with an antique crystal decanter filled with sherry.

"She doesn't know you. You have to make a good first impression," Morticia had insisted.

"Please, Mrs. Romani Queen," I began, clasping my hands together.

Is that how you were supposed to address her?

I breathed in the cold fall air. "I am coming to you for help. My life is a mess. I don't know what to do." I didn't want to be greedy. "Please just give me guidance, show me a path. Thank you for your time."

I waited for the incense to burn down. When it did, it took a second for my eyes to adjust. I could swear I saw someone move behind me in the graveyard.

Was it a ghost? Something worse?

I scooped up my bag and lantern to hurry back to my car. Of course, at that point, the lantern gave up on life, leaving me in the pitch-dark. Pulling out my phone, I fumbled with it to try to turn the flashlight on. A loud *creak* emanated from the woods bordering the west side of the graveyard. I stumbled.

I heard rustling that sounded like footfalls in the dry grass. Someone or *something* was definitely in the graveyard with me. I started to run, still trying to get my phone to work. The flashlight came on, illuminating a toppled gravestone just in time for me to trip over it.

"Crap!" I yelled.

My phone crashed to the ground. I was about to land on it when a pair of strong arms grabbed me, hauling me back.

"Vampires! Zombies!" I screamed, wriggling and trying to fight off my attacker.

"Penny, stop! It's me!"

I blinked. "Garrett?" I hit him on the chest.

"Ow," he said mildly.

"I should say ow," I said, shaking my hand. "Why is your chest so hard?"

"Why are you in a graveyard at midnight?" he retorted, grabbing my shoulders. "Are you hurt?"

"Just my phone," I said. He bent down to pick it up. "It's broken. Crap. Just my luck."

"Why are you even here?" he demanded. "You could have been hurt."

"I needed—"

"What could you possibly need?"

"I don't need to explain myself to you," I said shortly. I didn't want to tell him about the Romani queen. It seemed dumb in hindsight. The twins were crazy.

But then here was Garrett. Was this a sign? The wind blew, and the leaves rustled. Garrett's blond hair waved slightly in the wind. His eyes were the color of the moon. He reached out to stroke my cheek.

"You have chocolate on your face," he said.

"Long story," I said.

He kept stroking my face.

All right, Romani queen, I asked for a sign. Obviously you gave me one. Here it goes.

I let my hands slide up his chest. There was a sharp intake of breath. Almost inadvertently, Garrett leaned toward me.

"I thought you didn't want to go out with me," he said, his breath warm against my lips. Garrett's gray eyes were liquid mercury in the moonlight.

"I lied," I replied, closing the distance and pressing my mouth to his. It was a brief kiss, chaste, though I didn't want it to be.

I rocked back on my heels, about to escape back to the hearse. It was as if invisible spirits were pushing us together, like the magic in those angsty teen novels I had loved to read. Unlike in those books, though, Garrett wasn't some teen heartthrob. He was a full-grown man who wanted me unapologetically. Our breath was a silver haze in the cold air between us.

Garrett studied me for a moment, then he pulled me against his chest. His large hands moved slowly down my sides, and his breath clouded against my mouth as he bent down to kiss me. Though it was cold outside, I was warm in Garrett's embrace.

I moaned as his tongue caressed my mouth. The kiss was rich and smoky, like autumn. His hands moved up to my face, stroking me. He pulled back slightly to nip my lips then dipped down to claim my mouth again. The feel of his hard body against mine was more intoxicating than any boozy Halloween cocktail. If he had asked me, I would have gladly fucked him right there in the graveyard, ancestral curses be damned. Fortunately, he released my mouth before I could start dry humping him like a Chihuahua.

"A hot guy in a graveyard," I joked. "If I didn't know any better, I'd say you were a vampire!"

CHAPTER 30

Garrett

I had tried to make sure Penny didn't see me, but then she almost fell, and I couldn't have her hitting her head on a gravestone. I was sure people would know I was there, and I had just told my brothers she had rejected me. It would be all over the news. I would be blamed. I had probably left footprints in the graveyard or fibers or something. We couldn't have people writing crazy articles about the Svenssons; our businesses would never recover. I *had* to catch her.

Then she attacked me. I thought it was because she hated me, but then she kissed me. Then I kissed her.

Kissing Penny was addictive. She definitely didn't seem to hate me as I pulled her to me again. I bent down to kiss her, running my hands over her soft curves. She was warm under her wool cloak. Kissing her was better than I had imagined; she tasted like fresh apple pie.

"Do you want to take this somewhere less creepy?" she said when I pulled back.

"Like the hearse?"

She laughed. "Garrett made a joke!"

"I can be funny on occasion." I waited a beat. "You did say there was extra room to stretch out."

"I feel like sex in the back of the hearse is a big step. I'm not sure we're quite there in our relationship," she replied.

I wrapped my arm around her as we slowly walked through the graveyard. "What are you even doing out here?"

"Communing with the spirits."

"You don't strike me as a goth girl," I told her, guiding her around a fallen headstone.

"Please, you should have seen me in high school," she said. "I was full-blown emo, except I couldn't afford to go to Hot Topic and buy those pants with all the buckles and the *Nightmare Before Christmas* crop-top shirts. My tights had holes in them because they were the only pair I had."

"Did I just sense some emo gatekeeping from you?" I teased.

"Maybe just a little." She stuck her tongue out. I leaned over to kiss her again. The hearse was starting to look like a better and better option. But I needed to restrain myself. I didn't want to drive her away again.

"And you listened to Good Charlotte and My Chemical Romance?" I asked when I released her.

"Love those guys. I have a thing for moody, broody males." Her hand brushed my abs. "That's probably why I'm totally gaga about you."

I smiled in the dark. I'd never thought anyone would be crazy about me. "Did you dye your hair weird colors?"

"Of course! I was full-on blunder years," she said, leaning against my arm. "I was in foster care and desperate to fit in with some group, any group. I once attempted to do a black-to-pink fade. Morticia and Lilith tried to help me, but I could only afford the cheap hair dye from the dollar store. Spoiler, don't ever use that stuff. I think it was printer ink. It dyed my hair black, all right, but I ended up with black splotches all over my face, arms, and shoulders. I looked like a Dalmatian."

I clamped my lips together. "I'm honestly trying not to laugh," I said as she punched me playfully.

"Morticia has pictures somewhere. Periodically she'll blackmail me with them."

Her hand was back around my waist. She rested her head against my chest. "Did you have any embarrassing stories from your teen years? Or were you always the cold, calculating billionaire?"

I huffed out a breath that clouded in front of me. "Always cold and calculating," I said. "But not always the billionaire. When I was a teenager, my older brothers were in college. They weren't supposed to have guests, but I didn't have anywhere to live, so my brother snuck me into his dorm at Harvard. Whenever the maintenance people would come, he would make me hide up in the drop ceiling. While he was in class, I day-traded."

"That's where all your money came from?" Penny asked.

"And from other places."

"What about your younger brothers?"

"Weston, Blade, and Parker are the youngest of my mother's children. My dad didn't kick Parker out when he did us. We had to go back and kidnap him in the middle of the night. Remy had come back from Iraq and basically rolled off the airplane with his gun and headed to the compound to get Parker."

"Really? He seems so nice," Penny exclaimed.

"He's nice until you mess with his family. I think we all are. Well, I'm not nice."

"Yes you are," Penny insisted. "You take care of your other brothers. Did you have to go kidnap them too? Though I guess not if Davy was on the train."

"We don't need a violent Ruby Ridge-type standoff," I explained. "So now I basically buy my little brothers off my father."

"No Svensson sisters?" she asked carefully.

I ground my teeth but didn't answer.

In her hand, her cracked phone rang, the glow lighting up the graveyard.

"You need to get a new screen," I said, peering at it.

She fumbled with the phone. Was she trying to hide it from me? Why was she so flustered? She stabbed at the screen with a finger.

"Sorry about that." Penny was tense as we approached the hearse. She unlocked the door. "Do you need a ride home?" she asked, picking at a button on her coat. Her body language suggested she did not want to give me a ride. What had happened? Maybe I shouldn't have told her all the sordid details about my family.

"I'll run back," I said, stepping away.

CHAPTER 31

Penny

Of course my mother had to call me right as I was having a moment with Garrett. He walked me to the hearse then turned and ran at a loping pace back to the tree line.

Cursing, I yelled at Siri to call Trisha.

"How's my favorite daughter?" my mother said when the call connected.

"Wondering why you called her at one a.m."

"We need a teaser. I have to show something for an upcoming meeting. We really want to promote this article."

"I—don't know," I said, chewing on my lip.

"Look, just between us," she said dramatically, "magazine sales are down across the board. Everyone likes articles about cults and crazy families. You've seen all those TLC shows, right?"

"Yeah."

"The finance people said we need this article to save our bottom line this year. Several ad companies are interested in putting their products in this issue, but they want to know what's exactly is going to be in the article."

Despite the cold, my hands were sweaty. I felt nauseous.

"I'll see what I can throw together," I rasped. I wished the Grey Dove Bistro was open. I would kill for a donut Danish. And I had left all my cake with the Romani queen.

After I made sure the call was ended, I banged my head on the steering wheel. "I thought you were supposed to help me, Romani queen!" I yelled.

I couldn't sleep at all that night, and the next morning, I was up before dawn. Fortunately, the Grey Dove Bistro opened early. I was the first in line when Hazel walked up to unlock the front door. She smiled and hugged me.

"Rough night?"

"I need two, no three, pumpkin-spice lattes, large, extra whipped cream, extra caramel, and like four donut Danishes."

"Geez, you must have had a *very* rough night," Hazel said as I followed her into the café. "I thought you were party planning. It should be fun, not stressful."

"Ugh, that's next weekend. Crap. There's a lot I have to do still. Better make it four pumpkin-spice lattes."

I was finagling the door to the hearse open while juggling my coffees and bag of donut Danish when my phone buzzed.

Garrett: *Cars have arrived. One was delivered to your residence. Please burn that hearse.*

Penny: *This hearse is an antique. Besides last night you wanted to boink in it. I can't take that away from you!*

Garrett: *Boink?*

Penny: *I don't want to go into graphic detail about how I was going to be on my hands and knees in the back of the hearse while you fucked me, but I can if you want.*

Garrett: ...

Ugh, crap! I shouldn't have written that. I was operating on no sleep and too much sugar and caffeine.

Penny: *Ignore that. I get really horny when I'm sleep-deprived.*

Garrett: *Good to know.*

Penny: *Going to pick up the car now.*

I was feeling more than a little horny, thinking about sex with Garrett. I bet it would be good. He seemed like a man with impressive attention to detail.

I hurried back to the Victorian house. I didn't want the ghost to destroy the car. The brand-new black Tesla gleamed in the crisp fall morning sun. Thankfully, it didn't have a scratch on it.

"Ghost," I scoffed. "So dumb. It's just coincidence. I need to get a hold of myself." I guzzled the rest of my first coffee then started on the next.

I was jittery as I pulled up in front of the Svenssons' house.

"Get in!" I shouted over the pounding of the caffeine in my head. "I have to go buy pumpkins and make sure I have enough decorations and figure out what we're going to eat. I actually should have taken the hearse—then I could haul stuff. There's a lot of room in the back of a hearse, you know," I said over the blare of the Halloween music.

Garrett slid into the car. He turned off the music and then leaned over, pushing me back in the seat and kissing me hard. His hand slid under my shirt, cupping my breast.

"See," I murmured against his mouth. "If we had the hearse, we could just dive over the seat, and you could slip that in me." I palmed his cock through his pants. "It even has curtains."

"I can think of about five more places right now that would be better than fucking you in a hearse," he growled against my mouth, his hands starting to roam.

"We shouldn't right now," I gasped, pushing his hand away before it went even lower. "I need to go pick out some pumpkins. Don't worry. I'll drop you off at the office first."

I rummaged in the bag from the Grey Dove Bistro, pulled out a donut Danish, and took a big bite. He kissed me after I swallowed. "You can have a donut Danish. I bought a lot," I whispered to him.

"I'd rather kiss you instead. It tastes much better on you." Garrett sat back in his seat. "You know, I think I'll come pumpkin purchasing with you."

"You will?" I said, shocked, half-eaten donut Danish almost falling out of my mouth. "I thought you hated Halloween."

"I don't hate it. But I just know I won't get any work done if I'm thinking about you."

CHAPTER 32

Garrett

"I think I can make you love Halloween," Penny said as we drove away from the estate into the countryside. The rolling hills and the carpet of orange, red, and yellow leaves and the historic covered bridges did make this a picturesque part of the state.

"It's so beautiful out here," Penny sighed. "I just love this area."

"Ernest's farm is where I bought the hay bales and pumpkins that are in the PharmaTech lobby," Penny continued as we pulled onto a gravel drive flanked by two big signs depicting a large man holding up a giant pumpkin. For a weekday morning, there was a surprising number of people on the farm. The crowd included several school groups.

"Garrett!" several of my little brothers shouted.

Penny waved and hurried over to them, hugging each one and greeting them by name.

"Are you excited for the party next weekend?" she asked, a huge smile on her face.

"Yes! All our friends are coming!" Billy said, gesturing to the group of schoolkids gawking at the fields.

"Garrett's here helping me pick out pumpkins. Would you like to help?"

I love my brothers, but I came out here to a farm to look for pumpkins because I wanted to spend time with Penny, not babysit. But Penny waved them to troop around us to pick pumpkins.

"If you need pumpkins, we've got lots of pumpkins," Ernest said, approaching us with his hands in his overalls. The farmer was a large man. His overalls were embroidered with a scarecrow, and he wore a trucker hat.

"Amazing!" Penny said as Ernest led us to the pumpkin patch. "Okay, so I need fifty white ones, eighty orange ones, and ten of those gigantic pumpkins."

"Those are a little more expensive," Ernest said.

"Garrett brought his credit card." She smiled at me.

"I also have some blue pumpkins," Ernest said, leading us through the fields. "They're an heirloom breed, originally developed in this area."

"These look gray," I said. "Or am I color-blind?"

"They have a slight bluish tint," Penny said.

"They're not that cheerful," I told her, frowning.

Penny dramatically clapped her hands over one of the pumpkins. "Shh. You'll hurt their feelings!"

"Do you have black pumpkins?" I asked.

"We have some dark-green squash," Ernest offered.

I followed Penny around as she inspected every single pumpkin. The kids trailed behind us, pulling carts full of the ones we chose.

"Just buy a bunch, and we'll sort them out later," I told her.

"We're taking pictures of these, Garrett," Penny sniffed. "Sebastian is going to be at the house. We have to make sure we don't have a bunch of rabbit-chewed pumpkins out on display. Plus I need to have the right variety of pumpkins. Big ones, medium ones, small ones, giant ones."

"We had a good rain and a long summer, so we do have some real giant ones," Ernest said, leading us through another row of pumpkins.

"Wow, these are huge!" Penny said when we stopped in front of the biggest pumpkins I'd ever seen.

Penny took pictures of each large pumpkin.

"What are you doing?"

She glanced at me. "Hazel has opinions on which pumpkins I buy."

"That one looks like it's melting," Otis said. "You should buy that."

"I also have some square ones. Tried this technique I learned about where you grow them in a glass bottle," Ernest said proudly.

"I don't think we want any square pumpkins," Penny said.

"I might want a square one," I interjected.

Penny looked at me incredulously. "What could you possibly want with that?"

"You can name it SpongeBob," Henry said.

"Yeah, Penny," I said.

"Fine, I guess Garrett can have a square one, but it's not going to be at the party."

"I want a pumpkin so big I can carve it and live in it," Henry said as Ernest put stickers on the large pumpkins Penny wanted to purchase.

"No one is living in a pumpkin." I told them.

"So are we done?" I asked when Penny put her phone away.

"Uh, no. I'm here to work. If you want to go hang out with the kids, you are free to do so. I need hay bales and corn husks and leaves to make wreaths and fall brooms."

"Fall broom?"

"It's a decorative, nice-smelling broom. It makes the place seem cozy."

"We have bamboo, too," Ernest said. "Lots of bamboo. My dad brought some back with him from the war. Thought it would be nice to have and a cool thing to show his wife. Figured since it was a tropical plant, it would die out in the winter, but that never happened. Now," he pointed to the bamboo, bright green and waving in the wind at the edge of the property, "it's like a weed. Do you need any of that? It's free."

"Not that I can think of," Penny replied.

Penny spent the next hour picking through the various leaves and twigs she needed to make the brooms. The kids had already escaped to go run through the corn maze. I shifted my weight and looked up at the sky.

"All right, I think I have what I need," she announced.

I grabbed the handle of the cart and towed it to the house, where Ernest had a small store.

"Oof," Penny said when Ernest gave us the total. "Maybe we shouldn't buy so many pumpkins."

"I cannot go through that again," I said, brushing her hand away when she tried to stop me from handing over my credit card. "I spent valuable time picking them out. They are all coming home with us."

"We'll have all these pumpkins and hay bales delivered in the next few days," Ernest promised as I signed the receipt.

"I want to go through the corn maze," Penny said when we walked out of the little store. She grabbed my hand. "I love corn mazes, but I'm not that good at them. Though I think they're more fun to do when you're drunk and it's dark."

We wandered through the maze arm in arm. I wasn't even paying attention to where we were going. I was too absorbed in Penny. The red tendrils of her hair had escaped from the bun and blew around her face in the breeze.

"Um," Penny said after we had turned down one path. "I think I'm lost."

"If you touch a wall of the maze and start walking counterclockwise without removing your hand, eventually you'll find your way out of the maze," I told her.

"I don't want to be here all day."

"I thought you loved Halloween," I teased. We were in a dead end of the maze and finally alone. I pulled her to me, kissing her. My hand crept under her shirt, cupping her soft tits.

"If you didn't have those tights on," I whispered in her ear, "I'd make you come right now."

"For someone who doesn't want to have sex in a hearse, you sure seem okay with doing it in other places," she whispered.

I kissed her to slake some of the sudden desire I had to push her down and fuck her right there.

"Maybe spending an obscene amount of money on pumpkins has inspired me to live dangerously."

"If you didn't want to spend all that, you should have said." She wrinkled her nose.

It was adorable. I kissed her nose then her mouth.

"I need Sebastian to sell us that company, so enough pumpkins to raise a pumpkin army and enough hay bales to burn down my house are perfectly acceptable," I said, my hands drifting up under her skirt. Her thighs were warm under the tights, and she was even hotter between her thighs.

"Well," she said, kissing my jaw and rocking slightly against my hand. "Since you spent all day wandering around the pumpkin patch, maybe there's another pumpkin patch we could go explore."

"I really want to explore it right now," I said, nuzzling her neck.

"Garrett!" several little voices shouted. "We found you!"

"We're not playing hide-and-seek," I said to them, trying to keep the exasperation out of my voice as I released Penny. "You're supposed to find your way *out* of the maze."

"We did, but then we came back!" Oscar said.

"Maybe you can show us the way out?" Penny asked.

My little brothers each grabbed one of her hands, and just like that, they stole her away.

Penny looked over her shoulder and grinned at me. "I guess you're just chopped pumpkin now!"

CHAPTER 33

Penny

Garrett had really stirred my pumpkin-spice latte back there in the corn maze.

"Geez," I told him after we'd waved his brothers back onto the school bus. "I thought I was a little too old to be making out in the corn maze. That's what we did when we were teenagers."

"Who were you making out with in the corn maze?" Garrett asked. He didn't sound happy.

"No one, actually," I admitted, following him to our car. "The cool kids—the football players and the cheerleaders—did that. I was the weird foster kid in the back of the classroom. I didn't make out with anyone in the corn maze."

"You have now."

"Look who's smug! Maybe you can take me to one of those places you said would be better for a roll in the hay than the back of a hearse."

He half smiled. "I think I can work something out. You've earned a reward after that record-breaking pumpkin shopping trip."

"Maybe we—" I stopped short. We both stood there and stared at the car. It had been turned completely upside down.

"It's the ghost," I said after a minute.

"Sorry!" Ernest said, huffing over to us. "One of my guys was using a forklift on a fertilizer shipment and didn't put the prongs down."

"This is a brand-new car," Garrett said. He sounded shocked.

"The ghost made it happen," I said matter-of-factly. "You should buy an antique car, Garrett. Morticia and Lilith say that's what the ghost likes."

"I'm not catering to a ghost," Garrett scoffed. "Wait, what am I saying? There are no such things as ghosts. This is just a horrible coincidence."

"I'll call for a ride," I said with a sigh.

"When you said you were going to call for a ride, I thought you were ordering an Uber," Garrett said as a big black hearse pulled into the gravel parking lot.

Lilith was behind the wheel, silk driving gloves on, round sunglasses covering her eyes. She pulled the hearse alongside Garrett and me. Morticia cranked down the window and looked at us over her sunglasses.

"He's going to have to ride in the back," she said, giving Garrett the once-over. "He's too large to sit in the front seat. He's some sort of Viking throwback. "

"I'm not riding in the back of the hearse," Garrett said stubbornly.

"There are straps," Lilith said with a slight smirk.

"No," Garrett said flatly.

"We can squeeze," I told them.

"Honestly, how many pumpkin-spice lattes and donut Danishes have you had this week?" Morticia asked as she scooted over next to her twin.

"Not that many," I grumbled as I climbed onto the bench seat.

Garrett placed his hand on my ass as I climbed in. He gave it one caress, then he sat next to me. I was pressed next to him. He wrapped an arm around my shoulder.

"You really are a big dude," I told him.

"Like some sort of Visigoth mercenary," Morticia sniffed as she pulled the car onto the road.

I was very aware of Garrett's body pressed right next to me in the car.

"Don't forget, we're coming over to your house tomorrow to start setting up for the party," I reminded Garrett when we pulled up in front of the Svenssons' estate. As payback for the hand on my ass and just because I wanted to, I lightly caressed then squeezed his crotch as he opened the door. I smirked when he hissed in a breath.

He kissed me hard after unfolding himself out of the hearse. "I'm looking forward to it."

After Garrett was back in the house and I had scooted over to his spot that was still slightly warm, Morticia raised a thin black eyebrow. "I suppose the Romani queen came through."

The call from my mother came flooding back. I put my face in my hands. "Oh, I don't know. I think it's all worse!"

"What are you going to do?" Lilith asked after I told them about my mother's request for a sample article.

Lilith's angular face seemed even sharper. She and Morticia were the ones to put the pieces back together every time my mother let me down. I knew they didn't approve of my dealing with her.

"Garrett's going to be furious if I give her anything about his family," I said with a groan. "I can't stall for much longer."

"Just tell your mom you still need a chance to snoop through the house in order to put together a really nice package to attract a lot of marketers," Lilith said. "Maybe by then, the Romani queen will figure something out."

"Or the ghost could drop a tree on Garrett's car with you inside it, and then all your problems would just disappear," Morticia added.

"That's morbid."

"Happy Halloween!"

CHAPTER 34

Garrett

Penny was coming to our house the next morning to start decorating for the party that weekend. My little brothers were on fall break and were bouncing around, excited that they didn't have to go to school.

"Isn't this overkill?" Archer asked with a yawn. Hunter had forced him to wake up early.

"We have guests coming over," Hunter said, not looking up from the paper. "You can't be lounging about asleep. It's rude."

"When is Olivia going to start designing our cottage?" Archer complained to Hazel.

"She's busy with all your brothers' companies' other projects," she said.

"And those take precedence," Hunter added.

"You can always move into our cottage," Mace offered.

"Uh, no."

"Garrett needs a cottage for Penny," Billy said. "They were in the corn maze kissing."

My little brothers started giggling uncontrollably.

"Silence," Hunter growled.

"The corn maze?" Parker asked me. "*You* were in a corn maze?"

"I am perfectly free to go in a corn maze," I said, leveling my gaze at him.

"Yeah, Parker, this is a free country," Remy said.

"I'm going to work," Mace announced, standing up.

"Me, too," Archer said.

"You're going to go pretend to work," Mace said.

The doorbell rang, and all the kids jumped up, chairs clattering to the floor. They raced, yelling, to answer the door.

"Stop behaving like animals!" Hunter thundered.

"Penny's not going to want to be your friend," I told them, following them into the foyer.

I shoved them out the open doorway, expecting to see Penny. Instead it was Ernest.

"Where d'ya want these pumpkins?" he asked. Behind him was a huge flatbed truck packed with crates of pumpkins. There was another truck idling in the driveway, packed with bales of hay.

"What the hell?" Archer said, coming up behind us.

"That's a hundred dollars for a swear word," Hunter told him.

"Put it on my tab. Better yet," Archer snickered, "maybe I can just pay that in pumpkins."

"Remy," I called as I signed for the shipment from Ernest. "Can you do something with these?"

My older brother ambled over. "Where does Penny want it?"

"I guess around the back."

"Sure are a lot of pumpkins," Ernest said.

"It's a big house."

Penny arrived while Remy was directing my younger brothers to unload all the pumpkins, bales of hay, stalks of corn, sticks, and other fall decorations.

"Wow!" she said. "It didn't seem like that many pumpkins when they were out in the field, did it?" She sipped her pumpkin-spice latte. The creepy twins were with her, surveying the property.

"How are we going to unload everything?" Penny asked me, wide-eyed.

"We have two dozen strong-armed young men," I told her. "One of the few perks of having a large family."

Davy tried to pick up a pumpkin that was almost his size and toppled over.

"Stick to the little ones," I told him, hauling him upright.

"This is going to be a great party. I'm so excited," Penny said, clapping her hands.

"This is my first Halloween!" Davy told her as I dusted him off.

"It is?" Penny gushed. Davy grinned as she tickled him.

"No Halloween in the cult," Isaac said. I shook my head at him. Penny didn't need to hear all the sordid details.

"Do you want us to take any inside?" I asked her.

Penny said to Isaac, "Can you take some of those pumpkins into the house, please? Take the smaller ones, and choose a mix of colors. Also, don't set them on any wood surface; they will mess up the finish. Put them on a coaster or some type of protection."

We walked through the house, and Penny took notes on a floor plan. "So let's keep the party to the foyer, the living room, the sitting room, the conservatory, and the dining room. We'll also decorate that hall that leads to the bathrooms. We'll block people from going upstairs or into the library, kitchen, or other more private areas of the house."

"Wouldn't want anyone having some sort of steamy encounter, would we," I said, tone mild.

She blushed slightly. "No, we would not."

She ducked her head. Was the lust that blatant on my face?

"We'll have the games outside," she said as we walked back out onto the terrace. "There will be buffet stations set out in a few different areas, inside and out, along with bars. I'm sure all the parents who bring their kids are going to want a drink."

"Where's the haunted tiny house going?" Remy shouted over the roar of the tractor he was using to tow the tiny house Archer had bought over the summer off Craigslist.

"Don't put it close to the terrace; park it by the woods if you can so it feels like a spooky witch's house," Penny told him. He flashed her a thumbs-up.

"We'll put a bar here and another one over there, then savory snacks on the terrace, another inside, one over there, and a dessert table on the terrace as well," Penny said, sketching as she and I crisscrossed the yard.

"There will be a lot of kids. Archer invited the whole school," I told her.

"Where is the petting zoo going?" Otis asked as he lugged a hay bale past us.

Fuck. The petting zoo.

"Did you rent animals?" Penny asked me.

"Not yet. I was hoping they would forget about it."

"We have some taxidermy ones we can bring," Morticia offered. Or maybe it was Lilith.

"We need some live ones."

"Hey, Ernest," Penny called, waving him over. "Do you have animals?"

"Do you have any goats?" Remy added.

"Yeah, but the goats are mean. Devil creatures," Ernest said.

"Always wanted some goats," Remy told us.

"I'll bring you guys some chickens and a mini pig, except it wasn't actually a mini pig, and this gal ended up with a five-hundred-pound animal that liked to hop up on the couch and watch TV. She asked me if he could live on my farm. It got to be too much for her little apartment. Had to get him out with a crane. His name is Albert if you can believe it," Ernest said. "He's real friendly too. Polite as can be. When she dropped him off, he sat outside my front door, and then I just felt sorry for him and let him back inside. He has his own chair."

"I think that would be perfect, Ernest," Penny said after a moment.

"One more thing. My granddaughter has a miniature pony. Maybe she can bring him by?" Ernest said. "He's good with kids. She takes him to the children's hospital in Manhattan where she lives."

"Small towns, right?" Penny whispered to me when Ernest ambled off.

I wanted to pull Penny away and kiss her and do other things, but then Morticia and Lilith called to her.

"We're here to work," Penny said, rising on her toes to kiss me.

"I'll have to make it up to you later," I said, kissing her neck.

CHAPTER 35

Penny

"Oh, you're going to make it up to me later, are you?" I said. "I hope it includes you wearing a sexy Halloween costume."

"What constitutes a sexy Halloween costume for me?" Garrett asked.

I thought about that. "I guess you could wear one of those Spartan warrior outfits with the helmet, the leather armbands, and a cape. Ooh, and the leather sword carrier that crosses around your back, framing your glistening, oiled bare chest." I was starting to drool again. "Actually, that should totally be your Halloween costume."

"It's going to be freezing," Garrett said.

"Women dress in skimpy clothing all the time in the cold! You can take one for the team," I said, lightly punching his abs. He caught my hand and brought it up to his mouth. "Also, maybe add some tattoos if you really want to turn me on." Truth be told, I was already a little turned on. "Maybe we can shove Morticia and Lilith out of the tiny house and you can give me an idea of what you would look like half naked," I said to him as we walked hand in hand across the yard to the tiny house.

Unfortunately, when Morticia and Lilith saw us, they settled in for a very long and gruesome description of the haunted tiny house. It included dolls, spiders, fake body parts floating in jars, and lots and lots of fake blood.

"That's going to be… something else," Garrett said slowly as we walked out of the little building.

"Should there be an age limit on that?" I asked him.

"Probably…"

Over the next few hours, we decorated and set out pumpkins. I showed Garrett's little brothers how to make witchy fall brooms to hang up for decorations, and I made Garrett help me string orange and black streamers from the chandeliers inside.

"It's so convenient to have a tall person helping." I paused for a moment. "Are you sure you don't have anything more important to be doing?"

He stepped off the ladder he was using to drape crepe paper on the chandelier. He circled my waist with his hands. "I mean, of course I have something more important, but I'm not sure we should leave my brothers and the twins alone while I give you a happy Halloween."

"Boo!" someone shouted, making me jump.

"Crap! Hazel, you scared me!" I said, holding a hand to my chest.

"I knew there was something going on between you two!" she sang as she hugged me. "And people thought you were some sort of robot!" She wagged her finger at Garrett. "Look at you now—decorating, picking pumpkins. I bet you go all out for Halloween too."

Garrett's mouth was a flat line. Hazel was unfazed. "Make sure he dresses up," she told me.

"I have several options involving tattoos and various stages of undress," I promised her. Garrett grumbled behind me.

"Speaking of going all out," Hazel said. "I have sample food for the party. I want to see what you guys think."

Isaac and Bruno helped Hazel cart the trays into the dining room and set them on the buffet.

"I thought this was a sample?" I said.

"Yeah, but then I remembered the kids had fall break and would be hungry. Plus I find it's better to do the test run of catering-sized portions," she said, taking the cling wrap off the large metal containers. "Food turns out different if you cook in big batches or small."

"These are so cute!" I said, admiring the cookies while Garrett ordered his younger brothers to wash their hands.

"Did you make healthy food, or is it all sweets?"

"I have healthy dishes like a squash salad with dried nuts and cranberries. Though looking at all these pumpkins, you might be squashed out. I also have macaroni and cheese with lobster because that's amazing. And I have crab cakes for the adults."

I took one and stuck it in my mouth. "This is so freaking good! Best Halloween ever!"

After we ate and the kids helped clean up, Garrett pulled me aside.

"That table you wanted is upstairs. Come look at it before I bring it down."

"What table?" I whispered as Garrett pulled me into what was probably a servants' stairway. He tugged me upstairs, and we went into a small study.

"That was really unsmooth. Everyone could see that coming from a mile away," I said as he caressed my face.

Garrett was looking at me as if I were the king-sized Butterfinger candy bar in his trick-or-treat haul.

"If you were a jack-o'-lantern, I'd totally light your candle," I whispered to him. "It's a joke. You should laugh!"

He ignored me in favor of nuzzling my neck, kissing me right at the collar of my sweater. He kissed up to my jaw then to my mouth. I moaned softly as his hands made slow circles on my hips and up my waist to cup my tits through my sweater.

Garrett released my mouth to kiss down to my collarbone. I wanted nothing more than to feel his mouth on my rock-hard nipples.

"You know, I'm wearing a Halloween-themed bra," I whispered to him.

"You know, I might actually like Halloween if I see you wearing that," he whispered back then kissed me.

His hands were moving up under the sweater when we were interrupted by the sound of racing footsteps. Garrett leaned his forehead against mine.

"Penny! Penny! There's a disaster!" Billy and Oscar yelled, careening into the study.

"A disaster? How bad can it be?" I said as I followed them downstairs and outside.

We were greeted by furious squawking. Several of Garrett's brothers were chasing plump brown chickens around the terrace.

"What are those?" Garrett said, eyes narrow.

"First part of the petting zoo," Ernest said, dumping out another crate of chickens. "Chickens are delicate creatures. They need to get used to the area. I also brought some of their bamboo."

"What, why?" Garrett said.

"It makes them feel homey."

One squawking chicken slammed into Garrett's feet, followed by Davy.

"They can't just be loose on the property," Garrett said, picking up his little brother.

"Maybe we can keep them in the tiny house," I said.

CHAPTER 36

Garrett

"I think this looks great!" Penny exclaimed. It was the afternoon of the party. Penny, the twins, Hazel, and my brothers had spent the last two days decorating. Now the main downstairs rooms and the backyard looked like a Halloween paradise.

"We still need to find you a Halloween costume," Penny said.

She was dressed in a sexy little orange skirt and crop top. Her ankle boots had pumpkin pom-poms on them. I admired how her legs looked in the fishnet tights. They had a subtle pattern of bats on them.

"What are you?"

She struck a pose. "Pumpkin-spice latte!"

"You're certainly hot enough," I said, running my thumb across the bare stripe of her waist.

"I think it's a little bit tight," she said, adjusting her tits in the crop top. I still hadn't had a chance to finish what

I'd started. I was starting to have crazy dreams of dancing pumpkins and Penny in a skimpy witch's outfit. I'd barely had any sleep the past few days.

"I'll just stay as is," I told her. "No need to go crazy."

"No, no, no. I knew you were going to say that, so I brought you a costume from Mimi's house," Penny said.

"Your foster grandmother? I don't really want to wear one of her old dresses," I replied.

"No, silly! Mimi collected things."

"What things?" I asked. "This isn't some weird fetish thing, is it?"

"No!" She stuck her tongue out at me. "She collected things like dolls and puppets and animatronic teddy bears. She also had costumes. She used to be big in the community theater." Penny handed me a bag. "Go try it on. It should fit. It was made for Olaf."

"Olaf?"

"One of her many beaux."

In the bag were a pair of white riding breeches, a black waistcoat with tails, some sort of shirt made out of flimsy fabric with too many ties to be useful, a cane, a top hat, and a pair of black patent-leather riding boots. I was hoping the costume wouldn't fit. But when I pulled it on, it fit me like a glove.

"It's a little snug," I said, coming out of the powder room. "I don't understand—is this like the headless horseman?"

"Sweet summer child! You're dressed up like Mr. Darcy," Penny said gleefully. "You look so good! All the school moms are going to fall over themselves."

I looked down. The white breeches left very little to the imagination.

"Don't worry," Penny said, pressing against me. "I'll make sure they don't sink their claws into you."

The doorbell rang.

"Stop running!" Hunter bellowed as my younger brothers stampeded to the door. Penny and I headed to the foyer. The majority of my little brothers were dressed up as some flavor of superhero, so we had Batman, Iron Man, and Captain America all battling to open the door first.

"I swear," I muttered, stomping after them in the heavy riding boots.

"There's a pony!" one of my little brothers shrieked. They were all wearing masks, and I couldn't tell them apart.

"Hi!" A petite young woman greeted me with a wave.

"Oh, you do actually have a horse with you," I said, looking down.

"He's a pony," she said.

The miniature horse neighed. He was small. Davy could have sat on him like I would on a normal horse.

"Look, he even has on a Halloween-themed hat," Penny said, patting the beige pony and adjusting his straw hat that was festooned with orange, red, and yellow flowers. "I love horses! He's precious."

"This is Baxter," the young woman said. "I'm Amy."

"Come on through."

"He's housebroken," she said as the horse politely stepped inside. "I take him with me into children's hospitals."

My brothers crowded around the pony.

"Leave him alone," I warned them.

"It's okay, you can pet him," Amy said cheerfully. "But first let's see where we should be set up."

We led Amy and the pony to the backyard. The flock of chickens was roaming around. A large recliner sat elevated on a pallet. Albert the giant pig lounged on his throne, accepting treats from my brothers.

"He ate a whole veggie burger in one bite," Isaac told me in awe.

"Does Baxter need a chair?" I asked Amy uncertainly.

She laughed. "He's fine. I'll give him a break every thirty minutes or so."

"Did you guys have parties in the cult?" Penny asked when went up to the terrace to welcome more guests.

"Just doomsday watches," I told her. "It seemed like every other quarter the world was about to end."

"Aren't you glad it didn't?"

"You mean so I can wear too-tight clothes?"

"You look so good I could lick you," Penny said, running her hands over my hips.

"Honestly, I don't know how men back then even managed to father any children," I grumbled. "These pants are uncomfortably tight."

"But you look like a Halloween treat in them," Penny said.

"See, Edna, I knew I should have worn my Scottish barmaid costume!" Ida called out as she strolled out to the terrace.

"You're supposed to be playing a wicked witch," her granddaughter Olivia said. She was there to help Hazel with catering.

"Penny!" The two women ran to hug each other. "I haven't seen you since high school! You look good! I heard you were back in town." She stole a glance at me. "Wow, is that Garrett?"

Penny giggled. Olivia giggled. Ida and even Judge Edna giggled.

"I don't understand the joke," I said, frowning.

"Of course you don't," Penny cooed.

Sebastian was the next to arrive. He was dressed up as a vampire.

"I couldn't help but go all out," he said as he kissed Penny on the cheek.

I wanted to punch him in the face, acquisition be damned. Penny squeezed my arm.

"What a charming vampire!" Ida said loudly as Sebastian kissed her and Edna on the cheeks as well.

"This is my little brother Alfie," Sebastian said. Alfie looked to be about Billy's age, maybe eight years old or so. He, too, was dressed as a superhero.

"Welcome to our Halloween party!" Penny said, bending down to greet him.

"I like your decorations," Alfie said, pulling off his Spider-Man mask.

I whistled to my brothers.

"Come be good hosts," I ordered them. "You all can't just go off and play by yourselves and be antisocial."

"Come see the giant pig and the haunted tiny house! It's so cool!" Otis said, tugging Alfie across the lawn.

"Hm," Penny said. "I thought there was going to be an age limit."

"You have a haunted tiny house?" Sebastian said, obviously trying not to stare at all of my little brothers.

"It's fine," I told him. "You can comment on my brothers."

"Man, I wish I had a ton of brothers," Sebastian said. "I want to find a wife and have a ton of kids."

He better not be implying Penny. She is taken.

"Harrogate's the place to do it!" Penny said with a laugh.

"No kidding!" he said.

CHAPTER 37

Penny

"Where are the adult beverages?" Ida asked.

"Do not drink a lot, Grandma," Olivia chastised. "You're supposed to be manning the haunted tiny house. You can't be falling-over drunk."

I left them to bicker. More people were arriving. It was mainly families with school-aged kids. The moms all looked appreciatively at Garrett.

"I'm going to assume the Mr. Darcy outfit was your doing?" one young mom asked.

"I mean, I felt like we were all owed it," I said, handing her a drink.

"Nicely done," she said, toasting me.

I spent the next few hours making sure the kids weren't wandering off into the woods, that no one was feeding the chickens candy corn, and that no one dipped anything other than apples in the caramel. Albert the pig was a huge hit with the kids. He ate so much, I was sure he gained another fifty pounds. Baxter the pony reveled in his celebrity status. There was a line of people who wanted to plop their babies on his back and take a picture. The pony handled it all with aplomb.

Hunter stalked around, seeming to disappear and reappear like a vampire as soon as one of his teenaged brothers tried to sneak any alcohol. He lightly shook Isaac and Bruno, plucking the drinks out of their hands. "Here are trash bags. If you have time to drink, you have time to clean."

Hazel passed me, carrying a huge tray of more desserts. I followed to give her a hand in setting out the cupcakes.

"I thought I should keep the food simple," she said, "since the partygoers skew younger. I also made boozy tiramisu for the adults. It looks like a graveyard a little bit, doesn't it?" she asked, holding a clear plastic cup out to me.

"So good," I said through a mouthful. "I can't believe there are so many kids here. It looks like the entire school showed up."

Hundreds of kids in costumes raced around the grounds. I truly had a sense of just how big the Svenssons' estate was when I saw all the people out in the backyard with plenty of room for games and running around.

"The haunted house is a huge hit," Hazel said.

The kids at the party lined up and went into the tiny house a handful at a time. There was lots of screaming, but as soon as kids were tossed out, they ran back into line to do it all over again.

"Edna and Ida are giving stellar performances as creepy witches," she said.

"The parents sure appreciate the drinks," I said, motioning to a group of moms and dads on the terrace, sipping Halloween-themed drinks like Bloody Marys, poison-apple cocktails, and black-devil martinis. Sebastian was in the group, chatting with several of the other parents about the school quality.

"I think Ida does, too," Garrett said, approaching us with a cocktail in each hand. He handed one to me and one to Hazel. "Ida claims she's taking a break from her role as a witch. Edna is manning the haunted tiny house." I looked over. Ida and the twins were off to the periphery. Ida was tipping a flask into her drink.

"She better not get too drunk," Hazel muttered, heading over to the old woman.

"You did a good job," Garrett said. "Thank you. I appreciate someone who can plan complicated events."

"That's me! Party planner extraordinaire," I quipped.

"Party planning is a tough skill," Garrett said.

I laughed, feeling a little self-conscious, especially since once he found out about the article—and I was sure he would—this was all going to come crashing down around me.

"I need to grab something from the kitchen," I muttered, hurrying inside.

Even though Garrett made me horny as hell, I was still glad I hadn't actually slept with him yet. Somehow that seemed like a step too far, as if I was using my feminine wiles to trap him and exploit him. Better to keep a distance. I didn't want to hurt him any more than I was going to.

I rummaged around the kitchen, pretending to look for something.

"What are you doing?" Garrett asked.

I grasped the first thing near my hand. "Paper towels!" I blurted.

"Are you running away from me?" Garrett asked me, standing close but not too close.

"Of course not," I lied. He was so tall! I had to tip my head up to look at him.

"Good," he said, closing the distance and pushing me back against the counter.

"Don't you want to rejoin the party?" I whispered. "Aren't you having fun?"

"Almost," he said, hands coming up to rest on my hips. "There's one thing that will make it even more fun."

He kissed me hard, tipping my head back and grinding against me, pinning me between him and the counter.

"I wish that you weren't wearing tights," he breathed.

"I have to wear tights in the fall," I said. "You know, to stay warm."

"I think you're pretty hot right now," Garrett said. His hand trailed up under my skirt. I tipped my head back and moaned.

"You want to sip my pumpkin-spice latte?" I teased, kissing his jaw.

He grabbed me by the waist and easily set me on the island counter. It put my pumpkin patch right at perfect fucking height. He was hard as his hips pressed into me. His hands slid under my top to caress my skin. One hand moved up to cup my breast. He pulled my tits out of the low-cut top and pressed his mouth to a hard nipple, rolling it with his tongue.

"I guess I am getting pretty hot," I stuttered out as he sucked on the nipple, his hand sliding up my thigh. I bucked against his hand as he pressed it between my legs. "Maybe," I said then whimpered as his fingers rubbed me through the fishnets and my panties. "Maybe we should take this somewhere more private?"

"I'm not sure if we're going to have the chance," Garrett stated, straightening up.

"What?" I blinked, trying to get my bearings. I adjusted my top as Garrett cocked his head to listen. Footsteps headed in our direction.

"Albert's loose!" someone shrieked.

Garrett released me. I adjusted my skirt to hurry outside. The large pig had hefted himself off the recliner and was moseying through the party, straight for the caramel apple station.

CHAPTER 38

Garrett

It took me, Remy, and three of my other brothers to shove the pig back to the recliner.

By that point, the party had been going for hours, and I was ready for it to wind down. My little brothers were still wound up, and from the looks of the snack tables, all the kids at the party had gone overboard on the sweets and not touched any of the salads. Many of the parents felt the same. They were slowly hauling their kids out of the party.

Hazel had made little Chinese takeout-style boxes that were decorated with woodcut Halloween scenes that people could fill with snacks. We said goodbye to people as they left and urged them to take leftovers.

"Great party," Sebastian said, shaking my hand. His little brother waved to me. He had orange frosting smeared all over his face.

"I think someone might have overdone it."

"Best thing about Halloween is excess candy!" Penny said.

"I feel like he's going to regret it later," Sebastian said.

"Have him eat a salad," Penny said, tucking a red curl behind her ear. She and Sebastian laughed.

I wanted to scoop Penny up, take her to my bed, and claim her as mine.

I spent the entire evening obsessing over Penny. I wanted her to stay after the party ended and finish what I had started. Like a ghost, she haunted my thoughts. But she didn't strike terror, just plain lust.

My brothers didn't seem any the worse for wear the next morning. I fed them a savory breakfast—they had had enough sugar—then sent them outside to finish cleaning up and to catch one of the chickens that had wandered off.

I went up to the home office to catch up on work I had neglected due to Penny and party planning. Mace and Adrian were there as well, discussing the property situation for Thalian Biotech. I forced myself to concentrate on the task before me.

Several hours later, Archer threw open the door and announced, "They found the chicken!"

"Fine."

"You don't sound excited," he said, flopping down on the carpet.

"Well, Penny was wearing that outfit yesterday. I think he's frustrated," Adrian joked then gulped when I turned a cold stare in his direction.

"Don't forget," I told him. "You are still on my shit list. I have a ledger for each of you, and yours, Adrian, is bleeding red."

"Your pants were incredibly tight," Archer said, taking a broken cookie out of his pocket and sprinkling crumbs and sugar all over the carpet.

"I am trying to do business here," I snapped at him. "You all spend money like water, especially you, Archer. According to Mike, your conference center is hemorrhaging money, and I need to bring it under control."

"Dude, seriously, Mike exaggerates. Also, who had a truckload of pumpkins delivered just the other day?"

"Pumpkins are surprisingly cheap," I told him.

"Still, what are we going to do with them?" Mace said.

"Penny has several more Halloween events planned," I said. "I'm sure she has other uses for the pumpkins."

"Ah, young Halloween love!" Archer said, tossing a piece of the cookie into his mouth.

"I hope you're going to take Penny out on a nice date," Mace said with a frown. "She's a normal human being. It's shocking you managed to find someone nice who can also tolerate you."

"Not that shocking considering that you found Josie," I retorted. "Besides, we've gone out."

"To the corn maze and to Hazel's restaurant," Archer countered. "Up your game, Garrett. Take her out tonight."

I knew what Penny liked—well, not like that. But I would. No, I meant I knew she liked Halloween. I had the perfect date idea.

Garrett: *Go out with me tonight.*

Penny: *You mean come pick you up to take you out lol!*

Garrett: *Right. Please keep reminding me that I have no license. I feel like a fourteen-year-old again.*

Penny: *You sure didn't look fourteen in that Mr. Darcy costume. *wink emoji**

Penny: *Where are we going?*

Garrett: *A surprise*

Penny: *Am I supposed to drive with my eyes closed? What should I wear?*

Garrett: *Something normal.*

Penny: *Ok sexy rainbow glitter sparkles cat unicorn onesie it is then!*

Garrett: *If it's anything like the pumpkin spice latte costume, I'm not going to be mad.*

Penny: *What time are you picking me up, oh wait lol!*

Garrett: *I would say you're mean, except you're too sexy.*

Penny: *It's a special occasion, so I'll bring the hearse around in an hour.*

Penny showed up promptly at six. Thankfully, she was not driving the hearse. I had given her another car after the forklift had destroyed the last one.

"No ghost problems?" I asked.

"Nope!"

I sat in the car.

"What?" she said, looking at me.

I leaned over to kiss her. "We could just skip the movie. Archer owes me. I could snag us one of his fancy hotel suites."

"We're going to the movies?" Penny said excitedly.

"At the old movie theater in town," I said. "They're playing old horror films from the Fifties. I bought us tickets."

"I thought it closed," Penny said.

"It reopened recently. Svensson PharmaTech sponsored it."

She wrapped her arms around my neck and kissed me hard. One of my hands drifted down to rest on her ass. I wanted nothing more than to pull her panties down and fuck her right there.

"That's amazing! You're the best!"

"I didn't know you would be so excited about it," I said, wrapping a lock of her hair around my fingers.

"Wait, oh no!" she exclaimed, sitting back.

"What?"

"I have to go change. You should have told me!"

"You look fine."

"No. I have to wear my nineteen fifties Sabrina-inspired outfit. Hold on." She started the car and raced up the driveway.

"Penny, we're going to miss the movie."

"When is it playing?"

"An hour from now."

"Geez, overplan much?"

"I thought you might be one of those girls who is chronically late," I said.

"Hardly," Penny snorted as she turned onto the road. "If you're on time, you're late."

After a short drive into town, she parked the car in front of the rambling Victorian house. Though the day had been slightly overcast, it seemed as if there was a thunderstorm brewing right over the house. The whole building was dark wood with dusty windows. When we walked up the creaky porch, the temperature dropped about ten degrees.

"You can sit in there," she said, pointing to the parlor. "I'll just be a minute. I already know the perfect outfit."

I stood in the dimly lit sitting room. There was a fireplace on one wall flanked by dusty bookcases. There were several doors leading off into seeming darkness. The dusty chandelier above me tinkled softly. I looked up then back down and tried not to curse.

"Good evening, Garrett," Morticia and Lilith said in unison.

"I'm waiting on Penny," I explained.

They stood there, unblinking. "She's changing." In unison, they turned and disappeared down the hall.

Something brushed against my leg. A black cat meowed.

"I hope you're not a bad omen," I said to the cat, bending down to pet him.

"That's just Salem," Penny said.

The black tights hugged her legs, which was good, because the dark-red A-line skirt she wore ended high up her thighs.

"Do you like my outfit?"

"I love it," I said. "Take it off."

CHAPTER 39

Penny

I'll have to admit when Garrett said that, his deep voice rumbling around the room, I had half an inkling to strip down right there.

He kissed me, his hands sliding under the cape.

"Are you seriously going to do that in here?"

I shrieked. Salem startled and howled and sank his claws into Garrett's leg. He cursed as Morticia leveled her gaze at us.

"It's dirty in here. And people can see you from the street."

"I don't see how. These windows are filthy. Remind me that we need to clean them for the party."

"Leave them alone," Morticia said.

"If we had more light in here, we could get some plants," I suggested.

Morticia hissed. "Plants are gross and smell weird."

"Heaven forbid there's something green in here."

The old movie theater in Harrogate had been built in the 1940s, when the town was still booming in the post–World War II period. It was a beautiful old building constructed in the streamlined Modern style, with chrome and neon accents and a cantilevered awning. A vintage marquee announced the current features.

"Sweet! *Creature from the Black Lagoon* is playing," I said as we walked up to the building.

"Maybe that should be my Halloween costume," Garrett said.

"If you didn't like the Mr. Darcy costume, I feel like you won't like being in a heavy rubber suit that much either."

"I suppose you're right."

"This is amazing," I said when we walked inside. Fluted plaster details lit by hidden lights and draped in red curtains made it seem as if we had walked into a time machine. "I'm so glad I changed," I said as I soaked in the atmosphere. "The movie theater had been closed and abandoned when I was a teenager. Sometimes Morticia, Lilith, and I would sneak inside. I never imagined it could look like this."

Taking out my phone, I pulled Garrett down by his tie and snapped several selfies of us.

"I have to remember our first date," I told him.

"I thought the first date was pumpkin picking?"

"No, that was business," I said, looking around for the concession stand.

"Nowhere in my job description does it say go pumpkin picking," Garrett said, a smile tugging around his mouth.

"You had fun!" I teased him as I dragged him through the crowd. There were a lot of people out.

"The corn maze was the best part."

"We have to get popcorn," I told Garrett, pulling him to the concession stand line. "Can you fill it halfway then drizzle butter on it then fill it the rest of the way?" I asked the clerk when we finally got to the counter.

"This lady knows how to movie!" the clerk said as she fixed my popcorn.

"I also need a box of candy and a large Coke," I said.

Garrett carried my snacks as we went into the theater.

"They even have an usher!" I said in awe.

"Do you want the balcony or down below?" the usher asked.

"Balcony."

We found our seats, and I stuffed a handful of popcorn into my mouth. As I chewed, I noticed Garrett was looking at me softly.

"What?"

"I love how excited you are," he said, tucking a strand of loose hair behind my ear.

"Are you kidding me? This is the best date ever."

"The movie hasn't even started," he said with a slight laugh.

"Shh!" I said, kissing him as the lights dimmed.

Like in the classic movie theaters from the 1940s, this one played a Looney Tunes cartoon before the feature film. I laughed at Bugs Bunny's antics, Garrett's arm around my shoulders. The whole theater wasn't uncomfortably packed, but there were a lot of people. Everyone applauded when the film started.

I snuggled next to Garrett while Richard Carlson and Julie Adams pursued the creature. Garrett pressed his lips to my head when I screamed as the creature tried to kidnap Kay Lawrence. I applauded and whistled when the end credits rolled.

"Man!" I said when we walked out of the theater. "You'd think these old movies would be cheesy, but they're still kind of scary. Also, I wish I had a little more popcorn. Though I think some of it ended up on my coat." I dusted myself off.

"Dinner?" Garrett asked me. "There's a diner the next block over. They have hamburgers and milkshakes."

"Do they have the really thin shoestring fries? Because that's the only kind I like."

"Are you a french fry snob?"

"Totally."

The diner was in a 1950s style, with red vinyl-covered booths, white-and-black-checkered floors, and chrome accents.

"Ooh, they have milkshakes!" I said when we sat down and I looked at the menu.

"We have a special Halloween-themed milkshake," the waitress said.

"I will have that, fries, and a cheeseburger," I said, handing her my menu.

"Same for me minus the milkshake," Garrett said.

"You don't want one, hun? It's bright orange and has little candied bats on it," the waitress cajoled.

"You can have some of mine," I promised Garrett.

He made a face.

"So, is this the best Halloween season you've ever had?" I asked Garrett when the waitress left.

"I guess it is," he said, his gaze on me.

"Or is it going to depend on if you win that acquisition or not?"

"I feel confident about it," he said. "Sebastian seems as if he likes Harrogate. My little brothers managed to behave somewhat civilly to his younger brother, which is a plus."

"He posted pictures of the party on his Instagram account. That has to mean something."

The waitress came with our food.

"That is a nice-looking hamburger," I said as she slid the plates and shake onto the table.

"I debated about taking you to this place, which has milkshakes," Garrett said, "or this other place that has a jar of cheese sauce they dump over your burger and fries."

I was speechless for a moment. "I didn't realize that was a thing, and now I need that in my life."

"Next time. Promise," Garrett said.

I picked up my burger and thrust it at him. He looked confused. "You don't have a milkshake, so we're toasting burgers," I explained. He slowly picked his up. "To Halloween! And a successful acquisition!" I said as I tapped our burgers together.

And please, Romani queen, fix my life, because I can't write that article. Thank you.

I took a big bite. "Yum! I love the ones where the patties are smashed. I don't want a huge piece of meat I can't get my mouth around."

Garrett looked as if he was choking. He took a sip of water.

"That—oh, I didn't mean that. I'm sure I can fit my mouth around your meat," I said helpfully.

"I forgot your straw," the waitress said cheerfully. A metal pipe clunked on the table.

I looked at it and poked it suspiciously. "What is that?"

"A straw," Garrett deadpanned.

"No, that's some sort of murder weapon." I picked it up gingerly.

"I bet it's never been cleaned," Garrett said.

I made a face.

"Do you have any plastic ones?" he asked, taking another bite of his hamburger.

"I left them..." I thought for a moment. "Ugh, they're in the car that the ghost destroyed. I had them in the trunk." I sighed. "I'll just use a spoon. It's too thick to suck anyway."

There were more choking sounds from Garrett.

"You have a dirty mind," I scolded, pushing his water closer to him.

"Seeing you in that costume really tripped the wire on that one," he replied.

"What am I going to do about the straw situation?" I complained, taking a scoop of the thick orange milkshake.

"Welcome to my world. Small-town America, where unrequited and disastrous love has a nuclear fallout radius that affects everything."

"Yeah, this straw thing is not going to work for me," I said, picking up the long spoon that had come with the shake. I dumped a good portion of the salt shaker on my french fries, then used a fry to scoop up some of the shake.

"Don't make that face. Ice cream and french fries are the best," I scolded. I picked up a fry and scooped up some of the bright-orange shake and handed it to Garrett. He recoiled.

"Taste it," I ordered, making an airplane motion then popping the fry into his mouth.

CHAPTER 40

Garrett

The ice cream-covered fry wasn't that bad, I hated to admit.

"Is that a small smile I see?" Penny teased. "I told you it's good!"

I nodded. "It's good. I don't think I'd eat another one though."

"You need to have more fun. When people are released from cults, don't they go crazy and do all the things they've been missing, like Kimmy Schmidt on that Netflix show? Did you go to clubs or ragers when you left the cult?"

"No," I sighed. "But my brother Archer went hog wild with tattoos, fast cars, expensive art, and women. I was more concerned with building an empire big enough to crush my father."

"Wow. Well, it looks like you managed," she said.

"Almost. Not quite."

"What was your first holiday like after the cult?" Penny asked, taking another bite of the toxic orange milkshake.

"Weirdly enough, it was Halloween."

"Did you do anything fun?"

I thought back to that cold fall more than twenty years ago. "The winter had come early that year. Remy wasn't yet old enough to join the military. He and Hunter had procured money from... somewhere, and we all had taken a bus to Harrogate. We slept in an abandoned house. Harrogate had Halloween events, but it wasn't anything as extravagant as now. Remy found a pillowcase, and he was very insistent that I have Halloween. Mace still hadn't complete shaken off the cult conditioning, and he was convinced we were about to bring about Armageddon. Of course that didn't happen. Remy took me trick-or-treating. I collected an excessive amount of candy. Archer stole most of it, then he ate too much and got sick."

"That doesn't sound too terrible," Penny said.

I hadn't thought about that memory in years. Whenever I thought of fall, I always remembered the dread and the cold.

"Remy was really proud of that ghost costume," I said wryly. "He colored the eye holes with a black permanent marker."

"Maybe we should dress you as a ghost for old times' sake," Penny said.

"I thought you wanted me to be shirtless in a leather Roman harness."

"I mean if you're offering, I'm not going to say no to a shirtless man."

With all the innuendos at dinner, I thought for sure we were going to end the evening on a high note. But instead, Penny drove me back to my house. This was turning out to be the biggest issue with losing my license—I had no control over where we went.

"You want to come inside?" I asked her, kissing her and tucking a curl behind her ear.

"I don't know, I should probably get some work done," she said, slightly breathless.

"What work? You work for me," I retorted, pulling her close to me, reveling in her softness.

"We still have a lot left to do to make sure Sebastian sells you that company."

"Just take a night off," I said as I pressed her back against the seat.

She whimpered softly as I kissed her neck up to her mouth. I kissed her hungrily, needing her. I undid the red cape. *That's the problem with fall*, I thought. *Too many layers*. My hand cupped her breast, pinching the hard nipple and making her moan. Penny spread her legs slightly, and I pressed my other hand against the soaking panties. She bucked slightly against my hand. My fingers pushed under her panties. I wanted nothing more than to watch her come undone in my arms.

I stroked the hot wetness, Penny making high-pitched moans against my mouth as I teased her. "I want to see you come," I whispered against her mouth.

She bit her lip as I teased her clit.

In the dark, her phone lit up, ringing, and she started, pushing me off to grab for it. "I, um—I should go. Thanks for the evening. It was amazing." She kissed me lightly then practically shoved me out of the car.

"Clearly not that amazing if she just up and left," I muttered, watching her drive away. I wondered what I had done and stewed on it as I went into the house.

"I didn't expect to see you back," Archer said when I walked in. "Did you blow your date? Or maybe you're back because she didn't blow you!"

"Archer," Hunter reprimanded.

"I'm going for a run," I told my brothers and went upstairs to change. Then I walked out the front door. I could have gone on the trails around back, but it felt as if something was pulling me back into town. As I ran, slowly increasing my pace, I quickly warmed up in the cold.

Before long, I found myself outside of the old Victorian house.

CHAPTER 41

Penny

I wanted to stay with Garrett and have passionate, mind-bending sex, but then my phone rang, destroying the fantasy of the perfect evening.

My mother's name was on the screen. I knew she was calling about the article. I was jumpy, and I called her as soon as I parked the car in front of the old Victorian house. I could not afford to lose my license on top of everything else.

"There you are," my mother said sharply when she answered.

"I'm still working on finishing that sample article," I said quickly. "I'm trying to get some more information."

"You've been there for weeks. You were at the Halloween party, for God's sake!" she snapped. "I saw it on Instagram. You have to give me something. Don't disappoint me."

"They're not that interesting," I lied, slumping down on the floor. Salem came over to rub his furry black head against my arms. "I promise I'll have something together soon."

"There are people counting on you, Penny," Trisha said. "If the magazine doesn't do well this coming quarter, a lot of people will lose their jobs. It will be *your fault.*"

"Crap," I whispered after she hung up. I rested my head on my arms.

I stayed that way for several minutes until Morticia and Lilith hauled me to my feet. "We ran you a bath. We were out collecting herbs by the moonlight, and we put some in the water for you. It will calm you down."

"What am I going to do about the article?" I groaned as they prodded me upstairs.

"Did you ask the Romani queen for help?" Lilith asked as she deftly unbuttoned my cloak.

"Yes, sort of. Maybe I wasn't specific enough."

"She will come through for you," Morticia said.

"Should I go leave another offering?"

"You're too worked up for it right now," Lilith said. "Soak in your bath. It will do you good."

The bathroom glowed with tons of candles on every surface. It also smelled a little mossy.

"Are you sure?" I said, looking at the bark, dried berries, and leaves floating in the claw-foot tub. I slipped into the water after the twins left. Despite the smell, it was hot and relaxing, and whatever that tree bark was gave it a nice zing.

After my bath, I felt more relaxed and centered. I curled up under the comforter in my room.

"I just need to tell Trisha I can't do the article," I whispered to myself, eyes closed. The branches tap-tapped against the windows. I was cozy and warm. My mother couldn't hurt me. "I'll write a professional letter, give the money back."

The money you have already spent.

So I would wait until I got my next PharmaTech paycheck, then give the money back. I would be broke and unable to pay my loans, but I could make it work, hopefully. I still had a free place to live.

The tapping on the window was more insistent. I opened my eyes and screamed when I saw a dark figure in the window.

"It's the ghost!" I yelled and pulled the covers over my head. Then I realized that was dumb, pulled them down, and fumbled for my phone to call the police.

"Penny, it's me. Let me in," a man called, voice muffled through the glass.

"Garrett?"

I turned on my lamp, swung my feet out of bed, and hurried to open the window. The lead plate glass creaked as Garrett jumped into the round room.

"What are you doing here?"

"I had a momentary lapse in judgment and climbed up the side of your house. I would have climbed back down, but the ladder I used was knocked over in the wind," he admitted.

I blinked at him in the soft light.

"I'll just see myself out," he said. He didn't move. He was wearing a tight shirt that ended just under his elbows. I could make out the tendons and sinewy muscles of his arms. In the small room, his body loomed big. He smelled good and very, very male.

All the stress, the teasing that evening, and the zingy bath made me want one thing. "Since you're here," I croaked.

That was all the permission he needed. His muscles were hard under the thin workout shirt. I only had on a thin tank top and panties. They were bikini cut with smiling pumpkins. Cute, but not sexy.

"If I'd known you were coming, I would have put on something nicer," I joked, desperately trying not to seem self-conscious.

Garrett leaned back as his hands drifted through my slightly damp hair, caressing my face and moving to rest on my upper arms. "You look incredible."

"Well then, point for me!"

"If you keep wearing things like that, you might actually make me like Halloween," he said, his eyes intense gray in the lamplight.

"You should see the back of them," I said, turning around and leaning over to show the large laughing pumpkin painted like a bull's-eye on my rear.

I looked over my shoulder just in time to see Garrett grab my hips and press his face against the panties.

"Oh, so we're like that now," I gasped.

"I've been dreaming about this for weeks," he said, breath hot through the panties. My mouth was suddenly dry. Was this actually happening?

I leaned over as he mouthed me through the thin cotton, resting my hands on the antique oak nightstand.

Garrett pulled the panties down.

My last coherent thought was that I was glad I had shaved. I didn't want Garrett to get lost in the weeds on the way to the pumpkin patch.

Then his mouth was on me. It felt a thousand times better than his fingers. He licked me, spreading my legs and drawing a line from my opening to my clit. My head tipped back, and I moaned as he worked me with his tongue. He stroked up then back down, making this twisty motion on my clit. He licked and sucked on my clit while I strained back against him. His mouth pressed against me harder, and he sucked and teased my clit until I came with a cry.

"Fuck," I slurred, trying and failing to stand upright. Garrett wrapped a strong arm around my waist and looked down at me.

"Actually, I had it planned a little differently," he said, tracing his finger around my collar and down to the V my breasts made in my shirt. "I wanted to suck on your tits while I stroked your clit."

Garrett pulled off my shirt and cast it to the floor. His head dipped, and he kissed down the swell of my breast to the nipple, sucking and nipping it as his fingers stroked my pussy, making me wet and aching for him again.

I clung to him, my legs trembling while he stroked me.

Garrett pushed me onto the bed. He kissed me hard then was back at my tit, kissing one as his hand stroked the other. His hand trailed down to my pussy, where his fingers stroked the silky wetness, dipping into my opening then trailing up to tease my clit. My legs were spread for him. He moved up to kiss my mouth, his tongue mirroring the motions his hand was making.

"Fuck, I love your tits," he said, leaning up slightly to hover over me. "One day, I want to watch you touch yourself, stroke your clit, and tease those perfect tits while you tell me how bad you want me to fuck you," he growled in my ear.

He kissed me hard again then planted kisses back down to my tits, teasing and nipping one nipple then the other, all while his hand stroked my pussy. Two fingers dipped into my opening as his thumb rubbed my clit, making me whimper.

He kissed his way down, down to lick and tease my clit while his fingers were still inside, stroking me. My back arched, my fingers clawing in his short hair. One of his hands reached up to pinch my nipple. My breath came out in high-pitched pants as his tongue teased my clit, making twisting motions around it. One last swirl and I was over the edge, giving me visions of dancing pumpkins.

"Shit," I slurred before the pumpkins faded to black. "You didn't even take your clothes off for that egregiously amazing display. If I could work my arms, I'd totally give you a round of applause."

CHAPTER 42

Garrett

Penny was intoxicating. I wanted to curl up next to her and fuck her the minute she awoke. But then what if she regretted it? Maybe she was faking sleep so I'd leave. I paced around the small round room, feeling like a caged animal. Penny snored slightly, limbs sprawled, her large breasts rising and falling slowly. No, she was definitely asleep. I covered her with the comforter and turned off the lamp. Then I went to the window. I was thinking about trying my luck on the exterior of the building but then realized I was too drunk on Penny to risk it.

I didn't date a lot, or at all really. My family and company came first. I wasn't sure how this was supposed to go exactly, but I was a little put out that she had fallen asleep. Maybe that was a good thing. Archer would know, but I'd drink out of a metal straw before I even mentioned it to him. I crept downstairs—well, tried to, anyway. It was a creaky old house.

Thinking it would be less obvious if I went out the back door, I made it through the large house and down the back hallway. I eased open the back door and stepped onto the porch, letting out a breath.

I stifled a curse when the twins seemed to appear out of the fog. They were carrying a long, heavy bag full of… something. They paused, and we looked at each other.

"You never saw us," they said then hustled into the carriage house.

Shaking my head, I muttered, "I need Penny to move out of this creepy house."

Maybe I could buy her an apartment? But maybe she would think it was weird. Plus she loved this house.

Taking off at a steady lope, I was still hyped up from being that close to her. I wanted to scale back up the house to wake her up but decided against it. That wasn't very gentlemanly behavior. Besides, I could wait.

Penny was in high spirits the next morning.

"Man, today is a great day!"

"Is it?" I said, looking up. "It's sort of foggy."

"You know what I mean!" she said, pulling me in for a kiss. "You are amazing."

"Glad it met your approval."

As soon as we arrived at headquarters, I wanted to pull Penny into a closet and finish what I'd started the night before. Unfortunately, Mace was waiting for me in my office.

"Good news and bad news," he said.

"You know I hate it when you do that."

"I think we can assemble enough land with the belt factory work for the Thalian Biotech offices and facilities. However, we need city approval to build the offices there. There was a lot of pushback at the last town hall due to all our development in the historic downtown core. That being said, we have a meeting scheduled with Meg in an hour."

"And no one thought to tell me the deputy mayor was coming?" I growled.

"You were otherwise occupied," Greg said, pushing Mace aside.

He shook hands with Penny. "I hear you've been instrumental in helping to convince Sebastian to sell his company to us."

"This is Greg," I told Penny. "He is one of my older half brothers. He runs some sort of investment sideshow business."

"And who is offering the land for your use."

"Do we need to strategize for the meeting?" Parker asked from the hall.

"Hunter should definitely not be there," Mace said. "You know how he aggravates Meg."

Greg shook his head. "I seriously wish Hunter would get his act together. Well-placed groveling would go a long way to greasing the wheels of the city with Meg."

"What do you know, Greg?" Hunter spat, joining the group.

I looked at each of my brothers. Was this the perfect time to put my latest plan into motion? I thought it was. "No. Hunter absolutely needs to be at this meeting."

"He does?" Mace said. Honestly, my brothers were incredibly dense. It was a struggle trying to dumb things down for them.

"Yes. Someone go make sure the room is set up. Penny." She looked up at me expectantly. "Could you please go to Hazel's coffee shop and purchase one of those giant cups of pumpkin-spice latte, with extra whipped cream, the caramel drizzle, and the little cookie crumbs Hazel dusts on top?"

"Uh—"

"Also please purchase a selection of Halloween-themed desserts."

"Who are you, and what have you done with Garrett?" Mace said.

"You going to eat all that?" Parker asked, horrified.

I smiled. "Let's just say I've developed a sweet tooth."

CHAPTER 43

I returned with the coffee and treats right as Garrett and his brothers were settling down in the conference room. Garrett took the coffee and cookies from me and set them in front of Hunter.

"Get those away from me," he grunted. Garrett ignored him.

I was trying to ignore Bronwyn, who was at the meeting. She glared at me when I sat down next to her. I bet if I'd told her what Garrett had been doing to me the previous night, that would wipe the smug look off her face.

Garrett's older brothers were on their phones, but they stood up when Meghan, Hazel's sister and the deputy mayor of Harrogate, walked into the room.

"So glad you could join us, Deputy Mayor," Garrett said, pulling out her seat for her. "We know you're busy with the city."

"I can't believe I'm up here again for another one of the trademarked Svensson specials of trying to hoodwink the taxpayers of Harrogate."

"'Hoodwink' is a loaded term," Hunter replied coldly.

"What Hunter forgot to say," Garrett said loudly, "is that he's very happy to see you. He even went out of his way to buy you coffee and a Halloween cookie."

"I did?" Hunter said, looking shocked.

"The cookie is chocolate, and it even has a cat wearing a pointy hat on it," Garrett said as he handed Meg the bag and the coffee while we all looked on in shock.

"It was a very thoughtful gesture from Hunter, wasn't it?" Garrett continued.

Hunter looked behind him. It was comical, and I struggled not to laugh.

"Did you poison this coffee?" Meg asked suspiciously.

"Of course he didn't!"

"Why do you always accuse me of having the worst intentions towards you?" Hunter snarled, half rising out of his seat. Meg didn't back down.

"Oh, I don't know. Because you're a filthy, self-serving liar," she said.

"That doesn't mean I would poison your coffee!" Hunter shouted.

Garrett quickly moved behind him and grabbed him by the shoulder.

"Hunter was just trying to be nice. Extend an olive branch and all that," Garrett said, twisting his grip on Hunter's shoulder.

Meg sniffed the coffee.

"It's good," I said. "I drink a lot of those. It has the caramel drizzle."

"Unfortunately it has a ton of calories," Meg said.

"Calories schmalories," I cried. "It's the Northeast. Our people need some padding against the harsh winters."

Meg took a sip. Garrett relaxed his grip on Hunter.

"Don't ever touch me again," Hunter snarled to him.

"If we could talk about the land deal," Greg said, clapping his hands together.

"Yes, let's talk about that," Meg said. "You all want to put yet more offices and more light industrial space in the downtown. Eventually this place is going to be one big campus for the Svenssons."

"That's hardly—" Greg began.

Meg held up a hand. "I understand you all contribute a lot of money to the community, but there are some residents that don't think all that abstractly. They need to see a direct correlation to the development and their benefit. The city can't just railroad your developments through."

"So what do you want?" Parker asked. "A park, restaurants, a brewery?"

"Jobs," Meg said. "Personally, I would have said a clinic, but apparently there are people worried that it would attract the wrong sort."

I snorted.

"Yes, I know," Meg said with a sigh, "but something job related so that it seems like you're trying to help the larger Harrogate population would be nice. Don't you have some sort of small product you could make in a minimal amount of space? There are a number of the elderly who have failure-to-launch grandsons living in their basements who I'm sure would like to have somewhere to send them to learn some basic skills and develop a work ethic."

"We will look into that," Garrett assured her.

Meg stood up. "Thanks for the cookie. Oh, and those straws you were having someone smuggle into Harrogate? We confiscated them. Have a good afternoon, boys."

CHAPTER 44

Garrett

"That went surprisingly well," Greg said.

"It did?" Penny asked.

"No, it didn't. She took my straws!" I fumed.

"You went to high school with Hazel, right?" Mace asked Penny. "Any info or insight on Meg you could share?"

She shrugged. "My impression of her was that she was a very straitlaced, by-the-book type of person. But I'll think more about it. I think all the Loring girls are foodies, so bribing her with food seems like a good start. But Garrett seems to have that covered."

"Do you need my help for anything else, Garrett?" Bronwyn asked, batting her eyelashes at me.

"Penny's going to work more on the party plan for the next event with Sebastian."

"Maybe I can help." Bronwyn said.

"Sure, I suppose. Penny, maybe you can bring her up to speed." If I hadn't known any better, I thought Penny shot me a death glare. But then she and Bronwyn went off to talk.

I turned to my brothers. "We need to make it through the next few weeks. Sebastian has confirmed he is coming in for a Halloween party Penny is hosting at Morticia and Lilith's house."

"The creepy haunted house?" Mace asked.

"The house isn't haunted. There's no such thing as ghosts."

"Ida says it's haunted," Archer said. "Also, Hunter, I can't believe you bought food and didn't get me anything."

"I didn't buy it," Hunter said and glared at me.

"I'm helping you," I told him. "I'm going to fix your situation with Meg before you ruin us all. This land deal should have been a simple handshake. However, you have made it unnecessarily difficult."

"I bet it's all some devious plan to ruin Hunter," Parker said.

"You better not!" Hunter hissed.

"Of course I'm not! Besides, heaven help us, but a not-insignificant amount of our family net worth runs through Hunter. It's not like just getting rid of Adrian."

"Adrian is really trying to get better," Mace protested.

I shook my head slowly.

After I wrapped up with my brothers, Penny was still in a tense meeting with Bronwyn. I didn't want to disturb her.

While the acquisition was important, I had several other things on my plate.

I had contacts everywhere. It was part of how I was so effective. One of them was waiting for me at a teahouse in downtown Harrogate. The FBI agent was sitting at one of the tables in the back of the shop, sipping a cup of imported Japanese tea. We shook hands.

"Officially, I'm here about the business from this spring with Anke and the theft," Agent Donley warned.

"Of course," I said, waving his concerns away. "Anything you can tell me about my father?"

"Honestly," Donley said, "I think the guy must have some sort of lawyer or someone he's working with. He's *just* skirting the line of child abuse."

"Of course."

"Your father declared all the money you sent him on his taxes. I had forensic accountants look into him. He pays taxes on the property," the FBI agent said.

"What about welfare fraud?" I countered.

"He technically doesn't have his official residence with any of his wives, so they can legally collect government benefits. He's not running drugs. He's just an awful person. Unfortunately, there's no law against that."

"I need to rescue my sisters," I insisted.

"I would advise being sneaky," he said. "I was in the cult division at the FBI a couple years ago. Usually if you disband the cult, the mothers will take the kids and run off, and you can never find them. Sometimes they're absorbed into another cult, but a lot of times they simply disappear. Whatever it is you're going to do, do it very slowly and carefully."

I glowered.

"Probably a little too scary for Halloween," he joked. Agent Donley shook my hand. "Let me know if I can help. Thanks for the tip about the Russian spy."

CHAPTER 45

I could not believe that Garrett had foisted Bronwyn on me.

"I guess you're not as untouchable and special as you think," she said, flipping her perfectly straight hair.

I wanted to throw in her face how much attention, exactly, Garrett had given me last night. But I restrained myself. It was bad enough that I still hadn't found a way around giving my mother information on Garrett and his family. I definitely shouldn't be blabbing about what he and I were doing after-hours.

As if she knew I was thinking about her, my mother called me. I ignored it, though I knew it would make her furious.

"Is that him?" Bronwyn shrieked, grabbing for my phone.

"No, it's not," I said, snatching it back from her.

"You don't even know Garrett. I can't believe you'd think he would be into you," I shot at her.

"We went on a date," Bronwyn said smugly.

"Really?" I replied skeptically. "To where?"

"We had lunch in his office."

"So you didn't go on a date, you had a working lunch. You're delusional. You know that, right?"

"We had a connection," Bronwyn said, mouth screwed up in anger. "He likes girls like me! He said so."

"He did?" I said in disbelief.

"Yes."

"To you?"

"Not to me exactly," Bronwyn said, nose in the air, "but I heard Garrett talking to his brothers. He said he wants a sporty girl who eats healthy and is slim and has perfectly straight hair and nice clear skin."

I looked down at my body then kicked myself, because I knew that was what Bronwyn wanted me to do.

"You don't fit any of the criteria," she sneered. "Men like him don't date, let alone marry, girls like you. You're the tumble in the hay before he finds a real compatible woman who he can take to fancy charity balls."

"Are you going to help plan the party or not?" I mumbled.

"Not. I know it's going to be a disaster, just like you."

"Can I ask you a question?" I said in the car that evening.

Garrett grunted, not looking up from his phone.

"What is your ideal woman?"

"I always imagined myself with someone like a vegan marathon runner. You know, the crazy math types who count calories and macros, the sort of well-bred girls who only have trophy jobs and don't really need to work," he said absently.

My stomach churned. I thought I was going to puke. *Guess it's a good thing we didn't go all the way.*

"However," Garrett said, but his phone rang before he could continue. He answered tersely.

I sped the car up and screeched to a halt in front of the Svensson estate. Garrett unbuckled his seat belt and stepped out of the car. He signaled to me to wait a moment, but I slammed the door closed and drove away.

"Crap, I'm so stupid! I guess this is the sign I needed. You want that article sample, Trisha? *Fine.*"

As soon as I parked in front of the old Victorian house, I headed straight to the kitchen, poured a mug of bourbon liquor over good vanilla ice cream, raced upstairs, sat at my laptop, and began to type. I wrote a great two-hundred-word teaser about the aloof Svenssons. They were basically feral, having grown up in a cult in the desert, and were now raising their little brothers to be the same terrible, shallow men as they were.

By the time I had sort of proofread it, I was sloshed. It turned out the ice cream didn't do a lot to mitigate the effect of drinking straight liquor from a coffee mug. I was seeing Halloween spirits by the time I attached the article to an email and sent it to my mother.

"Screw you, Garrett!" I slurred, toasting the sent message with my empty mug. "See how you like this nonskinny bitch."

Then I slowly slid off my chair and onto the floor.

"There's an Oreo under my desk," I whispered. "When was the last time I ate an Oreo?"

"Do not eat that," Morticia said, her black boots appearing in front of me. She slapped my hand away.

I burped.

"I was going to have us start decorating for the Halloween party, but you are clearly not going to be any help."

CHAPTER 46

Garrett

When Penny drove away, I was slightly miffed. Maybe she had more work to do and didn't want to wait on me to finish my call. But I couldn't end it; I'd been waiting days for this call. I was on the phone with one of my contacts out west. I would bury my father.

My contact did not have much information, just speculation. I sat in the library and took notes over the hour-long call. My contact was an old Vietnam vet. He was crazy and lived off the grid. He refused to use the internet. I'd had to personally take him a satellite phone that I'd assured him could not be hacked.

On the call, he told me that my father had taken another wife, and that as far as he could tell, my sisters were still in the compound. He gave me a rundown of descriptions and license plates of everyone who went in and out of the compound. Then he went on a tirade about how aliens were putting metal shavings in his food. It was probably the peyote and sunstroke, but he provided good information.

"Any news from the western front?" Hunter asked as I sat in the club room, stewing over the phone call.

"Still not enough to hang our father."

"Don't drink too much. You have the Halloween party tomorrow. You need to put on a good face for Sebastian. We cannot let the Holbrooks win that company."

"Penny has it under control," I said. That reminded me, why had she been so abrupt in leaving? I needed to call her.

"One more thing," Hunter said, his face cold. "In the future, do not insert yourself into my personal life."

"When your personal life affects me, then yes, I will involve myself," I snapped. "I have given you warning after warning. Your situation with Meg has gone too far. I told you to fix it or I would."

"By buying her coffee?" Hunter said.

"Sometimes these things require a lighter touch," I retorted.

A lighter touch was how I decided to handle things with Penny. She didn't return my calls or text that evening. In hindsight, her question about the type of woman I was attracted to had been leading, and I'd clearly not answered correctly. I had been trying to answer truthfully and then end it with "And of course you're better than anything I could think of." But then my contact had called, and I'd missed that part.

I hoped to talk to her when she was in a more rational mood. She seemed to run hot and cold sometimes. I usually felt I was a good judge of people. Within minutes, I could get a read on them. With Penny, whenever I thought I had her pinned down, she always surprised me.

But the party at her house was tomorrow. I'd have to see her then.

When I knocked on the door of the large Victorian house the next evening, Penny answered. She was already clearly drunk. There weren't even that many people there yet.

She posed in the doorway. She was wearing a costume that could only be described as sexy witch. Low-cut corset top, fishnet tights, boots, a very short skirt, heavy makeup, and the requisite witch hat that was half pulled over part of her face.

"Am I welcome here?" I asked carefully.

"Where's your costume?" she asked, looking me up and down.

"I—"

She slammed the door in my face. The twins opened it back up.

"Penny has been drinking," they said.

"Clearly."

"Though she is on the larger side—college years and subsequent working years of too much stress eating will do that to a person," Lilith said, "she still doesn't hold her liquor all that well."

"I'm not that heavy!" Penny shouted, holding a Halloween cupcake in her hand.

Right. She was not over the comments I'd made in the car.

"I'm sorry, Penny," I said. "What I said in the car was true."

She raised her hand as if she was going to throw the cupcake.

"Don't throw the cupcake, Penny," Morticia said mildly. "I'll go find a butcher knife."

I tried not to gulp. "I didn't finish the thought, however. What I wanted to say was that clearly I am an unimaginative person, because I couldn't dream up anyone as wonderful as you."

Penny was immediately in my arms. She kissed me, tasting like buttercream frosting.

"Please don't get that cupcake in my hair," I murmured against her mouth.

"You are a little unimaginative, but you're so sweet," she said, pulling me inside. "Let's find you something to wear."

"Please, no more tight pants."

"I think Mimi had a bondage outfit," Morticia said. She and Lilith were dressed like Wednesday Addams in short black dresses, their dark hair in two plaits.

"I'm wearing a suit," I said. "I could be a vampire."

Penny looked me up and down. "Nope. I thought you needed to win that contract. You have to at least act as if you like Halloween," she said.

"So you're going to help me, and I'm forgiven?" I asked, resting my hands on her hips.

"Of course! Besides," she purred in my ear, "I haven't gotten the full Garrett Svensson treatment yet. I'm not going to throw that away over a dumb comment."

"She has remarkably low standards," Lilith said, tacking more fake spiderwebs over what looked like the very real ones on the grandfather clock.

"I want to drag you upstairs, but I think guests are arriving," Penny said, running her hands down my chest to my crotch.

"Put him in a costume," Morticia said. "Don't compromise your Halloween ideals for this joker."

"Besides, you owe her," Lilith said imperiously.

I followed Penny upstairs to a bedroom. It was stuffed with dolls. All the walls were covered with shelves, and they held doll after doll after china-faced doll. The lifeless eyes bored into my soul. The whole room smelled like lace.

"I was going to suggest we pregame in here. But..." she motioned around.

"It is creepy."

"Mimi has another room filled with ventriloquist dummies."

"Why?"

"Who knows?" Penny rummaged in a closet and pulled out a hanging bag.

"Is this where you found the Mr. Darcy costume?" I asked.

"Yep. There is a Mast the Meerkat costume, too, but I figured you wouldn't be happy about that." She unzipped the bag. "Ta-da! A Roman gladiator's costume. I think Mimi had it from a community theater production of *Julius Caesar*."

I stripped down.

Penny gasped. "Don't you want some privacy?"

"From you?"

"From them." She pointed to the hundreds of dolls.

"Actually, I think I might be able to mentally block them out if you want to give the costume a test run. Mind like a steel trap, you know." I tapped the side of my head.

"I don't think I can block the lifeless glass eyes out," she said. Her hand was clamped over her own eyes. But I noticed her peeking out between her fingers.

I pulled on the leather kilt, then I tried to put on the breastplate. "Are you sure this is going to fit?"

Penny came over. "Maybe we need to grease you up!" She giggled and tried to fasten the ornate burnished bronze breastplate on my torso.

"Your chest is too wide," she said finally. "I can't even fit it on you."

"What am I going to wear?"

"I guess you're just going to have to go shirtless. Tooo bad!" she sang out.

CHAPTER 47

Penny

All thoughts of "woe is me" were out the window with Garrett coming up to the third-floor ballroom to the party, shirtless and looking like something out of the *Gladiator* movie. I had managed to secure the short cape around his shoulders. His massive frame filled the room, and there was a definite ripple of attention as he passed. With his military-short hair, he definitely looked the part.

I squeezed his biceps. Part of me still sort of wished we'd braved the dolls. But then, this was a work party technically. I needed to schmooze with the guests—I shouldn't be sleeping with Garrett and leaving only the twins as hostesses.

Garrett went over to talk to Sebastian, who was standing with several of Garrett's brothers. A good portion of the PharmaTech employees was at the party. Apparently none of them had seen Garrett in all his glory before. One girl was pouring punch and completely missed the glass, splashing it all over her friend's shoe.

"Do you think this is sexual harassment?" Morticia asked, appearing next to me.

"What? Me?"

"No, *him* walking around shirtless," Morticia said.

"I mean, the women don't seem to mind."

"And some of the men seem pretty happy, too," Lilith added.

Bronwyn could not keep her eyes off him. I waved at her, and she glowered at me.

"How quaint. She's dressed as Edgar Allen Ho," Morticia said with a smirk.

"Is she still after Garrett?" Lilith asked.

"Of course."

"Poor girl is delusional."

Unlike the Halloween party at the Svenssons' house, this party was adults only. It was also borderline out of control. We were hosting it in the ballroom on the third floor of the Victorian house. Traditionally, the new middle class in the Victorian era had built grand houses with a ballroom on the third floor. It was seen as a status symbol. Though the house was big, it wasn't that big. The ballroom was modest, and we were packed in, with overflow spilling onto the stairs and down into the library and sitting rooms on the first floor.

People were pressed together very closely. I took full advantage of the situation to plaster myself against Garrett's bare chest. I stuck my tongue out and licked a stripe down one of his pecs. He grabbed my chin, tilting it up to kiss me.

"You keep licking me," he growled, "and I'm dragging you downstairs, dolls or no dolls."

Someone coughed behind me. Morticia and Lilith were there with trays of orange and black Jell-O shots.

Garrett's brothers Weston and Archer downed three each in succession then proceeded to jump onto a table and start dancing.

"Aren't you going to do something about this?" Greg yelled at Hunter over the music. Hunter pretended he couldn't hear his brother.

"Thanks for coming," I said to Sebastian, peeling myself off Garrett. I handed Sebastian a shot. He was dressed as the demon Crowley from *Good Omens*. He was wearing all black and had yellow snake-eye contacts.

"I hope we didn't ruin your wholesome image of Harrogate too much," I said to Sebastian. "We do like to party.

"Nice costume," Morticia said, sneaking up beside him. He smiled down drunkenly at her.

"Yes, very nice," Lilith said, coming up on the other side of him.

"Oh man, there are two of you? Or did you spike the Jell-O shots?"

Morticia and Lilith smiled feral smiles. "Don't worry," they said. "We bite."

"Stop scaring the guests," I admonished them.

"I really like your witch's hat," Sebastian said to me. "Looks authentic."

"This old thing?"

Garrett's arm immediately went possessively around my waist.

"Ah," Sebastian said. "I see. I thought there was something going on! Penny, if you ever decide you want a billionaire who's less blond and more dark haired, hit me up."

Garrett growled.

"He's kidding!" I told him.

Sebastian laughed and toasted us with another round of Jell-O shots.

Lilith changed the record over to some of the emo music from when we were teenagers.

"What!" Sebastian yelled above the heavy guitar intro. "This is my childhood!"

"I know, right! Come on, Garrett, let's dance!" I said, dragging him into the crush of people.

"I'm not sure I'm that good."

"It's just emo music. You jump up and down and make out on the dance floor. Surely you can do that," I said.

I clung to Garrett's neck, giving him sloppy kisses as I sang along to the familiar My Chemical Romance lyrics. It was warm in the ballroom with all the people, and after several songs, there was as slight sheen of sweat on Garrett's torso. I dragged my tongue through it. He grabbed the back of my neck, kissing me hard.

"Aren't you worried people will see?" I asked breathlessly.

"No. They're so drunk they won't care," he said. "Besides, I told you what would happen if you licked me again." Then he dragged me out of the ballroom.

His hand was on my ass as he half carried me to the nearest bedroom. The creepy dolls were still there, but then Garrett was kissing me, reminding me how good it felt to have him touch me, and I completely forgot we had the audience of hundreds of lifeless eyes.

"As soon as I saw you in that costume," Garrett growled. "I wanted to bend you over and fuck you."

"Funny, because as soon as I saw you in that costume," I panted against his mouth, "I wanted to straddle you and ride that perfect cock."

"You haven't even seen it yet," he said, sliding his hand under my corset to tease the pebble-hard nipple.

"I've seen it in my dreams," I said, reaching a hand under the leather kilt to cup his hard cock through the black boxer briefs. "And I want it in me."

"You need to have some patience," he said, kissing my neck. His hand slid up my thigh under the super-short skirt. He unlaced my black top, letting my breasts spill out of the too-tight fabric.

"Perfect," he murmured.

"Fuck me," I gasped as he kissed down the swell of my breasts.

He pulled one out of the lacy push-up bra and sucked it, rolling the nipple in his mouth until it was hard. The sensation went straight to my pussy, making me aching and wet. Garrett's mouth went back up to mine and kissed me hard while he stroked me through the tights and my panties.

"I need you," I whimpered against his mouth. He picked me up, and I wrapped my legs around him, cupping his strong jaw as our tongues tangled together.

He set me on the bed. My skirt was hiked up, and my tits were out, rising and falling as I breathed hard, half reclining on the edge of the bed. Garrett bent over me to kiss and nip my tits. His hand was back between my legs. I was splayed out, ready for him.

"I hope you don't like these tights," he whispered, "because I'm going to rip them."

The thin hatch pattern of the fishnets stretched then gave way. His fingers pushed through, moving the thong panties to the side so he could stroke my pussy. His fingers dipped into my opening, and he crooked them, making me whimper.

He stroked me with his fingers, rubbing and teasing my clit. Then he knelt in front of me, his breath hot against my pussy. I clutched at his head as he licked and sucked my clit while his fingers played in my opening. I was glad the music was loud so no one could hear my moans as he licked me.

He sucked and teased my clit with his tongue. I bucked against him, and he reached up, pinching and teasing my nipple as he stroked me. I could feel I was close as he continued to stroke me. My head was tipped back on the bed, and I moaned and panted as he brought me over the edge.

I lay sprawled on the bed, panting. Garrett, shirtless above me, looked like a mythical god. I reached out to run a hand down his chest then undid the leather kilt, letting it fall to the floor. He hissed as I slipped a hand into his boxer briefs. He was hard when I pulled his cock out. Garrett ran the tip along my tits then pushed me back onto the bed. I bit my lip, stifling a moan as he teased my clit with his cock.

I was settling in for an otherworldly experience when we heard someone yell out during a pause in the music, "Garrett? Garrett? Has anyone seen him?"

CHAPTER 48

Garrett

"Sorry!" Adrian said. "Mace wanted to know where you went." I stood outside the door while Penny hastily rearranged her outfit.

"Why does Mace even care?" I snapped. I swore I was going to lock my brothers in the bunker Remy had built.

"He said we're supposed to be entertaining Sebastian."

When Penny came out, she looked sexily disheveled.

"We should probably go back to the party," she said, cheeks flushed. "Or I can… you know… if that leather kilt is too tight."

"I'm perfectly capable of waiting," I said, guiding her back up to the ballroom. "I want to take my time."

"I'm glad we came back up," Penny said, elbowing me in the side. "Otherwise we would have missed *that*."

Hunter and Meg were *almost* dancing together. I rubbed my hands together. My plan was working.

Penny and I danced some more and made small talk with my employees. It was a little after one a.m. when people left. Penny shooed everyone who was left into the backyard where we sat around a firepit the twins had crafted.

At least Sebastian seemed pleased with the party. He was sprawled out on a wooden lounge chair.

"It's great how everyone just hangs out and seems to know each other," he was saying to Olivia and Hazel when Penny and I walked up. Penny had a fresh array of snacks and drinks to serve.

Sebastian's eyes narrowed slightly as I wordlessly offered him the tray of spiked apple cider. "Though, this town seems a little too perfect. You don't have some sort of annual deadly game of hide-and-seek or anything, do you?"

"Oh yeah," I deadpanned, "we totally just keep all the weirdos locked up while you're here."

"Honestly," Olivia said, "we sort of do. I've had to run interference to keep my grandmother from stalking you."

"Ida?"

"Yes."

"But you have to tell me about crazy stuff that happens here!" Sebastian said.

"You can't drive and use a cell phone," I muttered.

"Great plan!" Sebastian said. "It's safer that way. That's how my stepmother died."

We were all silent.

"Sorry to make it weird," he said. "She was a gold digger, but still. She was texting and driving. Fortunately, she didn't kill anyone."

"We have a straw ban, too," Penny added as she handed him a plate with cheese and crackers.

"I do not want to hear any more complaints about the straw ban, honestly," Meg huffed.

"Hunter thought you might like a drink," I said loudly to Meg. From across the firepit, Hunter narrowed his gaze.

"Stop trying to foist gifts on me that are allegedly from Hunter!" she snapped at me. "I can see by the confused and spaced-out look on his face that he has no idea what's going on."

So much for them dancing together. Maybe it was the alcohol.

"No," Weston insisted. "Hunter always looks like that."

"Yeah," Blade added.

"My new favorite Svensson brothers," Meg cooed at them.

"Bourbon hot chocolate? Spiked apple cider? Hungarian grog?" I said determinedly. I would not give up on my plan. Who knew what insane idea Meg would come up with next to punish Hunter and the rest of us Svenssons.

Meg took a cup of the grog.

Sebastian looked across the fire between Hunter and Meg. "Dang, are all the nice women here taken?"

"I'm not," Meg said.

Hunter looked murderous.

"You don't want Meg," I told Sebastian. Meg and Sebastian were not the plan. "She'll make you drink out of a metal straw."

"Maybe we could make biodegradable straws?" Penny said.

"I could make some out of bone fragments," Lilith suggested.

"As much as I want to discuss the chemical properties of a plastic replacement," Sebastian said, standing up, "I'm out. I have to fly to Germany tomorrow."

I stayed late to help Penny clean up, but really I was hoping to finish what I'd started in the bedroom.

"I don't know why we're bothering," Penny said as she slowly pushed a broom back and forth. "This house was already a disaster before the party."

"We can't have it too dirty," Morticia said. "We have a real estate agent coming by to look at it."

"You're selling it?" I asked.

"It's a lot of house," Lilith said.

Penny seemed a little sad. "I think I'm tired. Let's finish this up tomorrow."

"I'm assuming he's staying," Morticia said, pointing a sharp finger at me.

"I don't have a license," I said. "I can't drive home."

"Uh-huh."

Penny poured more hot chocolate into a mug and added a good pour of bourbon. "Carry me!" she said.

"I hope you're not going to be too drunk for what I have planned for you," I said, kissing her forehead.

"I can't let this bourbon hot chocolate go to waste," she said, sipping from the mug as I carried her upstairs. "I should have dressed up as Cleopatra!" She giggled.

"I don't care what you're dressed in," I said when I set her down on her bed in the round tower room. "Anything you have on I'm taking off."

She giggled some more. "Maybe we should go down to do it in front of all the dolls!"

"I don't care where," I said, pushing her back on to the bed. "I would even fuck you in the back of that hearse."

CHAPTER 49

Penny

The Romani queen just made things way more complicated. But one thing was simple. Garrett was perfect in the low lamplight. I studied him as I sprawled on the bed and sipped my bourbon.

"You know," I purred up at him, "I think this witch wants to ride your broomstick. I bet it's nice and stiff."

I straightened up on my knees and reached to undo the leather kilt for the second time that night. This time, I was totally getting my share of the Halloween treats.

Garrett pulled his boxer briefs down and reached up to take off the cape. Then he started to unfasten the leather bracers on his arms and the wide leather belt.

"Leave that. It makes you sexier."

"Only if you leave the witch's hat on," he replied, gray eyes heavy lidded.

"Done and done," I said, standing up and slowly unlacing the low-cut shirt. Garrett watched me like a predator as I slowly undid it and let it fall to the floor. Then I unzipped the short little skirt and shimmied it down. I slipped a hand into the waistband of the fishnet tights.

"Leave it," he said. He grasped my hips. "I want to fuck you with those on."

He tipped my head back, kissing me hard. He kissed down to the lacy bra, pulling my tits out and rubbing and kissing them. He undid the bra, letting it fall to the floor. Then he kissed down farther.

"Uh-uh," I said, placing a palm on his pec and pushing him back on the bed. "This witch is riding her broomstick."

Garrett sat back on the bed, watching me hungrily as I straddled him. His cock was hard and erect. I slipped my hand around it, stroking it.

"Nice and firm. Should be a smooth ride."

Garrett slipped on a condom as I positioned myself. His fingers were hard when he gripped my hips, steadying me as I rose up. I balanced on his shoulders. He used one hand to push the ripped fishnets and lacy panties to the side, then he was in me.

"Your cock is so big," I whispered against his mouth.

He tangled his hand in my hair as he kissed me hard. One hand cupped my ass, guiding me as I rode his thick cock. Every time I would slide down, his cock would stroke against my clit, making me cry out. I tipped my head back, and Garrett pressed his face against my tits, sucking and nipping the nipples as I moved up and down on top of him.

"Fuck. I want you to make me come," I said against his mouth as he kissed me.

One hand pushed under my panties to stroke my clit as he fucked me, his hips rising up slightly to meet me.

"I thought you wanted to ride the broomstick," he teased as he used two fingers to play with my clit.

"It's been a good ride, but I need the grand finale."

In one smooth motion, he tipped us over onto the bed. I was on my back, Garrett over me. His cock pulled out of me as he kissed his way down. He pulled my tights off as he licked me through the panties.

"Not like that," I whimpered, barely coherent as he teased me, the lacy panties pushed to the side and his tongue licking my clit.

I cursed as I came. Breathing hard, I half sat up, reaching for him. He was still hard, his cock glistening. I grabbed the belt and held him steady while I licked a strip up his cock, satisfied when he shivered.

"I wanted you to fuck me," I said, taking the tip in my mouth.

Garrett pulled me off.

"I would, except you've been a bad little witch."

"Oh yeah? Gonna give me my punishment now?" I purred. "Gonna spank me with that belt?"

He looked at me oddly. I pulled the witch's hat back on my head then turned around on the bed so I was on my hands and knees, my ass in the air for him.

"Take that belt off and show me how bad of a witch I am," I told him in my best sultry voice. The black lacy thong panties were soaking wet, and every motion made them rub against sensitive flesh.

Garrett looked as if he barely had control over himself.

"Don't you want to fuck my hot, tight pussy?" I coaxed over my shoulder.

I felt satisfied as I heard him unbuckle the belt. I wasn't some sort of BDSM type, but when else is a girl gonna let loose if not during Halloween?

Garrett caressed my ass, fingers pulling aside the lace panties slightly to tease me.

"You like it dirty?" he asked in that deep voice.

"Only when I'm drunk," I said, hissing as he hit me lightly with the belt. His hand cupped my ass then slid up my back to tangle in my hair. He moved closer to me, his cock brushing against my ass.

"Hit me again," I said, swearing when the belt made contact. Then his mouth was there, kissing the slight sting on my ass. He slid my panties down, planting little kisses along the slightly red skin.

I rested down on my forearms, the witch's hat tipping over one eye. I moaned loudly as Garrett pressed his face between my legs, tongue stroking me, mouth sucking my clit. His tongue traced up to dip into my opening then back down.

"You have to say 'trick or treat' before you get any candy," I said, turning my head to look at him and wink.

"Trick?" he said, stroking my clit and making me gasp. "Or treat?" he asked, ramming his cock into me.

I cried out, arching my back as he pulled out and thrust into me again.

"Crap, that feels good," I stuttered. He grasped my hips, fucking me hard. I made high-pitched little whimpers every time he thrust into me. His cock felt so good sliding in and out of my pussy. I was already so sensitive down there that I was getting close to the edge just from Garrett's cock.

I arched back against him every time he thrust into me. My hard nipples brushed against the bedsheets every time he fucked me. I knew he was close as the rhythm got faster, the thrusts harder. Knowing I was making him come undone was intoxicating. His hand reached around to tease my clit. I jerked against his hand then rolled my hips back against his cock. Gasping and panting, I could only moan as he fucked me and stroked me.

I could almost see the self-satisfied expression on his face when I came in a sweaty, moaning mess. Garrett gripped my hips, giving several powerful thrusts, then he came in me. He pressed sloppy kisses along my back and nuzzled my neck, whispering in my ear.

"Trick or treat. Thanks for giving me something good to eat."

CHAPTER 50

Garrett

One minute I was wrapped around Penny, the next she had half pushed me out of the bed, thrown my costume at me, and dragged me out the front door. The sun was just starting to rise, the sky a deep indigo.

She looked like a wreck. Was she sleepwalking?

"Penny, what's wrong?" I said as she tugged me to the car.

"There is something I forgot to do," she said.

"Can I help you?" I asked, smoothing out her hair.

"No! No, just you need to leave," she said, wrenching open the car door.

I studied Penny while she drove. She had a death grip on the steering wheel.

"Fuck my life," she muttered. She was stiff as she drove me back to the estate, speeding around curves.

"Penny," I said when she pulled up in front of the estate house. "Can you please talk to me? Is it something I did? Was it last night? Is it about what I said? You're absolutely the only girl for me." None of it seemed to register. She threw open the door, jogged around the car, and physically pulled me out.

"Thanks for the party! Had a great time. See you at work on Monday!"

I watched, stunned, as she drove away. I was still standing outside what felt like hours later but probably was only a few minutes when the front door opened and Hunter peered out. I blinked at him in the morning light.

"Where are your clothes? Why are you standing outside half naked?"

"I don't have my keys," I said, "or my wallet or my phone."

"What did you do?" Weston asked later when I had showered and dressed and was sitting at the dining room table. Even Archer was up. Apparently my relationship drama was enough to entice him out of bed before noon.

I opened my mouth then closed it. "It could be several things."

"Several?" Blade asked. "Do I need to make a spreadsheet?"

"No," Weston scoffed. "Spreadsheets aren't the answer for everything."

"Why don't you talk about it, baby brother?" Archer said after taking a big bite of a croissant.

"Leave me alone. I don't have to explain myself to any of you," I spat, suddenly feeling crowded.

I went out onto the terrace with my Bulletproof coffee. It felt like fall—not Penny's fun fall but the fall of my childhood, all dampness and desperation.

I sipped my coffee and watched the fog roll out of the woods on the grounds. Weston and Blade came outside.

"Hazel made eggs Benedict," Blade said, shoving a plate at me. Weston and Blade were younger than me by a couple of years. When we'd moved to Harrogate and my older brothers were looking for work, I had looked after them as best I could. I still tried to look out for them.

"You know, women, sometimes they get weird," Blade said, kicking some dead leaves that had blown on the terrace.

"Were you in love with her?" Weston asked bluntly.

Was I?

"I could have been," I said.

"You don't know if it's over," Weston said. "Maybe she ate something bad and needed you out or had her parents coming over and she forgot. It could be any number of things."

"It's her life," I said brusquely. "She can have me in it or not. I have bigger things to worry about." It sounded like overcompensation, even to me. I took the plate and carried it back inside.

Along with more eggs Benedict, there were bagels accompanied by an array of various dips and spreads laid out in nicely carved wooden bowls.

"Ernest dropped those by as thanks for buying all the pumpkins," Hazel chirped. Even with the late night, she still looked fresh. "He even carved them with little Halloween scenes. I'm going to take some pictures and put them up on

Instagram. He made them out of bamboo. Aren't they cute? Maybe you could take one to Penny as an apology present."

"I'm not even sure what to apologize for," I admitted.

CHAPTER 51

Penny

The only thing keeping me from sobbing as I drove back home was the fact that I needed to sound calm and professional when I called my mother. My hands were shaking as I scrolled to her contact in my phone.

"Good morning," she said.

"Did I bother you?" *Don't sound so meek,* I scolded myself. Whenever I talked to Trisha, I always turned into the little girl eager to make her mommy love her.

"Hardly," she said. "I'm running this magazine. I never sleep. Have any more juicy tidbits for me? The advertisers *loved* the sample, by the way. Nicely done! I always knew you were my daughter. We already had several firms order million-dollar spreads in the magazine, which is good, because now I don't have to lay people off."

Crap. I was such a terrible person.

"Actually," I said, leaning against my desk, my stomach flip-flopping, "I don't think I can do the article. I'll send you the money back."

"*Excuse me*?" The rage bubbled in my mother's voice.

I just wanted to shrivel up and pull the covers over my head. "I am so sorry, Mom," I whispered.

"Don't you *dare*. No daughter of mine would renege on her promise. Are the Svenssons putting pressure on you? I thought you were better than that, but I guess you're just a weak little girl."

I looked over at the bed, still rumpled. I half imagined I could make out Garrett's form. "Something like that."

"They found out? You stupid girl! They better not have found out. I need to call the lawyers. Harrington isn't going to like this."

"No, they don't know, but I think they'll find out. I just can't do it," I said, fighting back tears.

My mother sighed. I felt terrible. I wanted to take back everything and tell her of course I'd write the article. But I would feel even worse if I hurt Garrett. I never should have sent the tidbit. I had just thought at the time that he didn't want me. But after last night, it was clear that he did.

"Fine," she said disgustedly. "I'll work something out, *I suppose*, since I have to do everything. Just keep the money. I bet you already spent it, stupid girl."

"Are you sure?" I said, tears leaking down my face.

"Yes. I mean at this point, what does it matter?" she snapped.

"Let me know if I can write anything else instead," I said meekly.

"That won't happen."

After a cathartic crying session, I felt as free as a witch flying on a broom. Even though I didn't want to disappoint my mother or cost all those workers their jobs, I could not hurt Garrett or his family.

I took a hot shower and thought back to how crazy I must have seemed to Garrett, throwing him out like that. Oh my god! What if he thought I was disappointed? I tried calling him, but there was no answer.

I'll go over there later, I decided. *He might be asleep.*

I didn't want to be like Bronwyn, just showing up at odd hours. Besides, it was still early for a Sunday, and they had small children there. I didn't want to disrupt the routine.

Instead, I baked. I decided to make an apple cider mousse cake. We had a lot of apples left over from the fall party at the Svenssons' and apple cider from the Halloween party last night.

Salem meowed while I prepped the cooking area for filming. It was overcast outside, and not much light came into the kitchen. I had to set up several light stands. I felt momentarily ill when I thought about how much I had spent on these lights.

Think about nice things, I scolded myself, *like Garrett and this cake.*

I was making an intricate layer cake. The base layer was a lightly sweet, lightly spiced sponge cake. I put it in the oven while I cooked the apple cider over the stove and mixed it with gelatin to make a translucent layer. I took the sponge cake out of the oven and let it cool while I made a vanilla custard. I carefully scooped the seeds out of a vanilla bean and saved it for later—to flavor sugar, for example. The sponge cake was cool enough, so I cut it to fit the springform pan.

Once it was in place, I scooped in the custard, smoothed it, and placed it in the fridge. While it set, I cut up the apples and made a compote. After about ten minutes of stirring, I tasted it. It was a little tangy and sweet.

I checked my phone. No response from Garrett. Maybe I would take the cake over to the Svenssons. That was a normal, nonstalker thing to do, right?

I checked the cake. The custard seemed set, so I made sure it was in focus in the picture. I carefully placed a second layer of sponge cake for the middle layer. Then I spooned on the compote and set another layer of sponge circle on top. I let it sit in the fridge for thirty minutes while I wiped off the counter and sliced bright-red apple peel for a garnish and made the buttercream frosting.

I texted Garrett again.

Penny: *Making you a very elaborate apology cake! Because cake! And because I'm sorry and I really like you!*

I carefully removed the springform pan. I needed to concentrate. But I looked down at my phone. Why hadn't Garrett called me back? Was he angry?

I carefully spun the cake on the cake stand as I frosted it. When it was smooth, I placed the curls of apple peel so people knew what kind of cake it was.

I texted Garrett yet again.

Penny: *I'm coming over. Hope you aren't mad!*

No response.

Double crap! Why was he ignoring me? Was he angry? I spun around nightmare scenarios in my head of Garrett never speaking to me—or worse, telling me he hated me.

"Going to a Sunday-morning booty call?" Lilith asked as I placed the cake in the cake carrier.

"No, a cake call. Well, cake surprise call."

Morticia handed me a bag.

"What's this?"

"His things. Wallet, phone, keys."

Crap! No wonder he wasn't texting me back. At least now I had an excuse to go over to his house.

I cursed all my terrible decisions as I drove over to the estate. Was this it? It had just started to get good. I didn't want to lose him.

After I parked the car, I picked up the cake and looked down. I was still wearing my flour-covered apron. I was debating whether I should put the cake and bag down and escape back home before they noticed I was outside. But I didn't have time to flee. There was yelling, and the front door opened. Several small faces peered out at me.

"Cake! Cake! Cake!"

"Penny's here, and she brought cake!"

"Garrett, your girlfriend is here!"

"Did you just leave her standing there?" Garrett said, his deep voice cutting through his brothers' chattering ones.

"Hi!" I said breathlessly when he appeared at the door. He had a cup of coffee in hand and was wearing gray sweatpants, not the baggy kind, the kind where you get the outline of the good stuff.

He silently regarded me.

"I'm sorry about earlier," I said.

"It's fine." He shrugged. "It was just something fun. No need to be so serious about it."

"Oh, right," I said, my stomach dropping. "That makes sense—just some Halloween fun. I made a fall cake. Maybe your brothers want some?"

"Come in."

I stepped into the foyer awkwardly. Garrett leaned in and kissed me.

"Did you happen to bring my wallet?" he asked.

I held up the bag. He took it from me and kissed me again. "Thanks."

He took out his phone. I wrinkled my nose. He was going to see all my missed calls and texts of desperation.

I blew the tendrils of hair out of my face. "I'll just go take this to the kitchen," I said, holding up the cake.

It looked like there was a mass homework session going on the dining room. The youngest Svenssons were completing worksheets, while the high schoolers were doing complicated math problems. Weston, Parker, Blade, and Hunter were answering questions and giving tips.

"You guys want to take a study break?" I announced. "I have cake. I want to see how it tastes."

"Don't crowd her!" Hunter bellowed as Garrett came into the dining room.

His expression was neutral. What did he think of all my texts?

CHAPTER 52

Garrett

Any concern I had that Penny didn't really care about me dissipated when I saw the twenty texts and ten missed calls from this morning. I scrolled through the messages while she greeted my little brothers.

"I'll go in the kitchen and cut this," she said, my little brothers crowding around her.

I went around to the other kitchen entrance so it didn't look like I was following her. Penny opened the plastic carrier then carefully sliced into the fancifully decorated cake. Though my little brothers weren't making it easy.

"You're going to have some in a few minutes," I promised the boys, "but no one wants to eat anything you've all been breathing on. Here, take these dessert plates into the dining room. The last thing Penny wants is an audience while she tries to cut the cake."

"I somehow forget how many there are of you! It's like I can't count past ten!" Penny giggled. "I'm more worried I won't be able to split it."

"They don't need a whole tiered wedding cake worth of desserts," I said.

After handing out stacks of utensils and plates, I shooed the kids out of the kitchen. As soon as they were gone, I wrapped Penny in my arms, kissing her, reminding her of last night.

"You could just let them starve. We can go upstairs," I murmured against her mouth.

"You're not mad I kicked you out without your wallet?" Penny asked.

"No," I said, "but you can make it up to me anyway."

"You just look so comfy and soft and touchable. I just want to squeeze you," she said, slipping her hands under the waistband of my sweatpants.

"Cake!" Arlo and Otis said from the doorway, jumping up and down. I picked up the cake platter.

"You all need to stop acting like animals," I said as Penny followed me into the dining room.

The dining room was packed. Word had gone around that there was food.

"Wow!" Hazel marveled as she helped pass out the perfectly layered pieces of cake. "This is a beautiful cake. How did you create the layers so even? It's almost too pretty to eat."

"Patience is key, and putting it together really slowly," Penny said with a laugh.

"I'm glad you're back in Penny's good graces, Garrett," Archer said after scarfing down his cake.

"Archer," Hazel said "Did you tell Garrett and Penny about the surprise?" They exchanged a look.

"I'm slightly worried," Penny said.

"We entered you in the Halloween costume contest," Archer stated. "Hazel and I are of course the team to beat, but you know, good luck anyway!"

"I won the contest my senior year in high school," Penny said. "I am very competitive. You're going down, Archer!"

"Please," Archer snorted. "I have a foolproof Halloween costume idea. And an artist!"

"I'm not sure a contest is a good idea," I remarked. "I don't know if I can take any more tight pants or shirtless outfits."

"You finally found a normal woman who puts up with you. You have to meet her where she is, and if it's in a seasonal Halloween shop, then so be it," Archer said as he snagged a bite of cake off Davy's plate. Davy tried to stab him with the fork.

"Literally stealing food from children, Archer? For shame," Mace said.

"He doesn't need all that cake. I'm taking one for the team."

"Do you guys have any old costumes from when the Harrogates owned this estate?" Penny asked me after the plates were all cleared away. "Maybe you could find something you like better than the gladiator outfit."

"I'm sure we could go look for some," I told her, taking her hand and leading her to one of the back staircases. "Was that a little more subtle?" I asked, kissing her in the stairwell.

"Mm-hmm, nope!" she said with a giggle that turned into a shriek that I stifled with my mouth as I picked her up to carry her to my bedroom.

I usually hated having people in my space. Penny was different. It felt like she belonged there. And I wanted her.

"My brothers have a bad habit of interrupting, so this needs to be quick and dirty," I growled. I picked her up, bracing her on top of the dresser. I pushed her skirt up and pulled her panties down. They were the same ones from last night, the lacy black thongs. I threw them to the floor. I kissed her, crushing our mouths together as I pulled off my pants. I stroked her wet pussy as I put on a condom.

The dresser put her at the perfect height to fuck her. Her pussy was hot and tight when I thrust into her. She made little whimpering noises that drove me crazy. I kissed her hard, making sure to stroke her clit as I fucked her, bringing us over the edge at the same time.

"Better than a dirty martini," she said against my mouth as she kissed me softly.

CHAPTER 53

Penny

"Probably inappropriate to do that with your brothers in the house," I said against Garrett's chest. "Also I'm covered in frosting and smell like sex."

"Sex cake," he said absently.

"Would you eat that?" I wrinkled my nose.

"Your sex cake? Definitely."

I kissed him again then went into the bathroom to freshen up. Garrett watched me as I put my hair up into a messy bun. He slowly approached until he was behind me, unbuttoning my skirt and pulling it down. He pulled off my shirt and unhooked my bra.

"What happened to quick and dirty?" I murmured as he fluttered kisses down my back to the curve of my ass.

"I decided I'd rather take my time," he replied then pressed his face between my legs. I moaned, bracing myself on the counter. Garrett licked me slowly with his tongue, dipping into my opening, swirling around my clit.

"Don't take too long," I whispered. "I need you." I heard a condom package open.

Garrett stroked me, then he rocked into me, sliding out slowly, his fingers stroking my clit. The other hand cupped my breast, pinching the nipple as he fucked me slowly and deliberately.

I arched back into him, needing him to go faster. A low moan escaped from my throat, and Garrett tipped my head back to kiss me. I rocked forward, needing his fingers on my clit.

"Harder!" I begged.

He kept up that same excruciatingly slow rhythm. One hand fondled my tits then moved up to my neck to arch me back against him. My head tipped back, and he kissed me as he fucked me, his cock sliding in and out of me as he teased my clit.

I came like that in his arms, Garrett coming a few thrusts later.

"Much better," he said, nuzzling my neck.

I wrapped my arms around his torso, loving the way his washboard abs felt against my skin.

"I much prefer having you here," he said, kissing me softly.

"You know," he said after we had dressed and were heading downstairs. "There are still a few cottages left in the back acreage if the twins sell the haunted house."

"You want me to move into your compound?" I teased, turning to look up at him from the stairs. Garrett jerked back for a second. "Kidding!" I told him. "Besides, this is hardly a compound. It's like an all-inclusive, super fancy resort."

"I don't know about all-inclusive resort," he said, frowning, holding the door for me. Three of his brothers ran past us, screaming.

"Outside!" Garrett yelled.

"I haven't even seen all the trails and gardens you have back there. It must be nice," I said, squeezing his hand then helping him shoo his brothers outside.

"We just had the bridle paths redone," he said.

"Ooh, do you have horses?" I exclaimed. "I love horses!"

"No horses."

"You should get some horses," I told him. "Especially if you just had the bridle paths redone. Those are pricy—you can't just let them go to waste."

"We still have a stable," Garrett said thoughtfully. "Though I don't know if we want to turn this place into a barn."

He led me across the backyard and around a path to one of the outbuildings.

"You're not taking me somewhere to have your way with me, are you?"

"If I wanted to do that, I'd have stayed upstairs," he said, kissing me. He pulled back when we heard voices. Garrett led me into a large barn, where Remy, Mace, and several of his other brothers were looking at a green school bus.

"Why do you have a bus in your stable?"

"This isn't the stable," Garrett said, frowning as he studied the bus. There were cardboard fins duct-taped to it.

"That's the other building with the iron accents. This is the barn that Remy is using as a garage."

"The Holbrooks have horses," Remy said. "And goats. I could clear out some space for them."

"There are already too many people here," Garrett said. "We don't need an ark's worth of animals."

"Hey, you're welcome to use my hotel," Archer said from his spot on a lounge chair he had dragged into the barn. "Instead of sneaking around in sin. You're setting a terrible example."

Garrett sighed. "Why are you even out here?"

"We're trying to decide how to paint the bus," Hazel said.

"Does Hunter know about this?" Garrett asked with a smirk.

"You need to paint it with unicorns and glitter," Josie suggested.

"Or you could do glow-in-the-dark paint!" I said.

"Yes!" We high-fived.

"We could do chalkboard paint," Hazel said. "Then every day could be a new art day!"

"Is this a permanent thing?" Garrett asked.

"Honestly, the older you get, the more like Hunter you look," Archer said.

"Shut up."

"It's part of our costume," Adrian said, patting the bus while Remy beamed.

"You entered the contest?" I asked.

"Josie and I did. She's Ms. Frizzle, and this is the Magic School Bus," Adrian said. "Or it will be as soon as we paint it something nice."

"What are you in that scenario?"

"The pet lizard," Adrian said proudly.

"I love it!" I exclaimed, jumping up and down. "Garrett, we need to think up really awesome costumes."

"The only thing is, the bus in the show was yellow, but it transformed, so we need to have it transform," Josie said. "I'm trying to rope Liam and Platinum Provisions into thinking up something cool for us."

"Mace isn't doing a couples costume?" I asked.

"Adrian got first dibs," Josie said with a snort. "Plus there are times when I find Mace's OCD endearing and times when I don't. Also, what's the point of joining with a large family if you can't take advantage of it? My costume isn't just going to be a couple; there will be a dozen of us! Also, I don't think Mace wanted to be a lizard."

"I'm going to have a cool outfit and everything!" Adrian said, beaming.

"We should try to convince Hunter and Meg to do something together," I said.

"Way ahead of you," Archer replied. "Weston filled me in on Garrett's plan. Already filled out forms for them."

"Good," I told him firmly. "We have to take drastic measures. I'm not spending the rest of my life drinking out of a metal straw."

Garrett's family members looked at me.

"Wow, Garrett, you really found the perfect girl for you," Archer said.

"I know," he replied smugly, leaning down to kiss me.

"I don't see what the big deal is," Archer said. "It's just straws. Stick them in the dishwasher. The metal ones are better than the paper ones."

"Metal is just... you can't even clean it!" I said irately. "And the ones they had at the shake shop were bent, so you can't even get a brush in to clean the bend!"

"I'm getting a little teary-eyed, you're so perfect," Garrett said, nuzzling my neck.

"We could use actual straws," Remy suggested, pulling a piece of hay out of one of the leftover bales stored in the barn.

"I do not want to drink out of a piece of dirty hay," Garrett said with a scowl.

CHAPTER 54

Garrett

Penny's presence had chased away the chill and damp of the fall, but as soon as she drove off, it crept back in. I went up to the large home office. Just because Sebastian had appreciated the Halloween parties didn't mean that he was going to be okay with us shoving him in a back corner and not having any space for his employees. I needed to solve that problem very soon.

However, I was having a difficult time concentrating on where the Thalian Biotech facility could go and what sort of jobs we would even offer for working-class people in the greater Harrogate area. All I could think about was Penny. We had clearly crossed a hurdle in our relationship and come out fine. I had no idea why my brothers seemed to have such a difficult time with women.

I should do something nice for her, I decided.

But what? Jewelry and flowers? That seemed too pedestrian. I was a billionaire. Though I spent all my time working or taking care of my younger brothers, I should still be able to come up with something better in the gift department than trinkets and chocolates. I needed something personal to show Penny that I knew her well and appreciated her unique qualities.

The door to the office burst open.

"Davy was looking for you," Remy said gruffly, setting my youngest brother down on the soft carpet.

"I'm working."

"No you aren't," Blade said as he and Weston followed Remy in. "I didn't hear you typing."

"Maybe I was reading a spreadsheet," I retorted.

"Lemme see!" Weston said, rushing to my desk. He and Blade were Irish twins, born nine months apart. Their relationship was similar to Archer and Mace's, meaning that individually they were morons, but put them together, and it was as if they forgot how to act like normal human beings.

"He's not!" he said before I closed the laptop. "He's shopping."

"What are you looking for?" Mace asked, walking into the office from the door on the opposite side, Hunter scowling behind him.

"I hope it's a gift for Penny," Archer said, coming in and flopping down in Hunter's chair.

"Get out of my chair," Hunter snarled. One glare and Archer jumped up into Mace's seat.

"Oh, don't even complain," Archer said to Mace. "You're not working,"

"I was about to!" his twin exclaimed, trying to shove Archer out of his seat.

"Why are all of you in here?" I said, rubbing my temple.

"You don't want me here?" Davy said, looking up at me with ridiculous puppy-dog eyes. His lower lip even trembled.

I sighed. "Fine." I picked him up, setting him on my lap.

"Did I do it right?" Davy said to Archer.

"You did!" Archer said, clapping his hands. Davy broke out into a bright smile. "You're so smart," Archer said. "Have a cookie."

Davy took what appeared to be a leftover Halloween party cookie. He ate it happily, sprinkling crumbs all over my clothes.

"I've been training him!" Archer said proudly.

"You are a terrible person," Hunter said, shaking his head.

"What are you buying Penny?" Weston asked.

"I bought Hazel a whole café," Archer said, spinning around in his chair, "so just throwing it down that that's the gift to beat."

Mace grabbed Archer, trying to shove him out of the chair. "You really need to cut back on the sweets. Hazel is making you fat."

"You take that back!" Archer shouted, jumping up. Mace shoved him aside and sat in his chair.

"Maybe you could buy her some nice baking supplies?" Blade suggested.

"No," Weston scoffed. "You can't do that."

"What do you even know about having a girlfriend?" Archer said, rolling his eyes.

I tapped my pen on the keyboard. "I don't need any of your help."

"You should get Penny some goats," Remy suggested.

"No," Hunter said, not looking up from his screen. "And you better not be in here to beg for farm animals.

One of those petting zoo chickens laid an egg in my boot. It's ruined."

"You're lucky I'm trying the carrot approach to make you get your life together," I said to him. "Or there would be a whole goat family in your room eating your sheets right now."

"You should buy her a pony," Blade said, holding out his phone, which displayed a picture of a large black horse.

"Ponies!" Davy said, grabbing my shirt and smearing orange frosting all over it.

"Penny does like horses," I mused.

"You can't buy her a horse," Hunter complained. "Did you not just hear what I just said about farm animals?"

"Watch me," I told him. "And consider this a warning about the goats."

CHAPTER 55

Penny

After the party and hanging out with Garrett's family, going to work that Monday was rough. Now that I didn't have the article hanging over my head, I felt a lot freer. I stayed up all night baking and making videos. I was yawning when I pulled up in front of Garrett's estate.

He kissed me, the kiss promising intense pleasure. His hand briefly pressed between my legs. When he pulled back, he had a slight smirk on his face.

"What?"

"Nothing. I have plans in motion."

Unfortunately, those plans didn't include more kissing when we arrived at the office. Garrett had meetings all day.

Bronwyn was waiting by his office when we walked up.

"You wanted to see me?" she asked him, resting her hand lightly on his arm. I wanted to slam a pumpkin over her head, like they did in the cartoons.

"You're good with graphics and promotion," Garrett said to me as he set his stuff down. "I saw your website and your Instagram page. Josie, who is a marketing genius, is very impressed with your work. Maybe you can work with Bronwyn on a pitch presentation to the city. We're going to need to present at the next town hall, assuming Sebastian agrees to sell to us."

"Of course I can do that," I said, trying to keep the annoyance off my face. The last thing I wanted to do was spend any more time with Bronwyn.

She kept her smile plastered on her face until Garrett left, then she turned to me with a scowl.

"I know you have some sort of scheme going," she hissed at me. "All through high school, you were that weird kid sitting in the back of the room, drawing your little sketches. I always knew you were up to something. Now you breeze in here, and in not even two weeks, you have Garrett wrapped around your little finger. I'm going to find out what kind of fraud you're pulling."

"You are delusional," I said, shaking my head. "You're mad because he chose me, not you. Do you really think Garrett is going to suddenly wake up one day and see that you are what he wants? Think again."

"I'm going to dig until I find out what's going on," Bronwyn said. "I will turn up every secret, every terrible thing you've ever done, and present it to him on a silver platter."

"Maybe you could work on your own life," I shot back.

"My life is great," she sniffed. "I have a good job and a nice condo."

"But no handsome billionaire boyfriend," I said cattily.

"Why don't you stay here and think about how to spend Garrett's money, and I'll do the presentation," she said, flipping her perfect curtain of hair over her shoulder.

"I'll do the presentation," I snapped. "And I don't appreciate your implying I'm some sort of gold digger. You're the one who thinks of Garrett as a meal ticket. You were always like that in high school, going after the guys from the more well-off families."

"I can't help that I'm ambitious," she said, examining her perfectly manicured nails.

"You're not ambitious, you're a snake."

The rest of the day was tense. I managed to put together the outline of a presentation. Garrett and his brothers had settled on the old belt factory. However, we had to sell the site location to the townspeople to convince the city to approve our plans.

"Jobs," I muttered. "We need jobs. I wish we could do a clinic."

"Too much liability," Bronwyn snapped.

I wonder if we could propose some sort of makerspace, where people can rent out space to make jam or small products and whatnot.

I would run it by Garrett. I didn't want Bronwyn to steal my ideas.

His last meeting of the day was with us to go over the presentation. When we walked into the conference room, he was there with his brothers. Weston and Blade were already present and arguing with Garrett.

"I just don't understand why you have to give him that piece of land," Blade complained. "We already said we are moving our company here. We have to put it somewhere."

"You don't have to put it right at that spot," Garrett retorted.

"Where else am I supposed to put a huge consulting firm?" Weston countered. "This is outrageous! I'm complaining to Greg."

"I will find somewhere for you to put it but not there," Garrett barked.

"Penny, can you please tell Garrett..."

"Penny isn't here to listen to you complain," Garrett cut in. "Penny, could you run through the presentation, please."

"For the presentation," I said, "I tried to make it as positive and pretty as possible. I grew up here, so I know what people respond to." I flicked through the slides. "We start off with a historical comparison, look how much positive change the Svenssons have already brought to Harrogate, from the rail park to the art trail to the new convention center going in that will bring in jobs—which is the big keyword. The Svenssons have been great partners to the city. Thalian Biotech will be as well."

Garrett and his brothers nodded along as I spoke.

"To really hit home the jobs angle, Meghan mentioned we should provide some type of working-class factory job. I was thinking we could have a makerspace, to train the budding entrepreneurs of tomorrow."

"No!" Weston shouted.

"I think it's a fine idea," Garrett said, scowling at his younger brother.

"I know," Weston said, leaning back in his chair. "That's why I want it as part of my company space. It fits better with a consulting firm anyway. Sebastian isn't going to want a bunch of random people coming in and out of his facility. They like to lock it down so that people can't steal their research."

"Our company designed their security protocol," Blade explained.

"Of course a makerspace is a terrible idea for Thalian Biotech," Bronwyn said. "Penny, you need to think these things through. A factory would be much better."

"Yes, especially since there's one point person who owns it and manages the hires," Blade said, typing on his computer.

"Thalian can't just put up a big wall," I said. "We need to have some community-conscious element."

"So we're back to square one on the jobs."

"The presentation looks nice though. It's sort of minimalist," Weston added. "I appreciate it. I like your sketches and diagrams too. It feels authentic."

"That's the big buzzword these days!"

CHAPTER 56

Garrett

"We need to leave," Penny said, throwing me my coat after the meeting.

"We do?"

"Rehearsal, Macbeth. You're the star of the play."

"I always thought Lady Macbeth was the strong arm behind all the decisions," I said.

"She certainly had Macbeth by the balls!" Penny said with a laugh as we headed down to the lobby.

"Not that I wouldn't be okay if you decided to do a little ball handling yourself," I said, sliding a hand down her back to cup her ass.

"Seeing you on stage *does* gets me a little horny!" she said, doing a little wiggle.

"There are the two lovebirds!" Ida said when we walked in from the dressing rooms. The play was in a week and a half, and we had started dress rehearsals. Penny was dressed in the flowing robes of an Elizabethan lady. Her red hair was in a braid down her back. The costume was belted around her waist. I'd never thought of Elizabethan dress as particularly sexy, but on Penny, it looked stunning.

"Coming off not one but two successful Halloween parties," Ida continued. "I heard the one over the weekend was a real rager. Can't believe you didn't invite me—I really know how to get down." She did a surprisingly good imitation of what I supposed was twerking.

Ernest was there along with Art, fixing up the set. He waved when he saw us.

"Looks great!" Penny said. Ernest beamed.

"Enough chitchatting. Places!" Edna called out through a megaphone.

Ida, Dottie, and Bettina were all in full costume. They made convincing witches.

"They look so spooky, don't they?" Penny said, squeezing my arm.

"Yep, like scary old hags," I joked.

"I heard that!" Ida shouted in the middle of her line.

"Don't break character," her sister Edna scolded. "If Garrett didn't have to play Macbeth, I'd have him jump in and do your part."

Finally, Penny and I were on stage together. People think of *Romeo and Juliet* as a romantic play. But *Macbeth* is romantic in its own way. The Macbeths are a long-time married couple who know each other intimately. Then of course they start seeing spirits and plotting a series of murderers, but hey, love in the time of Halloween.

Speaking of romance, something stirred in me when I held Penny and recited the line, "my dearest love."

I wanted what the Macbeths had—not the stabbing and murdering, but the easy and deep and knowing love the two Macbeths had for each other. I wanted Penny with me for this Halloween and every one after. Plus all the other holidays, though I didn't care for them particularly. Maybe they would be more fun with Penny around.

The rest of rehearsal went well. I had to admit, fighting with the swords was actually quite satisfying. Between the costumes and the set, by the time I died dramatically, I felt very much invested in the play.

Everyone applauded at the end after the man who was playing Macduff paraded around with a disturbingly realistic version of my severed head that the twins had made out of wax and clay.

"I hope the twins didn't use a real skull as the base for that prop," Penny said as I walked with her out to the car. "We don't want to turn you off community theater. You're so perfect as Macbeth."

"And you're just perfect," I said, pulling her against me, breathing in the pumpkin-spice scent of her hair.

"I want you," I breathed against her neck. I pressed against her ass so she could feel the hard length of my cock through my pants.

"I guess we can go back to my place," she said breathlessly.

"No. I need you now."

CHAPTER 57

Penny

"I thought you didn't prefer quick and dirty," I teased, though my pussy was aching and wet with just the thought of him—and the thought of getting caught, if I was honest.

"Maybe I just need more data points," Garrett replied, bending down to kiss me.

"If you wanted to fuck me in the car," I told him when he released me, "I should have brought the hearse."

"I'm not fucking you in the hearse," he growled, opening the back door.

"You are a very large man in more ways than one," I said, "and I'm not sure if we can both fit in the back seat."

"Quick and dirty," he replied. I looked up. Archer hadn't completed all the parking lot improvement, and I had parked the car just outside of the ring of light of the last functioning bulb. Garrett ground his cock against me. My mouth felt slightly dry, and I wanted him immediately, right then and there.

I crawled into the back of the car, one leg on the floor, the other on the seat. Garrett ducked in behind me. He pushed up my skirt and pulled down my tights and panties. I panted, already wet and aching for him. He stroked me as he put on a condom, then he was in me.

Something about the angle, or the fact that we were fucking in a half-open car in a parking lot, really got me off. I was panting and moaning, not even trying to be quiet. Garrett kissed my neck and tangled his hand in my hair as he pounded into me. I ground my hips back against him as he fucked me, my breath coming out in high-pitched pants and curses, fogging up the window in front of me as his cock thrust into me. Garrett reached around to tease and play with my clit as he fucked me, the sensation making me moan loudly.

"You feel so good in my pussy," I gasped as he thrust into me. His cock slid all the way in, filling me, then out again. I bit my lip as his thumb stroked just right over my clit. I choked down a curse. Then he did it again. I was so close. His hand sped up, and his rhythm got faster and more forceful as he jackhammered into me. I came with a cry, and Garrett came shortly after.

The windows were fogged up like that scene in *Titanic.*

"I might have to have you fuck me in a car again sometime!"

"Just not the hearse."

The next afternoon, I was working on the presentation when Garrett came in with that self-satisfied smile on his face.

"You done for the day?" he asked.

I looked at the clock. "It's only 3:30, so yeah. What's up?"

"I have a surprise for you," Garrett said. "It's a really nice surprise." He seemed very pleased with himself.

"What is it?"

"You'll never be able to guess," he said smugly

"Hmm," I said as I packed up my laptop.

This couldn't be a ruse because he found out about the article, could it? I thought in a panic then forced myself to calm down. That was dead and buried. All of Bronwyn's threats wouldn't bring it up.

"Is it another kid?"

"No," Garrett scoffed. "Besides, my little brothers are not a nice surprise."

"The kids are nice!" I protested as Garrett helped me with my coat.

"Yes," he said impatiently, "but I wouldn't just hand you a baby and say, 'Here, Penny, take care of this, it's not even yours.'"

As soon as he said the word "baby," I was like, *Yes please!* Which was weird, because I had never been one to be like, OMG baby! But Garrett's baby, especially if it looked like his brothers...

"You just zoned out there," he said, kissing my nose on the stairs.

"I was thinking," I said, heading down the open staircase. "Is it another load of pumpkins? A stack of cupcakes? A giant cast-off wedding cake that the wedding cake maker had on hand because the wedding got canceled on account of the bride sleeping with the best man and you helpfully rescued an abandoned wedding cake?"

"You want someone else's wedding cake?" Garrett asked in confusion.

"I love wedding cake!" I exclaimed, clapping my hands as we walked through the lobby. "People act like fondant is nasty, but a good cake maker makes it a very thin layer then has a half inch of icing underneath. Plus wedding cakes are pretty with all the tiers, and you can have different flavors. You don't have to give me a *wedding* wedding cake, but what if it was a wedding cake but with say, Halloween decorations or something? Then I could have my cake and eat it too!" I snorted a laugh at my own joke.

"It's not a wedding cake," Garrett said slowly.

"Tell me!" I said when we were in the car. I had been parking farther away, just in case the ghost decided to blow the car up, so there would be as little collateral damage as possible.

"You have to guess."

I straddled him, kissed him, and started loosening his tie.

"I bet I can make you give me a hint," I said, unbuttoning his shirt. Garrett gritted his teeth as I kissed the V of bare skin of his muscular chest. I rocked my hips against him, feeling him grow hard.

"I'm not even wearing any tights," I whispered against his mouth, "so this will be a quick and easy fuck and a win for me when you spill what my surprise is."

"I have a strong will," he said, nostrils flared.

"Do you?" I purred, slowly unbuttoning my shirt. He swallowed, Adam's apple jumping with the motion.

"I know you like my tits," I said.

His hands moved up and down my sides as I pulled one breast out of my lacy bra then the other. Garrett buried his face in them, kissing the swells of flesh then sucking and nipping a nipple, rolling it in his teeth.

I ground against him, and his hand slipped under my skirt to caress my ass then trace the edge of lace panties to slip inside between my legs and stroke me. I gasped, whimpering, as he teased me.

"Now who's losing control?" he whispered.

I whimpered as he unbuttoned his pants, ripping a condom packet. I balanced on his shoulder as he teased me with his cock then slipped inside.

I moaned loudly, my head tipping back as I slid down, fully encasing him.

"That's the only problem with fucking in a car," he said as he moved me up and down to ride his cock. "Once you start in a position, you have to finish that way."

I moaned again as he teased my clit as I slid slowly up and down.

"Unfortunately, we can't be here all day," he whispered against my mouth, my tits brushing his chest. He pushed the seat back, giving himself enough leverage to tip me forward so he could thrust up into me.

I splayed on top of him, panting as he gripped my hips, his cock jackhammering into me. With every thrust, his cock rubbed against my clit, bringing me closer and closer to the edge. I rolled my hips against his cock in time with his thrusts, needing him to take me.

His large hand gripped my ass under my skirt as he fucked me, my panties pushed to the side. The motions made them rub my aching pussy, adding another layer of pleasure. That pleasure was suddenly cresting over me, and I cried out as it overwhelmed me. Garrett was the only thing holding me up as I trembled while he milked the aftershocks, hissing my name as he came.

I lay on top of him, panting, hoping no one had seen us.

"I can't believe you didn't break," I said when I finally could remember what day it was.

"It was close there for a while," he admitted.

I was still a little horny as I drove back to the Svensson estate. "Is the surprise sex toys?" I asked as I drove through the gate.

"No, but I'll put them on the list."

I laughed. "If you're taking suggestions, I want a whole platter of Chick-fil-A chicken nuggets—the big extra-large platter—with all the sauces all to myself."

Out of the corner of my eye, I saw that Garrett looked taken aback. "I feel like there's a pattern here of all your ideal presents revolving around food."

"Or sex," I reminded him. "I'm a simple creature. Feed me, do that thing with your tongue," I shivered. "And hand me a fun holiday-themed cocktail, and I am good."

"Oh well," Garrett sighed, dramatically for him. "I suppose you don't want the present then."

"I just can't think of anything better than a wedding cake all to myself, " I said as I followed him through the house and out onto the terrace.

"Shall I send them back, then?" he asked.

It took me a second to register. "Horses! Oh my god, you rented horses! Did you get them from Ernest? What are their names? Hi!" I said as the horses ambled over to us, curious if we had any treats. "Are you nice? Look at that pretty black coat! Aren't you a handsome boy? I haven't been riding in forever!"

I turned to jump up on Garrett and kiss him. Then I went back to petting and cooing at the large black horses. "How long do we have them for?"

"What do you mean?"

"From the rental agency."

"I own them."

I gaped at him. "You just bought some horses?"

"Actually, there are people online giving horses away for free," he said as one of the horses pushed his nose into Garrett's coat pocket. "An old lady owned these two, Merlin and Midnight, but she took a bad fall and is moving into a retirement home. So now they live here. She says they're friendly and well trained."

"You rescued horses?" I swooned and wrapped my arms around him, kissing him. "You have a hard shell, Garrett, but you're so soft and squishy on the inside."

He wrinkled his nose. "Don't tell anyone."

One of the horses stuck his velvety nose between us and chuffed.

"They're rideable and everything?" I asked, petting the horse.

"Yes." He pointed. "I had Remy bring out saddles. Western or English?"

"English."

Garrett snickered. "I grew up in the American West, so I'll just be over here silently judging your English saddle."

I put my hands on my hips. "I'll have you know I am a fairly good rider."

"I thought you said you were an emo girl in high school," he said, lifting a gleaming leather saddle onto the horse.

"Like many a tweenaged girl, I was also obsessed with horses. There's some sort of psychological study about how it's linked to when a girl first start realizing men are awesome and sexy," I said as I saddled the second horse.

"Oh!" I said after a moment. "I don't have boots or an outfit."

Garrett handed me several Hermès shopping bags.

"You really do plan for everything, don't you?"

CHAPTER 58

Garrett

Penny looked smoking hot in the riding outfit. The white pants hugged her curves, the navy-blue jacket pushed up her tits, and the patent leather boots ended just above her knee. She cracked the riding crop against her thigh.

"Ow," she said, rubbing her leg and looking at the crop accusingly. "That hurt more than I thought it would."

"Weren't you the one just asking for sex toys?" I teased her.

"Yes, but fuzzy handcuffs and cat ears, not dangerous ones—though if I'm drunk I like a little bit of a belt!" She winked at me. Then she immediately tripped on the stool I had put out for her. The horses were rather tall.

"Shoot, I really ruined the sexy illusion, didn't I?" she said, kicking the stool aside and putting her foot in the stirrup.

"Not in the least," I said, admiring her ass as she effortlessly swung up into the saddle.

True to her word, Penny was good at riding.

"This horse is awesome. Midnight, you're such a good boy!" she gushed, patting the horse. Then she kicked her heels and immediately took off down the nearest bridle path.

"Next year," Penny said when I caught up to her, "I want to have a haunted walk back here, you know, have a ton of tiny houses with different haunted themes. We'll light the paths with jack-o'-lanterns. It will be amazing!"

At that point, I was willing to say yes to anything she wanted.

Penny chattered on about her grand Halloween plans as we rode. It was chilly in the woods, but the horses didn't seem to mind. We rode at a more leisurely pace out to the fake ruins that had been installed near the turn of the last century as a feature landscape piece on the estate grounds.

"*That's* not spooky," Penny said as we approached what looked like a half-destroyed tower.

"There was a whole ghost story that went along with the ruins," I told her as we dismounted and tied up the horses by a small spring. "The Harrogates hired a semifamous fiction writer to tell the tale of a young woman whose family didn't want her to marry a rival industrial baron's son. According to this story, the family told the son that she had run off with a day laborer, and he believed them and thought she didn't love him. But really they had just locked her in this tower," I said, spreading out a blanket in the clearing by the ruins.

"That's a gruesome story. It doesn't even have a happy ending," Penny said, lying down and stretching out in the last rays of afternoon sun.

"But wait, there's more," I said, taking a bottle of champagne and two glasses out of a case in my saddlebag. "He's so heartbroken that he becomes a mercenary and fights in a war in Europe. Several years later, he's in a bar and happens to meet a traveler from Harrogate. This man tells the patrons a ghost story about how they would hear wailing on foggy nights from this very property. The rival's son is smart, and he has a hunch about what had happened. He sneaks back to the town then steals onto the estate grounds and follows the wailing to this tower. He sees her hair, blowing in the wind from the open window. His love is in the tower waiting for him! He calls to her, scaling the tower. But when he climbs to the top, he realizes that she is already dead of a broken heart. He's distraught. He has all his war gear with him and dynamites the big manor house and this castle. The Harrogates built their new house on the same spot, but the tower remains as a testament to their love."

"That is a creepy and sad ghost story," Penny said, taking a long sip of her champagne.

"Yes, but they're together in death," I said.

"Still…"

"Well, it's just a story," I told her, pouring her more champagne. "In reality, this used to be an old-growth forest that was clear-cut for logging. Harrogate won it in a back-room poker deal and built the large house, all the cottages and outbuildings, and then this fake ruin as a conversation piece. Though," I added, "Archer does swear the manor house is haunted. He claims the paintings watch him as he walks down the hall. Hunter thinks it's just because he eats a lot before going to sleep and that it causes nightmares."

Penny laughed and snuggled against me, lacing our fingers together. She looked so sexy in that outfit, the white pants hugging her curves. The boots added a hint of eroticism, and the little jacket nipping her waist gave her a sexy hourglass figure.

"I want to fuck you," I said bluntly.

"Here?" she asked, making a face. "It's cold outside."

"You let me fuck you in the car," I countered.

"That was inside of a car," she retorted. "I'm not really an outdoor person. I like baths, nice hotels, Netflix, cups of tea, and warm cake."

"I bet I can convince you," I said as she poured another sip of champagne.

"Doubtful," she said, taking a swallow. She turned to look at me, her tits straining in that tight jacket. I wanted to rip it open and release them.

"Bend forward," I whispered. She took another swallow of the champagne, then I took the glass and set it aside.

"It's a little too cold for reverse cowgirl," she said, getting on her hands and knees, her ass round and perfect in those tight pants. I wanted nothing more than to fuck her like that. I pressed my hands between her legs and was rewarded with a slight moan. I unbuttoned the tight pants, allowing enough slack that I could slide my hand in. Penny shivered as I stroked the hot, wet heat of her pussy.

"Still not convinced?" I murmured as she bit her lip to stifle a whimper.

I eased the pants down along with the lacy white panties. The glistening pink flesh was revealed, and I pressed my face into it. Penny gasped, trying to spread her legs more for me, but she was hindered by the pants. She cursed and bucked as I slowly licked her, taking my time to draw out every trace of pleasure.

I sat back upright. "So?"

"So fuck me!" Penny begged.

I stroked her with one hand as I unfastened my pants and put on a condom. Then I eased inside of her. She was very tight; the angle made her pussy squeeze around my rock-hard cock.

She whimpered as I slowly drew out and entered her again.

"I want you to fuck my hot pussy, Garrett. Please fuck me hard," she begged.

I reached forward and tangled my hand in her hair as I thrust into her again. She cried out.

"Shhh," I said, thrusting into her again. She bit down the cry, her panting high-pitched as I fucked her. I increased the rhythm and felt her shudder, her pussy hot and tight around me.

"Your cock feels *so good*," she moaned as I gripped her, one hand in her hair and the other holding her hips steady so I could fuck her into a pleading, shuddering mess. I moved a hand to her clit, stroking her in time with my thrusts. I wanted to make her come. I loved the little pants she made, her chest heaving, her legs trembling as I made her come undone.

She rocked against my hand and back against my cock. I could tell she was close by the little noises she made. It was driving me to the edge. I felt her come around me, and in a few short thrusts, I was done.

"Like the outdoors now?" I murmured, kissing her neck.

"Maybe you should put a hot tub out here," she said, sticking her tongue out, her hair clinging around her face in slightly sweaty tendrils.

CHAPTER 59

Penny

"We still need to figure out our Halloween costumes," I said to Garrett after we rode back to the house.

"Maybe we could be Jack and Sally," he suggested. "From *The Nightmare Before Christmas*."

"Yes!"

"But do you think we'll win with those costumes?" Garrett asked with a frown as we dismounted and walked the horses to the stable.

"I thought you didn't care about Halloween," I teased.

"I'm competitive, and I want to beat my brothers," he admitted.

I looked over at the horses, the beginnings of an idea forming. Garrett unsaddled them, and I found brushes and hoof picks.

"They seem happy in their new home," I said as I brushed my horse.

"Come by and ride anytime," Garrett said seriously.

I grabbed his crotch. "Oh, I plan to ride quite often."

Before we could become too distracted, there was chattering and yelling outside.

"I want to see! I want to see!"

"Don't scare them," Garrett said to his little brothers as they ran into the stable. The horses snorted and stamped.

"Can we feed them?" Arlo asked.

"Maybe just some carrots."

I left the Svenssons after helping the kids feed the horses. The large animals seemed pleased to be the center of treats and attention.

"Where are you off to?" Garrett asked.

"I have to think about our winning Halloween costumes. Also, I have some videos to edit. I can't just hang around here all day."

"You could," Garrett said with a heavy kiss.

Breathless, I had to push him away before I changed my mind. I didn't want him to think I was a gold digger, just trying to ingratiate myself with his family. Bronwyn's words had hurt more than I cared to admit. Even if Garrett said he didn't mean it, he *had* said I wasn't really the type of woman he had envisioned himself with.

Morticia and Lilith were in the carriage house behind the old Victorian mansion.

Covering my eyes, I waited until Morticia had finished welding a sculpture of some sort of monster before approaching her.

"I have an art project for you."

"Are we going to lock Bronwyn in a cage? Or maybe one of those iron masks so we don't have to hear her insult you every other minute."

"I don't think we can just lock people up," I said.

"You can if you try hard enough," Lilith replied, her eyes black and intense.

"I need Halloween costumes for Garrett and me."

"Hmm," Morticia said as I described it and sketched it out. "You actually came up with something intriguing."

"I think we can manage that. It's definitely creepy."

Lilith rubbed her hands together. "Deliciously creepy."

"Leave everything to us," Morticia promised.

I was feeling very relaxed and satisfied after the horseback riding and the other riding.

A bath was in order. I loved the old claw-foot tub in the downstairs bathroom. As much as Morticia and Lilith insisted on their various herb concoctions to use in the water, I wanted a good old-fashioned bath bomb. I had been saving a Halloween-themed one for a special occasion. Fizzing, it turned the water bright orange. I stepped into the tub, sinking up to my neck, tipping my head back and closing my eyes. I had classic Halloween movies playing on my laptop. The old-timey voices murmured in the background as I stretched out in the water.

I was half dozing in the warm water when I felt hands grab me. I shrieked. "It's the monster from the Black Lagoon!"

"What?"

"Oh my god, Garrett, you scared me half to death! What are you doing here?"

"Shhh," he said. "I don't want the twins putting some sort of curse on me. Besides, you said you liked tubs. And I'm assuming sex in tubs."

He kissed me, mouth warm. His hand slipped into the water to cup my tits, which floated at the surface, then down between my legs. I sat back, spreading my legs for him.

"Anyone ever got you off in a tub?" he said, teasing my clit.

"I've gotten myself off," I gasped.

He kissed me hard. "Show me."

I placed one wet hand on his chest, pushing him back and leaving a wet palm print he didn't seem to notice.

"First," I said in my best sex kitten voice, "I stroke my tits like this. My nipples like it when they're played with." I stroked my tits, pushing them up and pinching and rubbing my nipples. I made a little whimper at the pleasure stirring in me.

"Then," I said, one hand still on my nipple, "I lean back, like this, letting my hand slowly go down, imagining that it's your hand. You slowly spread my pussy, teasing me softly first, dipping in my opening, feeling how wet and aching I am for you, then back up to my clit." My eyes were closed, lost in the awakening of pleasure. I bit my lip, imagining Garrett touching me.

But he was there. He kissed me hard, his hand replacing mine, stroking me. My hips moved in little circles as he teased my clit, stroking down my pussy to my opening then back up. He kissed along my collarbones and up my neck back to my mouth, his tongue echoing the motions of his hands.

I didn't have the leverage to really roll my hips against his hand. I could only make small motions, gasping as he brought me over the edge of pleasure and made me cry out.

"The rest of the fantasy," I said when I was able to talk again, "was that you pull me out of the tub and fuck me."

"Sounds dangerous," he said, rubbing his thumb over my nipple. "Slippery tile and all that."

"You know what else is slippery?" I said, reaching for him.

"What?"

I splashed water on him, laughing.

"Fall hazard," he said and took off his wet shirt.

"Didn't you ever see *The Shape of Water*, where she floods the bathroom and fucks the creature from the Black Lagoon?" I retorted, leaning on the edge of the tub, watching him undress.

"Her tits weren't as nice as yours," he replied, gathering my tits up in his hands and pushing them together.

I took his cock, hard and erect, and rubbed it between my breasts. Garrett hissed. "How about you fuck me like this?" I purred, the water on my tits letting his cock easily slide between them. "Can't say this is a safety hazard."

He clamped his lips tighter.

"Don't tell me you never wanted to do this," I said.

Garrett grabbed my breasts, his thumbs teasing my nipples as he slowly thrust between them.

It was so erotic. I put one hand on his firm buttock, the muscles jumping under his skin as he slowly thrust between my tits. His thumbs on my nipples sent jolts to my pussy. One hand snuck below the water as I stroked myself in time with his thrusts.

"*Fuck*," Garrett said and pulled me straight out of the water, silencing my shriek with a kiss. "Watching you touch yourself is going to send me straight over the edge."

CHAPTER 60

Garrett

I refused to have sex in the bathroom, but I wasn't above fucking Penny in the doll room, which happened to be the closest room to the bathroom. I threw her on the bed and ripped open a condom packet then pushed inside her. Between her sexy cries and thinking about her touching herself, I couldn't help but fuck her furiously. I teased her clit, rubbing and pinching it in time to my thrusts. She came quickly, which was good, because between watching her touch herself and sliding my cock between her perfect tits, I was half gone already.

"Mmmph," Penny moaned as I kissed her deeply. "You're better than any bath bomb."

I woke up wrapped around Penny. The room was freezing, but she was warm snuggled against me.

I kissed Penny awake, and she opened her eyes and shrieked slightly. "They're watching us," she whispered. One hundred lifeless doll eyes stared at us.

"I was going to suggest we go again," Penny said, "but this is a little too much Halloween even for me."

I kissed her. She still smelled faintly of pumpkin from the bath bomb.

"What time is it?"

"I have no idea."

"We're going to be late for work," she warned.

"I own the company," I said. "We can't be late."

I watched Penny dress slowly. I hadn't taken my time last night fucking her, and watching her shimmy on her panties made me aching and hard. Penny gasped when I kissed her neck, pressing my cock in between her legs. I teased her tits, rolling a nipple in my fingers as I put on a condom.

I slipped my fingers between her legs. She was still wet and slick from last night. She moaned and widened her stance, tilting her ass up slightly, begging me to fuck her.

I thrust into her and was rewarded with that little high-pitched pant. Her head tipped back as I fucked her. I needed her, and I grasped her hips as she rolled back against me. In the slickness of her pussy, I played around her clit, loving how she bucked against my hand. She came with a cry as I furiously rubbed her clit, the shivering in her pussy and the way it squeezed around my cock making me come with a curse.

I kissed her sloppily. "I feel like we need a nicer place to do this."

"I think the twins are selling the house soon, so who knows? You may get nostalgic for the dolls and spiderwebs," she said lightly.

After we dressed, I followed her downstairs, my hand on her lower back.

"I have cake for breakfast," she said. "I think the twins have granola. They said they also had dried crickets from Mexico."

"Crickets are a good source of protein," I remarked as Penny rummaged in the cupboards.

"If I find out you've been eating crickets, you will never kiss me again," she warned. "I'm eating cake," she said, taking a slice out. "I don't know what you're eating."

"Cake?" Archer said.

"What—why are you here?" I said to my brother as he came into the kitchen from the opposite door, arm in arm with Hazel.

"We brought sustenance," he said. "We even ordered you an iced coffee."

"How?"

"I told him to," Morticia said, coming in with Lilith.

I glared at my brother.

"We're working on Hunter and Meg's Halloween costumes," Lilith said.

"You're not the only one who can plot!" Archer said. "*I'm* going to be the one to put Meghan and Hunter back together!"

"That was my plan."

"The coffee and small snacks were your plan, and it would be fine except for the fact that it sucks. You can't be subtle. You need the big gesture. Hence the joint Halloween costumes," my older brother said.

"They're not going to go for that."

"Drink your coffee. All that sex makes you a little slow. You need to hydrate."

I took the iced coffee and frowned. There was a paper straw in it. It had already started to disintegrate. I fished out little pieces of paper.

"What are their costumes?"

"It's a surprise!" Hazel said. "I'm convincing Meg to wear hers, and Archer's going to convince Hunter to wear his."

"Great," Penny said. "Then they'll be back together and I can drink a milkshake without all the extra fiber."

CHAPTER 61

Penny

The big Harrogate Halloween festival was in two days. Over the past week, Garrett and I had spent time rehearsing, hanging out at the old Victorian house or his estate, and working on costumes.

"I can't believe how much more relaxed Garrett is," Weston said the Thursday before the festival. Garrett's Manhattan brothers had come into town for the festival, mainly to help corral the kids.

"You always see me tense because dealing with you and your bullshit stresses me out," Garrett retorted.

"This is going to be the best Halloween ever!" I said to Garrett. I was putting the finishing touches on his younger brother Ellis's costume. He wanted to be Rocket the Raccoon, and none of the store-bought costumes was going to do it for him.

"You're such a Halloween snob," Weston teased Ellis while I adjusted the straps on the space suit.

"Do any of your other brothers need help?" I asked Garrett.

"Hazel is working on their costumes. I think the kids are more interested in the food and games than in the Halloween costume contest."

"Speaking of," I said, lowering my voice. "Is the coast clear? I want to try the costumes on the horses."

Garrett was going to be a Nazgûl, or Ringwraith, from *Lord of the Rings*. The Nazgûl were the phantom ghost kings who were cursed by the rings. They wore black capes and hoods, carried swords, and rode horses. They were creepy and terrifying and made a perfect Halloween costume. I was going to be Arwen the elf princess because I wanted to look pretty and ride a horse.

"Along with the armor, Morticia and Lilith made these special harnesses and saddle blankets for the horses," I whispered to Garrett when we were in the stables. "Hopefully Merlin doesn't freak out with your costume."

Merlin was a patient horse and allowed himself to be bribed with apple slices while I fitted the harness to him. Garrett shrugged on the black robes, put the plate-metal greaves on his legs, and swung onto Merlin. I stood on a stool to arrange the stiffened black hood of the artfully tattered cloak around Garrett's head.

"Ooh!" I exclaimed, stepping back. "You look sooo creepy!" I couldn't make out Garrett's face. His tall form and broad shoulders filled out the cloak. He had Merlin walk a few paces. "You look like you just stepped out of the movies."

Garrett brandished the sword that Morticia had made.

I shivered. "It's chilling. We are so going to win."

Midnight's harness wasn't as elaborate. It had the intricate, feminine Celtic swirls of the elves. In the movies, Arwen's horse was white, but Midnight was dark, not a nice cream color. But it would have to do. I wasn't dyeing my hair, either. But I did have pointy elf ears and a curved sword.

After making Garrett take pictures of me so I could see the full effect, I packed the costumes back up. Garrett carried the boxes into the house after the coast was clear.

"I guess I'll take this to my room," he said, going into the house through a side door, not the main doors that led out onto the terrace.

"Your room is so much nicer than mine," I said, squeezing his bulging biceps.

"What? I kind of like the cobwebs, the asthma-inducing layer of dust, and the creepy puppet that's hanging from the ceiling," he said as we walked into his room. He set the boxes down and wrapped me in his arms, pulling us down onto his bed.

I hit him lightly then buried my face against the spot on his chest.

"I wish Morticia and Lilith weren't selling it," I said, trying to keep the sadness out of my voice.

"It needs quite a bit of work," he said.

"Yeah. It's probably for the best. The house will go to someone who can properly take care of it."

Garrett stroked my hair.

My phone rang as I lay against his chest. I leaned over the bed, rummaging in my purse, Garrett's large hand on my hip. It was my mother. I immediately canceled the call, or tried to anyway. I heard her shout hello before I managed to hang up. She called back immediately. I sent it to voicemail.

"I have to go," I said to Garrett. I jumped up, grabbing my purse and racing for the door.

"Oh, okay, fine. I'll see you tomorrow," he said, following me.

"Sure, tomorrow," I lied. "I just—I have to bake my cake for the contest. I forgot! I'm so dumb sometimes!"

I drove back to the Victorian house as if the wheels were on fire. As soon as I parked the car, I called my mom. "What do you want?" I said.

"That's no way to talk to your mother."

"Well then I guess this discussion is over," I snapped.

"Please, Penny, stop being so dramatic. I need you to send me the notes and any other material you had on the Svenssons."

"I told you I didn't want anything to do with that. I'm not working on the article," I said, my stomach sinking.

"I know that," she said. "But I told you I already promised our advertisers a certain type of article. I'll have someone else working on it. So send me what you have."

"No," I said firmly. All my life, I'd only wanted her to accept me. But now that I had something worth losing, my mother's opinion of me suddenly didn't matter.

"No?" she said. Anger tinged her voice. "There was a contract. We paid you to do research. The research legally belongs to us. Hand it over, or I will get the lawyers involved."

I felt like crying. If I was sued, Garrett would definitely find out. Then he would trace the article back to me.

"I'll send you what I have," I said, feeling defeated.

"That's a good girl. Send it to me soon, love!"

After ending the call, I went up to my computer, looked through my notes and deleted the worst of the information, and then sent the files to my mother. I felt as if I was going to puke.

Going down to the kitchen, I tried to calm down. I did actually need to bake a cake for the Halloween festival. I decided on a pumpkin-caramel Princess Charlotte cake. They always looked impressive, and baking always soothed my nerves.

CHAPTER 62

Garrett

Penny didn't come pick me up the next day. She texted and said she was baking then going to help with the big Harrogate Halloween festival setup. I probably should have helped set up, too, because I managed to get absolutely no work done.

That evening, I made Weston drop me off at her house. The lights were off, and I heard Salem meowing on the other side of the door when I pulled the chain on the doorbell. No one answered.

"Just leave me here," I told my brother.

"Are you sure?" he asked, looking apprehensively at the bare tree that blew ominously in the breeze. "I think it's going to rain."

"My car is unlocked," I said, pointing to the Tesla that was parked in front of the house. "I'll sit in it if it starts pouring."

Thunder cracked and lighting flashed. Weston shifted his weight. "Hunter's not going to like it if you get hit by lightning."

"I'm fine."

"You must really like Penny," he said as he headed back to his car.

I sat in the rocking chair on the porch and texted Penny.

Garrett: *I'm at your house.*

Penny: *How very stalkerish of you.*

Garrett: *Sorry. I can leave. I don't want to make you uncomfortable.*

Penny: *I was being weird yesterday. Ignore me.*

Garrett: *I can't ignore you.*

Penny: *You might be able to jimmy the lock and go inside. I think it's raining.*

Garrett: *I won't melt. If it gets bad I'll wait in the car. I don't want your neighbors to call the cops on me.*

Penny: *I'll be there soon. There was a tiff on whether the giant pumpkin stand was going to be closer to the town hall or if the giant onion booth was going to be closer.*

Garrett: *Sounds like a serious problem.*

Penny: *You have no idea. I thought there was going to be a brawl!*

I watched the rain pour down. Actually it was blowing sideways, and I was getting soaked. I pulled my collar up and stepped off the porch. I would wait this out in the car.

There was a crack. Lightning lit up the sky. If I hadn't known any better, I would have said the electricity almost sketched the form of a skeleton. It hit the tree. A branch arced, crackling with white lightning that sent it crashing and burning into the car with a pop. The car was on fire!

I watched it burn for a moment, hardly daring to believe what I was seeing. A fire truck screamed in the distance. It pulled up in front of the house with a black hearse close behind.

Penny jumped out, a look of horror on her face as she ran to the burning car. I sprinted down the cracked path and grabbed her, pulling her back.

"What are you doing?" I shouted.

"Oh my god, Garrett!" she said, looking up to me wide-eyed. "I thought you were in the car and the ghost killed you!"

"Ghost?" Clint, one of the firemen, said as he and his men sprayed a deluge of water on the car.

"Yes," Morticia replied, adjusting her sunglasses. The orange flames reflecting in the lenses made her look demonic. "The ghost doesn't like new cars."

"Sounds like you need the Ghostbusters!" Clint said and laughed as he sprayed more water. The fire was out as quickly as it had begun.

"I'm so glad you didn't get burnt up in the fire," Penny said, hugging me and burying her face against my chest.

Lilith shrugged. "We do have the hearse, so it wouldn't have been all bad."

Salem was howling when we went back into the house. Morticia and Lilith disappeared then came back with several bundles of leaves and lit them on fire. Salem sneezed and rubbed his face against my pants leg.

"What is that?" I asked, coughing at the thick white smoke.

"Sage," Morticia replied. "We need to cast away the evil spirits." They smudged me with the smoke then handed Penny a bundle of leaves.

"Walk around the house with that."

"Okay." Penny grabbed my sleeve. "You probably need to towel off, don't you, Garrett? You're drenched."

As soon as we were upstairs, I took the sage from Penny and doused it in the glass of water on the nightstand.

"We're supposed to burn that!" she protested.

"I have a better way of banishing evil spirits," I said, taking off my wet shirt.

"Oh yeah?" Penny said, reaching up to put her hands around my neck. "We should stick together then, you know, for safety, so the ghost doesn't get us."

"Yes we should," I said, bending down to kiss her. She ran her hands down my chest, and I easily lifted her up onto the dresser.

"Morticia said there are Wiccan rituals where sex summons spirits or something like that," Penny told me.

"I already have my sex goddess right here," I whispered to her, sliding off her panties. I kissed her mouth as I unbuttoned her blouse, then kissed down to her tits.

"I'm feeling moved by spirits already," she said with a whimper.

I hiked her skirt up more and spread her legs so I could press my mouth against her pussy. She bucked against me, so I held her hips in place while I slowly traced her pussy, dipping my tongue into her opening and then slowly swirling it up to her clit.

"Fuck me," Penny begged, red hair in sweaty tendrils around her face. I leaned back, making her curse.

"If we're banishing spirits, you have to be methodical," I said simply, returning to tease and lick her into a sweaty, whimpering mess. When she was soaking wet, her pussy hot and aching, I undid my pants and threw them on the bed along with my boxer briefs. Then I slowly teased her with my cock.

"Put it in me," she moaned.

"What about finesse?"

She sank her nails into my biceps. "I want to fuck."

I slipped on a condom as I pinched and teased her nipple. Penny panted with anticipation, then I slowly slid into her. Penny wrapped her arms around my neck, kissing my mouth and jaw sloppily.

"You feel how hot and aching and wet I am for you, don't you?" she moaned against my mouth. "I love feeling your cock in my pussy."

I sped up, kissing her, grinding her against me in time with my thrusts, making sure to angle my cock so it slid against her sensitive clit, making her shudder. I knew she was close with the way her legs tightened and trembled around my waist. The whimpering cries turned into short pants, then she came with a loud moan, taking me over the edge with her.

I kissed the side of her head. "I definitely felt a cosmic shift."

CHAPTER 63

Penny

"Today is the day!" I said, sitting up in bed in excitement. It was still dark outside. Fortunately the rain had stopped, and I could see the full moon setting under the tree line.

"Garrett, wake up," I whispered, shaking him.

"You're like a kid on Christmas," he murmured.

"Better! Today is the Halloween festival. "

He pulled me down, pushed me back into the bed, and straddled me. He bent to kiss each breast then down to my pussy, still wet and slick from the previous night. With a few strokes of his tongue, he had my pussy aching for his cock. I arched my back, moaning as he teased my nipples while he traced patterns on my clit. He tormented me, almost making me come then bringing me back down.

I heard him rip a condom packet, then he was easing into me. I moaned, spreading my legs for him, needing his cock. He fucked me slowly, keeping an excruciatingly steady rhythm while he teased my clit, played with my tits, and kissed me, his tongue swirling in my mouth. I was clinging to him and trembling when I came, my legs wrapped around Garrett, coaxing him to come inside me.

"You should just move in so you can do this every morning," I said breathlessly. "You could spend every Halloween like this."

After breakfast, one of Garrett's brothers picked him up.

"I'll see you over there," I said, kissing him goodbye. "Wear something festive!"

The Halloween festival was spread out all along Main Street and the town square. The streets were closed off, and the Svenssons had even made sure the train wouldn't need to go through during the day of the fair. It was a big event, and people from all over came into Harrogate to participate.

Booths selling Halloween candles, scarves, decorations, and other crafts were setting up along the street as I walked to meet Hazel in the town square. The stage for *Macbeth* was already set up. Workers were sweeping off the leftover rain.

The cakes—along with fruits, vegetables, pies, and other foods—were being displayed for voting near the pumpkins.

"What a pretty cake!" Hazel said as she took mine from me and set it down in the glass case with the number. The whole fair was to raise money for Harrogate. If you spent fifty cents, you could vote on a cake. You could also bid on a cake to take home.

"Yours is really pretty, too!" I said, admiring the tiered naked cake decorated with pine cones and orange and red flowers. "I just want to take a huge bite."

"I really want to eat them all!" she said, giggling.

Garrett came up to us, wrapping his arms around me as I was admiring the giant pumpkins.

"Are you going to make a giant pumpkin pie?" he asked, kissing my neck.

"Mmm, pumpkin pie. I haven't had a real Thanksgiving in forever," I said, refusing to think about my mother and about how wonderful Thanksgiving at Mimi's had been.

"You can have it at our house. Usually we order Chinese food."

"You eat Chinese food? On Thanksgiving? Uh, no. That is not going to work for me. Come on, let's look at the booths. We have to change for the costume contest soon," I said as we walked arm in arm down Main Street. The festival was packed.

"Usually I avoid the fall festival," Garrett admitted. "I didn't realize it was such a big deal."

"It's a huge deal," I said as we stood in line at a food truck selling lángos.

"Have you ever had this?" I asked Garrett, ordering two. "It's Hungarian. It's fried bread with sour cream, garlic, and grated cheese. It's basically all my favorite food groups."

"Apple cider! Hot apple cider! Two dollars! Support the Harrogate art retreat!" Ida yelled over the crowd as she roller-skated past us, wearing a bright-orange catsuit. Let's just say she did not look like anyone's Fall fantasy.

Garrett bought two, peeling off one-dollar bills from a wad of cash.

"Going to a strip club later?" Ida asked.

"No."

"I know of a good one! I'm actually thinking of doing a geriatric stripper class," Ida said, twirling on her skates. "You know, it's supposed to be good for your hips."

I sipped the drink so I wouldn't have to say anything. "Oh my goodness, this has a lot of alcohol in it," I said, coughing.

"Of course it does!"

"Ida, it's nine in the morning," I said. "I'm going to be drunk."

"No judgment here!" she said, skating away.

"I hope she didn't sell that to children," Garrett said with a frown.

"Too late," I said as I saw several of Garrett's brothers walking through the crowd. Archer had an armful of apple cider cups. He had several of the youngest Svensson brothers on leashes.

"Are you drinking all of that?" Garrett asked scowling.

"Dude, I had no idea it was alcoholic before I bought the whole tray from Dottie. I think she had been sampling the cider, if you know what I mean." He gestured to Garrett to take the tray. Then he proceeded to untangle the leashes on the kids.

"What am I supposed to do with these?" Garrett complained.

"Give me those," Meghan said, approaching us and holding out her hand for the cider. "I told Ida she can't sell any more. We aren't serving alcohol at the fall festival. This is a family event."

"Well shit, if there's no alcohol at this festival, I'm definitely not giving these to you then," Archer said, taking the tray back from Garrett.

The pumpkin judging was happening in thirty minutes. I bought a hot dog with the works, and we assembled in the stands. The rest of Garrett's brothers were there, along with Sebastian and his little brother Alfie. Ida, who was more than slightly tipsy, narrated as the pumpkins were measured.

"Now folks, the largest pumpkin ever was over two thousand pounds. Let's see if any of them are that big," Ida announced as the pumpkins were weighed. "Wow, eight hundred pounds! It looks like Ernest is the winner. Since I know none of us can math good, we have a visual. Would the best-looking group of brothers in the Northeast please step forward? I want to see how many Svenssons this pumpkin is equal to!"

The pumpkin was wheeled onto a balancing scale. Ida corralled Garrett, Hunter, Archer, and Mace to stand on the scale.

"Oh, not quite. Do you have a small Svensson to make it even?"

Davy scurried over, and we all laughed as Garrett picked him up.

"Perfectly balanced!" Ida shouted as one of the reporters from the newspaper snapped photos.

"What's with the onions?" Garrett asked me as we went to watch the next competition. "It seems random."

"Oh, it's a big surprise. You'll see!" I said as we watched them measure and weight the onions. Art had the largest onion.

"He just had one giant pot, and all he grew was an onion," Ida said into the microphone as Mayor Barry handed him the trophy, "but there you go. Concentrate on one thing, and ye shall be rewarded."

Up next was the pie contest. Jemma won with her beautifully decorated apple pie. She had carefully cut out a fall scene from the piecrust.

"This is so pretty!" Hazel said as we admired it. "I love the detail. You should come work at my shop!"

Hazel won the cake contest, which was no surprise. But I was the runner up. The newspaper reporter took pictures of us with our cakes.

"You won this cake," Ida said to Sebastian.

"Which one?"

"Both!" Ida exclaimed.

"What are you going to do with two cakes?" I asked.

"Eat them!" he said.

"A man after my own heart!" I turned to Garrett. He was scowling. "You should have bought me some cake."

"How about I eat your cake later," he whispered in my ear, making me blush.

CHAPTER 64

It was late afternoon, and the costume contest was starting soon. Penny and I went back to the Victorian house to change. Remy had driven the horses to the house. He didn't like crowds but was happy to help on the periphery. We dressed and made sure the horses were happy in their costumes. Then we assembled at one end of Main Street. The mayor was up on the grandstand in the town square to announce the contestants as they passed.

"First up, we have Josie and an unnamed number of Svenssons as Ms. Frizzle and the Magic School Bus."

The horses snorted as the old school bus trundled down the street. Josie and my brothers had painted it and added fins to make it look like a rocket ship. Periodically, the boosters would shoot flames. Tristan was driving. Josie and several of my little brothers were on top of the bus on a little balcony. Josie's dress was festooned with rockets. Adrian was seated next to her dressed as a lizard, though he looked more like Godzilla.

The crowd cheered as they waved.

"Next, we have Snow White, the Seven Dwarfs, and Prince Charming," Mayor Barry announced.

"I should have taken one of those horses," Archer said as he passed us.

"I almost didn't recognize him," Penny said to me. "He dyed his hair."

Archer was dressed like a Disney prince with a cape, brown boots, and sword. He bowed and mugged for the crowd. But they only had eyes for Hazel. She was dressed in the bright sapphire bodice and golden skirt of Snow White. She danced down the street, and seven of my youngest brothers, dressed in little fake beards and carrying pickaxes, scampered after her like ducklings.

Eli, dressed in a witch's costume with a large fake nose and heavy theater makeup, crept after them.

"That is so adorable!" Penny said, applauding. "I should have taken one of your brothers as Frodo."

"Next we have Hunter and Meg as Bonnie and Clyde," the mayor announced over the PA system.

Meg had been helping Hazel keep the seven dwarfs in line. She looked around in shock when her name was called and shook her head.

But Hunter pulled up in a pristine Ford Model T. He was carrying a fake old-time machine gun and a bag full of chocolate money. He was dressed very suavely in a pin-striped suit. Meg also looked the part in her felt hat and flapper.

"Ready for your big moment?" Hunter said, holding out a hand.

"You were signed up," I told her.

"Come on, Meg, do it for the Harrogate Trust." Hunter's smile was soft.

"Fine," Meg said, patting her hair into place. It had been pinned to look like she had a short bob. "Just this once. Oh, and I'm driving the car." She got behind the wheel and blared the horn. Hunter hung out the window and tossed chocolate coins out to the crowd.

"Up next, we have another Svensson," Mayor Barry boomed over the sound system. "Garrett and Penny as the Nazgûl and Princess Arwen." Since the characters interacted during the chase scene, Penny sent my horse down the street first, and I followed a few paces behind. The crowd loved it.

"We're so going to win," Penny said at the end of the parade route. "Though, I have to admit, even though I knew it was you in the costume, it still was a little creepy to have a faceless demon bearing down on me."

After the parade was over, we assembled back at the grandstand. Two of the dwarfs were crying, and the witch and the lizard looked a little tipsy.

"I thought you confiscated all the alcohol," Hunter said to Meg. She scowled at him. So much for pushing them back together.

"All the votes are in," Mayor Barry said. "The winner is... Snow White!"

"Yay!" Hazel cheered, jumping around with my little brothers in a circle.

"Geez. Pimping our little brothers out for a cheap win," I said to Archer.

"Hey, I had to dye my hair. I don't think this is ever going to come out!" Archer retorted as the photographer lined them up to snap pictures.

"Wow, this is amazing!" Sebastian said. "What a great event!"

"It's not over!" Penny called. "Time for *Macbeth*."

CHAPTER 65

Penny

"This is going to be so much fun!" I said, feeling giddy when we were backstage. We didn't have a real theater; it was more of a temporary structure. Garrett and I were just off to the side behind a wall. I peered out to look at the crowd. Several of Garrett's brothers saw me and waved.

The sun had already set, and several lights illuminated the stage. In Shakespeare's time, theater sets had been fairly minimal. The Harrogate community-theater rendition of *Macbeth* included the stage, the actors, the elaborate costumes, and a handful of props. Among the crowd, there were several carts that sold meat pies, cider, ales, and other semihistorically accurate snack foods.

"*Places!*" Edna hissed. She was a judge experienced in wrangling lawyers in her courtroom, and her voice tended to carry. I noticed several people in the audience sat up straighter.

The lights began to dim, and Ida, Dottie, and Bettina went out to the stage. Remy helped them carry out the cauldron.

Edna banged on a drum that sounded like thunder. The lights went all the way down, and the dry ice in the cauldron smoked, hissed, and popped. Ida cackled and said, "When shall we three meet again?"

The play had begun. *Macbeth* had always been one of my favorite plays. Nothing could beat spooky witches, crazy prophesies, visions, blood, and gore. It was always a crowd-pleaser.

When Garrett and I were onstage together, I felt the electricity between us. I realized I wanted nothing more than for this to be our life. Okay, not plotting to murder our best friends and going crazy, but the fall festival, being a team, his family, our weird friends, the town. It felt like home, like this was the place I belonged, and Garrett was the man I was supposed to experience it all with.

At the end of the play, we all took our bows.

"Thank you all for a wonderful Halloween celebration," Edna called out. "We'll see you out trick-or-treating next week."

"Don't tell me you didn't have fun," I said to Garrett as he pulled off the chain-mail costume.

"It was sort of fun." He leaned in and kissed me. "I'm so glad I met you."

"I'm glad I met you too."

We went back to his family hand in hand.

"I guess I should head out," Sebastian said, Alfie in his arms. "The fall festival was really cool. It's so great that the whole town comes out, and all the tourists."

"But," I told him, "if you're going to move here, you can't leave now. Only tourists leave now. Residents stay for the best part."

He raised an eyebrow.

"We drink cider and eat cake and onion rings. There's a late-night onion ring-frying session."

"That is so random."

"I know, right? But that's why we have the biggest-onion competition."

Most of the tourists were making their way to the train station or to their cars. We locals all went to a side street, where there were firepits set up. Hazel was at the cart, stirring batter, while her sister sliced onions. I joined in to help.

"So this is a contest?" Garrett asked, separating the rings.

"Only in so far as you see how many you can eat!" I said as the first batch of onions was dunked into the hot oil.

"I'm exhausted," I said, yawning after Remy dropped us off at the Victorian house. He'd come back with the bus to ferry people around. It still had all the rocket-ship attachments on it.

"Gonna take some time getting those off," Remy said cheerfully as he pulled open the bifold door. "Welded all that on."

Garrett carried me upstairs then laid me on the bed and slowly undressed me. "I think you deserve something after that Halloween extravaganza."

"Do you love the holiday now?" I asked as he kissed me, slowly unlacing my top. "I even wore festive lingerie."

"I think I could spend every Halloween like this if it was with you," he said seriously.

He kissed his way down my body, sliding my clothes off. He pressed his face against the Halloween panties, pushing them to the side to stroke my pussy. My breathing quickened and my heart raced as he stroked me then eased the panties down.

I spread my legs for him, moaning as he kissed my pussy, licking my clit, sucking it, teasing it, bringing me over the edge. I came with a cry. "You should warn a girl," I said as Garrett removed his pants and boxer briefs. I admired the view as he pulled on a condom.

"I love fucking you after you come," he said, his deep voice sending shock waves through me. "Your pussy is so tight and hot." He turned me over, teasing me with his cock, making me moan. "I love making you come again, just with my cock."

He pushed inside me, and I cried out. My pussy was aching for him. He reached forward, cupping my tit, pinching my nipple as he thrust into me. He was right—I was going to come again just from his cock. I moaned, rocking back against him. Garrett slowly thrust into me, taking his time, drawing out the pleasure.

I spread my legs wider, begging him to take me harder. He maintained the same slow, steady rhythm.

I knew what would speed him up. I reached down to stroke and rub my clit. Garrett grabbed my hand, pushing it up above my head. My tits were pressed against the bedspread, and my ass arched up as he fucked me hard, making me cry out with every thrust.

His balls slapped my ass as he took me. My pussy throbbed, needing release. I moaned low in my throat, and

Garrett nipped my neck. He pulled back slightly, grabbing my hips to jackhammer into me. I could tell he was close, the sensation and the angle sending me over the edge, and I came with an honest-to-god scream.

CHAPTER 66

Garrett

The rain woke me up the next morning.

"I love being inside when it's raining," Penny murmured. "It's so cozy."

She stretched up to kiss me. I held her and kissed her softly.

"I'd say we should stay here all day," I said, "but I have a surprise planned."

After we dressed, we went down to the kitchen. The twins were in there, and there was a pot of… something boiling on the stove.

"The carcass of your car is still sitting out in front of the house," Lilith said, not looking up from the large pot. "We have a realtor coming by today to look at it. The car is detracting from the property value."

"You're still selling?" Penny said.

"You're welcome to buy it," Morticia replied.

"Maybe your sugar daddy can buy it," Lilith said, turning to stare at me.

"You take that back, Lilith," Penny said. "That's not why I'm with him!"

"If the house comes with the two of you, then no way," I said. "I don't need you putting hemlock in my coffee."

"I suppose you don't want any of this then," Morticia said, scooping two mugs full of the liquid out of the pot. She and Lilith went out to the back porch.

"I love my friends," Penny said. "But honestly, I would like for once in my life to have my own space. When I lived in the city, I shared a room, like a literal room, with two other people. Now at least I have my own room, but I have to share the house with an army of ten thousand dolls."

"I feel the same way about my brothers," I admitted. "Love them, would do anything for them, but it would be nice to have some peace and quiet."

"Ah well," Penny said, getting up and bypassing the bubbling pot to grab a tea bag. "It's nice to dream."

I looked at her blankly. "Or we could just leave."

"Leave?" she said as she boiled water.

"I have a condo in the city. We could go there for a few days." She looked at me in shock. "Unless you don't want to," I said, backtracking.

"Sorry, you lost me at 'condo in the city,'" she said. "Did you mean a condo of your very own, or do you have a bed in a condo?"

"It's mine. I don't even share any walls with another condo. I have the whole floor of the building."

"You really should have led with that!" Penny said.

I left her to pack and had Weston pick me up. He looked rough.

"I don't know what Ida put in that cider," he rasped.

"You're a lightweight," I said with a smirk.

"Clearly."

When we were back at the estate, I packed a bag then dragged Blade out of bed to drive a new car back to Penny's. Then we were headed to Manhattan.

"OMG, Garrett," she said as she sped down the road. "It's almost Halloween!"

"You're not tired of it?"

"Never!" she shouted and turned up the music. Jack Skellington was singing about Christmas.

"See," I said, "this isn't a Halloween soundtrack."

"Picky, picky. Oh, if we're going to Manhattan, we have to stop by the Halloween Emporium. It's a pop-up holiday shop. They change names and stock based on the season. They have nice, high-end stuff. It's not like the Halloween stores in the mall. I want us to be Jack and Sally for trick-or-treating next week."

"Doesn't he just wear a suit?" I said, frowning. "Why do I need a costume? I have a pinstripe suit."

"And I'm sure you look very handsome in it," Penny said, "but this store supposedly has a Jack Skellington head, and you need a bat bow tie. Also they have Sally's dress and tights."

"You already have the red hair, at least," I said, tugging one of her curls.

On the drive over, I did research. If I was taking Penny to Manhattan, I wanted to make a good impression. She was quickly becoming an important part of my life. I wanted to keep her in it, and part of that was making her happy.

CHAPTER 67

Penny

"This store is better than I imagined! I could live here!" I exclaimed when we had driven the hour and a half into the city. The store was in an old converted warehouse, and it was filled with Halloween. "I want all of these things," I said.

"You want to live in a Halloween store?" Garrett asked as I picked up a Halloween snow globe. "Why would someone even make that?" He sounded confused.

"Look, they have a ton of creepy costumes!" I said, hauling him around the store. "There's the bunny from Donny Darko."

They also had a lot of sexy costumes, I noticed, in another area of the store. There were sexy versions of any animal imaginable, which was really just the same corset with the tails and ears swapped in and out. I held one of the costumes up to my torso.

"Have you ever fantasized about…" I checked the tag. "A sexy capybara?"

"The giant rodent?" Garrett asked with a frown.

"Maybe let's not," I said and put back the costume.

Another section held more mainstream sexy outfits, like a 1950s pinup girl.

"You like this one?" I asked, holding up one of the costumes. It was black leather with lace accents. There was a face mask that looked like a Batgirl mask.

Garrett's face was perfectly neutral.

"Sorry," I laughed, putting it back. "I keep getting distracted."

Garrett followed me through the store. There was a whole section dedicated to *The Nightmare Before Christmas*.

"This is what I need!" I found Sally's dress and tights, which made it looked like she was stitched together. "They even have the sewing basket and the bottles that she used to spike her evil master's soup."

Garrett carried all my selections as I looked through the shelves. I found Jack's bat bow tie.

"Unfortunately, they don't have any of Jack's pumpkin-head masks left," I said.

"Thank God," Garrett muttered under his breath.

I squeezed his firm buttocks. "I'll just have to put makeup all over you then," I said, sticking my tongue out.

He kissed me. "I don't want to ruin my suit."

I felt a little sick when the clerk rang up the purchases. I knew the Halloween Emporium was high-end, but I had only bought a few things. How was it so expensive? I fumbled for my credit card. Hopefully I had enough to pay for it.

But Garrett handed over his credit card.

"You don't have to," I said. "This was my idea."

"Let people do nice things for you, Penny. You deserve it," he said as the clerk bagged up the costume items.

"This day has been awesome!" I said, putting the bag in the back seat and starting the car. "Where to now? Your mysterious condo?"

"Turn at the next street and keep going straight. I'll tell you when to turn."

Garrett navigated me to a nondescript brick building. I parked in the garage and followed him to the lobby. He nodded to the doorman and swiped a key card at the elevator.

"So how does that work?" I asked. "One person on each floor? You must never see your neighbors."

"All my neighbors are my brothers. This was the first major real estate investment Greg and Hunter did together."

"A real piece of Svensson history right here," I quipped.

The elevator dinged, and we stepped out into a private lobby. I was starting to internally freak out. Private lobby before the condo? The Svenssons were really living large in Manhattan if they had that. The lobby held plants in front of a large window and a little bar area with refreshments.

"This is nuts," I muttered.

"I think the architect's intention was if that you had a party or something, you would place security and coat check here."

"Throw a lot of swanky parties lately?" I asked as he punched in a number on the high-tech keypad next to a heavy metal door.

"Yes—the fair with the haunted tiny house and all the chickens you held at my estate."

"That doesn't count! That was for kids. It wasn't swanky."

"You are of course free to host a party here," Garrett said.

"I don't know, this building looked a little small from the outside," I remarked.

"It is a very long building," Garrett said as the large metal door whooshed open.

"No kidding!" I said in awe when I walked into the condo.

My experience in New York City thus far had been a small step up from that of the rats and the pigeons. When I had lived in Manhattan, it hadn't been anything like what I'd seen on TV. There were no fancy prewar apartments with super-high ceilings and fireplaces and tall windows. Instead, there were converted tenements, moldy wallpaper, and pipes that leaked and, in the winter, coated the walls with ice. There were crazy neighbors and fights in the street below a tiny window that let in no light on account of the brick wall that was a foot across from it.

Garrett's condo was movie-star living—or actually, I supposed, it was billionaire living. It featured huge windows and tall ceilings with the original wood structure visible. Plush carpets with geometric contemporary patterns soaked up the sounds of my footfalls. It was so quiet. The double-paned glass in the large windows hardly let in any street noise. The large balcony that looked over a side yard was filled with plants. It also had a chaise lounge. There was tea sitting out. Garrett poured me a cup.

"This is like a cozy little oasis. Tea and snacks? " I said, eating a perfectly tiny cream puff. "It's like magic."

"It's really an overzealous doorman," Garrett said with a small smile. "My brothers aren't here a lot, and I think he likes to plan fun little gestures whenever he has the chance.

He takes care of the plants and lets the cleaning people in. He's a nice guy. His kid is at Harvard with a few of my brothers. We set up a scholarship fund to pay for his education."

"That's so nice!"

"He's a good dad."

"Sounds like it!"

"Better than mine," Garrett said, face dark.

I held his hand. "My mom is a scummy person too."

Garrett kissed me. "Maybe we should have some alcohol. I think I need it after that Halloween store."

"I make a good whiskey sour," I told Garrett. "Where's your alcohol stash?" I said, walking back inside. Garrett pointed. There was a whole bar with a wall of expensive liquor along with a hammered copper sink and a wine fridge and everything.

"This is insane! Now all I need is a baking kitchen."

"There's a catering kitchen," Garrett offered.

"Shut. Up. Why is this condo so huge?"

"It was designed for entertaining—fundraisers, business parties, the like. The design isn't really geared toward families. As you can imagine, it's a pain whenever my little brothers are in town. There aren't that many bedrooms."

"It's nice to have another kitchen, though," I said. "What do you do with all this space?"

"I know Weston skateboards in his."

"You can hear him?" I asked, mixing the drinks. "You would think there would be soundproofing."

"There is," Garrett said. "You can't physically hear it, but I know when he's up there, and I know when he's skateboarding."

Laughing, I snuggled next to Garrett on the couch and handed him his drink.

"I want a beanbag chair," I said.

"Why?"

"I've never had one. I always wanted one as a kid. And I never had the space in any of my Manhattan living situations. This place is big enough. I could have three and just sprawl out on them."

"You are very easy to please," Garrett said against my neck.

I snorted. "You got me off in like three minutes this morning. I am a simple, simple creature." I sipped my drink. "This is nice. This is exactly what I needed."

"I know you said you're simple," Garrett said after a moment. "But I did have an actual plan for this evening."

"A party?"

"A charity ball."

"You want me to be your bland socialite plus-one at a charity ball?" I said with a laugh.

"Not if you're going to be that way about it," he said.

"Are you kidding? Of course I want to!" I exclaimed. "A sexy cocktail dress, smoky eye makeup—I'm down!"

"Well, too bad, it's not a bland function—it's a costume ball."

"Even better. Oh, shoot! I should have bought something at the costume shop," I said. "Why didn't you tell me?"

"This is a little more high-end. I had costumes shipped over here," Garrett said with a slight smirk.

"You did?" I said, jumping up.

"They're in the master bedroom."

"Is this some ruse to get under my skirt?" I asked, hands on my hips.

"I mean, always, but no, there is legitimately an outfit in there. And mine as well."

Leading me to the master suite, Garrett opened the closet. It was legitimately bigger than any of the Manhattan apartments I'd stayed in.

"Geez, you have a lot of suits," I said, running my hands through the perfectly ordered racks of clothes.

"Can't have too many suits."

A deep-purple dress on a padded hanger swung from a wooden hook in a wardrobe. Garrett handed it to me.

"Hopefully this fits. I got your measurements from Dottie when she was making the costumes."

The dark-purple dress had a Spanish influence, with ruching and black-lace edging.

"Bathroom is through there," Garrett said.

The bathroom was even more impressive than the closet. It had a huge tub. Just to see if I could, I stepped in and stretched out full-length.

"It would be like a coffin except it's a tub," I said aloud.

"What?" Garrett yelled through the door. "Does the dress fit? If it doesn't, there is a limited time frame to make other arrangements."

"I can't tell if you care if it fits or if you're trying to find an excuse to watch me get dressed," I said. "These things take time. I have to do my hair and makeup first."

Because the dress had a Spanish vibe, I put my hair half up in a side bun. Then I did heavy, dramatic makeup with a smoky eye. Satisfied, I shimmied into the dress. It had a built-in bra. I was a little worried it wouldn't hold everything up. Especially with all the cake I'd been eating, I was extra busty.

"I think you need to help lace me up," I said, opening the bathroom door.

Garrett came over to me and laced up the corset. I adjusted the dress then slipped on the black stiletto heels.

Garrett tied the mask around my face. It was a delicate black silk. I looked sexy and mysterious in the mirror. I played with the lace fan, admiring my reflection as Garrett dressed.

"Ready?" Garrett asked, standing there in a tux with tails.

I studied the tux. "Wait—oh!" It had white bones painted all over it.

"It's like Daniel Craig in that James Bond movie!" I exclaimed, clapping my hands together. "The one that started on the Day of the Dead. Oh. My. *God,* you look freaking hot!"

Garrett smirked and pulled a skull mask out of a box. It had black silk ribbon to tie it. Somehow that made him look even more fuckable. One gray eye winked at me through the mask.

He slipped a top hat onto his head and picked up a cane. Draping a fur cape around my shoulders, he offered me his arm.

"Also," Garrett said as he inspected the mask in the mirror. "One more thing I forgot to add... we're crashing this ball."

CHAPTER 68

Garrett

A part of me didn't even want to go to the charity ball. I wanted nothing more than to fuck Penny in that outfit. The way her breasts in the tightly laced bodice of the dress swelled above the neckline... the way the slit exposed part of her leg, revealing the creamy skin... But Penny was excited.

"Whose charity ball are we crashing?" Penny asked happily. She looked mysterious in the mask. I leaned down to kiss her but couldn't make contact. The skull mask covered my jaw and mouth, and while I could speak in it because the jaw piece hinged, I couldn't make out with Penny. Though I did try.

Penny giggled as the mask brushed her face. Her mask only covered her eyes, so she reached up and kissed me on the skin of my jaw right at the edge of the mask.

"Careful," I said. "Or I might just have to fuck you before we even get to the elevator."

She shivered and clung to my arms.

"Don't tempt me. Besides, didn't you know that my absolute dream is to go to a fancy masquerade ball?"

"This will be fancy, all right," I said as we walked out the door.

"We won't get arrested for crashing, will we?"

"Let's hope not."

"It's Halloween. The saying is 'trick or treat' for a reason."

The doorman already had a limo waiting when we arrived downstairs.

"Oooh, a limo, and it's an SUV limo," Penny said, shivering slightly as we stepped outside. It was freezing. It was definitely late October. The wind whistled through the canyon of tall buildings as I helped Penny into the limo.

Penny leaned against me once I sat down beside her.

"Champagne?" I offered, pouring her a glass.

"Oh my god, this limo has a bar in it? So. Cool. This is the first time I've actually been in a limo," she said, pushing at the buttons like a kid.

But when she sipped the champagne and posed seductively, she was all woman.

"You ever had sex in the back of the limo?" she purred.

"Can't say that I have." I couldn't really kiss her, but I could do other things. "The drivers talk though," I whispered in her ear. "Maybe we should give them a show." I let my hand slide up the hem of her dress.

"The Kennedy Arts Center," the driver said a little too loudly.

Penny coughed and downed the rest of her drink, fanning herself. "That was a quick ride."

"My condo is in a desirable part of town," I said. The limo driver opened the door, and I helped Penny out.

"*Wow*," Penny whispered. She hung onto my arm as we followed well-dressed couples through the large bank of doors, following the signs for the Holbrook Foundation's Annual Fall Masquerade.

"Holbrooks?" Penny hissed. "Like, the Holbrooks that your entire family hates?"

"The feeling is mutual," I whispered back.

Penny was a little antsy when we approached the people in black suits who were checking invitations.

"We don't have..."

"Shh," I said.

"Welcome to the masquerade," a woman greeted us. "Thank you for your patronage. May I see your invitation?"

"We'd like to purchase tickets at the door," I said smoothly.

The woman taking the tickets looked at her partner in confusion. "Let me see if we can accommodate you," she said, tapping on her tablet.

I pulled a wad of hundred-dollar bills out of my tuxedo breast pocket. "I would like to remain anonymous. This charity endeavor is very near and dear to my heart. As such, I would also like to make a donation. For a good cause."

The woman looked at the cash. *Would she take it?* She took it. "Thank you for your support," she said, smiling and handing Penny and me two cardstock letters with gold embossing.

I led Penny into the large hall.

As soon as we were out of sight of the entrance, Penny pulled me into an alcove.

"Oh my god. That was insane. I'm done. I'm sweating like a pig." She fanned herself. "I can't handle that much stress."

"Relax," I said. "We're in. I'll get you a drink."

A server magically appeared, and I took two champagne flutes from the tray. Penny gulped hers down.

"You're going to be tipsy."

"I'm sweating so much this is going to go right through me." She handed a server her empty glass and took another. "How did you even know about this ball?"

"My brothers regularly crash it."

"I feel like it's not crashing if you buy a ticket," she remarked.

"If we did it under our names, Hunter would find out," I said, sipping my own drink. "Greg would be pissed. Besides, according to Archer, the Holbrooks throw amazing parties."

Penny and I slowly walked around the perimeter of the room. Archer was right, I decided. The Holbrooks did throw a nice party.

"Look at her costume," Penny said. She had a whole plate of various hors d'oeuvres that the servers were passing out.

"This miniature crab cake is amazing. Can you unhinge your jaw enough to eat it?" she asked, feeding me a bite. "Also, have I told you how freaking sexy you look in that costume?"

"That is a really nice costume," a young woman said. "I'm jealous!"

"I'm double jealous," said the dark-haired man next to her. "I should have thought of being James Bond!" I peered at him. He had the jaw and coloring of a Holbrook. Which one was he?

"Oh, Carter, you'd have to be blond to pull that off!" his date said.

So he was the screwup. It seemed that Allie had been a good influence on him. From the stories, Carter should have been drunk as a skunk right now. But he seemed remarkably sober.

"Honestly, Allie, it's like you don't even care about me." He held out his hand. "On behalf of the Holbrook Foundation, thank you for coming." He peered at me. "You're not one of the Davenport cousins, are you?"

"No—"

"I'm Penny!" Penny chirped. *Speaking of drunk.* I nudged her slightly. She looked at me doe-eyed. "And that's James Bond."

Allie and Carter laughed.

"Lucky girl!" Allie toasted Penny.

"I guess I shouldn't have given my real name," Penny whispered after Allie and Carter strolled off to talk to the Burbanks.

CHAPTER 69

I couldn't believe I was at an actual, honest-to-goodness ball. There was even a live band. They were playing jazzy renditions of popular songs.

"The food is amazing," I said, taking several more of the crab cakes the servers brought by. "You want to dance?" I asked Garrett, finishing the rest of my champagne.

"Are you done with your snack?"

"I guess so. Here, eat this last one." I waved it in his face.

He ate it with a snap then led me onto the dance floor. I felt so glamourous. Garrett was striking in the black tux and tails.

"I thought you said you didn't know how to dance."

"I can do basic moves," he said, twirling me around the floor.

"This is a little more than basic," I told him.

"It's just a pattern," he said, pressing me toward him. "You just follow the steps. Simple."

Garrett was all lean grace. I had had enough champagne that I was at that happy spot of sexily sloppy and not sick drunk.

We danced for several songs. Then Garrett pulled me away. We walked around the room, admiring the costumes and the scenery, then we went outside. There was a courtyard off the main event space. Outside were several firepits and dessert stations.

"Look! High-end s'mores," I told Garrett excitedly.

"They're organic and handmade," the server explained. "These are freshly baked graham crackers, and the chocolate is imported from Switzerland."

The marshmallows had been dyed pale colors and cut into shapes like bats, pumpkins, and witch's hats.

Garrett sat in one of the deep wooden chairs and pulled me onto his lap. "I'm trying to keep you from falling into the fire," he said.

"I'm not that drunk," I scoffed, almost impaling my hand with the skewer. "Whoops. It slipped!"

I toasted the marshmallow. It puffed up beautifully. I took a bite, moaning around the warm, gooey treat.

"I think you're supposed to make a sandwich out of that," Garrett remarked, drawing little circles on the back of my neck.

"I eat everything separately," I said. Garrett snorted. "Do you know a lot of people here?" I asked, taking a bite of the marshmallow then the chocolate then the graham cracker.

Behind his mask, his eyes narrowed slightly. "I think that's Grant Holbrook, with his wife Kate," he said, motioning to a man and woman dressed as Victorian Era nobility. "And that's, ugh, my brother Weston. Come on. If the Holbrooks find out he's here, he's going to be thrown out. We don't want to be caught up in that. It would be incredibly inconvenient."

Garrett took a bottle of champagne and flutes, motioning me ahead of him. Then he paused, handed me the glasses, and took a whole tray of snacks from one of the servers.

"And that's how I know you truly understand me," I said, reaching up to kiss him.

"I just don't want you to pass out when we get home. I still have more things planned," he said, mysterious behind the mask.

We snuck out through a back door and down several halls.

"Are we allowed to be out here?" I whispered as we walked down a back hallway.

Two men in servers' outfits approached us. One said, "Sir, I'm sorry, but the party is that way."

"Hey Garrett, is that you?" his colleague asked.

"Diego." He and Garrett did a fist bump. "It's fine." The other server shrugged and walked off.

"Security just made the rounds, so you should be good. Just let me get that tray and those glasses off you when you're done."

"Sure thing."

"Who *are* you?" I whispered when we were out of earshot.

I thought I saw Garrett smile under the mask. "He does some work for me."

"What type of work?" I asked.

"Eyes-and-ears work."

"Remind me never to piss you off," I said after a moment.

"You could never," Garrett said emphatically. "You're perfect."

He led me up a grand staircase. The walls were covered in mirrors. I admired our reflections. Garrett looked smoking hot. I looked pretty good, too, very sexy and mysterious. Off the landing, there was a large room with floor-to-ceiling windows overlooking the courtyard off the large event hall. The trees with fairy lights cast a faint glow into the room. The music drifted up from the event below, filtering faintly through the glass. Garrett sat on the floor, and I lay back, resting my head in his lap.

I sighed then poked him. "So..."

"So, what?"

"Are you a Halloween fanatic now?"

"I suppose."

"Do I sense pumpkin-spice lattes in your future?" I teased.

"I wouldn't go that far. But I do have something else planned that is in line with Halloween."

CHAPTER 70

Garrett

"So," Penny said, curling up against me when we were in the limo. "Did I change your mind?"

"Hmm? Change my mind about what?"

"Still want a marathon runner who eats vegan food?"

"Hell no. If you ever left me, I'd just wander around in a circle, dreaming of your curves and tits and legs wrapped around me." I kissed her or tried to through the mask. I reached up to take it off.

"Not yet," Penny said. "I'm really turned on by it." She planted kisses along my neck and the exposed part of my jaw.

When the limo stopped in front of my condo building, she ordered, "Carry me!"

"I thought you said you weren't drunk," I told her, picking her up.

"Oh, I'm drunk," she said, licking my ear. "And very, very horny." Her breath was hot against my ear.

In the elevator, she kissed the mask then my jaw and down my neck to nibble at my earlobe.

"I'm going to have a very happy Halloween," she purred, undoing my bow tie. "Maybe we should play trick-or-treat. Or are you scared?"

I pressed her to me, letting her feel my hard cock. "Never."

"Ooh, treat then!" she said, as I half carried her off the elevator. I could barely punch in the numbers on the keypad. "Yes, definitely treat," I said, feeling like I was about to lose all self-control.

The package I had ordered was sitting in the master bedroom when we stumbled in. Penny had practically ripped my jacket off me.

"Don't you want your treat?" I said, breathing hard.

"I'm about to have it right now," she said, pressing her tits against me.

I gestured to the package.

"Oh, *oh*!" she exclaimed. "You got me a present, Garrett!" Penny clapped her hands when I handed her the large, flat box.

"Nicely done! Look at the wrapping paper!" It was silver with witches embossed on it. The whole thing was tied with a huge orange-and-black bow.

Penny carefully unwrapped it.

"I'm sort of impressed at your hand-eye coordination," I remarked, "considering how much you drank."

"You will be very impressed in a little bit," she said, smirking to herself.

"You probably drank two bottles of champagne."

"Yes, but I'm made of sturdy stock. I basically store the alcohol in my boobs," she said, jiggling her chest. The lace-up back of her dress was half undone, and I wanted to tear it the rest of the way off her. But more, I wanted to see her in the costume.

"You really have jumped on the Halloween train," Penny said as she pulled out all the pieces.

It was the sexy bat costume from the Halloween Emporium. There were fishnet fingerless gloves, thigh-high leather stiletto boots, and a short corset with a scalloped edge shaped like a bat.

"I'm going to treasure this forever," Penny said.

"It's more of a one-time-use outfit, because I plan on ripping it off you," I growled.

CHAPTER 71

Penny

I went into the bathroom to change. It was always touch and go with big boobs and lingerie. I might rip it before Garrett ripped it off me. I pulled on the little shorts, though they barely counted as shorts. They rode on my waist, cut high in the back into basically a thong.

I laced up the corset then put on the bra. It had a thin strap under the boob, a strap on either side of the boob to frame each of my breasts, then one strap to cover the nipple. My large breasts strained out of them, but the bra stayed intact as I buckled the halter strap.

I pulled on the thigh-high stiletto boots and the fingerless fishnet gloves then looked at myself in the mirror. I looked pretty hot if I did say so myself. Also, thinking about Garrett taking all this off me was making me pretty wet.

I walked out of the bathroom and posed. Garrett was half undressed, barefoot, sitting in a chair. He was half hard through his boxer briefs; his chest was muscular under the undone dress shirt. Garrett's gaze was more intense than a werewolf's as he stood up and stalked over to me. Taking off his dress shirt, he examined me head to toe then back up again.

"I think I'm going to really like fucking you like this," he said. His deep voice sent shivers through me.

"Not if I go first," I said, placing two fingers on his chest and pushing him back to the chair. "You can't pose like that, tease a girl, then just think you're going to turn around and fuck her." I straddled him. His cock was hard through the trouser material. I ground my hips against him, making him curse. In retaliation, he sucked my nipples through the fabric, tongue slipping under the strap.

His hand snuck under the panties, rubbing through the wetness. I ground against him, needing him to fuck me just like this. I kissed him, and he pulled me back down, crushing our mouths together.

"Fuck me," I murmured.

"No."

"*Fuck.*"

"You can't just tease a guy then expect him to just spread your legs and fuck you, can you?" he said, faint smile playing around his mouth.

"Oh, I know how to push your buttons," I said, one hand creeping up to rub my rock-hard nipple through the bra fabric.

He cursed, kissing me again. "*Fuck.*"

"That's the idea."

He pulled me off him then set me down. "My condom is in my shirt pocket."

"What happened to being a good planner?" I said, sashaying over to the nightstand and bending over it, posing, my ass seductive and perky due to the heels. "I'll just be here waiting."

"Got it," Garrett said. He came over to me and pressed his hand against my pussy, rubbing me through the panties. "I want to fuck you just like this," he growled, rubbing my pussy, spreading the wetness to tease my clit as he put on the condom.

He pushed the panties to the side, then he was in me. His hand moved to stroke my clit as he slowly fucked me. His hand still rubbing my clit furiously, he cupped my breast with the other, pinching the nipple, still very slowly fucking me. His objective was obviously to make me come.

"Not fair," I gasped as I felt myself approach the edge. In the tall heels, my legs trembled. "You need to come too."

"I have self-control," he said, nipping my neck.

I gasped as I came, bucking against his hand. I noticed his cock was still hard and erect when he turned me around, hands at my waist on the corset.

"You know how much I love to fuck you," he whispered against my mouth. "I want to make this last."

He pushed me back onto the bed, kissing my tits, hands back under my panties. I panted and moaned against his mouth. He eased off the panties, throwing them to the floor. He scooted me back on the bed. I spread my legs for him, the heels digging into the mattress. He bent down, kissed me hard, then ripped the strap that went over my nipples, leaving the ones that framed my tits.

"Much better. I needed better access," he said, nipping and rolling one nipple then the other in his mouth.

I moaned and gasped, digging my nails into his back.

He stood up, gripped my hips, and then fucked me. The little straps holding my boobs didn't do much to hold me in, and my boobs bounced as he pounded into me. Then Garrett stopped, still inside of me. I moaned, delirious with pleasure, as he sucked my tits, planting kisses and pinching the nipples with his thumb and forefinger.

"Fuck me," I whispered hoarsely.

"Not if you ask like that," he said. Then his cock was out of me. He kissed down, down, to press his mouth on my clit. I moaned as he swirled my clit with his tongue, making a flicking motion as he licked a line to my opening where his cock had just been then back up. He fingers pushed inside of me.

"I want your cock," I moaned.

Garrett hummed against me, making me curse. He sucked my slit, crooking his fingers inside me. I sweated and panted as he teased me. I felt my body tighten, and then I came.

"I'm not sure if I have any Halloween candy left," I gasped.

"I think you might have a little left for me," he said, kissing me deeply and rubbing his thumb over my nipple. Then he slowly slid back inside of me. He went excruciatingly slowly, drawing out every shiver, every hitch of my breath. I arched against him in time with his thrusts, long, high-pitched moans escaping my mouth.

I thought I was about to come again when he stopped then flipped me over, my legs splayed like a Playboy bunny pinup. Garrett caressed my breasts, rolling the nipples through his fingers. Then his mouth was back, licking my pussy but barely teasing my clit. If he'd really gone for it, I think Garrett could have made me come right then and there. I moaned low as he pulled back and positioned himself behind me and grabbed my hips.

He fucked me as hard as I had been begging him to, and it was all I could do not to cry out with every thrust. He was fucking me so hard and fast, and I was so wired from the previous times he'd made me come, that I didn't even need him to stroke my clit. I hung on to the bedspread as he fucked me. Legs trembling, I came with a cry and a shudder. Garrett thrust into me a few moments more, drawing out the aftershocks. I felt him come in me, and then he sprawled on the bed beside me.

"You know," he said, pulling me over to lie on his chest. He ran his fingers through my hair.

"What?" I whispered, sticking my tongue out and poking his pec muscle.

"I think you have converted me to Halloween."

CHAPTER 72

Garrett

When I woke up, Penny was sprawled next to me, her red hair half covering my face. She smelled slightly smoky and sweet, like roasted apples. The halter bra with the straps framed her tantalizing breasts. I kissed her awake. She stretched like a cat against me.

"Want you," she murmured.

We lay side by side, facing each other. Penny's sleepy smile changed to one of pleasure as I stroked her pussy, teased her clit, kissed her neck, and kissed down to her tits to twirl a nipple to a hard pebble in my mouth. I pulled one of her legs up over my waist and teased her with my cock. I kissed her deeply as I pulled on a condom. Then I entered her. Her pussy was hot and wet from last night, and I slipped in and out, listening as her soft whimpers became moans then cries as I stroked her clit, drawing out the pleasure. I kissed her as we came in unison.

"Good morning," I said, touching our foreheads together.

"I'm starving," Penny said.

I kissed her. "I thought I just satiated all your hunger."

She laughed. I would never get tired of hearing her laugh.

"Let's get brunch!" she decided.

"I can have it brought up."

"We're in Manhattan!" Penny exclaimed. "We have to be out."

There was a brunch place nearby, Fire and Bread, that Penny wanted to try. I had Carlos organize a private room for us. Just because I had to go out didn't mean I was going to be sharing Penny.

"Yum!" Penny said when the servers brought out a huge spread of bagels, lox, and cream cheese, along with eggs Benedict and fresh pastries.

"And all-you-can-drink mimosas!" the server said.

"I'm a simple person," Penny said when we were alone. "Feed me, fuck me, booze me." She poured hollandaise all over the eggs Benedict.

"There's a crab-cake version as well," the waiter said, bringing in another plate.

"Best weekend ever!" Penny said, taking the plate.

"After all that party planning, you deserved a break," I told her, compiling a lox bagel.

"I can't tell if you're being snarky," she said, waving a piece of crab cake at me, "but I am going to take it as a compliment."

"Hey!" I told her, holding up my hands. "Sebastian is supposed to make a decision on who he's going to sell to in the next couple of days. If he chooses Svensson PharmaTech, your parties and making him feel welcome will be a big part of that."

"Did you ever figure out the factory site?" she asked, taking a sip of her mimosa.

"We have another meeting with Meghan when we're back in Harrogate. Hopefully Hunter will have stayed away from her."

"Bad blood?"

"Bad relationship." I grimaced. "My brother can be harsh—he had a bad childhood. But mainly he's a dick."

"Let's take the long way back," Penny said after we finished.

"It's nice to be in Manhattan when you're not scrounging for work," she said as we passed by a little park.

"I'll make sure you never have to scrounge for work," I said, kissing the top of her head.

She wrinkled her nose. "I'm being a brat. I don't want to just sit at home all day, mooching off someone else."

I leaned down to kiss her mouth.

"If you want to sit around and bake cakes and throw parties, you can absolutely do that."

"Penny, my darling daughter, it seems you've found the perfect man, haven't you?" a woman called out.

Penny froze, completely tense.

"Penny didn't tell me she had a boyfriend!" The older woman had Penny's red hair, but she didn't have any laugh lines. Her smile was fake. I immediately disliked her.

"Hi, Mom," Penny said, her mouth a tense line.

"I'm Trisha," she said, extending her hand to me.

"Garrett," I said suspiciously.

"Your reputation precedes you. Penny, maybe you can invite me over for dinner so we can catch up?" she suggested with a laugh.

"Garrett has to go," Penny said, practically shoving me away. "He's a very important man with very important things to do."

"I thought you were in foster care?" I said quietly when we were back at the condo. Penny was silently packing.

"I was."

"So, she didn't look like a drug addict or mentally ill," I said carefully.

"Nope, just run-of-the-mill sociopath. Didn't want to be a mother. Dumped me with my father. He didn't know what he was doing. He died, and the state foster care took me. She ran off to Greece with her younger, richer boyfriend. Came back to the country when I aged out of the system."

"I'm sorry."

"It doesn't matter," she said brusquely. "We should think about how we're going to convince Meg to sign off on that factory!"

Penny brainstormed ideas in the car on the drive back. She was trying to be easy and breezy, but her hands were clenched on the wheel at the three o'clock and ten o'clock positions, when normally she had one hand at the five o'clock. Her shoulders were tense, and she was grinding her teeth. I hated to see her upset.

"I'm fine, honestly," she said when she dropped me off. "I should go make sure Morticia and Lilith haven't kidnapped someone in the basement. Thanks for the fun weekend!"

CHAPTER 73

I was so furious at my mother. What had she been playing at, accosting me in the street? I internally debated with myself then called her. She picked up on the third ring.

"My wayward daughter, who is too busy snagging herself a billionaire to help out her own mother. What a surprise."

"Stay away from me and stay away from Garrett," I warned. "Don't run any articles about him or his family."

"Or what?" my mother spat. "You'll sue? Call the police? Then he'll know it was you."

I gulped. Garrett couldn't know that I'd had anything to do with my mother's plot.

"Don't worry," Trisha said. "When we publish something—*and we will*—it will be anonymous. No one will have to know. You can be the little plump gold digger after his money, and no one will be the wiser."

"You are a terrible mother," I hissed.

"And you are a disappointment of a daughter." Her voice lowered. "Men are there to be used. You know that in your heart. That's why you're after him and not a man like your father."

I felt sick when I went into the house after the call. Trisha had just ruined the entire magical weekend for me.

Maybe Lilith and Morticia would know what to do. I shuffled dejectedly through the house. When I opened the back door, I heard children screaming in terror. I ran across the backyard. The twins couldn't *actually* be doing some sort of demon sacrifice, could they?

When I ran into the workroom on the bottom level of the carriage house in the backyard, Morticia and Lilith were operating some sort of torture device.

"What are you doing?" I yelled. The twins, along with two of Garrett's little brothers and Parker Svensson, all looked up at me, their eyes big through giant goggles.

"We're making dart guns. We're going to sell them to kids all around the world," Billy said seriously.

Oscar added, "We decided it would be better than paper airplane launchers."

"It's bamboo pulp," Morticia said as she unscrewed the machine. Steam blasted. A single striped straw came out.

"We're trying to make it more like plastic to get the aerodynamics right," Billy said.

"I added a little secret chemical to the formula." Parker smirked. "It pays to be the smartest person in the family. I have two PhDs, did you know that?" he bragged.

"I do now."

Morticia made a gagging motion.

"Who's your favorite older brother?" Parker said to Billy and Oscar.

"You are!" they cheered.

Billy put a paper dart in the straw and blew it. It zoomed past my head to stick in the nearby wall.

"Success!"

"That seems dangerous," I said. "Does Garrett know about this?"

I didn't have the energy to chase after Garrett's younger brothers. My mother was slowly destroying my life. Again.

"I think," I said after the Svenssons had left, "maybe I need a tarot reading."

Morticia nodded. "Where is the sage?"

She and Lilith set up in the dining room. Lilith lit candles and poured me a cup of bitter tea.

Morticia had me cut the deck. She laid out death, the tower, and the devil.

"This isn't good," she muttered.

"What's not good?" I practically yelled.

"An enemy will come into your life," she said, tapping the cards.

"Already happened," I said, blowing out a breath and sitting back in my chair. "It's my mother. She's trying to ruin me."

"You're out of balance," Morticia continued. "Catastrophic failure is in your future."

"What should I do?" I wailed.

Morticia handed me a bundle of herbs and sticks. "Take this out and burn it."

CHAPTER 74

Penny was in a somewhat better mood the next day when she picked me up.

"Recovered from the weekend?" I asked after I kissed her. "I heard my little brothers were at your house."

"They're making a dart gun," she said.

"Honestly. They all want to be entrepreneurs, and they come up with the worst ideas," I said.

"They want to be like you. It's adorable," she said with a bright smile.

I kissed Penny once we were alone in the office.

"You know what I could go for?" she murmured against my mouth.

"There's a storage closet nearby," I suggested, sliding my hands along the curves of her hips.

"Hmm, normally yes, but maybe tonight. I need a pumpkin-spice latte. You want anything?"

"The usual."

"I see if I can find a plastic straw on the black market."

I smiled to myself as she danced out of the room. My phone dinged.

Bronwyn: *Can we talk about the project?*
Garrett: *Sure*

Five minutes later, Bronwyn came into the office. She shut the door and smiled.

I stood up. "Please open the door," I said firmly. "We have gone over this."

"I'm not here to seduce you, Garrett," she said, tossing her hair. "I would say it's because you're impervious to it, but well..."

"Well what?" I narrowed my eyes.

"I have a few little tidbits about Penny, the so-called love of your life, that may make you rethink your image of yourself."

"I don't understand."

She smiled with pity and derision, then she set a folder on my desk. I stared at it. Bronwyn opened it. "Read this," she said, pointing to an article.

I skimmed it, my heart sinking. "It's about my brothers and me." I glared at her. "Did you write this as some sort of blackmail effort?" I snarled.

"No. This is the beginnings of an article going in next month's issue of *Vanity Rag*. Written by none other than Penny," she said.

"I don't believe you." I paced around the room.

"I thought you might say that," Bronwyn said imperiously. "I have a sorority sister who works for the *Vanity Rag*. Ever since Evan Harrington's investment firm bought it, he's been urging them to make more money. Their meal ticket is you and your family. The key is Penny. She's not who she says she is. She's a journalist. She's a liar. She doesn't love you."

"This could all be fake," I countered, willing myself to believe it.

"What about this?"

Bronwyn pulled up a video on her tablet. It was of a conference room full of people, including Penny's mother. They were talking about how this article about the Svenssons and their polygamist cult was going to blow the new issue's marketing profit out of the water.

"I told Penny she could have a book deal, TED talks, interviews on all the morning shows..." Trisha was saying.

"Turn it off," I snapped. I still couldn't believe it. I sat down at my desk, trying not to show how shocked I felt. "I need time to review this. Thank you for bringing it to my attention."

"I know," Bronwyn said, face a mask of sympathy, "how tough this must be. Please know that I am here for you in your time of need. Let me know if there is anything I can do." She squeezed my arm lightly and left.

Penny would be back soon. I needed time to figure this out. The kicker? I needed Hunter.

He and Mace were downstairs in a conference room. Greg was there, too, as was my wayward older brother Gunnar, who ran a reality TV production company. Its most popular show was *The Great Christmas Bake-Off*. With his shaggy hair and cool pothead vibe, Gunnar never seemed concerned about anything, even when his production company was hemorrhaging hundreds of thousands of dollars a day. But even he looked shaken when I threw the folder on the table and told them what Bronwyn had said.

My brothers sat there in grim silence after I finished.

"How did you let this happen, Garrett?" Greg asked finally.

I shook my head. I couldn't say anything. I was supposed to be in control. I was the puppet master. But I had been played.

"It's going to be all over the news," Mace said. The shock was wearing off, and the anger was setting in.

"It would be one thing if it were just rumors, but she's been embedded for *weeks*," Greg hissed. He turned to Hunter. "This went on right under your nose."

"It was Garrett," Hunter argued. "I thought he of all people would have done an extensive background check on whoever he brought around our family."

"She seemed so nice."

Gunnar patted my shoulder. "Stop ragging on him. We need to do damage control. We can worry about taking Garrett down a peg later. This article can't go out."

"I told her everything," I groaned.

"Jesus, Garrett, you barely knew her. You just met her a few weeks ago," Greg said coldly.

"She seemed so nice and understanding." My whole world was crashing down. It was like the fall when we were kicked out of the compound, and the realization was setting in that actually we were kind of fucked. The chill of the air, the death and desperation.

"We need to fire her," Mace said. "Actually, we should go to the police."

"Gunnar, you're the one with media contacts," Greg said, making a list. "Try to get the article pulled. We also need to come up with a contingency plan, just in case we can't."

"You don't understand," I said, trying not to hyperventilate. "I told her *everything*. She knows about how I'm trying to ruin our father, and she knows about our sisters. They'll publish it, and we'll never get the rest of our siblings back."

Mace gaped at me in shock. I felt sick.

This was bad.

CHAPTER 75

Penny

The Grey Dove Bistro was busy when I walked in. Hazel waved.

"I started Garrett's iced coffee order," she called.

"I sort of don't even want to buy it for him, " I said, rolling my eyes. "He's just going to complain about the straw."

"I have straws made out of paper, metal straws, and actual straw from a plant," Hazel offered.

"Garrett is going to complain about all of them."

"Then he cannot have coffee."

"Can I have a donut Danish?"

"Pumpkin cheesecake?"

"Yes please!"

"How many, two?"

"A bag. I'm going to take some to the office." I declared. Actually, I was probably going to eat all of them myself then have a massive sugar headache. But I was still upset about my mom, and hey, I was a stress eater.

I took a big sip of my coffee. The thoughts about my mother were making me nauseous.

"How do you make this so smooth?" I asked Hazel.

She winked. "You don't want to know. You'll run screaming to the nearest treadmill."

"Ignorance is bliss!"

I munched on the donut Danish as I drove back to the office.

After everything Garrett had done, I felt bad that I didn't have his favorite straw. It seemed like such a small thing, but it always made him happy. I checked online, but the stores were all out of stock.

"Why can't they make a nonplastic straw that's like plastic? Oh!" I exclaimed, a pumpkin-spice latte–induced epiphany hitting me.

I drove back to the old Victorian house and half jogged around to the back, where Morticia and Lilith had their workshop.

"Is something on fire? I don't think I've ever seen you run that fast," Morticia said mildly.

"Ha ha, and just for that, you don't get a donut Danish."

"We don't eat donut Danishes. They're puffy and cute," Lilith sniffed.

"This is a blackberry chocolate donut Danish." I took it out of the bag.

Morticia's eyes widened. "It's black like my soul. I need it." She held out her hand. I sighed and handed her the treat.

She bit into it. "Inspirational."

"I need a favor," I said. "I need that straw you made for Garrett's brothers."

"We have several. The little Svenssons are trying to mass-produce them." She and Lilith gave each other knowing looks. "The poor children. They try so hard."

"They're, like, ten years old. Give them a break."

"We have high standards," Morticia said as she handed me a couple of the straws. "I don't know how many more there will be, though. We were not paid to make them."

"So you did it because they were cute?"

The twins scowled.

"Oh my god! I knew it! You love children."

Morticia sniffed and took another dainty bite of the donut Danish.

I stuck one of the straws into my coffee and took a sip. "It's pretty good. Has a nice mouthfeel. Garrett will appreciate that."

"Gross."

I parked the car in Garrett's spot and skipped into the building. I couldn't wait to show him the straw and see what he thought.

"Garrett! You wouldn't believe it! Geez, how could I be so dumb. The answer was right in front of me—"

But Garrett wasn't in his office.

I checked his calendar; he wasn't supposed to be in a meeting. Sticking the straw in his iced coffee, I wandered around the office, looking for him. I found him in an out-of-the-way conference room. Several of his brothers were there as well. None of the Svenssons seemed happy. I wondered if I should interrupt them.

Garrett looked up at me, his face a cold mask, eyes unreadable.

I turned to leave and almost ran into Bronwyn.

"There you are," she sneered. "I guess I arrived just in time for the grand finale, when Garrett finally boots you out and I pick up the pieces. He's going to see how terrible you are, and I'll be the kind, sweet, marriageable girl who exposed your lies."

She swung open the door.

"I don't understand," I said uncertainly. I felt as if everything that was good in my life had become unmoored and was floating away, and I didn't know why.

"My contact sent me more information about the article," Bronwyn announced to the room.

I wanted to collapse on the floor. Instead, I set the coffee down in front of Garrett. My hands were shaking so badly, I was afraid I would drop the cup.

Twisting my hands, I said, "Garrett, please, this isn't what you think. I can explain."

"Famous last words," he said, staring at me, gray eyes flat.

I swallowed.

"Congratulations," Garrett said, standing up from the table.

"What?" I was confused.

"You pulled one over on me. Not easy to do, but you did it. Now that I have my emotions under control, I can admire the thought you put into developing such a complex scheme. If you weren't trying to destroy my family and potentially have the half siblings I have remaining in my father's cult compound hidden away where I can't find them—or worse—I would say I was impressed."

"Garrett, I would never!" I begged. "I told them not to run it!"

"Bronwyn gave me the article snippet that you wrote and sent to your mother." Garrett set the printout down in front of me. "Did you write this?"

"Garrett, please let me explain—"

"Did you write this, yes or no?"

"Yes." Tears pricked in my eyes.

"Did you send it as an email, yes or no?"

"Yes," I croaked.

He set another sheaf of papers in front of me. "Are these your notes?"

I nodded. My nose was running. I couldn't speak because I was going to start sobbing.

"And did you send this email, yes or no?" Garrett asked in a clipped tone.

The sobbing started.

"Stop crying," he said coldly. "You're not sorry you did it. You're sorry you were caught."

I fished in my purse for a tissue.

"Normally I would find some sort of suitable punishment, but now we are in damage-control mode. Needless to say, you're fired. But do keep in mind that I'm probably going to sue you." He scowled at me. "Which admittedly isn't going to be worth much. But I can make sure you never find a job anywhere in the Northeast again, so there is that."

"Garrett!" I sobbed out. "I didn't mean to."

"But you did."

I reached out for him.

Bronwyn slapped my hand away. "He said you're fired. Get out, or I'm calling security."

Her smile was triumphant as I started the walk of shame to collect my things. I didn't have much—just my Halloween decorations and the rest of my latte. I swept it all into the trash can and picked up my purse.

I was crying so hard as I left the building that I could barely text Morticia and Lilith.

Penny: *Can you come pick me up from PharmaTech? I need a ride.*

Lilith: *Ghost destroy your car?*

Penny: *More like Bronwyn ruined my life. She found out about the article somehow. Garrett was furious, obviously. Now I'm fired.*

Morticia: *We'll be right there.*

I sat on the curb waiting.

"How did this happen?" I whispered. Of course it had been too good to be true, like everything in my life. After bouncing from foster family to foster family, I'd thought I'd finally found somewhere to belong once I met Mimi. Then she died. And now I had thought I could make something real with an amazing man, and it was ruined! "I'm cursed. I'll die alone, poor, and miserable."

Right on cue, a hearse pulled up.

"You look like garbage," Morticia said as Lilith rolled down the window. "Get in. We have a special Hungarian tea blend called Black Cat's Curse. It will make everything, including your problems, memories, and possibly bladder control, seem very far away."

CHAPTER 76

Garrett

Seeing Penny sob in front of me almost made me reconsider. She did seem sorry. But then, she did write the article and the notes and, more importantly, sent them to the magazine.

"If she'd truly had second thoughts, she never would have sent the documents," Greg stated. "Or she would have come clean earlier."

I slumped back in the chair. I never slump—bad posture leads to dowager's humps and other back problems later in life. Yet there I was, slumping.

"Can I get you anything?" Bronwyn asked sympathetically.

I blinked. Why was she still here? "No, thank you."

She stroked my face. I wished it was Penny.

"Thank you, Bronwyn," Mace said firmly. "I know you and Penny were working on the presentation. Sebastian is coming into town in the next few days. We need to have something to pitch to him and the city so that he knows we are committed to having land available."

The detached and rational part of me noted that Bronwyn had left after Mace finished talking. Since Sebastian was coming into town, Penny would have had something fun, memorable, and festive planned. I wondered what we were going to do now.

Mace and Archer looked at each other.

"Stop doing that silent twin communication thing," I said irritably.

"We just think you should probably go home and lie down," Archer said.

"I have work to do."

"Just take a break, Garrett," Mace cajoled. "When our company first started, you would literally sleep in the office for weeks on end."

"That was to get away from you."

"Garrett—"

"Stop trying to tell me what to do," I spat at Mace.

Hunter stood up. "Come on, Garrett. You need a rest. I think this day is over for you."

My older brother picked up my iced coffee then dragged me by the arm.

"No."

"Stop it," he said mildly and shook me like he had when we were kids.

When we arrived back at the estate, Remy hugged me.

"Stop it. Don't touch me."

He just hugged me tighter. "Sometimes things are like that. Take a nice hot bath."

"I'm not taking a bath," I snarled. I refused to stoop that low in my heartbreak. And that was what it was: heartbreak. Penny had broken my heart.

I changed into my running clothes and went outside. Maybe I would go for a ride. Animals were supposed to be good for your mental well-being. The horses snorted when I went to the stable. I wondered if they missed Penny.

Was everything going to remind me of her? There was only one thing to do—push through. I supposed I could fight for her, but the reality was, there was nothing there. It had been a trick.

Maybe there's a good explanation?

There's not. She sent the emails. You saw the proof.

I left the horses in favor of a run. My lungs burned as I sprinted through the property, steering clear of the castle ruins and the fence that brushed up against the cemetery side.

Fuck, she really had been everywhere in my life.

When I returned to the house, Billy and Oscar were scowling by the door, holding my coffee cup. The kids must be back from school.

"This is our dart gun," Oscar said accusingly.

"Excuse me?" I said, trying to grab the cup from him.

"You can't drink out of it. It's our product," Billy insisted.

I counted to ten. I did not have the patience right then.

"This is a plastic straw." I snatched the cup out of his hand and took a sip of the now not-so-iced coffee.

"No, it's made out of a bamboo composite."

"Whatever," I said, moving around them. I held in my hand the last iced coffee Penny would ever buy me.

It was my night to cook. I almost started to reach for the phone to text Penny.

Never again.

"I'll cook," Hunter told me when I went into the kitchen. "Or rather, I'll order food. Go lie down and stop drinking coffee so late. It's going to fry your brain."

I couldn't go to my bedroom; it still smelled like Penny. I settled on the conservatory. It was filled with plants we had brought in from the cold. My little brothers were in there, shooting each other with darts. They always wanted to be where one of the older Svenssons were was. The company was distracting enough, at least.

I lay there trying and failing to keep from running through each memory I had of Penny. I finally gave in, turning over my memories, looking for any signs I had missed. And they were all there—her immediate interest in my family, the teasing, the calculated way she bought me drinks, hosted parties, planned fun outings. I thought it was her caring personality, but really she was cold, cruel, calculating. But how did she make it seem so real?

"You want pizza?" Davy said, wandering in. He shoved the plate in my face. Actually it was over my face, because the pizza fell in my hair.

"I'm not hungry."

"I can give you a different kind," Davy said as he pulled pieces of pizza off my hair.

I went back to mulling over Penny. Every single memory was tainted. What's worse was I hadn't seen it coming. It was the oldest trick in the book. A pretty young woman uses sex and nice feel-good feelings to make a man fall in love with her. Then, *bam*, she has him by the balls.

I should have seen it coming.

Hunter came into the conservatory, frowning. "Garrett."
"Garrett!" Davy shrieked next to my ear. I winced.
Hunter blinked. "I just received a very odd phone call."

CHAPTER 77

Penny

"How did this happen?" I sobbed as Morticia drove me down the hill from Svensson PharmaTech.

Lilith petted my hair.

"It's Bronwyn," Morticia declared.

"She's always had it out for me," I said, wiping my nose. "She had everything—a nice house, loving parents, and she even dated the high school hockey team captain. But she always tries to make my life miserable."

"Just think of this as a natural disaster," Morticia said. "The tarot cards did warn us."

"We thought the Romani queen would be enough to combat it, but she wasn't," Lilith added.

"I can't believe Garrett thought I would want to hurt his family. I would never," I said, dabbing my eyes with a tissue.

When we were back at the house, I tried calling him. He didn't answer, so I left a painfully pathetic message. "Please,

Garrett," *sob* "I just," *sob, snort* "I care about you so much and," *hiccup*, "your family—"

Lilith grabbed the phone before it could get any worse.

"You need alcohol for your nerves. You're hysterical," Morticia said, patting my hand. "We'll prep the fainting couch."

The twins led me into the formal sitting room, and I stretched out on the balding green velvet couch. Lilith pressed a mug of hot alcohol into my hand.

"This isn't a cocktail."

"It is a cocktail," Lilith said. "What you call cocktails are actually mixed fruit juice for little girls. This is a real cocktail. Alcohol, alcohol, more alcohol, and a pressed citrus peel."

I took a sip, and my throat burned.

"This will help you get over him," Morticia said.

"I can never get over him!" I wailed.

Morticia looked disgusted. "Love. Remind me to never fall into it."

The doorbell rang. An obnoxiously chipper voice sang out, "We just wanted to come by again and have a look around."

"Who is that?" I croaked.

"Oh, hi, Dottie," I said when Lilith led her into the room. "What are you doing here?"

The senior citizen beamed at me. "I have my real estate license. This is the first house I'm selling. We have a lot of interested buyers!"

"You're actually selling?" I asked the twins, trying not to puke up the alcohol. I'd only had one sip, but even that was too much.

"We told you we have to sell," Morticia said impatiently. "You could buy it, but you quit your magazine job, and you just got fired, so..."

"You are cold-blooded."

"Go buy a lottery ticket," Lilith said with a snort. "You're not the only one with debts."

Dottie tapped her fingers together and patted her practically blue permed hair. "The buyers already put down an offer—all cash. Here is the contingency paperwork."

I couldn't believe it as I watched the twins sign the papers.

"I'll just bring the family round in a bit!" Dottie said, taking the papers and leaving.

"I need to get out of here," I said, pushing off the fainting couch. "Can I borrow the hearse?"

"What for?" the twins chorused.

"My mother is going to run that story. I need to beg."

"What you need to do is go over her head," Morticia said. "Who owns the magazine?"

We looked online. "It said Evan Harrington's investment firm bought it," I said, looking at Wikipedia. There was a picture of a handsome, square-jawed, brown-haired man.

"He looks like a grade-A douche," Lilith remarked.

"Better wear your good bra, not the one with the elastic all strung out so your boobs are down by your waist!" Morticia called as I ran upstairs.

I grumbled and changed. Then I teased my hair and grabbed my best fuck-me heels. I had basically just lost everything I cared about. I wasn't going to let the same happen to Garrett.

The sky was gray and overcast as I drove to Manhattan. The hearse couldn't go all that fast—it had a tendency to fishtail. People honked and rolled down their windows to curse at me as I crept slowly down the freeway.

"I'm in the far right-hand lane!" I screeched as I tried to drive and crank open the window so I could yell at the critics properly.

I was frazzled when I pulled up in front of the Harrington Investment tower. I parked the hearse and handed the keys to the valet. He looked between me and the large black car.

"Lady, what the hell?"

I ignored him.

"I need to see Mr. Harrington," I said when I marched into the building.

The receptionist rolled her eyes. "You can't just go up to see Mr. Harrington. He is a busy man."

"When is his next appointment?"

She snapped her gum. "Um, for you? Never."

"This is important!" I practically shouted.

The receptionist pushed an intercom button. "Security."

"Hey, Shonda. Oh, hi, Penny."

"What are you doing here?" I said.

It was Sebastian. He had a bag from the Grey Dove Bistro in one hand, his phone in the other.

"I need to see Mr. Harrington. She won't let me up," I begged. "It's an emergency; I'll be quick."

Shonda crossed her arms and rolled her eyes.

"Evan is my best friend. We were roommates at Stanford," Sebastian said. "Here, I'll take you up. If that's all right with you, Shonda?"

"I guess."

I tried to calm down and think about what I was going to say as we rode the elevator up to the top floor.

"Evan!" Sebastian called, waving to the personal assistant and walking into Evan Harrington's office.

I tried to stand up straight and stick those tatas out, as Ida would say.

"Who is that?" Evan said, frowning.

"Penny," Sebastian said mildly.

Evan had the look of "What the ever-loving fuck?"

"Penny from the Queen of Tarts ASMR videos," Sebastian added, setting the bag of food on Evan's desk.

A smile broke out on Evan's face. "Oh, wow, you're the best. Literally changed my sleep. You should see my graphs. I'm giving a TED talk about it."

"That's great! Listen," I said in a rush. "I am here to throw myself at your mercy."

Evan looked less than pleased with the offer. "I'm engaged, and you have a dead grasshopper in your hair."

I shrieked and batted at my hair. Something flew off.

"Eh, I think it's not dead," Sebastian said, rummaging in the paper bag for a lemon tart.

"Oh my god. Listen, *please*, I need your help," I explained. "Your magazine, the *Vanity Rag*, is publishing an article about the Svenssons. I was supposed to write it, then I realized I couldn't, and now my mother is going to publish the article anyway, and Garrett's little siblings are going to be trafficked to South America."

Evan had a dark look on his face. Was he mad I had tried to insert myself into his business?

"Please!" I begged, clasping my hands. "I can write you a different article, a better article. I will do literally anything. I have no shame—I will shave my head, go on a cruise dressed as a clown, walk topless in Times Square, road trip by camel, try to sneak into Buckingham Palace—*literally anything*. Just please don't print that article."

Evan looked coldly at me.

Sebastian glared accusingly at Evan. "Evan, how could you? Are you some sort of sociopath?"

"I had no idea this was going on at the magazine," Evan said in a clipped tone. "I assure you we will not be running that article. The last thing I need is for the Svenssons to come after me. We will straighten this out right now."

We marched downstairs and down the block to where the magazine offices were. As soon as we stepped out of the elevator, gasps echoed through the open office. My mother jumped up and hurried over to us when she saw him.

"Mr. Harrington!" my mother exclaimed. "What an honor."

"Trisha, were you spearheading this Svensson article?" Evan asked, smiling. It didn't reach his eyes.

"Yes. We have millions of dollars in advertising money lined up," she said brightly.

"You're fired," Evan said and gestured to the security guards, who were hanging in the background. "You could have had us all sued to the moon and back."

My mother turned to me with all her anger and hate on her face. "You! You ruined this for me! What kind of daughter are you?"

"I'm not your daughter," I said defiantly. "Real moms don't act like you."

My mother looked down her nose at me. "You have been a disappointment from the day I met you."

"The feeling is mutual," I spat.

"All these people," my mother said, gesturing around the room, "are going to lose their jobs. When they're homeless and their kids don't have health insurance, that's on you."

"Is it though?" I countered. "The Svenssons are awesome, but they honestly aren't that interesting. Even if it was a scandalous article, it would only help you with this quarter. What about the next, and the next?"

"Don't pretend you know anything about the magazine business," my mother sneered.

"I know about digital brand building," I countered. Building my Queen of Tarts brand had been a good crash course.

"Spoiler: if you all had used the magazine as a loss leader and concentrated on building digital traffic these last few months, you could have made tons more money. But you can't think creatively, Trisha. Now the *Vanity Rag* is failing, but you're not going to use the Svenssons to prop it up for one more quarter. You need to fundamentally change the structure of the business."

"That doesn't help us now," my mother stated as the security guards shooed her away. "We're going to lose the advertising money that would have paid their salaries this quarter."

Several of the magazine staffers were watching us, worried looks on their faces.

"You need to do something, Evan," Sebastian warned. "It's almost the holidays. See, this is why I never chase easy money."

Evan looked annoyed.

Sebastian scowled at him. "Who held your hair while you puked after that party?"

"Fine. We will come to some agreement with the advertisers," Evan said irritably.

"Don't worry, Penny," Sebastian said. "Evan will work it out. He can come up with good ideas every once in a while!"

CHAPTER 78

Garrett

"What call?" I asked.

Davy picked an olive off my cheek and ate it.

"Davy, stop it," Hunter said, obviously disgusted. "You're worse than Archer."

"Hey," Archer said, wandering in with Mace. "I heard that!"

"So what does he think?" Mace said excitedly.

"What do I think about what?" I asked, sitting up. A pepperoni slice fell on the floor, and Davy pounced on it. Remy wandered in, chewing on a slice of pizza, and grabbed Davy before he could eat it.

"Evan Harrington just called me," Hunter said.

"The investor?"

"If you can call him that," Hunter scoffed. "He owns *Vanity Rag*, the magazine that Penny was going to write the article for. He says he had no idea it was planned and that it won't run at all. Apparently Penny was in his office earlier today. She threw a grasshopper at him and offered to wear a clown suit on a cruise and break into Buckingham Palace."

"I don't understand," I said.

Archer rolled his eyes. "Ugh, Hunter can't tell a good story. I heard the whole thing on speakerphone. I don't know what Penny threatened, but Evan sounded a little nervous. There was a very definite undertone of 'please don't sue me,'" Archer crowed.

"But I thought Penny and her mother wanted to run the article," I said, confused. "Why was Penny trying to convince him not to do it? She was going to be paid tens of thousands of dollars—I saw it in the email."

"I mean if someone came into my office and threw bugs at me, I'd give them whatever they wanted, too," Mace said with a shudder.

"Yay!" Remy exclaimed. "Davy, isn't this exciting?" He picked up Davy and tossed him into the air.

"What—what are you doing?"

"You were wrong about Penny!" Remy beamed. "She's okay. You can be a couple again. She made you so happy."

"She still wrote the article," I countered.

"It's not running," Mace argued.

"She lied," I said, crossing my arms.

"Doesn't everyone?" Hunter shrugged.

"I can never trust her," I said flatly.

"I puked in your bed after that crazy party two years ago, and you said you would never talk to me again, yet here we are," Archer said.

"Ugh, I forgot about that."

"I really drank a lot that night."

"It was disgusting."

"But you love me, and it's okay!" Archer wrapped his arms around me. I pushed him off.

"At least go talk to her," Remy said. "Penny said she was sorry, and most importantly, she made amends."

"You're the so-called rational one," Hunter said. "Prove it."

I couldn't back down from a challenge. I peeled myself off the lounge chair.

"Better shower first," Mace suggested. "You can't show up covered in pizza."

One shower later, I was standing in front of the old Victorian house. A storm was gathering above me. I could smell it. Penny loved thunderstorms. She said they made her feel cozy.

I'd sent Mace away after he dropped me off. I didn't know how long I'd be. There was a car in front that I didn't recognize. Was it Penny's? Would she hear me out? Or was she angry at me still? I didn't want to lose her. I knocked on the door—or almost knocked on the door. Morticia opened it a crack before I could make contact with the peeling paint.

"The house has been sold," she said. "No more offers are being accepted at this time."

"Excuse me," I growled, pushing my way inside. "Where is Penny?"

"Gone," the twins stated.

"Gone where?"

"This is our new house, mister," a pug-nosed kid said, stamping his feet at me. "You need to leave."

"You sold the house?" I asked incredulously. "Penny loves this house."

"We're going to have the whole thing covered in shiplap, mirrors, and those blond wood cabinets from Ikea," the kid's mom said excitedly.

"You're going to let them do that to the house?" I hissed to the twins.

"They made a good offer," Lilith said with a shrug. "We're about to sign."

"I'll make you a better offer," I said to Morticia. I hated losing. Penny would definitely never forgive me if this house was sold to people who were going to paint it rainbow colors.

"You're too late," Dottie said.

"It's our house now," the kid's father said. "We're under contract. Only the buyer can cancel the contract."

Lightning flashed, and the lights flickered. The old organ in the music room wailed, the sound vibrating through the floorboards.

"What's that?" the kid screamed, clinging to his mother's leg.

"It's the ghost," I told them seriously.

"This house isn't haunted! Don't tease these poor people, Garrett," Dottie reprimanded.

Thunder boomed. Dottie crossed herself nervously. Salem stood at the top of the stairs and yodeled. The wind howled, the shutters banged, and outside, leaves and branches started swirling around ominously. Was that a tornado forming?

"It's just a dust devil," the father said uncertainly.

"It's the ghost," the twins said, slowly turning in unison, eyes unfocused, and talking in their creepy shared voice.

The miniature cyclone outside swirled furiously, picking up the mailbox, a chair, and finally the couple's car. Dottie and the buyers all screamed as the car was smashed down on the sidewalk. For good measure, another bolt of lightning came down, striking the car and immediately turning it into an inferno.

"Still want to buy this house?" I asked, smiling toothily.

"Honey, I think we should maybe think about another place." The wife's skin was pasty from fear.

"Yes, I think that would be best," the man said, swallowing visibly.

"The contract has a clause that you have to pay if you're backing out," the twins said.

"I will pay it," I told the couple.

"Fine," Dottie said, tearing up the contract. The couple wandered outside in shock. In the distance, sirens wailed.

"Way to ruin my first sale!" Dottie yelled to the house, shaking her fist.

"You scared away our buyer," Morticia said, crossing her arms.

"The ghost did," I said mildly. "Shall we go to my estate so I can write you a check?"

CHAPTER 79

Penny

I drove back to Harrogate feeling not necessarily relieved but definitely better. Yes, I had kept Garrett's family from being dragged through the tabloid mud, but it wasn't going to make anything right with Garrett. He hated me. I would never see him again.

I drove back to the Victorian house. There was a scorch mark on the sidewalk and a SOLD sign out front.

"Fuck," I said. I went up to the door, hands trembling. My key still worked, at least.

I slowly packed up my bags. I didn't have much. A lifetime of moving around and living on a twin bed in a room with two other people in Manhattan hadn't left me with much.

This house was the only place that had ever felt like home. Sure, it was a little weird and too big and was a little—okay a lot—dirty, but I loved this house! I didn't even know where I was going to go. I wanted to go apologize to

Garrett, but I figured I shouldn't bother him. He probably hated me and never wanted to see me again.

I texted the twins.

Penny: *I have my stuff out of the house. I guess you sold it?*

Morticia: *Yes, it has been sold.*

Penny: *Where do you want me to leave the hearse?*

Lilith: *Can you come pick us up? We're at the Svenssons'.*

Penny: *The Svenssons'? I can't go there.*

Morticia: *You can stay in the car. We'll wait for you outside.*

But when I pulled up in front of the huge estate, the twins weren't waiting outside. I texted them. I didn't want to sit in front of the Svenssons' house any longer than was necessary.

Someone knocked on the window of the hearse, making my heart jump. Was it Garrett? Nope.

"Sebastian."

"Hi, Penny."

Evan was there too. He waved to me.

I opened the door of the hearse. "Why are you here?"

"We came to talk to the Svenssons. Can you come with us?" Evan explained.

"No, I'm not coming! They hate me," I said, chewing on my lip. I refused to cry.

"Garrett likes you. Plus, I'm still worried they might sue me. The Svenssons can be nasty fuckers. There are so many of them too." He shook his head. "I can't believe Trisha. And she already sold the advertisers on this. "

"I'm sorry I ruined your business," I said, looking down at my shoes.

"He should have been more involved," Sebastian said. "That wedding is messing with your brain, Evan."

"Actually, it's my fiancée," Evan muttered. "Wait, I shouldn't have said that."

"Not too late to back out!" Sebastian reminded him.

"We're not discussing this again," Evan growled. He took the steps up to the door two at a time. When he rang the doorbell, I braced myself.

The screaming and running started immediately.

"Good grief," Evan exclaimed.

I could hear Garrett on the other side of the door, yelling at his little brothers to stop behaving like wild animals. I almost cried just hearing his voice.

"I shouldn't have come," I stammered. Wait, actually I was crying.

Sebastian put his arm around me.

The door opened, and Garrett's little brothers spilled out.

"Do you have pizza?" they chorused.

"You already ate!" Garrett snapped. Then he looked up, finally noticing me. His face changed from indulgent annoyance to fury.

"Garrett, I'm so sorry—"

"Don't touch her!" he snarled.

Sebastian stepped back.

"You don't have to be rude!" I said, hands on my hips. *Wait, did he just say "Don't touch her?" Fuck that.*

Tears forgotten, I yelled, "You can't be possessive! You fired me! Not that I didn't deserve it, but for fuck's sake!"

"That's a bad word!" Garrett's brothers shrieked. "It's a fine!"

Garrett crossed the wide stone porch and swept me up in his arms, kissing me.

"I'll pay for her," Garrett assured his brothers, ushering me inside.

Evan and Sebastian followed uncertainly.

"Dang, this is a nice house!" Evan commented.

"Can I help you with something, Evan?" Garrett asked coldly.

"Well, well, if it isn't Evan Harrington," Hunter said, sitting at the dining room table, looking like the Godfather. The rest of Garrett's brothers fanned around him.

I looked between them. There sure was a lot of testosterone in the room all of a sudden.

Morticia and Lilith sauntered in. Morticia was studiously ignoring Davy, who clung to her black gothic skirt.

"Ready to go?"

"There's a small child on you," I said, pointing.

"If I pretend he's not there, maybe he'll go away."

"Hi, Penny," Davy said. Then he yawned.

"They need to go to sleep," Garrett said. "You should state your piece then leave."

"Garrett's had a difficult day," Weston said, standing up to shake Evan's hand. "Seriously, Garrett, Evan is a client. Can you act like you weren't raised in a cave?"

"I'm really confused..." I said.

"Evan's here to make sure you Svenssons aren't going to sue him," Sebastian explained.

"You came all the way for that?" Garrett said in disbelief.

"I have a meeting tomorrow." Sebastian said, "with the city. Evan wanted to see the property. I'm about ready to make my decision."

"I believe we have a solution that will be viable to everyone," Greg said smoothly.

Did they? When I'd left yesterday, they didn't.

"Also," Evan added, looking at me.

"Stop staring at my girlfriend," Garrett snapped.

"I'm not your girlfriend!" I shrieked.

"You're not? But why?" He looked slightly hurt.

"Garrett, I thought you apologized," Greg said reproachfully.

"She didn't pick up her phone. Penny, I'm sorry," Garrett said, gray eyes intense, as if I was the only thing in the world right then. "I overreacted. I was terrible and irrational."

"You shouldn't be apologizing, I should be apologizing!" I cried. "I put your whole family in danger. You must hate me."

"I don't hate you! I love you!" he said, taking me in his arms. "You are the best thing to ever happen to me. I want to spend every Halloween with you."

I started crying. "I love you, too, and I thought I ruined this and that you would hate me forever!"

"You don't buy houses for people you hate," Lilith stated.

"What house?" I wiped my eyes.

"It's a nice apology house," Archer said, grinning.

"A random house?" I was totally confused.

"Gosh, you're so dense, Penny. Garrett bought Mimi's house," Morticia scoffed.

"You sold it to Garrett? And you bought it?" I turned to Garrett.

"The ghost wanted it to happen."

"It was fate," Morticia said matter-of-factly.

"And we get free rent and use of the carriage house forever until the end of time," Lilith told me.

"They literally made me write that in the contract," Hunter explained.

"Oh. I need to sit down."

"You can have your job back, obviously," Garrett said, pulling out a chair for me.

"I don't know," I said. "I did technically screw up, and besides, I was hired through a temp agency."

Evan cleared his throat.

"They're having a moment here, Evan," Archer said.

"Penny, while I'm sure being a temp for these guys is exciting, I have a better proposition."

"No," Garrett said, shaking his head. "I don't want to lose you again. I need everything I love within a twenty-foot radius of me at all times for the foreseeable future."

"Great," Archer said. "We're all going to go snowboarding, and you can babysit if that's how you feel. They can sleep in your room."

"Okay, fine. That was an overreaction."

"It's sweet that you care," I said, hugging him.

"Penny, I want you to come run the digital marketing department for the *Vanity Rag*," Evan stated.

"I'm not qualified!" I protested.

"Your ASMR baking videos are amazing, you have an active fan base online, and you understand digital marketing. I was thinking about what you said, about the magazine being a branding loss leader. I think its brilliant and the kind of disruptive thinking my investment firm likes."

"Oh, but what about the advertisers?" I asked.

"Yes, that's going to be a problem, but we cannot run the article. Fear of a lawsuit aside, I'm not going to drag people through the mud like that, especially not kids."

"We appreciate that," Garrett told him.

"I can still do the clown suit and storm Buckingham Palace," I offered.

"I think I have a better idea," Garrett said.

CHAPTER 80

Garrett

I couldn't believe Penny was back. I had wished she was there, then she just appeared on the doorstep. I hadn't realized how horribly dark everything had been when I thought we were done until she showed up.

I had been willing to just throw Evan out with a stern warning of a lawsuit, but Penny seemed worried about the workers. I realized that this might be a good opportunity to have Evan owe us a favor. Besides, I already had this plan in motion, just in case. As soon as Hunter had told me Evan had called him about canceling the article, I had started scheming. I knew we couldn't be too careful. After what had happened with Penny, my new rule was that every plan was going to have nested contingencies.

"Gunnar," I said. My older brother looked up. "*The Great Christmas Bake-Off* is still beginning filming after Thanksgiving, correct?"

He gave me a grin and a thumbs-up. "You bet!"

"Evan, would the *Vanity Rag* be interested in special access to *The Great Christmas Bake-Off*? The Svenssons are providing space in one of our towers for filming and hosting the contestants. You would have as much access as you wanted."

"We are?" Greg interjected. "It better not be in the Svensson Investment building."

Evan looked thoughtful.

"It would be a great way to kick-start the digital brand!" Penny said excitedly. "But we would need double the drama from what was in the last season."

"Oh, there will be drama," Gunnar assured her. I knew he was about to launch into his pitch. "We're going to have crazy contestants, more baked goods than you can possibly eat, and a Frost brother."

"Which Frost brother?" Penny said with a laugh.

"Belle is throwing Owen under the bus. She said she was planning on doing it anyway, for ratings," Gunnar replied.

"If I'm going to be working on it, you should make a guest appearance," Penny suggested.

"We'll see. I don't do well on TV."

"But you did so well in the play!"

"Some Svensson brothers will be there," Gunnar told Penny, "in some capacity."

"I think we could pitch that to advertisers," Evan said, nodding. "What do you think, Penny? Are you on board?"

"Ah—" She glanced my way.

"Don't look at me," I said. "It's your job. I'll support you in whatever decision you make."

"Are you sure?"

"Of course. Besides, someone over there has to run things properly. And it may be good for our family to have someone who runs an international magazine."

"Great!" Penny said. "I accept. I have a ton of ideas that will make this super awesome!"

"Let's schedule a meeting for next week."

"All's well that ends well," Archer said. Evan and Sebastian had left after hashing out more details of *The Great Christmas Bake-Off* with Gunnar and Penny. "My work here is done."

"You literally did nothing," Hunter said.

"Is there any pizza left?" he asked, rummaging through the empty boxes.

"Can we please have a ride back to the house?" Morticia said with an exaggerated sigh. "Otherwise we're taking the hearse and stranding you here."

"I don't know if it ends well yet," I reminded my family. "There's still the issue of the land."

"You said you had it figured out," Penny said.

"Uh." My brothers and I looked at each other.

"We do in spirit," Archer said.

"We need Sebastian to sell us the company," Greg said, "so you all need to figure something out in the next five hours."

"It's going to be a long night," Mace said. He handed me my iced coffee. "This is watery, but I know it's the only kind of coffee you drink."

Penny's face lit up when she saw the cup. "I think I might have an idea!"

CHAPTER 81

Penny

We could hear Ida talking loudly from down the hallway when we all trooped into city hall the next morning to talk to Meg. Sebastian was with us.

"So you think the city will give its support for this development?" he asked.

"We already own the land," Hunter said. "If they don't, we'll sue."

"I see why Evan was worried about a lawsuit—you guys are sue-happy." Sebastian said. "Unfortunately, I cannot have Thalian Biotech embroiled in a high-profile legal case."

"Also, my conference center is going to be in operation in the next year," Archer said. "I don't need the bad publicity."

"They'll sign off on it," I assured them. "This is a great idea."

Billy and Oscar were there, as were Morticia and Lilith. It was a toss-up as to who was in a worse mood about wearing nice formal clothes.

"Why can't you reverse the ban?" Ida was saying as we stopped in front of Meg's office. "I drink half a gallon of plum juice every day. The paper straws are wreaking havoc with my digestion, Meghan. It's like World War III every morning—"

"Ida—ugh." Meghan looked at Hunter. "I can't believe it, but I must say I'm actually glad you're here." Meg shook Sebastian's hand. "I'm pleased you're considering Harrogate for your business."

"We want to win," Hunter told her, "and the city is the only thing standing in the way of making a brighter future for Harrogate."

"You just want to win because you're a brat," she said, crossing her arms.

"Care for an iced beverage?" Garrett asked, offering her a cup of iced coffee.

"Let me guess, this is from Hunter?" Meg said, taking it.

"Actually it's from Straw Boys, the newly founded bamboo straw company started by local residents."

"They're biodegradable," Morticia said, zero emotion in her voice.

Meg inspected the straw and took a sip. "This is better than the paper ones," she admitted.

"They all worked together as a team," I said, "to create these straws. They're revolutionary."

"Who's going to be running it?"

"We will!" Billy and Oscar piped up. Meg looked to Hunter.

"Parker will *heavily* assist them," he assured her.

"He will?" Parker muttered. Garrett kicked him.

"You're okay with sharing your facility with this factory?" Meg asked Sebastian.

"Yes ma'am," he confirmed. "I think it's great that your town cares so much about the environment."

"If these straws will keep me from having to listen to that"—she pointed at Ida—"then I'm all for it."

"There won't be pushback from local residents?"

"No one tells people this, but I basically run this town," Ida bragged. "I can have fifty angry seniors with signs in front of any establishment in ten minutes—an hour if it's after senior special day at the diner. That clam chowder is good, but geez."

"Thank you, Ida," Meg said loudly.

"Great! I think I've found a new home for Thalian Biotech," Sebastian said, shaking Meg's hand then Garrett's.

"Let's go sign some documents," Hunter told him.

"I guess that's that," I said aloud when I was standing in front of city hall. "Time to go home!"

"No. I need an iced coffee," Garrett said behind me.

I whirled around. "I thought you were signing papers?" I asked, confused.

He shook his head. "It's not like the movies. First we sign essentially a promise note. Then there's going to be months of negotiations and legal obstacles to work through. Hunter's the lawyer, and that's his job. So now I need coffee."

"I'm fired. And I don't have a car. I drove the hearse over here. I know how much you hate the hearse."

"I'm feeling very Halloween today," he said with a small smile.

We walked arm in arm to where I had parked.

"I can't believe I missed the straws," he said when we were at Hazel's, waiting for the coffee.

"You were distracted," I said.

"Apparently," he replied, leaning down to kiss me.

When Garrett had his coffee and we were back in the hearse, I drove the opposite direction back to the estate.

"I thought we were going to the office?" he asked.

"I need to thank the Romani queen first," I explained. "She made this all possible."

"Back to the graveyard?"

"It's not as spooky in the middle of the day," I said as we pulled up.

Wrapping my red cape around my shoulders, I walked across the cemetery to the grave site. Garrett stood beside me as I left a bag of donut Danish on the gravesite and mouthed a silent *Thank you*.

"You know," I whispered as I walked back to the car with Garrett, "we haven't done it in a hearse yet. *There's curtains.*"

He frowned.

I opened up the back of the hearse and climbed in. "A mattress and a cooler and you could live in here," I said.

"No," Garrett said, glaring at me from outside.

I slowly unbuttoned my top. Kneading my breast, I pulled it out of the bra.

"Mmm, I guess I'm just going to do this all by myself then, because I am so freaking horny right now."

"I have self-control," Garrett said, nostrils flaring.

I pushed my hand up my skirt and slowly eased off my panties. I leaned back against the back of the seat, hitched up my skirt, and spread my legs. My fingers had barely touched my pussy before Garrett was in the hearse.

"Gotcha!"

"Is this the part where you take me off to your haunted mansion?" he growled against my mouth.

"I have to entrap you with my sexy feminine wiles first," I teased.

One hand between my legs, Garrett stretched me out in the back of the hearse. I moaned as he stroked me. I had missed him, and I wanted it hard and fast. I wanted to take him all in and be with him forever.

Garrett must have felt the same way, because he rolled on a condom, stroked me again, then was in me. The car bounced as he fucked me, every thrust claiming me, reminding me that I was his.

I panted against his mouth, my legs wrapped around him as he took me. I came with a cry, Garrett thrusting into me. He stretched out the aftershocks, then I felt him come. After, Garrett rested our foreheads together.

"Actually, I don't think we should do that again," I said, nibbling on his lower lip.

"Fuck?"

"No! That every day. In a hearse though? Probably not. It smells a little weird..."

CHAPTER 82

Garrett

"Man, you had it all wrong!" Archer said cheerfully that evening.

It had taken a while to sign the documents. They still hadn't been finished when Penny and I arrived back at PharmaTech. Sebastian's lawyers had wanted several last-minute changes to a contract. It was three words, but Hunter spent five hours arguing with the law firm about it. The kicker was that Sebastian's lawyers were our brothers Josh and Eric. Hunter had helped them start their firm, so he was especially peeved they were giving him a hard time.

"Nothing like having Svenssons on your side!" Sebastian said as he signed the last document.

"Let's go celebrate!" Penny said.

I wanted to go somewhere private and celebrate some more with Penny. But I supposed business came first.

"The Grey Dove Bistro now has a liquor license!" Hazel said when we walked inside.

"You made a good choice," Ida said, almost falling off her stool.

"Ida's been helping sample the cocktails," Archer explained, offering her his arm.

"I don't need your help, mister!" Ida said and almost tipped over.

"So you're officially a Harrogate resident!" Penny exclaimed, hugging Sebastian.

I tried not to seem outwardly jealous. Then she hugged me *and* kissed me. I felt much better.

"We need more good-looking men with money in this town," Ida said, following us upstairs to the private dining room. "It's getting a little incestuous with all these Svenssons."

"They're not so bad," Penny said, running her hand through my hair.

"You boys hungry?" Hazel asked. "We have food ready to go."

"I'm always starving," Archer said.

"You're supposed to be helping," Hazel said. "Freeloaders don't just get to eat."

"Halloween-themed cocktail?" Penny asked, taking a tall glass full of black and orange swirls off a tray. "They're called harvest moons."

"Can I just have a normal drink?" I asked.

"Embrace the Halloween spirit," Sebastian said to me.

"Two more days until Halloween!" Penny reminded me as Hazel directed Archer to place trays of fries, sliders, and other bar snacks on the long wooden table.

"How do you handle all the trick-or-treating?" Sebastian asked.

"We split into squads. It's a whole production," I explained, taking a duck slider.

"Sounds like fun!"

"Morticia and Lilith are running the haunted room in the Victorian house. They'll block off and decorate the foyer so the kids can have an authentic—but shortened—haunted house experience. Everyone has to go by," Penny said excitedly.

"I thought you two were going to be living there now?" Archer said, setting down another tray of food.

"It needs some drastic repairs," I told him. "Morticia and Lilith will continue to live there while the carriage house is renovated, then we'll start on the main house."

"We also need to get rid of the ghost," Penny added. I nodded.

"Wait, you actually believe in the ghost?" Hunter asked me.

"Of course I do," I told him. "He's destroyed several of my cars and drove out those other buyers."

Penny leaned against me. "I don't think it's a real ghost. It's just some Halloween fun."

"Do you know who is haunting the house?" Sebastian asked the twins.

They shrugged. "One of Mimi's old boyfriends. He was always into old cars. Would never shut up about it."

"Her boyfriend? I thought it was someone scary like the headless horseman or a serial killer or something. It figures that it was Bobby," Ida declared, setting down an empty glass and picking up another one. "Don't tell me Bobby's been haunting your house. Of course he would. He was always insufferable. Well, I'm going to take care of this right now. He can't just be haunting people willy-nilly."

"What about the food?" Sebastian asked.

"This won't take long," Ida assured him. "Keep my drink on ice for me, would you, sugar?"

"I'm coming with to see this ghost banishment," Hazel insisted, wiping off her hands.

"Don't you need like salt or holy water or something?" Penny asked as we all followed a tipsy Ida downstairs.

"No," Ida declared. "If it's Bobby, he just needs a stern talking-to."

We followed her the several blocks to the old Victorian house that was now mine and Penny's.

"Bobby!" Ida yelled when we stopped in front of the house. "Now Bobby, you listen here! You can't go around haunting people."

"Is this a normal occurrence in Harrogate?" Sebastian asked.

"She's very drunk," Penny told him. "So yes. Yes, it is normal."

The wind picked up.

"I think this house must be in some sort of geographical depression," Penny said to me. "It has strange weather patterns."

"It's a ghost!" I said decisively. "All evidence points to a ghost."

"I mean it, Bobby!" Ida shouted above the wind.

I suppressed a shiver as the temperature dropped.

"I knew your mama! She was a good woman!" Ida said loudly, shaking her fist at the house. "She wouldn't want you carrying on like this. Get out of there! Go haunt someone else. Oh, you know who you can haunt? Myrna. I was supposed to win the big bingo prize last week, but I didn't, and I know it's because she cheated!"

The wind howled, and the shutters on the house clattered. I closed my eyes against the dust and leaves that were kicked up.

"I mean it, Bobby!" Ida threatened.

The wind subsided, and the clouds opened up, light from the setting sun shining on the house.

"It still looks creepy," Hazel said, "though a little less so."

"I think I need another drink," Ida said.

CHAPTER 83

Penny

We were twenty-hours out from Halloween. It was chaos in the Svensson household.

"How do you all not have costumes? You all had them for the Halloween party two weeks ago!" Hunter said irritably as Garrett and I helped his youngest brothers try on their outfits.

"They need new costumes, Hunter," Garrett said.

"Why?"

"Because that's how things are done on Halloween."

"You don't even like Halloween," Hunter scoffed.

"I'm a Halloween convert," Garrett insisted.

"I don't have time for this. I need to figure out who is running that bamboo straw factory."

"I don't want to do it anymore!" Oscar said.

"I thought you were an entrepreneur," Garrett said.

"I'm going to start a different company."

"Someone else can run this one," Billy said firmly.

"Not it!" Parker called out.

"I'll give you an intern," Hunter offered. "A couple of our brothers should be graduating from Harvard soon."

Parker groaned dramatically.

"I'll help," Remy said gruffly. "Just until you find a more permanent solution." He was hot-gluing feathers on Nate's radioactive duck zombie costume.

"Remy needs to be the next Svensson brother to get hitched," Archer declared.

Hunter sighed.

"I would rather it be Hunter," Garrett said.

"You could do another themed costume with Meg and hand out candy at her house," I said, waving to Henry to come over so I could fix his costume.

Hunter scowled slightly.

"Make sure everyone checks their schedule," Garrett said. "I have an itinerary, your assignments, and your squad of children in your inboxes. We're not mobbing houses all at once. There are two kids per adult."

The majority of his adult brothers had come in from Manhattan, either to pass out candy or to chaperone trick-or-treaters.

"Weston, are you even listening?" Garrett snapped. I giggled as Garrett's younger brother unwrapped a piece of candy.

"That is Halloween candy, Weston. You put that back right now. I created a formula to estimate how many pieces of each we need. You're throwing off my counts," Garrett snapped at him.

"Ugh your counts."

He threw another piece at Josh and Eric, who were trying on their Halloween costumes.

"Our squad is themed," Josh told me. "We're all going to be werewolves."

"It that why Kenny is getting a brand-new costume?" Hunter asked.

"I think ours is better," Blade declared. "We're all going to be the Avengers."

"You all need to dress up," Garrett said to Isaac, Bruno, and several of the other teens who were lounging on the sofa.

"Halloween is stupid," Isaac said.

"Halloween is a huge deal in Harrogate. Everyone has to participate. You could go to the Grey Dove Bistro to help. Rose and Minnie are going to be there handing out candy, too," I told them. "They're going to be disappointed if you aren't in costume."

"Neither of you better even look at them!" Hunter warned.

The teen boys jumped up, gears spinning. "We need costumes! Penny, help! What do we do?" they begged.

"You can always be a ghost or a zombie," I said. "That's just makeup and tattered clothes."

"We need something that makes us look nice," Isaac complained.

"Vampire?" I suggested. "Dark elf? Viking warrior? Spartan?"

"They're so scrawny!" Archer laughed. "They can't run around shirtless!"

"None of you are running around shirtless," Hunter declared. "I don't want people getting sick."

The doorbell rang, and I had to physically restrain Henry before he went tearing off to the front door.

"I thought you were going to break them of this habit," Greg said to Hunter.

"Maybe it's part of the charm of our household," Hunter snapped.

"They can't behave like animals," Greg said, crossing his arms.

"Archer turned out okay."

"Did he?"

"The deputy mayor is here!" Andy announced.

Meg walked in, heels clicking on the floor.

Now that I knew that there was a thing between Hunter and Meghan, I was enthusiastically aboard the train of trying to get them back together.

"You came all this way to see Hunter?" Billy asked.

"I can assure you that is not the case," Meghan said firmly. "I thought I'd stop by with some good news for you all. Due to his community service with the play, Garrett has earned his license back early."

"Finally," Garrett said.

"Don't talk on the phone and drive!" Meghan ordered, handing him the license.

"Curbside delivery?" I asked.

"I thought Garrett might need it, since the town is basically shut down for Halloween tomorrow and then it's the weekend. Also, I understand Penny is starting a new job. We want her to concentrate on that, not drive Garrett around," Meg said, laying the paperwork out on the dining room table. "I'm a big fan of *The Great Christmas Bake-Off*!"

"We're going to have a bunch of exclusive content," I promised while Garrett signed his forms. "It's going to be amazing. After Halloween, Christmas is my all-time favorite holiday!"

CHAPTER 84

Garrett

"Are you honestly already thinking about Christmas?" I asked Penny late Halloween afternoon.

Since she didn't work for Svensson PharmaTech anymore, Penny had spent the morning in my office on the phone with Dana Holbrook, my brother Gunnar, Belle Frost, and Evan Harrington, talking strategy about the magazine interfacing with *The Great Christmas Bake-Off*.

"I've been in contact with several of the employees at *Vanity Rag* who have digital journalism experience," Penny said. "They're going to do photography, make videos, and write fun content. It's going to be so awesome!"

She went back to smearing theatrical makeup on my face.

"But tonight is all about spooky stuff. And I need you to look amazing. We're finally going to be Jack and Sally!"

Penny was carefully completing my Jack Skellington look.

"I really don't want that on my face," I said, shifting in my seat.

"Hold still," Penny ordered, applying more black paint around my eyes. "Everyone else in the squad is dressing up. Andy is Dr. Finklestein, Billy is Oogie Boogie, Oscar is the Cyclops, and Nate wants to be the mayor of Halloween Town. I'm Sally, obviously. I even had my hair blown out." She spun around, her red hair flowing behind her in a long curtain.

"I like it," I said. "But I think curly and crazy suits you better."

"You're so sweet! I'm too lazy to get it blown out every day anyway." She beamed and went back to caking white makeup on my face.

"While I'm working..." She stuffed a tablet in my face. "You need to learn these lyrics. We need to win the contest."

"What contest?" I asked, trying not to sneeze from the smell of the face paint.

"Apparently your family is ultracompetitive, and Weston thinks we need a squad contest. Obviously we're going to win. Hazel is doing Cinderella and the whole set of transformed animals. We're going to sing 'This is Halloween.'"

"I feel like we should practice," I said, memorizing the lyrics. I'd heard the song enough times while driving to work with Penny that I probably already knew it by heart.

After putting the finishing touches on our costumes, Penny and I took our squad downstairs and assembled in the foyer. I surveyed my brothers. Josh and Carl had a Wild

West theme, while Mace and Josie were corralling some sort of menagerie of animals.

Remy pulled the bus out in front, and we all crammed in.

"Holy smokes, Archer," Weston said, shoving our brother up the steps of the bus. "Being engaged to a restaurant owner has wreaked havoc on your waistline."

"I like him fat!" Hazel called out.

"Harsh, Hazel," Archer said, adjusting his Prince Charming costume. "Garrett, you're truthful—do I look like I've gained any weight other than even more muscle?"

"Maybe it's all the carbs," I said. "It makes you puffy."

"This family is going to hell in a handbasket," Archer complained.

"A hundred dollars, Archer," Hunter said. "You know the rules."

"Meg is handing out candy at her house," Remy said over the roar of the engine. "We will drop your squad off there first, Hunter."

"Please stay on your designated routes," I told my brothers as the bus rumbled down the street. "We will not have all the Svensson kids moving through the town in one big pack like locusts or zombies."

"Oh!" Archer said, raising his hand. "Group Halloween costume next year—all of us dressed as zombies like *World War Z*. We'll roam around as one big horde."

"No."

"It would be so cool!"

"We're at your stop, Archer," I said as we parked in front of the Grey Dove Bistro. The teens were already there; Remy had dropped them off earlier with huge boxes of candy to hand out.

"Man," Archer said, "I can't decide if I look sexy with dark hair or incredibly sexy." He blew his reflection a kiss as Remy opened the doors.

There were already crowds of people on the street when Remy let us off near the town square.

"Harrogate is known for Halloween!" Penny gushed as we stepped out. "People come from all over to go trick-or-treating!" She snapped several selfies of us until my brothers started protesting.

"Oh, I hope Hazel and Morticia have enough candy," Penny said, adjusting my bat bow tie. "It's a crime to run out of candy on Halloween."

"They're going to run out?" Billy asked in concern.

"I'm sure you'll collect more candy than you thought possible," I assured them.

"We have to hit every house!" Oscar said excitedly.

"There are a ton of businesses. I think pretty much every business or resident downtown hands out candy. It's a Harrogate tradition," Penny told them. "We're going to trick-or-treat for three hours, then we're going to a party."

"Another party?"

"Absolutely!"

We made our way down Main Street. The first stop was Ida's General Store.

"Well, don't you look a treat! Garrett, is that you under all that face paint? You know, Halloween is big in Harrogate, but Christmas is pretty big too. We do a rendition of *A Christmas Carol*. I bet you'd do a mean Ebenezer Scrooge," Ida said.

"I'll think about it."

"You've been bitten by the theater bug," Ida crowed, elbowing me. "I know it when I see it. We're kindred spirits."

She handed the kids some candy.

"We didn't say 'trick or treat,'" Henry protested.

"Oh, my bad! Give me the whole spiel," Ida said.

"Trick or treat!" they chorused.

"Now sing for her!" Penny commanded.

The kids made it through one verse of a very off-key, warbly rendition of "This Is Halloween."

"Well, they have heart," Ida said as she tossed more candy into the kids' bags.

"And for the adults," she stage-whispered, slipping Penny and me mini bottles of rum.

"We can't do drunk trick-or-treating," I said to Penny under my breath. "Ida is out of her mind."

"She's a local character." Penny giggled.

"I don't know," I said as we strolled down the street three hours later, the kids running ahead in front of us. "Maybe Halloween is better drunk."

"My feet hurt," Penny complained. "Next year I'm dressing up as an old lady or another costume where I can wear comfy tennis shoes."

I twisted off the top of a miniature rum bottle and handed it to Penny.

"I think someone ten houses ago was handing out those little shots of basically colored sugar water," I told her. "You could steal one off the kids and use that as a chaser."

"I'm taking it straight," Penny said. "Cheers!"

Penny and I clinked bottles. A ragged-looking father across the street raised his own bottle to us.

"Oh, thank God, I think that's the Victorian house—our house!—there in the distance," Penny said.

I started to lead the kids around the back.

"I want to see the haunted house!" Andy screeched. He had been sneaking candy as we went, and he was amped up on sugar.

"You're about to go home and go to bed if you can't act like a civilized person," I warned him.

He and my other little brothers scampered up the steps. "Trick or treat!"

"Oh my god!" Penny exclaimed. "Is that a fire?"

CHAPTER 85

Penny

"It's perfectly contained," Morticia sniffed.

"It adds atmosphere," Lilith added.

The hearse was parked strategically in the front yard, a coffin half falling out. There were bats hanging from the trees and a cauldron bubbling in the front yard. An ogre stirred it periodically.

"Is that water?" I asked Lilith. I could never tell with the twins.

"You're ruining the scene," she chastised. Remy was there, dressed as the ogre. Garrett looked at him oddly.

"What?"

"Usually he doesn't like crowds. Maybe this is different because he's dressed up."

Remy spooned some of the bubbling liquid out and let it plop back into the pot. "We're eating this tonight!" he told us cheerfully.

"The haunted room looks amazing!" I gushed at the twins. "It's just like how Mimi did it!" I spontaneously hugged them. They reacted like cats who had fallen into the tub.

"Of course we were going to go overboard with the spooky," Lilith said, pushing me off. "You can't have Halloween without the haunted foyer."

Andy looked around, eyes bugging out of his head. A skeleton mounted to a wall turned to scream at him. He shrieked and clung to me.

"This is so spooky!" I said, shivering slightly.

"Look, Nate, a rat!" Billy said, pointing.

"That's not real, is it?" Garrett asked.

"His name is Buzzard," Morticia said. "Don't worry, he's very intelligent. He'll tell us when he's feeling overwhelmed. He has a little hut to hide in, but he likes the kids."

"Salem's not going to like that, is he?" I asked.

"Oh, he's going to live with you all," Morticia said lightly, "so it shouldn't be a problem."

"He is?" Garrett sputtered.

There were more trick-or-treaters coming, so I pulled Garrett's little brothers away, and we went around to the backyard. A fire was going, and sausages were roasting. The café lights made the space feel cozy. Archer was already there with Hazel, rubbing her feet.

"I need another drink, Archer," she groaned. "Never again will I go trick-or-treating with heels on."

"You're telling me," I said, plopping down next to her.

"Spiked apple cider?" Garrett offered.

"Happy Halloween!" I toasted. "Let's do it all again next year!"

The kids all spread out their hauls on the long farmhouse table.

"We have ingredients for s'mores and hot dogs," Parker said, "though maybe I should wait on the s'mores," he added as we all looked at the insane piles of candy the kids had collected.

"Penny! Penny! Look at all my candy!" Davy said, running up to me. The pillowcase dragged behind him on the ground. He had so much candy he couldn't even pick it up.

"I think you might have overdone it," I said.

"No kidding!" Josie said.

"Oh, you were smart," I told her. She was dressed like a zookeeper with comfy khakis and sturdy boots.

"Yeah, I am not a walking-in-heels person. I am a sitting- or possibly standing-in-heels person."

Garrett picked up Davy and sat him at the farmhouse table. Davy climbed up to stand on top of it. He clapped as Garrett dumped all his candy out before him.

"Wow, you collected a lot!"

Davy immediately threw himself on top of the pile.

"I mean," I said, "who hasn't wanted to jump into a pile of candy?"

"Davy, you smooshed most of it," Garrett said.

"I want to eat all of it!" he shrieked.

"You should probably space it out…"

"Actually," Parker interjected, "dentists believe that it's better if you eat as much of the candy as you can all at once. It's better for your teeth to have one sugar shock as opposed to having candy every day for months. I've been working with a lot of them for that new toothpaste we're developing at PharmaTech," he added.

"You heard him," Garrett announced to his brothers. "Eat as much candy as you want!"

They high-fived and started attacking the loot.

"At the very least," Garrett said as Andy stuffed a huge Snickers into his mouth, "they'll be so sick after this that they won't want to touch it."

"I'm not cleaning it up," Mace declared, pouring more rum into his apple cider and snatching one little tiger before he could throw a candy wrapper into the fire. "Put it in the trash bag," he ordered.

I sat down next to Garrett on the porch swing.

"Harrogate has certainly improved Halloween since the last time I went trick-or-treating when I was a kid," he said, sipping his cider.

"I can't believe you hadn't passed out candy or taken your brothers since then," I said, wrapping my arm around his waist. Garrett nuzzled my hair.

"I was busy, and I also didn't want to deal with the bad memories," he admitted.

"Now you have nicer ones hopefully."

"Absolutely," Garrett said, kissing me. He peered at me then rubbed at my face. "You're covered in white paint."

I laughed. "So now that you're a Halloween convert, we need to think about how we're going to remodel the Victorian house."

We looked up. The house was silhouetted against the full moon. It creaked ominously.

"It looks like a lot of work," Garrett said.

"It will be worth it though! We'll have a nice home, and we can host crazy Halloween parties."

"Could take a while to be done," Garrett said.

"You don't want to live in the house with all the creepy dolls until then?" I teased, leaning against Garrett's chest.

"Not particularly. Maybe we can buy a condo, an apartment, or take over part of the wing of the house—there's the whole east wing that hasn't even been renovated yet," he said carefully. "Though I'm sure my family is too crazy for you to want to live there for any extended period of time."

"I drive around in a hearse and live in a haunted house," I reminded him. "I think I can out-crazy you."

"Former haunted house," he said, smiling and kissing me again.

"You won't get overwhelmed with all my Halloween stuff? I want a whole room filled with stuff for Halloween," I told him.

"You can have as much Halloween stuff as you want," Garrett promised me. "I love you. I want you to have pumpkin-spice lattes to your heart's content."

"Aw! You know what I love more than pumpkin-spice lattes and Halloween?"

"Christmas?"

"No! You, Garrett!"

The End

A SHORT ROMANTIC COMEDY

IN HER Pumpkin Pie

CHAPTER 1

Penny

I breathed in the cold smoky air. It had been several weeks since Halloween, and things had finally started to calm down. But that meant…

"We need to start planning for Thanksgiving!" I announced, walking into the dining room with the pile of crepes Hazel had made. "Thanksgiving is almost here. We need to talk about the menu, the guest list, the decorations. Oh! We should have all the kids make those turkey handprints. Those are so cute!"

The Svensson brothers all looked at each other.

"Oh, I'm sorry," I said. "You guys probably have your own Thanksgiving traditions. I just get excited. You know me! I've never met a holiday I didn't love."

"But you have the magazine," Garrett said in concern. "Aren't you going to be working? You can't plan a whole

Thanksgiving dinner and ramp up for *The Great Christmas Bake-Off* specials at the same time."

"The only thing I want is deep-fried turkey. I can only eat it once a year. You are not taking this away from me," I warned.

"We don't really do turkey," Parker informed me.

"What? I need to sit down! I think I'm going into shock. What do you mean, you don't have turkey on Thanksgiving?" I demanded. "Do you have ham? Roast beef? Brisket?"

"We usually just order Chinese," Garrett said.

Hazel, Josie, and I all collectively gasped.

"That is *not* happening," we chorused.

"The kids have never had a real Thanksgiving?" I asked.

"We're trying to make money here," Garrett snorted. "This house isn't cheap."

"We're having the biggest, most insane Thanksgiving ever," I said. "No excuses. We're not eating Chinese. We are eating three kinds of turkey, macaroni and cheese, cornbread stuffing, vats of gravy, mashed potatoes, and cranberry sauce—not the canned stuff."

"I like the canned sauce!" Josie protested.

"We will have multiple kinds of cranberry sauce," I decided.

Josie cheered. "This is going to be amazing!"

"But you're working," Garrett insisted.

"Just to be clear, the three of us," I motioned to Hazel and Josie, "are not the only ones cooking. You all aren't going to just show up and mooch. You need to help."

"I don't know," Hazel stage-whispered to me. "They may be too far gone. Maybe we should concentrate on the babies!"

Garrett found me as I was about to drive into Manhattan to meet with Evan Harrington about the magazine.

"You don't have to do this," he said seriously. "I don't want you to think you have to take care of us."

"I'm not trying to come in here and completely disrupt your lives. I know you all took good care of your brothers," I said, wondering if he was mad. "I won't do it if you don't want to."

"That's not what I said," he replied tensely.

"I'm going to be late. Just let me know what you want to do."

On the drive to Manhattan, I wondered what was going on with Garrett. Unlike Halloween, Thanksgiving was one of those holidays where any repressed family tension bubbled to the surface.

Maybe my own annoyance was poking through. It mainly revolved around the fact that I hated that I had to commute into New York City. It was hours a day that I missed out on. I felt like I saw more of Evan Harrington and the *Vanity Rag* staff than of Garrett.

"*The Great Christmas Bake-Off* is starting right after Thanksgiving," Evan said once we were all at the morning meeting. "Let's try to remember, we are putting the focus on the digital content. *The Great Christmas Bake-Off* moves fast. We need all hands on deck."

"Traditionally in magazines," I told them, "the digital content is supplemental. Just remember, here the magazine is supplemental to the digital content. It's a new way of looking at things, but I think it's way more effective and profitable."

After the meeting, Evan pulled me aside. "Penny." His tone was serious. "I need to talk with you. Look, I know you think this *Great Christmas Bake-Off* thing will pay off—"

"It will," I said firmly. "We have a lot of social media interest."

"Good, good."

Evan looked a little distracted. "Listen, I have a lot of investors, and you know how they are. To put it bluntly, they think the magazine is a bad asset. We need some short-term cost cutting."

I had worked in journalism long enough to know what that meant. "You mean firing people."

Evan nodded. "Or some type of dramatic cost reduction. Just want to give you a heads-up if you see any deadweight around."

"But it's almost Christmas."

Evan shrugged helplessly.

The very thing I had wanted to prevent was happening.

CHAPTER 2

Garrett

"Penny sure is spending a lot of time in Manhattan," I said, pacing around the conference room. We were supposed to be having a meeting about Blade and Weston moving their company ThinkX to Harrogate.

"Of course she is. She has a job there," Weston said in annoyance. "Josie is there a lot, too, because she's working for us."

"You don't think she's cheating on you, do you?" Blade asked.

"I don't know—I mean, no, of course not. She's working."

"That's right, she's working. It's all business. Evan is engaged," Weston reminded me.

But his fiancé was a real piece of work—a true bridezilla if rumors were correct. Penny was so much better. What if Evan wanted an upgrade? What if *Penny* wanted an upgrade?

Evan was extroverted and lived in a luxury penthouse, not with his excessively large, crazy family.

Stop being weird, I ordered myself. I had a tendency to obsess about things. I was being paranoid. There wasn't anything between Penny and Evan. I sat down and forced myself to calm down.

"Your company."

"We need a nice headquarters," Blade said. "We have a lot of people who travel, since it's a consulting firm. We need a nice, attractive space that they can come back to and looks nice on our website."

"Like the old Mast Brothers factory," Weston said pointedly to Archer.

"No! I need all of the square footage for my conference center," he yelled.

"No you don't," I told Archer. "We can carve out space for offices. In fact, we *need* to in order to make your financial pro forma work."

"We have the Art Zurich Biennial Expo lined up," Archer protested.

"That's one week out of the year," I countered. "What are you going to do the rest of the time? This conference center is going to cost hundreds of thousands of dollars a month to operate. You need a baseline financial cash flow. Office is a good base to have."

"Ugh!"

"They're creative offices," Greg said. "That works nicely with the conference center."

"No," Archer said defiantly. "This is my baby."

"Are you kidding me, Archer?" Greg snapped. "I paid for the conference center."

"You paid for *some* of the conference center," Archer retorted. "Besides, I have a vision."

"And I have a vision of turning a profit. Find more office tenants—not just ThinkX. On another note, before I forget," Greg said. "I want ham at Thanksgiving."

I looked at him blankly.

"I heard Penny was planning an intense Thanksgiving. I want ham."

"Turkey is traditionally served on Thanksgiving," I said automatically.

"People eat ham, too," Greg countered.

"I don't know if that can be accommodated," I told him.

"Make it happen."

"I've designed an app," Blade said, "so we can track what food is going in. We already have fried turkey, smoked turkey, and baked turkey. We can add ham. Anyone can log in and add to the list."

"See, Garrett? Blade is a team player," Greg said.

"None of you has ever had Thanksgiving," I grumbled. "You can't just start dictating the menu."

"Also, I'm not sure giving everyone free rein with the list is a good idea," Hunter said with a frown as he scrolled through it. "There's… vegetable curry listed, along with hot dogs and beef jerky."

"None of that is Thanksgiving fare. We need to cut those line items. We're going to have to have a family meeting. This is ridiculous," I stated.

I texted Penny after the meeting.

Garrett: *People are overrunning Thanksgiving. I heard Henry request hot dogs. I think we should have a meeting.*

Penny: *OK I'll be a bit late.*

I resolved to make this Thanksgiving as painless as possible for her. But I still wanted it to be memorable, just in a good way. Penny loved holidays, and I wanted this to be the best Thanksgiving she'd ever had.

I called Blade into the office late that evening before the family meeting. His company, ThinkX, was a consulting firm, and it handled logistics for Svensson PharmaTech, saving us millions of dollars every month. If anyone could bring Thanksgiving under control, it was Blade.

"I know you're busy," I said when he and Weston came in.

"Thanksgiving?" Weston asked.

I nodded.

"This is a major operation," Blade said. "Food service is no joke. We did software for FoodCo, the big catering company that serves stadiums, colleges, and hospitals. That's where we adapted the Thanksgiving app from."

"Good," I said. "This needs to be perfect."

Exactly an hour later, I had everyone assembled upstairs in the ballroom. Remy had rows of seats set out. It was where we normally had family meetings. This Thanksgiving situation needed to be a formal family meeting.

I was starting to worry that Penny wouldn't show up.

Maybe she's at Evan's apartment, or she took one look at the list of random stuff on the app and decided she didn't want anything to do with me. I resisted the urge to start pacing. Mace paced when he was anxious. I refused to stoop that low.

"So sorry I'm late!" Penny said, running in, slightly breathless.

I kissed her. Her cheeks were flushed.

"So everyone excited for Thanksgiving?" she said, clapping her hands.

"I want egg salad," Arlo said, raising his hand.

"Listen up," I told them. "This is Thanksgiving, not Random Food Day. There are certain foods that are not Thanksgiving foods and will not be served."

"We're starting new traditions!" Penny protested. "We can have different foods. If not for dinner, it can be part of the appetizer hour."

"Appetizer hour?" I said in horror.

"Yes," Penny said. "Thanksgiving has four courses: appetizers, dinner, then dessert, then leftover sandwiches and leftover dessert. Four."

"So you want..." I scrolled through the list. "... chicken nuggets with purple ketchup for the appetizer course, the main course, or dessert?"

She made a face.

"We are going to have a lot of poultry, Henry. We'll have chicken nuggets another time," she said to my younger brother.

I nodded. "That's what I thought."

CHAPTER 3

Penny

I was starting to wonder if I was getting a little too ambitious with Thanksgiving. We were sitting around the dining room table with the app, spreadsheets, and menus. Blade, Garrett, and several of his other brothers were there. Blade had set up a whole network with server space to save recipes and inspiration images. It looked more like a military operation than a fun, wholesome meal-planning session.

"I'm estimating," Blade said, "with all our friends and family, that we have two hundred and fifty people coming, many of them adult males."

"We're going to need one and a half pounds of turkey per person," Garrett said. "So that's three hundred seventy-five pounds of turkey."

Josie and I looked at each other. "That's a lot of poultry," she whispered.

"From my research, the fifteen- to eighteen-pound range is ideal for a turkey," Garrett continued, looking at his notes. "So that's twenty-one turkeys."

"That's a lot of turkeys."

"That's all roast turkeys," Blade said. "We're also smoking some and deep-frying some, though they will be smaller."

"Better order more though, because we want leftovers for the sandwich course," Weston added. "I think Eli and Tristan could eat an entire turkey between them."

"How are we going to cook twenty-one turkeys?" Josie asked, looking at me wide-eyed. "There are only four ovens in the kitchen."

"The café can hold three," Hazel said grimly. "Ida and Olivia are coming to the dinner. We can put one in their oven, and we can put one in Meg's oven."

Garrett blinked at me. "I ordered more ovens."

"You what?"

"I bought a trailer that is designed for mobile catering. I bought several ovens and warming racks. You can cook large amounts of meat in them, as well as side dishes."

"Oh." I was a little shocked.

"What? You said that we had to step up," he reminded me.

"I meant like hosting a fun meal-planning session and scrapbooking it."

Blade looked at me over his laptop. "I don't think we can scrapbook our way out of this."

"I ordered three hams from the farm Ernest's brother runs. He also has country ham. That was put in the appetizer category," Weston said.

"I want shrimp cocktail," Hunter added. "And oysters."

"You're going to make everyone sick," Garrett snapped at his brother.

"We'll keep it cold."

"The fridge isn't that big," Josie muttered.

"I bought two trailers just in case," Garrett said. "I've also ordered an industrial-sized fridge and a freezer to go in the second."

"It's like having a fairy godmother but for cooking," I remarked. "Just snap your fingers and bam! Thanksgiving! This is going to be great! And to think I was about to throw in the towel and say screw it, let's order Chinese."

"You already promised Thanksgiving!" Archer exclaimed. "You can't just take that away!"

"We're making food orders now, too," Garrett said. "Everything will be delivered two days before."

"Perfect."

"Chloe and Jack are coming down the day before to help cook," Josie added.

"Well," I said "It sounds like everything is squared away."

"Everyone has their assignments," Garrett said, standing up and taking his laptop.

I followed Garrett upstairs. He was tense. I didn't know what was wrong.

"Do you not want to do Thanksgiving?" I asked him in concern.

"No, of course I do," he said, stopping to gaze at me. "I want you to be happy."

"I want you to be happy, too," I said, placing a hand on his arm.

"You make me happy. I want this to be perfect for you."

"Thanksgiving is always imperfect and messy," I retorted. "That's part of the charm of the holiday."

"Yes, but there should be a baseline," Garrett said with a crooked smile. "Like no raw turkey and the food should be hot."

"Sorry you're having to plan more than I thought you would," I said sheepishly. "I've just been busy."

Garrett kissed me. "You don't have to do it all. I'm here to help you, Penny. We're a team, right?"

"Of course!"

I lay on the bed while Garrett showered. I thought about joining him, but I didn't want to be with him just for a moment; I wanted us to spend our whole lives together. To do that, I needed Evan to move the *Vanity Rag* to Harrogate. It was the perfect solution. It would save money, and I wouldn't have to commute.

Then Garrett and I would be together forever.

CHAPTER 3

Garrett

My speech about being a team was put to the test the next morning. Penny and I were going grocery shopping.

"I can order food online," I reminded her as we walked out to the car, bundled up against the chill. "And not just from Amazon. I can have anything from any specialty grocery store anywhere in the world here within twelve hours."

"Yes, but," she said, "there are certain things I don't trust the online delivery on, like eggs. I have to have farm-raised eggs. Who's going to deliver those?"

"There are twenty different options," I said through gritted teeth. "One even has profiles of the chickens."

"All the cold stuff, too!" Penny said, buckling up. "You don't know how long it's been sitting out. The fish! I can't have shellfish delivered. What if it makes people sick? I would go to hostess hell."

We spent the next five hours going to store after store. I wanted to complain about all the driving, but then Penny was so excited to go shopping.

"I don't see the lobster," Penny said in concern when we were at a fishmonger an hour away.

"Lobster?"

"Yep!" Penny nodded. "I'm making lobster macaroni and cheese."

"I never understood how macaroni and cheese is a Thanksgiving food."

"It totally is," she insisted as the fishmonger handed me a dripping box. Scratching noises filtered out of the holes on the side. I set it in the back seat on newspaper while Penny laid down a tarp in the trunk. Then I dragged over a bag of oysters as big as me and loaded it into the back of the SUV.

"Now we just need eggs."

Ernest was sitting on a hay bale when we pulled up at his farm.

"Happy Thanksgiving!" Penny said, hugging him.

"You're my last pickup," he said. "Got your ten dozen eggs and also the country ham."

"You're coming, right?"

"Yes ma'am, looking forward to it. Bringing my granddaughter, too," Ernest said, wheeling the cart of eggs carefully to the car.

"Of course!" Penny said as I tried to fit all the eggs into the packed SUV. "This is going to be amazing! It's going to be the best Thanksgiving ever!" she enthused as I carefully pulled the car out into the street.

"It's weird having you drive," she remarked. Her phone beeped.

"Hazel said Chloe's coming in early tomorrow morning to cook. And Remy says the trucks are there. I want to bake the pumpkins tonight," she chattered. "Oh! Ice, we need ice."

After packing the car full of ice and returning to the estate, I had my younger brothers help unload.

"We should do as much as possible tonight. Though there are things I don't want to start cooking until tomorrow. I don't want people eating day-old food. This app is amazing by the way," Penny said to Blade.

"We weren't going to make the kids help until tomorrow," I said. "There might be a revolt." Plus I didn't mind. It was the most time I'd spent with Penny in the past few weeks.

I went with Remy to check on the catering trailers then found Penny. She was in the kitchen, making pie fillings and cutting up deep-orange sweet potatoes.

"We're having three different types of sweet potato dishes tomorrow," she said brightly.

"Seems carb heavy," I said as I washed my hands.

"Yes, carbs! That's the best part about Thanksgiving."

"I'm going to clean the pumpkins," I told her.

Yes, the Halloween pumpkins were still in play. Penny had spent the morning knocking on the pumpkins and sniffing them to see which ones were still good for pie. She picked the smaller ones because they were sweeter, but they were still decently large pumpkins. There was also going to be pumpkin bread, pumpkin mousse, and pumpkin soufflé.

"We have a lot of pumpkin," she remarked as I inspected the pumpkin and raised a cleaver.

"Maybe we should do this outside?" she suggested.

"It's freezing outside."

"If we had some goats, we could feed them the pumpkins!"

I raised the cleaver again.

"Wait!"

"You're going to make me chop off a finger."

"Oh no! Just save the seeds. I want to toast them." She reached up to kiss me. "Thank you! Love you!"

"Love you too."

I wish I could have been happier to spend time with Penny, but I couldn't shake the feeling that something was happening that I was missing. She would periodically text someone but was being cagey about who it was. She was also angling her phone away from me, holding it like a poker hand.

You're being as paranoid as Mace, I told myself.

Later, when we went to bed, she immediately curled up next to me and went to sleep.

Do not check her phone.

I wasn't going to stoop to that level. But I couldn't put the awful thought out of my mind enough to sleep. I barely slept a couple of hours before the alarm blared and it was Thanksgiving morning.

"Thanksgiving dinner is in eight hours, people," I said early Thanksgiving morning. "It starts at two p.m. sharp with appetizers. Everything will be prepped and in the oven by that time." My brothers were all lined up in the dining room. They all wore hairnets, aprons, and nonslip shoes and were stifling yawns.

We had stainless-steel prep stations set out in the kitchen. Knives had been sharpened. There was a set of silverware that Remy had found buried under the house when we moved in that I'd had several of the teenagers polish yesterday.

"I love a man in uniform!" Chloe said, coming into the house with several trays of dough. Jack Frost followed her, toting a large box of what smelled like cookies.

Chloe hugged everyone.

"I'm turning command over to you all," I said.

Penny made a face. "I don't have catering experience, so, Hazel and Chloe?"

"Right then," Chloe said, tying her apron and pointing to my brothers. "You all are prepping salad, you're starches, you're cutting veggies, and you three are at the meat station. Places!"

"We made all the cakes yesterday," Penny said as she and Chloe made sure my younger brothers were properly chopping, slicing, and dicing. "But I think pies are best fresh."

"Absolutely!" Chloe agreed. "I cut the piecrust ahead of time. We'll put it in the fridge to make sure it's really cold."

"These are so beautiful!" Penny exclaimed. "Look at how intricate those are. See, Garrett? She cut out a whole fall scene."

Chloe slid the trays into the fridge and went to correct Isaac's knife work. Penny went with me outside.

"Are we seriously deep-frying turkeys?" Greg demanded when he saw me. "They're going to burn the house down."

"As long as they're room temperature when they go into the oil, it won't start a fire," Penny said. "Also, deep-fried turkey is amazing." The air was pungent with smoked meat as Hunter opened the lid of the smoker to help Remy turn the birds.

"How is the smoked turkey?" I asked.

"We have three birds in the smoker," Remy said. "They are almost done. Been smoking since yesterday evening."

"Good stuff!" Penny gave him a thumbs-up.

"Did you buy my shrimp?" Hunter asked.

"In the fridge," I said, going off to check the temperature of the fish.

"Ready for Thanksgiving?" Remy asked, coming into the truck with two trays of stuffed mushrooms.

"I'm glad you have Penny," he said gruffly. "She's been good for you. I'm glad you're happy."

"I don't know how long it's going to last. I think she found someone better," I said darkly.

"Just go talk to her," Remy urged. "She has a lot on her plate with the job."

"I think she's just tired of this family," I admitted.

"You won't know until you talk."

CHAPTER 5

Penny

I went upstairs to the ballroom to start looking at the decorations. We should have had them all out days ago, but the *Vanity Rag* job was sucking up so much of my time. I had been texting with Evan all yesterday, trying to convince him that moving the office to Harrogate was a good idea. It would have been easier to call, but he was at his crazy fiancée's house.

I'd had the kids make crafts, but they were haphazardly piled on a table. There were wreaths made from handprints and the little turkey table toppers. I also arranged orange and red chrysanthemums in some antique crystal vases I'd found.

"We're going to have to serve buffet style," I said to myself. "Probably two lines. I need to find some people to move the tables. We'll have one on each side of the room. We should have at least two of everything. Should we have servers?"

My phone rang.

"Hey, Evan!"

"Can you talk?"

"Yeah, totally!" I said, my voice echoing around the ballroom.

"Shhhh," Evan hissed. "I can't have my fiancée hear. I swear she's crazy. I'm hiding in the attic. So I ran the numbers past my CFO. He thinks moving is good, but my COO is worried about space in Harrogate. I know Sebastian was saying it was difficult to find space when he sold to Svensson PharmaTech."

"That was because of the factory portion," I assured him. "For you, it shouldn't be a problem. I think they're building new office space somewhere though. I'll ask Garrett."

"Have you been talking to him?" Evan asked.

"No, he doesn't know anything," I whispered. "He'll flip out when I tell him."

"In a good way," Evan said. "I would assume he's not been liking your long commute."

"Yeah, totally."

Something that sounded like a harpy from hell screeched at the other end of Evan's phone call.

"My fiancée is calling. Got to go!" he said and hung up.

"Penny?" Garrett called. "Do you need anything?"

"No, I'm fine!" I replied.

"Is something wrong?" he asked.

"Well, I'm a little worried about the buffet placement and the table placement," I said, waving a hand.

Garrett caught my arm. "Penny, look, I think we need to talk."

"About what?"

"About what you're doing with Evan," he said grimly. "I know he's great and fun and everyone likes him and you are spending a lot of time with him..." His mouth was a thin line. "I just—you're the best thing that's ever happened to me. I'm not giving you up without a fight."

"Huh? I don't understand," I said, looking up at him in confusion.

"Are you happy here? With me?" Garrett asked, searching my eyes.

"Of course I am!" I said.

"I mean, I could understand if you weren't."

"Why?"

"This place is a madhouse."

"It's just Thanksgiving," I said with a laugh. "Besides, I'm hardly ever here."

"I know," he said unhappily.

"But that's all going to change," I insisted.

Garrett's face was perfectly neutral.

"Evan just gave the go-ahead to move the *Vanity Rag* headquarters to Harrogate! Isn't that exciting?"

Garrett gaped at me in shock. "Oh, *that's* what you were doing?"

"What else would I be doing?"

"I don't know," he grumbled and looked out the large floor the ceiling windows in the ballroom. "You were spending a lot of time with him and on the phone with him... Sorry," he said. "You don't need to deal with me and my issues."

"I love you, and your issues are my issues. You should have told me you were concerned!" I cried.

"I'm sorry for thinking poorly of you," he said formally.

"Apology accepted. Now for the forgiveness part."

He gave me a sideways look.

"I need you to help find office space. I was hoping to put it in Archer's conference center, but he says he needs all the space."

Garrett snorted. "Hardly. Just tell me what you need, and we'll make it happen."

"You'll see a lot more of me!" I reminded him. "I hope you can handle it." He kissed me.

"You know," Garrett said, "I was prepared to make it up to you in another way."

"Hey, I love a two-part apology."

I pulled him into the small, secluded sitting room off the ballroom.

"I want you to fuck me," I whispered, pulling my dress off over my head. It was a soft jersey material that pooled on the floor. I lay back on the fainting couch as Garrett softly closed the door and locked it.

I rubbed a nipple through my bra, watching Garrett's eyes go almost black with desire. My hand slowly went down to my pussy. I spread my legs, giving myself better access.

"What? You're not going to come over here and give me a hand?" I asked, breath hitching as my hand slipped under the black lace panties to stroke myself. I was quickly becoming wet.

"I think I'll just watch," he said mildly.

I moaned then slid my panties off, tossing them to the floor. Spreading my legs again, I stroked the wet pink flesh, giving Garrett a good show.

"You know what I'm thinking about?" I whispered. "I'm thinking about you watching me touch myself, tease my clit." My other hand went up to my nipple, and I tossed my head back. "I'm thinking about you watching me tease myself, pleasure myself, until you can't stand it and you completely lose control and then you punish me for it."

"I am perfectly in control," he growled, grabbing me up and spinning me around. I was propped up on the fainting couch, my chin resting on the low back. There was a mirror in front of me, and I watched as Garrett stroked me, saw the pleasure on my own face. He took off his belt and unbuttoned his shirt. His clothes went on the floor, and I admired his chiseled body, the ripples of muscles on his arms, the washboard abs that felt so good against my skin. He picked up the belt, hitting me lightly across my ass with it. I jumped. He caressed the slightly red skin then bent down to kiss it.

"That enough punishment for you?" he asked. I moaned as he kissed lower to lick the glistening pink flesh. "Pretty sexy." He stroked me with his hand while he rolled on a condom. Then he pushed into me. He braced one hand on the back of the fainting couch. The other teased my nipples as he fucked me then moved down to tease my clit, making me cry out.

"Shh," he said, kissing my neck.

In the mirror, his face was fully in control. Mine was a mess of pleasure, sweaty hair, and lip biting as Garrett fucked me and teased me and stroked me, bringing me crashing over the edge. I panted as he thrust into me a few more times, shuddered, then released inside me.

"This is turning out to be a very nice Thanksgiving."

CHAPTER 6

Garrett

After finding out what had been distracting Penny, I felt a lot better about Thanksgiving. I wouldn't say I was excited, but I could tolerate it. Especially if there was more of what we had just done.

"We should get back to work," Penny said. Her skin was still flushed, and she smelled amazing.

"Or we could not," I suggested.

"Guests are coming in two hours."

"Fine." I opened up the checklist on the app and went around marking things off while Penny went downstairs to finish the pies.

"One hour!" I barked. Several of my brothers were upstairs in the ballroom, setting up the appetizer area. The huge room had tall mahogany pocket doors that could be used to close off a space for cocktails during a formal event. It also had a full bar.

"Maybe we should have hired a bartender," Penny said, chewing on her lip.

"I already have one of my brothers assigned to it," I said. "Carl's been on Greg's bad side lately, so maybe that will straighten things out if Carl's the one handing Greg alcohol."

Several of my brothers were carrying the highboy cocktail tables up from storage. "Don't scrape the floor," I warned them.

The salads were done, and the fridge was packed with food that was waiting to go upstairs.

When I went back to the ballroom, Penny and Josie were finishing up the decorations.

"Oh, crap! I still haven't done my makeup," Penny said.

She had pumpkin filling on her cheek. I wiped it off.

"You look great."

"I'm covered in flour."

"It makes you look soft and cozy," I said, leaning down to kiss her.

"Soft? Cozy?" She felt my forehead. "Have you been eating that shrimp?"

"What's wrong with the shrimp?"

"I'm teasing!" She laughed.

I leaned down and kissed her again. She tasted like pumpkin spice.

Penny came back from showering and changing as I was counting down to two p.m.

"Guests should be arriving soon," I said.

"People usually show up slightly late for parties," Penny assured me.

The timer went off, and the doorbell rang. I braced myself for the stampede and the inevitable yelling from Hunter. In their nice clothes, my brothers did a more or less stately walk to the front door.

"Welcome to the Svensson residence. May I take your coat?" Nate asked as Ida, Olivia, and Edna were escorted inside.

"Weird smile, but A for effort," Archer said.

"They're so polite and well-behaved," Edna remarked.

"Hunter must have put the fear of God into them."

"I told you we were early," Olivia said to Ida as I escorted them to the ballroom.

"Please have a cocktail."

"Thank you for coming!" Penny said, hugging them. "Happy Thanksgiving!"

"We brought wine."

"We have a lot of alcohol!"

"Good!" Ida said.

The doorbell rang again, and more townspeople arrived. Penny went back to the kitchen to put the final touches on the appetizers while I went to greet the guests.

Up in the ballroom, Hunter was chatting with the mayor. Barry was looking a little pale and sweaty but otherwise seemed engaged.

"What a wonderful idea," he said, shaking my hand; the other held a plate of snacks. "Wonderful food as well. You all did a fabulous job."

"Maybe you should just have some salad," Meg, his grandniece, said in concern. "The doctor said you need to eat healthier."

"It's Thanksgiving! It's a time of excess!" Mayor Barry insisted. "I'll take another of those fancy fall cocktails."

"A Kentucky mulled cider?" I asked.

"That's the one!"

Meg sighed. Hunter looked at her softly.

I wasn't sure if my plan to push them back together was working. Meg didn't seem as annoyed with Hunter as she normally did. Considering she hadn't thrown her drink on him yet, I would regard it a win.

"You didn't have anything," Penny said, scooting under my arm and smiling up at me. "Here." She held out a stuffed mushroom. "They're very tasty. Chloe made them."

Isaac came by, carting a tray of little glass cups holding small servings of shrimp.

"Shrimp cocktail! Shrimp cocktail!"

Hunter reached for one at the same time as Meghan.

"Ooh, I think their fingers touched," Penny whispered to me. "We should lock them up together somewhere just for an hour."

"That could go horribly well or horribly wrong," I said.

"Are you talking about Hunter?" Owen, Jack Frost's brother, asked. "I don't know why he doesn't man up and grovel. Look at what's happening with poor Evan. He's about to marry a man-eating harpy. Hunter's an idiot to throw away things with Meghan. If he wasn't such a vindictive piece of shit, I would make a play myself."

"No you wouldn't," his sister Belle said, coming up and clinking glasses with Penny. "You're such a poser."

"I'm a billionaire," Owen scoffed. "I run a huge company."

Belle snorted. "When was the last time you went on a date?"

"I'm busy. I work."

"Almost time for Christmas," Belle said to Penny. "*The Great Christmas Bake-Off* starts filming in a couple days."

"We still need another Frost brother," Penny said mischievously.

"Not it!" Jonathan Frost yelled from across the crowded room.

"You brought your whole family?" I asked Owen, looking for his other two brothers, Matt and Oliver.

"Can't leave them by themselves in New York. Usually we just eat Chinese food for Thanksgiving."

"Same," I said.

"Speaking of food," Penny said, taking my plate, "we need to make sure everything's ready for dinner."

I followed her down into the kitchen. Remy was checking the temperature on the twenty-one turkeys that were resting on the long kitchen island. Weston and Blade were carting in trays of macaroni and cheese, corn-bread stuffing, and sweet potatoes with marshmallows.

"Why do they have candy on them?"

"Because that's awesome! You can't see it, but underneath the marshmallows," Penny said, "there is another layer of candied walnuts. So delish!"

She looked around. I went through the dishes, checking everything off against the list on the app.

"Don't drop them when you're carrying the platters," she said as Weston lifted a turkey onto a cart. "That would be the worst—having a turkey tumble down the stairs."

I smiled. "Obviously we're going to use the elevator."

"You have an elevator?"

"Two actually," I said. "One goes up to the ballroom, then there's another at the end of the west wing."

Penny picked up a salad bowl, and Remy pushed the first load of turkeys to the elevator.

"This is a huge elevator."

"It's a freight elevator," I explained. "We installed it in case we were going to host fundraisers."

"That never happened," Weston added.

"We're totally having more parties if there's all this capacity," Penny said. "You could fit a car in here!"

Chloe was upstairs in the ballroom, arranging cakes and pies on the massive dessert table. Hazel was straightening the casseroles that had already gone up and making sure the warmers were working.

"Let's put those turkeys over here," she called. "Which one of you boys is good with a knife?"

We all pointed at Remy. He beamed.

I helped unload the trays of food. Through the closed huge mahogany doors, we could hear people talking and laughing. My phone alarm rang. "Fifteen minutes," I said.

Eli and Tristan came up with the final load of food, and we spread it out. Remy was carving turkeys at one of the long buffets. Greg had set up at the other one.

"You know how to carve a turkey," Penny admired. "You're so neat and fastidious."

"I used to do food service," Greg sniffed.

"After the cult," I whispered to Penny.

Greg scowled. "Yes, that. And it was the main impetus for my building an investment firm worth tens of billions—so that I would never work food service ever again."

"We appreciate your sacrifice," Penny said and not-so-subtly snuck a piece of the smoked turkey. "Remy, this is amazing!" She stuffed a piece into my mouth.

The final alarm sounded.

"Throw open the doors!" Penny said, clapping her hands. "It's time for Thanksgiving!"

CHAPTER 7

Penny

"This is so amazing," I said as people streamed in. "There are so many people, and it's all our friends and family!" People lined up at both stations, and I went around greeting people I had missed at cocktail hour.

I hugged Morticia and Lilith. "I saved the turkey gizzards for Salem," I said. "Thanks for coming!" I exclaimed, hugging Ernest's granddaughter Amy.

"I brought Baxter. He's out with your big horses. I hope that's fine."

"I hope they're being good hosts."

"They're big horses, though Garrett's a big Svensson, so I suppose you need a large one! I brought some flowers too. Chloe put them out on the dessert table."

"They're gorgeous!" I gushed. "Ernest showed me your greenhouse on his farm."

"He's nice to let me grow them there."

"She's selling herself short," Ernest interjected gruffly. He was wearing a suit that was ever so slightly too small, and he'd combed his hair back and shaved. He looked a little drunk but happy.

"Her flowers are the biggest moneymaker the farm has. Kept us afloat during the recession."

"I mainly do weddings," Amy said. "I'm with the group Weddings in the City."

"You're doing Evan Harrington's wedding," I said.

Amy's expression suggested she was having flashbacks to a war. "... Yes..."

"His fiancée is something else," I added.

"Sure is." Amy took a deep breath. "When you and Garrett get married, hit us up. I could make this place amazing for a reception. We'd have the ceremony outside, tons of flowers."

"Oh, he hasn't even—we haven't talked about that. I only just met him."

"When you know, you know!" Amy winked. "I've done enough weddings to know when people are well and truly in love!"

As much as I wanted to start planning a wedding, I had a lot on my plate, including finding stuff to put on my plate.

Mimi had been a good hostess and refused to eat a bite of food until all her guests had been served. I'd already snuck a few bites of turkey, so I wasn't as great as she was, but I still waited to make my plate until I was sure everyone had been served enough of all the dishes.

"Hungry?" Garrett asked, handing me a plate.

He served me slices of turkey. Remy had gone to sit next to Meg's friend Susie.

After I had piled food onto my plate and found my seat, I stood up and clinked my glass.

"Thank you all for coming and spending Thanksgiving with us. I know we've had some trials this year. There were a number of cars that were destroyed. People lost their licenses, but we had a lot of wins. And a big part of that is that we all work together, more or less. After you finish eating, please don't forget about desserts. There's a ton, including pumpkin pie made with pumpkins and eggs from Ernest's farm."

Ida raised her hand. "And there's more alcohol!"

After dessert, we set up the espresso machine and served slices of fruit.

"I hope everyone's still hungry," I said. "We will be setting out slices of roast turkey and smoked turkey. There are also freshly baked rolls for sandwiches, and we also have—drumroll please—deep fryers. Yes, we are deep-frying turkeys. Will we burn the house down? Who knows, but if you step out to the downstairs terrace, you'll find out!"

"At least the fire department's here," Archer called out, and Clint stood up and waved.

People chatted and wandered out to the balcony overlooking the back terrace. Some guests trooped out downstairs to the terrace. Garrett and I stayed up on the balcony, holding hands and wincing as Remy heated up the oil.

"He better not burn anything down."

The oil smoked when Remy dunked the first turkey in. We all cheered.

"I'll drink to that," Garrett said, clinking our glasses together.

"What are you thinking?" I asked him.

"I never really thought about it, but this sure would be a nice place for a wedding."

I felt giddy.

"You think?"

"I mean, you know, logistically speaking." He smiled down and kissed me.

"Turkey time, round two!" Remy called out, pulling the first turkey out of the boiling oil.

"Hell yeah!" shouted several of Garrett's brothers who had come in from Manhattan that morning and had been basically drinking all day.

Garrett shook his head. "They better not fall in. I'm not spending the rest of Thanksgiving in the emergency room."

Greg carved the first turkey on the terrace. The horses had gotten loose and were moseying around on the grounds. The kids pet them and fed them apples.

Amy was sitting on the steps, chatting with several of Garrett's brothers, who flocked to her like territorial hummingbirds. She was weaving flowers into wreaths as they flirted with her.

"It's like they've never seen a woman before," he growled.

"Hey!" Hunter yelled before Garrett could do it. Hunter pointed to a platter. "Take this upstairs," he ordered them.

"I think this was the part I was looking forward to all day," I said when Garrett's brothers came up with the tray of fried turkey. I'd put most of the leftovers into the fridge but left out turkey, dressing, and cranberry sauce for sandwiches. I'd also set out pots of various aiolis and stacks of smaller plates along with some fresh salad and tangy vinaigrette. We'd had a lot of carbs.

Garrett selected a few pieces of fried turkey for me, and we went back onto the balcony. He wrapped a blanket around both of us, and we watched the next turkey being lowered into the oil. This one didn't fare so well, mainly because Remy was upstairs making himself a sandwich, and one of Garrett's drunk brothers sloshed the turkey into the oil. There were screams as some of it splashed and spattered, setting the dried plants in a nearby planter on fire.

"Fire! Fire!" Davy and Henry screamed as Hunter sprayed the planter with a hose.

"Never a dull moment," I said.

"I knew that was going to happen."

"Yeah," I said, "but sometimes the best things in life come out of a big mess. Like this fried turkey. And you, the man I love most in the world."

"And you, the woman I love most in the world. You lived in a haunted house full of dolls when I found you," Garrett said, smiling. He leaned down and kissed me. "I'll take haunted houses, flaming balls of turkey, and insane parties every day if it means I can spend it with you."

The End

Acknowledgements

A big thank you to Red Adept Editing for editing and proofreading.

And finally a big thank you to all the readers! I had a great time writing this hilarious book! Please try not to choke on your wine while reading!!!

About the Author

If you like steamy romantic comedy novels with a creative streak, then I'm your girl!

Architect by day, writer by night, I love matcha green tea, chocolate, and books! So many books…

Sign up for my mailing list to get special bonus content, free books, giveaways, and more!

http://alinajacobs.com/mailinglist.html

Made in the USA
Las Vegas, NV
02 October 2024